The Darling

—

LORRAINE M. LÓPEZ

THE UNIVERSITY OF
ARIZONA PRESS

TUCSON

The University of Arizona Press
www.uapress.arizona.edu

Printed in the United States of America
20 19 18 17 16 15   6 5 4 3 2 1

ISBN-13: 978-0-8165-3183-7 (paper)

Cover designed by Leigh McDonald
Cover photo adapted from *Reading* by Alexander Lyubavin

Publication of this book is made possible in part by the proceeds of a permanent endowment created with the assistance of a Challenge Grant from the National Endowment for the
Humanities, a federal agency.

Library of Congress Cataloging-in-Publication Data
López, Lorraine, 1956– author.
    The darling / Lorraine M. Lopez.
        pages cm — (Camino del sol : a Latina and Latino literary series)
    ISBN 978-0-8165-3183-7 (pbk. : alk. paper)
    I. Title. II. Series: Camino del sol.
PS3612.O635D37 2015
813'.6—dc23
                            2014041932

♾ This paper meets the requirements of ANSI/NISO Z39.48–1992 (Permanence of Paper).

The Darling

Camino del Sol

A Latina and Latino Literary Series

For Judith Ortiz Cofer

She was always fond of someone, and could not exist without loving.

—*Anton Chekhov, "The Darling"*

The Darling

La Cariña

On her wedding day, Caridad Delgado pined for a dead man. He was a doctor and a playwright, a charismatic raconteur sought after for parties and weekends in the country. Of course, he was older than she. Most successful men, dead or living, were much older than Caridad, just eighteen on that Saturday in late June 1975. Weeks ago, she had razored her one photograph of him from a library book. A heartbreakingly handsome man, Anton had a smooth brow, thick dark hair, and a patrician's nose under which he sported a neat moustache and triangular beard—a *reasonable* amount of facial hair. His image flashed in her mind's eye as Caridad now hurried through the cobblestone vestibule to find a restroom. In the picture, Anton's eyes glimmered with attentiveness and wit behind round wire-rimmed lenses. "An engaged man," he'd claimed, "is neither this nor that; he has left one side of the river and not yet reached the other."

Surely a bride-to-be is more *that* than this. After he'd wed, Anton wrote, "If you are afraid of loneliness, do not marry." Exiled from home, alone in a hotel, he died from an ailment of the heart at just forty-four. His wife Olga said, "Fitting he should end his days with a glass of champagne and silence." Over seventy years later, Caridad longed for the man who promised "you *are* what you believe in." Unsteady in heels, she clip-clopped, wobbling like a colt through the corridor, her ivory gown billowing and snapping with each step. The sole of one shoe skidded over a slick stone, and Caridad palmed the dank wall to catch herself.

"Caridad," a deep voice called out.

She turned back, peering through her wire-framed glasses. Near an exit stood a man dressed in an olive-drab uniform and holding a garrison cap. The soldier, black haired and acne scarred, squinted at her, and a luminous smile split his swarthy face. "Remember me?"

Caridad had no idea who he might be. "Of course, I do," she said.

"It's me, Martin. Martin Pineda. Your mother took care of us when my folks had to go to Mexico."

"Martin!" Caridad cast her mind back to the summer when the six Pineda children invaded her mother's small duplex after their parents were summoned to Mexico for a family crisis. "How nice to see you," she said. "How've you been?"

Martin shrugged, his lumpy face still stretched into a now-familiar grin. The Pineda children all shared their father's small-eyed, large-jawed face with a jutting brow — "the Cro-Magnon look," as Caridad's eldest sister Felicia had observed. Caridad herself had been a fair child, with hazel eyes and wavy black hair. She was a favorite among the adults in her young life. Family friends and relatives would often stroke her hair and caress her cheeks, murmuring "cariña," an endearment that her teachers echoed in English, more often calling her "darling" or "sweetheart" than by her difficult-to-pronounce first name. Caridad had been sharp in school, sent to the upper grades for reading, while Martin floundered at grade level. Despite this, her mother and Señora Pineda had hoped for a match between their two children. Caridad had been aghast, and even Felicia had ridiculed the idea, saying, "We hope Caridad can do better than *that*."

"So you're getting married," Martin said.

Caridad glanced at her gown as if taking startled notice of it. "I guess so."

Martin's laughter spilled out, echoing in the hallway. He'd grown much taller than his diminutive parents, and his chest had expanded, tapering into his trim midsection. Martin now held himself erect, modeling such ramrod posture that Caridad drew her shoulders back.

"I'm glad you could make it," she said.

A flush shadowed his face. "I'm, uh, I actually wasn't invited. I heard you were getting married, and I'm on furlough this weekend, so I thought I'd come by to congratulate you." He dug into a pocket. "I brought you something." Martin held out a sheet of notepaper.

"Thanks." Caridad took it from him. Not a poem, she hoped. Caridad, who loved literature, suffered poems written for her, verses that rhymed words like "love" and "above," "you" and "true." These were nearly as excruciating as songs sung for her by one former boyfriend who played guitar, songs she'd endured with a smile frozen on her face. For Christmas, her fiancé Jorge had presented her with a design involving the color wheel that he'd painted—she *knew*—as an exercise for an art class. On top of being undesired, the poems, songs, and painting, supposedly presented in her honor, garnered attention and praise for the boyfriends composing these.

"It's just a letter," Martin said.

"Oh!" If he included a return address, she would write him back. Caridad, who loved to write, was an avid correspondent. She overwhelmed pen pals with long and speedy replies and was always on the lookout for someone new with whom to trade letters.

"You know what," Martin said, "I'm kind of jealous of all this." He gestured at the chapel's dank walls. "We're the same age, and here you are, already taking this step into the future. I don't know if I'll ever—"

"You will, Martin. You'll fall in love one day and—"

He laughed again. "That happens all the time. When you get married, you have to stop that, don't you? You're supposed to stop wondering who you're going to meet and what's going to happen next. You even have to forget about those you hoped to know more." He cleared his throat. "Anyways, you don't need to hear this. Not today."

"Since you're here," Caridad said, "why not stay for the wedding?" She extended an arm like a game show hostess, indicating the direction of the chapel as if offering this to him as a prize. Martin's laughter pinged against the walls, chinking like coins spilled by a rich man. "How unbearable at times," Anton had observed, "are people who are happy."

"Wish I could." Marin drew her near. "But I have to go."

Caridad yielded to his embrace and the kiss he planted—not on her cheek as she expected, but fully on her lips. The moist surprise of it sent a surge of warmth through her. Martin withdrew, issued another prehistoric grin, and pivoted to slip out the exit behind him. In his wake, Caridad reached for the knob as if to follow him. Then she stopped herself and spun away from the door.

When at last she slipped into the tiled restroom, Caridad scanned it from floor to ceiling. The transom window was angled open near the ceiling, affixed to rusted chains. If she stood on the aluminum trash can, she could just reach the window and maybe snap those corroded chains. Once she hoisted herself out, though, Caridad would have no choice but to leap twelve feet or more to the pavement. Discouraged, she gazed into the flecked mirror. Her reflection stared back, a vacant expression on her face. Olenka, again. With a jolt, Caridad recognized the sweet emptiness described in Chekhov's story about a good-natured woman ever-searching for love.

She shook her head as if to loosen the thought. Guests would be filling the chapel by now. Caridad pictured her mother's apple cheeks blanching if she learned her daughter had run off. And Jorge—how would he feel if she climbed out a window to catch a bus for Barstow, or even Vegas? He would be shamed and wounded. Plus, Caridad had no money for bus fare. The blank look on her face wavered. Her eyes stung.

She had removed her glasses and was reaching for the paper-towel dispenser when her sister Esperanza burst through the door. "Are you okay?"

Caridad nodded, but a sob tore from her throat.

Esperanza bolted the outer door to the ladies' room before gathering Caridad in her arms. "What's wrong? Tell me."

"What if this isn't love? I mean, maybe I don't really know what love is, and now I'll never find out." She told Esperanza what Martin said.

"Is *that* what's bothering you?"

"Not just that." Caridad told Esperanza about her namesake, the other "darling," about how Anton's tender cipher now haunted her. Then she tried to describe that awful moment in the supermarket, but she began weeping instead.

Esperanza assured her that every bride experiences doubts. "Why, I didn't just cry about it," she told Caridad, "I swiped a handful of Valium from my mother-in-law's medicine chest and a bottle of tequila from their bar." Her soft lips thinned into a tight smile. "I was going to lock myself in that vacant house next to theirs. They might not have found my body for days."

Caridad pulled back to regard her sister's round face. Her shining eyes, snub nose, and plump cheeks suggested cheerleader, prom princess, radiant bride—all the things Esperanza had been—never hinting at such despair.

"Can you imagine?" Esperanza gazed in an unseeing way over Caridad's shoulder. Then she grinned. "And, hey, look at me now. If

I'd gone through with that, I would've missed your wedding, Dah-Dah," she said, using her childhood nickname for her baby sister.

Caridad drew a shuddery breath.

"So what's this about some *story* you read?"

Now, there was no way for Caridad to explain how a piece of fiction had hammered her so. How Olga Semyonovna—Olenka—had leapt from the page to superimpose her image on to nearly every reflective surface, hijacking Caridad's thoughts, even disrupting her sleep until she longed to cry out, like the young boy at the end of the story: *Get away! Leave me alone!*

"I guess it's nothing," Caridad said.

Esperanza turned on the tap. "Rinse your face." She cranked the dispenser and tore off a paper towel for her sister. Soon Caridad was again a smooth-faced young bride. Even if her eyes were puffy, her lashes dense with crystallized tears.

"You look nice," Esperanza said. "Are you ready?"

Caridad nodded, and her sister ushered her into the corridor, her minty breath tickling her ear. "There's always divorce."

With organ chords buzzing in her bones, Caridad gazed beyond the array of faces now turning toward her. Votive candles in ruby jars guttered and glowed near the altar. Acrid incense stung her nostrils, and the low murmur of voices swarmed her ears. The thick-walled chapel swooped and swerved. Caridad's knees loosened. Her eyelids fluttered, and she swayed. With rustling sounds and the patter of swift footsteps, Mama rushed to her side. Her staunch embrace held Caridad upright until the vertigo passed. Then Caridad glanced at the face near her own, and she was—at last—astonished by love, lofted onto its warm and pulsing back as if it were a winged horse she could ride skyward.

"M'ija, you are pretty as a plum," Mama said, still holding on to Caridad.

Caridad surveyed her mother's seamed and shiny brow, her dark eyebrows, her long nose with its small bulb at the tip, her mouth now crimsoned and waxy, and her curly brown hair, freshly dyed and styled to frame her wide face. "You are the one," Caridad murmured in a voice too low for her mother to hear. "It's *you.*"

"Ready?" Mama asked.

With the next swell of music, Caridad linked arms with her mother and lurched toward the altar, where Jorge Benitez stood near the first pew. Her groom's eyes were wide and fearful, but a toothy grin cleaved his dense beard. Beyond Jorge, Caridad's sisters—Esperanza as matron of honor and Felicia a bridesmaid—stood across the aisle from the two groomsmen: Jorge's former roommate, Mike, and best friend, Noah. Jorge had lobbied for Caridad to include Noah's wife, Geraldine, as a bridesmaid. But Caridad had refused, just as she'd rejected Jorge's suggestion that *his* father give her away. "I want my mother," she had insisted, not minding that she sounded like a petulant child saying this.

Now, as she clung to Mama while taking one measured step after another, Caridad imagined they could take these stilted steps backward in time and place. She and her mother would retreat to the parking lot, returning home to earlier in the day, then weeks and months back, all the way to when the four of them lived in the duplex—maybe popping corn before a movie or cleaning house on a Saturday, the radio blasting over the vacuum's roar—instead of step-pause, step-pause, step-pause, advancing on the candlelit altar where Caridad would have to let go.

It's kind of a blessing for a bride when someone gets drunker than she at the wedding. For a while, this had been hard to call, with Esperanza bringing Caridad flute after flute of champagne at the Mexican restaurant where the first reception was held. She spent much of that celebration holding court in the lounge area of the ladies' room that was separate from the stalls. In this talc-scented antechamber, Caridad had arranged herself on a vinyl chaise, pounding down champagne and chatting tipsily with those who dropped by to visit or to urge her to come out and join the party.

The odds were then good that Caridad would be the most intoxicated person at her wedding, but Jorge's teenaged sister Emma gulped down more champagne than she could handle. Now Caridad watched her new sister-in-law with gratitude at the second party—for select guests—in the backyard of the Benitez family home. Emma wrenched free from her father as he was leading her into the house. Red-faced, she shouted something that Caridad couldn't hear over the music, and Mr. Benitez backed away. Jorge's cousin took his place and managed to steer the girl inside. "Here's to you, Emma," Caridad whispered. She lifted her champagne flute and sipped its dregs.

"We should probably switch to coffee or water," Esperanza said. They sat under a tent rented by Caridad's new in-laws for the occasion. Esperanza had been matching her drink for drink, and now she was hiccupping beside her sister with the soft persistence of a tree frog.

Caridad's drunkenness, as if weary of her company, was retreating of its own accord, fading into a dull headache. The band broke for intermission with a clamor of instruments and static from the speakers. Voices and laughter filled the void. The tent had been erected over the paved patio, extending beyond the concrete slab and over the dense lawn. Caridad and Esperanza sat in folding chairs (also rented) in the grassy section, and Caridad had slipped off her heels, so the blunted blades pricked the soles of her feet. Esperanza draped an arm over her sister's shoulder. "Listen to me," she told Caridad. "You're going to be happy, okay? Just like me and Rey." Esperanza's cheeks dimpled fetchingly. The tight curls she'd steamed into her brown hair now dangled like loose corkscrews.

Esperanza fluttered fingers at her husband, who appeared under the tent to retrieve beer from an ice chest. His shirt was rumpled and darkened with sweat stains that formed half-moons at his armpits and the triumphant shape of a torch in the middle of his back. "Isn't he the greatest?" Esperanza said when Reynaldo sent a glazed look in her direction.

Reynaldo Ochoa, according to Felicia, was at least "three kinds of dickhead," and then she'd list all three: "He's a total moron, about as sleazy as they come, and the dude is a dog. Face it—a *big* one." No, Rey wasn't the greatest, but he was hardly a complete dog. The truth had to be somewhere in between. If pressed to choose, though, Caridad would side with her eldest sister. She trusted in Felicia's honest impressions, even if they sounded cruel. When Felicia's boyfriend gave her garish earrings for Christmas, instead of thanking him with a kiss as Caridad had done to show appreciation for the unwanted color wheel, Felicia had demanded to know where he had bought the gilt-and-glass baubles. "I'm taking this clownish shit back," she'd said.

And where was he now, that boyfriend? As if there were a chance of spotting him, Caridad scanned the weddings guests. Jorge's grandmother, her nimbus of white hair covered by a dark mantilla, wagged a gnarled finger at her son, Dionisio, Jorge's teetotaler father, who with

7

his one glass eye was more of a grim Cyclops than a god of wine and celebration. Behind them, Caridad's new mother-in-law, Blanca, bustled about in a snug bronze dress. Jorge's friends stumbled into the tented area for drinks, as glassy-eyed as Reynaldo since they had likely all smoked joints together in one of the cars parked in front. Various dressed-up and uncomfortable-looking cousins, aunts, and uncles from both sides of the family milled about, paper plates and plastic cups in hand. Mama stooped to chat with a shorter woman while casting concerned glances Caridad's way. Near the sliding glass entrance to the house, Felicia harangued a shriveled old man, and at the buffet, Noah was loading a plate with canapés likely intended for his wife, Geraldine, who'd planted her generous backside in a chair near the box fan. Jorge, with crumbs in his Amish-style beard, stood beside his friend, popping glistening mushroom caps into his mouth.

Yes, where was Felicia's boyfriend with poor taste in earrings now? Long gone, that's where. If Felicia had barged into that church restroom instead of Esperanza, Caridad might not be here now, sipping flat champagne and gawping at guests like meerkats at the zoo. Felicia would have led Caridad out of the restroom and paraded her to the parking lot, hissing "fuck off" at anyone who ventured a curious look. Then Felicia would have driven Caridad home, telling her that Jorge, in her opinion, was "kind of boring, seriously out of shape, and not too smart," a description she often followed up by asking, "And *what* is up with that beard?"

"There's always divorce," Caridad now quoted Esperanza's words and raised her flute again. Band members tramped onto the plywood platform built by her father-in-law, settling unfinished drinks and picking up their instruments.

Esperanza winked at Caridad. She also lifted her flute. "To divorce!" she said, startling the drummer. He knocked his beer can against the cymbals, punctuating Esperanza's toast with a jangling crash.

Days after the wedding, Caridad and Jorge sat on the linty green carpet in Noah and Geraldine's disheveled living room and opened gifts. For their honeymoon, Jorge had planned a backpacking trip near Lone Pine in the Sierra Nevada, so he'd urged Caridad to petition her relatives for camping equipment as wedding presents. His extended family came through with Swiss Army knives, aluminum cookware, canteens, even a Coleman stove. But Jorge's grandmother, ignoring the directive, presented Caridad with a mourning veil identical to the mantilla she'd worn to the wedding. Caridad's family likewise gave the couple what they felt like giving: towels, linens, kitchenware, and small appliances. One beloved aunt, though, troubled to find a lantern, an item on Jorge's list, but instead of an army-surplus model, she'd given them an antique oil lamp, an intricate floral design etched into its glass base. "Useless," Jorge said.

Aware of Geraldine's acquisitive gaze, Caridad grabbed the lamp. "*I* like it."

So far, Geraldine had snapped up a handheld mixer, a toaster, towels, and a salad bowl set. These gifts were duplicates, and Geraldine had been swift in asking for them outright. Since Jorge's friends had transported the gifts in their van and stored them at their house, Caridad couldn't begrudge this. As Jorge read cards and tore away wrapping paper, Caridad noted who gave what in a steno pad. She looked forward to composing thorough thank-you notes.

His back against the sofa where Geraldine was ensconced, Noah also sat cross-legged on the floor, huffing on a bong. "I've often longed to take a stout party of men into the Sierra Nevada," he said after the last gift was opened. He drew on the bamboo pipe, the water chamber bubbling like an aquarium filter.

"What about women?" Geraldine put in. "You forget women."

A party of stout women, thought Caridad. *Why, Geraldine could lead that.*

Noah passed the bong to Jorge, who took it, saying, "You and Geraldine should come with us to Lone Pine."

Caridad's eyes grew so wide with disbelief that they burned. She transmitted a series of furious thoughts to Jorge, who avoided her gaze. Geraldine and Noah didn't even glance in her direction. Once Caridad grew accustomed to the couple's odd appearance, she'd been awed by the way they spoke, their diction a sharp contrast to the dopey utterances of her high school friends. She'd been almost as impressed by the couple as she'd been by Jorge, an aspiring artist in college when she'd met him. Over time, though, her admiration for all three had dimmed.

She thought of Anton's letter to a friend, in which he claimed that all he honestly wanted to say to people was: "Have a look at yourselves.

See how bad and dreary your lives are!" What would happen if she quoted this? Maybe they'd laugh the way they did when Geraldine's parakeet cursed. More likely, just as they didn't see her, they'd fail to hear what she said.

"I can't go." Geraldine nudged Noah with her bare foot. "But you should."

Jorge thrust the bong at Caridad, though he knew smoking weed made her anxious. Now all three watched her, scrutinizing this exchange. Caridad grasped the bong. Noah and Geraldine would talk, Jorge had told her once. They would think she was uptight and judgmental if she always refused a toke. They were like conscientious parents, making sure a child ate all her vegetables. Caridad huffed mightily, searing her lungs. Soon she lost track of the conversation. The words twisted away like wisps of sweet smoke wafting from the pipe. She drew her long legs to her chest, wrapped her arms around them, and waited in silence until Jorge said it was time to leave.

On the drive home, Jorge dropped a thick hand on her thigh, startling her. "I'm glad you didn't make a big deal about Noah coming with us to Lone Pine."

Caridad gaped through the windshield at two rapidly approaching orbs of light. Fuzzy dots at first, the bright spots sharpened, piercing the darkness with luminescence as they loomed closer and closer like headlights of an oncoming truck. She squeezed her eyes shut and kept them closed until they reached home.

The trip to Lone Pine in mid-July gave Caridad time to think over the small problems that had been cropping up since before the wedding, troubles easy to suppress as long as she was busy with school and work. Things she could forget entirely when she and Jorge were in bed, two bodies rocking together in the dark. Esperanza had told her years ago how she enjoyed intercourse only with Rey, claiming this as the sign of true love. Before they married, Rey would borrow money from Esperanza without paying it back, and he'd vanish for days without calling. He'd often return her from dates distraught and weeping. One night he stood outside the window to the bedroom she shared with Caridad, drunkenly insisting, "I shine, but you never see me shine." Over and over, Esperanza denied this. His shine, she'd said, was *all* she saw.

Fourteen-year-old Caridad, unable to sleep through this, lacked the nerve to tell them both to knock it off. But she'd made up her mind then that she would never allow a lover to hold her in such thrall. She was eager to shed the inexperience that would make her beholden in the way Esperanza was to Rey. Caridad's first time had been with Edmundo, a younger brother of one of Esperanza's friends, in the back of his cousin's van that was parked at the beach. The experience had not only been gritty and painful, it had also scared Caridad. The bestial look on Edmundo's face as he plunged had alarmed her. Later, before dropping her off at home, he'd taken a gilt chain from around his neck and handed it to Caridad, as if offering restitution. The chain held a medal depicting the Holy Family. Edmundo didn't call or try to see her after this, and Caridad soon lost it. Fair enough. She had no desire to kneel before a window to convince Edmundo that she saw his shine.

After a few other hasty trysts that left her feeling numb yet embarrassed, Caridad grew more inclined to believe her sister when she equated sexual pleasure to true love. At seventeen, Caridad met Jorge, a college friend of Rey's. Jorge listened to Caridad. He seemed to care about what she had to say. And when Jorge, who had been affectionate and gentle, managed to spark pleasure in her, Caridad suspected she was in love with him. In the early days of dating Jorge, she couldn't eat much or concentrate too well for the queasy ticklishness in her stomach. Love-sick, she told herself. This must be lovesickness.

Though sometimes she'd imagined living with Jorge, when he proposed to her, Caridad had gasped for breath, as if drowning. Mistaking hyperventilation for euphoria, Jorge later told his friends, "I took her breath away." This was similar to the sensation Caridad had experienced when Jorge decided to move to Echo Park from the Valley to be closer to her after they'd only been dating for a month. Dread and obligation had coiled around her, constricting like a python. But just as Caridad couldn't tell Jorge—an adult who could live wherever he chose—not to move near her, she later lacked the words for refusing his proposal without the risk of losing him.

The small car chugged along the highway, Jorge driving and Noah in the backseat, holding forth on various topics. In a tone of weary superiority, Noah used obscure technical terms whenever he could, and he relished being asked what these meant. But sometimes he misspoke words, like "hyperbole," which he pronounced as "hyper-bowl," conjuring for Caridad the image of an excitable Tupperware container. Yes, Noah, as Felicia often noted, was a "know-it-all shit-sucker," and as such, the confounding friendship he shared with Jorge was oftentimes unendurable to her. The identical beards, for one thing, prompted people to ask if the two were brothers, though Noah was a freckled redhead and Jorge was olive-skinned with dark brown eyes and hair. After Caridad first met Noah, she'd asked Jorge if he'd grown his beard to look like his friend. He'd hotly denied this as if they'd both, spontaneously and coincidentally, decided to adopt the Amish look, those *hyper*-beards.

Noah now leaned forward to say something to her.

Could he possibly need *more* room? She'd already scooted her seat as far as it would go, cramping her legs. "Beg your pardon?" she said.

"*Beg your pardon?*" Jorge affected a shrill falsetto. "Daydream Believer," he said, using his pet name for her.

"I *said* that this area is directly above the San Andreas Fault," Noah told her. "If there's any seismic activity, this stretch of highway will be blown to smithereens. An earthquake of just point five on the Richter scale could have the force and magnitude of a nuclear blast. No one here would survive it."

"Is that so?" Caridad said. What did Noah expect her to do with such information? Faint away with fear? Urge Jorge to speed up the car? Should she commence saying a rosary? They liked to frighten her, Noah and Jorge did, with threatening tidbits like this. They were like older brothers in this way, bedeviling a kid sister. Caridad affected a huge yawn. Then she opened the glove box to organize its contents, hoping Noah would again leave her alone.

She pulled a clutter of road maps onto her lap, smoothing one to bend it into its creases. Jorge once marveled at this ability of hers. "Who'd have thought," he'd said, "I'd meet the one female in the world who knows how to fold a map." And she had given him a wry look. How typical of Jorge, though, this amazement over simple things she could do, as if Caridad were a dog clever enough to operate a forklift. Whenever she offered a suggestion that Jorge found useful, his eyes would widen in surprise and he'd say, "That's *actually* not a bad idea."

She flapped out another map, and a crumpled sheet of notepaper tumbled to the floorboard. Caridad grabbed it. Martin Pineda's letter! She'd balled it into the long sleeve of her wedding gown and tossed it into the glove box when they'd left the church for the first reception. In the blur of events, Caridad had forgotten all about it. She now recalled the warm thrill of Martin's embrace, that moist kiss. Caridad stuffed the note into a gap between the buttons of her shirt, where the paper chafed her midsection as the small car chugged north.

Jorge parked near the mouth of the trail, and the three of them climbed out of the car to don backpacks, canteens, and baseball caps before beginning the three-mile trek to the campsite. Noah inaugurated the hike by lighting a joint and expressing his doubts that Caridad could keep up with their pace. She pretended not to hear him and waved the joint away, ignoring Jorge's pointed look. The inclined trail was steep, but Caridad, with her long legs, had no trouble keeping up with the two chunky stoners. At one point, she overtook Jorge and then Noah, who'd been leading the way. She kicked a stone into his shin when her boot flew up over a root, but she acted as if she hadn't noticed this. Caridad led the way until Noah sped up, red-faced and grunting, to pass her. She wasn't about to make a contest of it, so she slowed her pace and took in the view.

The afternoon was clear and sharp with color. The air smelled fresh rinsed, and the ground was spongy after a recent rain. Birdsong and insect chirps made soft music after the harsh roar of the highway. Iron-streaked cliffs rose in the distance, and a glassy ribbon of water glimmered at their base. Wild flowers grew in undulating pastel swaths, a lacey rickrack bordering the tall grasses. Up close, these were pink, yellow, and light violet, some with full blunt blooms radiating from neon hubs and others with petals clustered like tiny grapes. From her horticulture class, Caridad recognized meadowfoams, fiddlenecks, and the bright confetti of popcorn flowers. "*Plagiobothrys*," she murmured, admiring the first and most enduring blossoms of spring. Caridad gazed over the rims of her glasses, and the splotches of color transformed into pastel daubs, a blur of astonished faces in an impressionist painting.

"Watch out for poison oak," Noah called over his shoulder. "It's everywhere."

"And snakes," Jorge said.

Noah stopped and unscrewed the top of his canteen, signaling a short break. "The northern Pacific rattlesnake is indigenous to this region."

An insect thrum filled Caridad's ears, but was there a deeper sibilance, a hissing underlying this?

"Black bears, too, can be deadly," Jorge added.

"As are mule deer," Noah said.

"Mule deer?" Caridad pictured a hybrid creature, a long-muzzled and antlered beast that brayed. Even so, how could any kind of deer pose much of a threat?

"More attacks on humans by deer than bear in any given year." Noah removed his baseball cap to fan his florid face.

"Don't forget ticks," Jorge said.

"That's right." Noah nodded. "The deer tick is a vector for Lyme disease. You can be bitten without even knowing it. A lot of infected people don't find out until it's too late. Lyme causes meningitis and Bell's palsy, loss of control of one or both sides of the face."

Caridad gasped, raising a hand to her cheek.

Satisfied, Noah and Jorge stowed their canteens. Noah pivoted to resume leading the hike. A bank of charcoal-bellied clouds scudded overhead, shrouding the sun and draining the blooms of color.

At the campsite, Noah draped a tarp over the branches of a nearby tree and stretched out under that while Caridad and Jorge cleared away stones and twigs before assembling their tent. The tarp would suffice for him, Noah claimed, suggesting he was more rugged than they, when really he was just too lazy to set up a proper tent. Before nightfall, Jorge built a fire, over which Caridad heated canned beans, which they ate with bread. Jorge and Noah then roasted wieners and discussed the scabby psilocybin mushrooms that Noah had procured, which they would consume in the morning.

"There's enough for all of us." Noah jutted a thumb at Caridad. "I mean, if she wants to try some."

"You really should," Jorge told her. "It'll be so cool."

Wordlessly, Caridad banked the fire with a green switch sheared from a fallen branch, stirring the glowing coals to stoke the blaze. In the firelight, the two men looked more like brothers than ever, their sooty faces shining and those look-alike beards dipping and rising as they spoke. As the night grew darker and colder, they covered up with blankets and huddled closer to the fire, with Caridad in the middle. They sipped tequila, and Noah lit a joint and passed it to Caridad.

While she was handing it to Jorge, something warm scrabbled under the blanket, burrowing into the leg of her cutoffs. She jerked away, kicked off the covers. Caridad zinged the darkness with her switch, its tip glowing from the fire, and she whacked the intruding creature.

Noah yelped. He drew his right hand to his chest, shielding it with the other as if Caridad were likely to lash out again. She tossed the switch away, unsure if this had been an accident or if Noah had deliberately reached into her shorts.

"Why'd you do that?" Jorge asked Caridad, who shrugged in reply.

Noah examined his wounded hand, and Jorge fished the first-aid kit out of his nearby backpack. The tequila's harsh aftertaste tickled the back of Caridad's throat. She coughed and clapped a hand over her mouth, but still she snorted with laughter, tears filling her eyes. As such, the apology she managed was probably not too convincing to Noah or Jorge, who gaped at her, round-eyed with alarm.

In the morning, though, Caridad found no amusement in Noah's one-armed efforts to gather firewood. His right hand, bound in a mitt of gauze, was suspended in a knotted kerchief sling. Had she really injured him? Jorge seemed to think so. When they'd crawled into their sleeping bags last night, he'd turned his back to her and began snoring within minutes. Now he avoided her eyes as he helped Noah collect kindling in the chilly mist that had settled over the campsite like a diaphanous gray scarf.

Her shoulders, still aching from the weight of her pack, tightened anew. Sure, Jorge irritated her, but what if she likewise annoyed him? What if he'd been performing the same calculations as she had during the drive, tallying irritations before deciding that he no longer loved *her*? What if he now regretted marrying her and planned to ask for a divorce? All those wedding gifts to return! She'd have to move back home, sleep alone in her narrow bed—with no one to love her at night, no one to kiss her and call her "Daydream Believer," a nickname she *actually* liked. Caridad anticipated her mother's disappointment, Esperanza's pity, and Felicia's unsurprised satisfaction. "I knew it," her eldest sister would say. "I told you not to marry that fuck-head."

The note from Martin! What if Jorge had found it? What if in it Martin had proposed a clandestine meeting? And what if, after reading the note, Jorge drove right past their exit on their return to the Valley, heading to Echo Park instead to return her, like an unwise purchase, to her mother's house. Caridad slipped back into the tent. She pawed through the rumpled clothing she'd worn the day before. She flapped out her shirt. Where could it be? *Where?* She was rummaging through her backpack when Jorge called her to breakfast.

"Look, I'm sorry," Caridad told Noah as he spooned up instant oatmeal. "It was an accident, I swear." No point in explaining why she'd struck him—Jorge wouldn't believe her. "So," she said, "when are we going to try those mushrooms?"

With his uninjured hand, Noah produced the plastic bag from the pocket of his windbreaker, and Jorge's eyes at last met Caridad's, a slow smile forming on his face.

Noah predicted that soon after ingesting the psilocybin mushrooms they would "regurgitate the contents of their upper intestines." The tough bits tasted like burnt cork, but the mushrooms didn't upset Caridad's stomach, though she overheard Noah and Jorge retching in the distance. She'd lost sight of them when she wandered away on her own. From time to time, her ears filled with sounds of fluids slopping over rocks. Splashing noises blended with the groaning wind and gurgling creek. The soft plosion of mud underfoot combined with the fluty ululation of birdsong—all of it evoked a disrupted digestive tract. How had she overlooked this arrhythmic intestinal music in nature before now?

And why had she never noticed the leaf-people? How could she have missed the many hobbit-sized creatures comprised of twigs and branches and cloaked in many layers of dark foliage? They couldn't speak, of course. They had no mouths. But they beckoned with leafy limbs. Caridad followed them to a meadow carpeted with wild flowers, a vivid tapestry of blooms in different shapes and sizes. At the edge of the meadow, the leaf people pointed. *Look, look.* Caridad read their thoughts, which were somehow her thoughts, too. *See that? See?* A white flash lofted past, somersaulting over the wild flowers and then jerking like a kite. Caridad squinted. It was Martin's letter, twisted like an elongated bow tie. Cheered on by the leaf-people, Caridad lunged for it. But just as she was about to snatch it out of the air, a downdraft sucked it into a steep burrow. She peered in from the edge. Within the shaft, leaf people clung to earthen walls, thick with shaggy roots and vines. At the bottom, maybe ten feet down, the stark paper glowed in a lemony strand of light.

The leaf-creatures summoned her. *Remember Olenka*, they said without speaking, *and the supermarket. That thing on his neck!* They shuddered, leaves rattling, as if they had been there, standing beside Caridad when Jorge reached up for a peach at the top of a display. His beard rose with his chin to reveal a dark roseate pustule, distended as the head of a newborn mouse somehow hatching from his neck. Caridad had recoiled, certain that under his bunchy beard many more pustules erupted, kin to that king-sized carbuncle on his neck. Like her, the leaf-beings could see him straining for what was fresh and unblemished, as long as he bearded over his own damage. With Caridad, they'd later cringed at his outburst when the checker bowled the peach so it struck the counter's ledge with a squishy thud.

Come on, they urged her now. *Just one step, that's all. Too late for Olga Semyonovna, but not too late for you*, they told her, shaking their dusty green manes. Caridad pictured the mild Russian wife, her simple heart an empty vessel waiting to be filled with a husband's passions, and Caridad remembered arguing with Jorge's father in support of his art when the old man suggested Jorge set it aside to teach. How much easier it was to champion his desire than to dare speak her own: to be a writer herself like Anton, to compose the kind of stories that she loved to read, to remind the world that it was bad and dreary, but that stories—when told well—could be sublime.

She flexed her ankles, despite her stiff boots. Like a high diver poised at the lip of a springboard, she bounced on the balls of her feet. Instead of focusing on the spot where she would land, Caridad clenched her eyes shut. And she leapt.

Emergence

———

Dr. Pearce told Caridad to let him know if the blade became too hot. Seated upright with legs extended on the table, she nodded. The doctor flicked on the electronic saw that vibrated with contact on her cast. Warmth emanated from this, countering the chill in the pallid exam room. Tendrils of dust wafted where the blade ruptured the plaster. How hot was too hot? How would Dr. Pearce hear her over the buzzing handheld saw? She would have to touch his tanned forearm. Caridad glanced at his heavily lidded gray eyes. Anton Chekhov had been a striking-looking doctor, too. While his eyes were attentive, Dr. Pearce's jaw was slack, his mouth open. He had the dark piratical looks that are irresistible to many, coupled with a carelessness that was disturbing in a doctor. A yellowed button on his lab coat dangled like a jaundiced spider, his face was shadowed by stubble, his dark hair oily and uncombed.

Anton! How long had it been since she'd thought of him? The broken leg, the summer, the new semester, and especially a Shakespeare seminar—sparking a new infatuation—had all intervened since her preoccupation with Chekhov's stories. She used to have his words at the tip of her thoughts, and now only one phrase, the ending of "The Lady with the Dog," bobbed to the surface of memory: "the most complicated and difficult part of it was only just beginning." The saw's heat intensified. Caridad focused on the plaster cracking apart and her bony leg emerging, knobby but downed with fine dark hairs—a pale and tender hatchling.

Dr. Pearce warned her to take it easy. She'd have to build up her leg muscles through exercise. He produced a few pamphlets and a daily exercise chart. Caridad skimmed these gladly. She enjoyed lists, rules, and regimens. Hadn't she followed the doctor's instructions exactly in protecting her leg as it healed? Though at first the crutches hurt her underarms and caused her shoulders to ache, she became so adept that the sight of these, now propped against a chart illustrating the vascular system, released in her a surge of nostalgia.

Caridad would also miss the sympathy she'd drawn as she pegged along, swinging between her crutches to get to classes and work. She thought of Leland McWhorter, who saved a first-row seat for her in the auditorium where her psychology class met, and Barry Ketchum, a corny middle-aged student who carried her books from her Shakespeare seminar to her next class and then lingered, making bad puns until the professor arrived. At least she'd be done with that, but Caridad flashed on Leland's emerald eyes and the hank of sun-bleached hair that spilled over his face when he set the crutches at her feet.

"The bone's fused well," Dr. Pearce said. "Keep up with your physical therapy and avoid falling off any more cliffs, and you'll be fine." He winked.

Caridad didn't bother correcting him. It hadn't been a cliff at all, but a deep shaft into which she'd leapt to retrieve a letter she'd ultimately lost in the excitement of being rescued by Boy Scouts and then airlifted to a nearby hospital. That night, nine weeks ago, she was already watching *Jeopardy!* on the wall-mounted television in a hospital room, her leg encased in plaster, by the time Jorge and Noah burst through the door, looking like old-time prospectors with windburned faces. She'd signaled them to sit in the scoop chairs near the bed and to shush. The contestants were working their way through "The Bard," a category in which Caridad felt competitive. "Who is Oberon?" she'd called out, but before she could award herself dollar points for being correct, Jorge and Noah began asking so many questions that Caridad gave up, switching the television off with the remote control.

Noah wanted to know if she'd told anyone about the mushrooms they'd eaten. Caridad had been tempted to fan his anxiety, to torment him and Jorge in the way they provoked her. But they'd leave her alone sooner if she told them the truth, so Caridad admitted to keeping mum about this. She'd also refused all medication, in case it might interact badly with the hallucinogen. Her leg was throbbing by then in an excruciating way, as if Lilliputian miners drove pickaxes through her flesh and muscle, striking the shinbone until it reverberated, thrumming clear to her teeth with each blow.

Relieved, Noah ponied up to her bedside. He stroked his beard, sprinkling debris on the covers as he offered information on fractured bones with a focus on worst-case scenarios, including amputation. Caridad hoisted herself on her elbows, a hot white flash zapping her like an electric current. "I need *rest*," she said, before settling back into the pillow, eyes closed. Noah mumbled something about shock, which he said was "potentially fatal," but after a few moments, they'd shuffled out. Caridad flipped on the television in time for Double Jeopardy!

"Is your husband here to drive you home?" Dr. Pearce now asked.

"What? Oh, no, my sister's taking me home."

"In a day or so, you should be able to drive."

Caridad nodded, wishing she knew how.

A nurse appeared to replace the borrowed crutches with an aluminum cane. Leaning on it, Caridad limped into the waiting room, where Felicia sat, paging through a *Reader's Digest*. With her large brown eyes, tawny skin, and willowy shape, Felicia would be the loveliest of the three Delgado sisters, if not for her tendency to scowl, roll her eyes, and speak in a loud hectoring voice. Felicia now gathered up her purse and stood. "That only took for-fucking-ever."

After they made their way out the door, Felicia glanced below Caridad's gauzy skirt. "Ugh! Your leg's all withered and pathetic looking. You better shave that sucker and *fast*. Wear pants until it looks normal."

"It's pretty awful, I know," Caridad said, "but the bone has fused well."

When they reached the elevator, Felicia pumped the button marked with a down arrow. "I still don't get it."

"Get what?"

"I don't get why you were alone when you fell. Even though there were three of you since you took that jackass Noah with you on your honeymoon. I don't get *why* you took that jackass with you on your honeymoon in the first place, or why anyone in her right mind would spend a honeymoon in the woods. I just don't get *any* of it."

Caridad tapped the down button.

"I think honeymoon," Felicia continued, "and I think room service. I think candlelit dinners, champagne, and chocolates on the pillow. I do *not* associate honeymoons with sleeping on the ground and marching like a soldier." She gestured at Caridad's leg with the *Reader's Digest.* "Or broken legs."

Caridad gasped. "You took Dr. Pearce's magazine!"

"There's an article in here on the pancreas that Mama should read."

"You can't just steal things," Caridad said, secretly thrilled by her sister's minor theft and her dismissive attitude toward camping.

"And I don't get why Jorge couldn't bring you to this appointment," Felicia said. "He's not working, and he doesn't have class on Tuesdays."

Caridad shrugged.

A graduate student, Jorge collected unemployment on the sly. But on this day, he'd promised to help Geraldine build hutches for the rabbits she bred. Caridad insisted he follow through with his plans when she told him the appointment had been rescheduled. She needed some time away from him after their conversation that morning.

The day before, Noah had announced to Jorge that he and Geraldine planned to experiment with open marriage, "fortifying commitment to one another by developing a polyamorous relationship." He then convinced Jorge that he and Caridad ought to do the same. Over breakfast, Jorge brought up the idea, relaying Noah's suggestion that the couples try a foursome. While he was speaking, Caridad kept expecting Jorge to laugh, to say "gotcha" and tell her it was all a joke. Instead he'd fixed his eyes on the tabletop, repeating Noah's reasons why this would strengthen their relationship. The phone rang, and despite the cast, Caridad had been first to hobble for it. When the doctor's assistant asked her to come in that day, Caridad made up her mind to call her sister for a ride to the clinic.

Felicia punched the elevator button again. "Are there stairs?"

Caridad shoulders seized and her eyes filled. What if she slipped on the steps and rebroke her leg? While she'd managed well with the crutches, no way did she want to lumber on them for several weeks more, her leg outstretched before her like a length of wood. She pressed the button again. The elevator grumbled in an indecisive way, but a spaghetti strand of light seeped from the space between the doors and they slowly pulled apart.

After Felicia dropped her off at the guesthouse she and Jorge rented, Caridad changed into blue jeans and a tank top. Then she stumped about with the cane, collecting materials to paint the wall hanging she'd constructed for a studio art class. Jorge had urged her to enroll in the course, hoping she would become interested in art the way he was. Once in the workshop, Caridad enjoyed it. For her midterm project, she'd planned to construct a female torso out of bricks and mortar, as if a woman's headless, limbless body were bursting forth from institutional confinement, the bricks molding to her shape as she emerged. But terracotta bricks proved too heavy for mounting on the plywood backing, and these were too porous to stick to anything without mortar.

Caridad found a solution as she waited for Jorge to finish up in the ceramics lab one day. Lightweight kiln bricks adhered to the backing with epoxy, and they were soft enough to file and sand, forming breasts, stomach, hips. Now she was ready to paint the work, but the blond bricks she'd experimented with had soaked up color, resulting in a pinkish hue, a shade that suggested a female torso breaking into a powder room. Only an inexpensive brand of oxblood tempera, close enough to terracotta, held its color on the bricks, but the cheap paint rubbed off easily, even after drying.

When it was painted, Caridad would spritz the work with fixative spray, though she was unsure if the aerosol acrylic would work on paint. What a great thing if it did hold color and prevent smudging on more than just charcoal and pastel sketches. She imagined applications for the spray beyond art. Couples could mist each other with it to keep one another vibrant, their edges clear and defined. Nothing could go blurry. Caridad thought of the paper she was writing on Shakespeare's sonnets, the preoccupation with the ravages of time and the yearning for immortality in those verses. Although his poems composed a bonding solution of sorts in their ability to capture and preserve the observations of one great man long gone, the Bard would likely have appreciated a can of such stuff to spray over himself and those he loved.

Caridad, too, wished for some way to keep Jorge in sharp focus, the way he'd appeared when she'd first met him—sophisticated, mature, and even attractive. He'd had an attentiveness of expression in those early days that made Caridad feel as if what she had to say mattered. His brown eyes curved into quarter-moons when he laughed at her silly jokes. He'd rush home from class, and he would often take her to bed as soon as he arrived, and after they would talk and talk until it grew dark outside. Now when he returned home, he would kiss her cheek and pick up the newspaper to read the sports pages. If only she had sprayed that earlier draft of Jorge with something like fixative . . .

Caridad shook her head to release the silly thought. She propped the back door open and lugged out a crate containing the paint, brushes, rags, and a jar for water. Then she set the wall hanging atop a card table. She dipped her brush and stroked the kiln bricks with tempera, planning to fill in the spaces between the bricks with caulking putty once the paint was dry. The first coat soaked in a bit more than she liked, so Caridad repainted, saturating each brick. Radio music wafted through the bedroom window, the volume turned low so as not to disturb their elderly Cuban landlords who lived in the main house just yards away.

She'd already provoked them once by asking what was so bad about Fidel Castro anyway. After taking a survey course in Latin American politics, in which she learned that the dictator had nearly eradicated illiteracy and crime and developed a top-notch health-care program on the island, Caridad was curious why her landlords despised him. But the old man had given Caridad a withering look and shuffled off while his wife released a high-pitched stream of Spanish, like a teakettle whistling on a stove, as she vowed to shit on Fidel before naming members of his cabinet, friends, and family she would likewise defecate upon if given the chance.

The guesthouse was Caridad's first home apart from her mother's cluttered duplex. The maple-paneled living room and bedroom, the light and airy kitchen, and the closet-sized bathroom—all of it was neat and cozy, thanks to Jorge, who kept the paneling polished, the floors mopped, and the countertops, mirrors, and fixtures gleaming. He had also decorated the guesthouse with belongings he'd brought from the place he'd rented before moving here. While Caridad had vetoed the cartoonish black-light posters he'd had hanging in that room, she didn't mind the installation of his heated water bed or the bookcases he'd built. On their shelves, he'd arranged vessels and sculptures he'd crafted in the ceramics lab along with various potted plants Caridad had acquired from her horticulture class. In the center of one bookcase, Jorge displayed a large fishbowl terrarium in which he grew a bonsai that he himself had stunted, training the branches to twist laterally. He had a teensy battery-operated vacuum for suctioning dust from the glass, so it sparkled on the top shelf, greeting Caridad like a dazzling face whenever she returned home.

She also enjoyed the small backyard, an apron of concrete fanning out to a grassy patch separated from the yard of the landlords' house with chain-link fencing. They'd planted tomatoes and squash along the back fence. On warm evenings, they dragged out chairs and a hibachi to grill skewered vegetables for her and chicken or steak for Jorge. They would sip beers while their food seared, talking or listening to music through an open window the way Caridad was doing as she painted her wall hanging.

She recognized the first chords of a sentimental song as she painted, the lyrics lamenting a lost love. Slowed by the mournful song, Caridad applied final strokes of oxblood to the bricks, and the first line of a sonnet came to mind: "Music to hear, why hear'st thou music sadly?" She imagined herself regretting lost love, though she couldn't think who she might miss in this way. Probably not Jorge, who, after only a few months of marriage, had just proposed sharing her with his friends. How suggestible Jorge was when it came to Noah's ideas! No doubt he longed for an older brother, a surrogate for his weak-willed father. But this was too much. In a way, Noah pushed Jorge to choose between friendship and marriage, and he hadn't chosen her.

Reflecting on Jorge's connection to Noah, Caridad considered different ways of loving. Shakespeare's sonnets covered a range of romantic connections, from youthful muse to longtime companion—a few of his amorous verses even seemed to be directed from one man to another. Though she'd never experienced that once-in-a-lifetime lightning flash of attraction described in the song on the radio, Caridad knew—maybe too well—the commonplace closeness that Shakespeare now and again described. For her, this meant a day-to-day thing involving laundry, cooking, and dishwashing, a familiar affection that endured despite the bad haircut she'd once given Jorge, the eye-smarting stench that sometimes trailed him out of the bathroom, that persistent acne on his neck and back—oh, she could go on and on.

Shakespeare described a mistress's eyes as being nothing like the sun, and that seemed fair enough. But eyes not being like the sun, wiry hair, and even dun-colored breasts were little compared to that choking stink, those pustules, the way Jorge cracked his knuckles—all ten of them—and then his jaw and neck before starting again with his thumb, next the index finger . . . until Caridad yearned to slip off her shoe and smack him just as repeatedly on the head with it. She considered writing a sonnet about bad smells, pimples, and joint popping. She tried out a few verses, working through the meter in these. Then she rubbed her chin with her wrist, wondering what rhymes with "boredom"? *Whoredom? More dumb? Sore thumb?*

Caridad plunged her paintbrush into the jar of water nearby, pink-tinted clouds billowing as she stirred, and she hummed along with the radio. Despite the sad song, alone in the backyard that afternoon, she was pleased with her wall hanging. The sun warmed her bare shoulders. An occasional breeze bore the fragrance of burnt sugar from nearby magnolia blossoms, blending this with the scent of fresh-mown grass. Caridad cast her eyes upward and asked aloud of the mid-September sky, "Shall I compare thee to a summer's day?" As if in response, the tinny pitch of children's voices lofted from a few yards over, along with the repeated *thwack-thwack-thwack* of a bouncing ball. Beyond this, the regular whoosh of cars on the freeway sounded much like the susurrus of waves cresting and breaking.

Over these pleasant sounds, she didn't register the side gate opening until its rusted hinges squealed. Caridad glanced up, and Noah, wearing rumpled khakis and a short-sleeved shirt, appeared at the edge of the paved apron, the gate banging shut behind him.

"I knocked in front," he said. "You didn't hear me, so I came around back."

Caridad doused the paintbrush again, fanning the bristles at the bottom of the jar.

"A colleague dropped me off here to wait for a ride home. I took the car for an oil change this morning, and Jorge is driving Geraldine to the garage to retrieve it. They should be here soon, and Geraldine will spirit me home. No doubt Jorge has apprised you of all this."

If Jorge had mentioned this, the information had been eclipsed by the polyamorous bombshell he'd dropped. Still, Caridad nodded as if she'd been expecting Noah.

He pointed at her leg. "Ah, they've removed the cast. How was that?"

"Fine," Caridad said, glad she'd changed into Levi's when she returned home.

Noah squinted in the sunlight, his face pinkening with the heat. Then he grinned at her. "What's this?" He approached the card table. "This is *very* handsome work."

Before she could warn him not to touch the wall hanging, Noah had his hands on it. He was cupping the brick bosom when the gate shrieked open again. Jorge and Geraldine appeared in the backyard. Noah lunged away from the piece and raised a rust-stained palm to greet his wife and friend.

"So you told Jorge no *and* yes?" Esperanza asked her that Saturday while they waited in line at Foster's Freeze for lemon slushes to satisfy her sister's latest craving. When a teenaged boy pivoted away from the counter bearing a chocolate-dipped cone, they advanced a few paces, cars whizzing by on the boulevard behind them.

"I told him yes and no," said Caridad, reluctant to continue the conversation they'd started in the car.

"Yes and no?"

Caridad lowered her voice. "I said yes to the first thing and no to the second."

"No to the second . . . now that was the—oh my god. The *foursome?*"

In front of them, an elderly man wearing a tweed ivy cap cast a curious glance at them.

"*Shush,*" Caridad hissed. "Lower your voice."

"But that would mean you'd have to—*yuck!*" Esperanza frowned in distaste. "Noah has the skin of a piglet, a spotty little piglet. It would be like . . . *having intercourse with a piglet.*"

Now a woman with a toddler shifted sideways for a look at the sisters.

"Will you keep your voice down?" Caridad said. A lowrider Chevy pulled into the adjacent parking lot, mariachi music blasting from its open windows, seconds too late to drown out her sister's penetrating voice.

"And *her,*" Esperanza said in a stage whisper. "You'd have to do something, like, with your mouth *on her.*" She grasped Caridad's forearm. "Oh, Dah-Dah, that woman is awful. She's pushy and rude and just awful!"

"I said *no* to the second thing. *Remember?* I'm not doing any of that."

"Did I tell you she's been calling me?" Esperanza's smooth forehead crimped like gathered silk. "She calls and calls. Did you give her my number?"

"No, dummy, you did. Don't you remember? You gave it to her at my wedding. I told you not to." Caridad nudged her sister forward.

Single-minded Esperanza couldn't walk and chew gum at the same time, let alone walk while talking. "Why's she calling you?"

"She wants to observe the birth."

"*What?*"

"She's trying to get my permission so she can watch the baby being born."

"*No*, no way." Caridad knew well how Geraldine behaved with her animals when she "mated them," which she accomplished by jamming their sex organs together, the large woman mouth breathing the whole time. And when her rabbits gave birth, she'd gawk through the chicken wire, so as not to miss a speck of blood, a millimeter of placenta. Geraldine was far too interested in reproduction. She had no business bringing this disturbing fascination into Esperanza's delivery room. "Tell her no."

"I *have*," Esperanza said. "Every time she calls, I tell her that I don't want anyone but Reynaldo and of course the hospital people in the delivery room with me, but she keeps calling to see if I've changed my mind." Esperanza's dark eyes shone, her soft chin wobbled.

"Don't worry." Caridad clutched her sister's elbow to steer her forward. "We'll tell Felicia to call her."

"Let's get her a slush, too." Esperanza wiped her eyes with a wrist. "We can go right over to get Felicia to call that woman because I really can't take it anymore."

Caridad handed Esperanza a tissue from her bag and stepped to the counter to order.

"Now, what was the first thing?" Esperanza asked as they bore their drinks to the car.

"Open marriage," Caridad told her, "the polyamorous thing."

"That must have felt terrible. How could Jorge even *bring up* with such a thing? I'd be devastated if Reynaldo suggested this." Dog though he was, Rey was unlikely to coax his wife into participating in his extramarital activities. "That must have hurt you," Esperanza said.

"It really wasn't that bad." But now a knot tightened in her throat, and Caridad swallowed hard before saying, "Though the foursome thing makes me want to throw up, I can see some potential with the polyamorous stuff."

"So you said yes to that?"

"You bet I did."

Standing before the kitchen sink in her mother's house, Caridad felt like Gulliver or Alice in Wonderland just after taking a bite of the cake labeled *Eat Me*. The Formica countertop, cabinets, and basin appeared to have shrunk since the last time she'd been home, while Caridad had somehow *expanded*. Even the dining table, chairs, and stove seemed dollhouse-sized to her. Surely the guesthouse she and Jorge rented was much smaller than this. Had she then imagined this room larger while she was away? Her hand, pouring the syrupy dregs of her slush into the sink, flashed before her like a flesh-toned paddle. Or had she somehow increased in size? "Do I seem bigger to you?" she asked her mother, who was stirring beans on the stove nearby while Caridad's sisters phoned Geraldine from a bedroom.

"No, m'ija. Why? Oh my goodness!" Mama surveyed Caridad's midsection. "You and Esperanza both? When, tell me when?"

"What? No, no, *no*."

"I thought maybe . . . you're so quiet."

"Believe me, Mama, I'd tell you first, if it was anything like that."

"Es que, you are so misteriosa. I thought maybe *that* was your secret." She squinted at Caridad. "You used to be such a chatterbug."

"Chatter*box*, Mama." Caridad drew an arm over her mother's soft shoulder. "Don't worry about me. Really, I'm fine." She inhaled her mother's unmistakable scent—crushed coriander, tea roses, and traces of sandalwood soap. Caridad closed her eyes and she was five again, standing on the back porch, clinging to her mother and burying her face in her soft belly, clothespins in the pockets of Mama's housecoat jutting against Caridad's cheek. The memory of being safe and warm was so pervasive that she longed to stay in this shrunken kitchen now redolent with the aroma of bubbling beans and garlic, to remain here in her mother's house. It wouldn't take much. She could ask Felicia to take her to pick up her things while Jorge was on campus. Caridad pulled away from her mother, drawing breath to suggest this when Felicia burst into the kitchen, Esperanza in tow.

"What a twisted bitch!" Felicia said.

Mama cupped her ears. "Cuidate, muchacha. I didn't raise you to curse like a salesman."

"*Sailor*, Mama," Esperanza said.

"This woman, this *friend* of Jorge's wants to horn in on the baby's birth. She's trying to get ringside seats to the main event." Felicia's eyes widened with outrage.

"¿Que dice?" Mama asked Esperanza, who explained about the pestering phone calls.

Lips compressed, Caridad's mother drew back, doubling her chin. "Pues, I hope this is the end of it."

"Oh, it better be," Felicia said, "or I'll drive out there and seriously fuck that woman up." She grabbed her slush and drew noisily on the straw. Then she turned to Caridad. "I really don't know what Jorge is doing with such stupid friends, or why you put up with that." Felicia's eyes flashed as she redirected her hot feelings toward Caridad. "Seriously, who's going to respect you if you don't respect your own damn self and make people act right?"

Esperanza collected her purse and keys from the table. "I've got to get the car back in time for Rey to play basketball at noon. We'd better go," she told Caridad. "Unless Felicia wants to drive you—"

"Actually, Felicia doesn't want to drive anyone anywhere," Felicia said. "I can't *believe* you don't drive! This is L.A., you know, not some sleepy pueblo where you can walk barefoot to the zocalo in minutes. You need to get your damn license and start driving like a normal person."

"Déjala," Mama told Felicia before turning to Caridad. "But, m'ija, you should learn to drive. Ask Jorge to teach you. He's so patient and kind." Mama smiled as she often did when she mentioned her son-in-law's name. "I bet he's a good teacher."

Caridad nodded, glancing down at the pale flippers that were now her hands.

Just over two weeks later, on a Sunday afternoon, Caridad ironed a muslin peasant blouse. She would tuck it into her straight-leg Levi's to offset her narrow waist and slim hips, and she planned to wear her long hair down so it would swing with her stride. In a camisole and jeans, she set up the ironing board in the living room where Jorge hunched in an armchair, staring into a thick paperback. He'd begun reading fiction lately, at last showing interest in the books Caridad loved. Now he was plowing through *Anna Karenina* in a determined way, though his face was set in an expression of contempt, as though he resented Tolstoy for coming up with the idea for the novel in the first place.

Caridad glanced up at her wall hanging, which was mounted over the chair where Jorge sat. How awful it would be if the bricks came loose and crashed down on his head. Noah had been right, though. It was a handsome piece. She'd repainted the places that he'd touched. This made the color richer and deeper, more oxblood than terracotta, even better than she had imagined. She misted her blouse with water and then ran the hissing iron over the fabric. The fragrant steam called to mind cloud-swollen skies on a summer afternoon just before the first raindrops patter down to sizzle on the cement.

"What time is he supposed to be here?" Jorge asked.

Caridad checked her wristwatch. "Not for another fifteen or twenty minutes."

"I'm going to be pissed off if he's late."

"*Why?* He's not coming to see you." This was awkward—her husband waiting with her for her date to arrive.

"It's rude to be late," Jorge said. "Shows lack of consideration."

Caridad shrugged. Leland had been so laid-back in making the date that he didn't seem to care whether she accepted or not. When she told him she was married, he'd lifted an eyebrow as though intrigued, and after she explained about the open marriage, he'd said, "Cool." He might easily be late or not turn up at all. "Even if he doesn't come and I have to take the bus to Fairfax," Caridad told Jorge, "I'm going to see that movie." After learning she was in a Shakespeare seminar, Leland had invited her to see Zeffirelli's *Romeo and Juliet* with him at the Laemmle Theatre.

"I can take you."

"No thanks." Caridad pulled the warm blouse over her head and tucked it into her jeans. Then she collapsed the ironing board and stowed it in the closet with the iron. She brushed and brushed her hair until the dark waves crackled with static. Standing before the bathroom mirror, Caridad regarded her reflection. An ordinary face, she thought, distinguished by its lack of distinction apart from her hazel eyes, an unexpected contrast to her dark lashes, eyebrows, and hair. Her glasses muted this, making her even more commonplace and approachable to people like Jorge, Barry, and even Leland. Unlike Juliet, nothing about Caridad "doth teach the torches to burn bright!" She pinched color into her cheeks and turned away from the mirror. After packing her glasses in her purse, she was ready to go. As Jorge had predicted, Leland was late. While she waited, Caridad sat across from Jorge and listened to his complaints about *Anna Karenina*.

"She's so selfish," he said. "I mean, her husband's really not *that* bad. All that stuff about Levin and local politics and agriculture—do we really need all that? I don't get why this is supposed to be such a great book."

"Maybe you should have started with something less complicated," Caridad told him, a thread of meanness tightening her voice.

Jorge glanced up, his dark eyes round with surprise. Ruddy splotches bloomed above his beard as if Caridad had slapped him. He cleared his throat. "This isn't what I meant, you know. This isn't what I had in mind when I brought up open marriage."

Caridad gazed into her lap. She plucked a strand of hair from the denim and released it to sail to the floor. He'd said this a few times before, explaining that he'd just hoped they'd grow closer to Noah and Geraldine, deepen their relationship by getting to know their friends and themselves more intimately. Jorge would go on and on before winding up with an accusation: She'd taken things too far. He'd never wanted the marriage opened *this* much. At which point, Caridad would observe that either a thing is open or it's not. "You open anything up," she'd told him, "and something's liable to get out."

Jorge now held up the book as if offering it in evidence. "Don't you know how much I love you? I would do anything for you."

The old Caridad, the Caridad she was just over a month ago, would have rushed to his side, enfolded him in her arms, and insisted she loved him, too. But that Caridad had slipped away—something had cracked apart, the space widening just enough for her to wriggle through. This new Caridad remained seated, tensing and releasing the leg she had broken, the habit of exercise difficult to shed, though the break had mended so well that Dr. Pearce had cleared her to take tennis in the spring.

"Anything," Jorge said again. "I mean it. I'll do whatever you want."

She considered Noah and Geraldine, the things people never should ask of one another—giving up friendship had to be among these. How could she expect Jorge to surrender a relationship that was likely to prove more enduring over the long course of his lifetime than his now tenuous connection to her? And even if he gave up his friends, Caridad knew it would be impossible for her to unknow what she had discovered about Jorge and about herself during the brief time they'd been married.

Caridad glanced at the bookcase, her face reflected like a hologram in the luminous glass bowl housing the dwarf tree. She dropped her eyes. A patch of sunlight poured through the open window, funneling dust filaments glittery as stardust and blanching the flat gray carpet. Caridad and Jorge sat motionless, grim as Victorian portrait models. A mower coughed twice before rumbling over a nearby lawn, and the neighbor's dog, scraping the links of its heavy chain against the concrete, woofed at this.

A fist pounded on the front door, and they both jumped.

Renew and Renew

In early November, Caridad and Esperanza's friend Darlene married her longtime boyfriend Sergio. After the church service, Caridad trailed Esperanza and Reynaldo into the reception hall. They made their way past buffet tables laden with platters of cold cuts and cheeses bedded on lettuce, cut-glass dishes heaped with pickles and olives, baskets of rolls and breadsticks, and trays of fruit and julienned vegetables radiating like spokes from hubs of glistening dip. Recessed in a shrine-like alcove, the cake—a multi-tiered monument under a thick façade of buttercream frosting and corniced with sugary rosettes—glowed under soft lighting. Caridad's stomach rumbled, and she coughed to disguise this. Esperanza turned to her. "Are you all right?"

"My throat's a little dry." But Caridad's mouth went juicy at the sight of dark green champagne bottles arrayed on shelves near the buffet.

"Let's find our table," Esperanza said, "and get something to drink." She took her sister's arm as if Caridad were too weak from thirst to walk, but then Esperanza whispered in her ear, "Dah-Dah, I feel dizzy."

Caridad clasped her sister about the waist, buttressing her back as she guided her through the hall, now echoing with voices and footsteps and chairs scraping the bare floor. She towed Esperanza close behind Reynaldo's navy blazer as he plowed ahead, parting clusters of guests. Rey then stooped over various tables arranged in the hall, checking place cards for their seats. Esperanza's satin dress, a burgundy maternity gown, slithered against Caridad's silky shift with each step. She paused to reinforce her grip when Reynaldo at last beckoned them to a table in back.

Once they were seated, Reynaldo produced a handful of butterscotch disks. He opened one and popped it between Esperanza's lips. "Gestational diabetes," he said.

"*Diabetes?* Like Mama?"

Esperanza shook her head.

"It's just that the hormone levels interfere with the insulin. Once the kid's born, she'll be okay." His shining moment—*at last, some shine!*—of husbandly solicitude drawing to a close, Rey scanned the reception hall. "Hey, there's Memo." He stood and then leaned to kiss Esperanza. "Keep an eye on her," he told Caridad before heading away from the table.

"I just need to eat something every few hours," Esperanza said. "I haven't had anything since lunch. What time is it now?"

Caridad glanced at her watch. "It's after four." Caridad hadn't eaten anything more than a leathery slice of pizza for breakfast. The pizza had been left over from supper with Leland McWhorter, their last date before his stint as an Americorps VISTA volunteer in the Mississippi Delta. That morning, Leland had slipped away for an early flight so quietly that she had been surprised to awaken to an empty pillow beside hers.

Esperanza fixed her with a sharp look. "Have you seen Jorge lately?"

Caridad shook her head.

"Do you think he's here?" Esperanza surveyed the hall.

"Of course not."

"Darlene and Sergio came to your wedding."

"*I* invited them. Darlene is our friend, not his." The past few weeks had shown Caridad that when newlyweds separate, husband and wife take with them what they brought into the marriage, from personal belongings to friendships. Her throat had clotted when Jorge crated his terrarium bonsai, but when she considered the absence of Noah and Geraldine from her life these days, it was with relief, not regret.

"Why won't you two work things out? Marriage isn't always easy, but it's *worth* it." In the background, Rey's honking laughter rang out, followed by a feminine titter. Esperanza's face tightened, but she said, "You have to compromise, make sacrifices even. Sometimes the hard thing is the right thing to do."

"And sometimes the hard thing is just the hard thing to do." Caridad was tired of hearing about marriage as work from Esperanza and Mama, as if it were an unpleasant chore, as if all she had to do was roll up her sleeves and go at it the way she'd scrub a floor and *wah-la!*—as she'd say when playing magician as a child—she would again desire Jorge, whose touch had repelled her in the end, like the unwanted advance of some creepy cousin. Caridad pushed back her chair. "Let's get something to eat."

Before she rose from her seat, the bride and groom burst into the hall to an explosion of applause. Someone chinked a spoon against glass, and the guests grew silent. While servers scurried about pouring champagne, the best man muttered a lengthy but inaudible toast to the married couple. A waiter filled all six flutes at the table where only Caridad and her sister sat. When Esperanza pushed hers away, Caridad whisked it to her lips for one sly gulp, reserving her own flute to lift for the toast. As the best man droned on, the champagne's tingling warmth blunted the sharp edge of her hunger. Even so, after glasses had been raised and Caridad drained a second flute, she and Esperanza bolted for the buffet. There, they filled their plates, constructing towers of crudités, cheeses, fruits, and bread that were barely architecturally sound in their defiance of gravity.

When they returned, an unfamiliar gray-haired man and woman were seated at their table, a pair that Caridad took to be siblings or a couple married so long that man and wife resembled one another. Both were spare and stringy with smallish heads of close-cropped ash-colored hair. She left it to Esperanza to sort out who they were, while Caridad sipped Rey's champagne. She then cast a covetous glance at the full flute before the vacant seat near hers. Just as her hand traveled toward it, a bright blur scudded in the periphery. The scent of lilacs gusted near, and gloved fingers landed on her outstretched arm.

"Darlene!" Caridad stood to embrace the bride.

"You look beautiful!" Esperanza told Darlene.

But veil askew, flushed in the face, and wearing false eyelashes, Darlene looked blinkered and blundering. After exchanging greetings, the bride reached around to produce a slender dark-haired and moustachioed man who'd been lurking behind her vast tulle skirt. "This is Seth Dunbar," Darlene told them. "He plays guitar in Sergio's band."

"Bass," Seth said. His thinning black hair gathered into a ponytail, Seth had the expressive eyes of a silent film star. Caridad pictured a legionnaire's cap obscuring his receding hairline and skimpy ponytail and more dramatically framing those limpid eyes.

"Bass, whatever." Darlene shrugged. "He's sitting at your table, so take care of him, hear?" And with another whir of tulle, she disappeared into the sea of suit jackets and pastel dresses in the direction of the buffet.

Leading Seth into the guesthouse that night, Caridad was glad that she'd tidied up for Leland's visit the previous night. At least the bathroom wasn't disgusting, and the kitchen, apart from the empty pizza box on the counter, wasn't too bad either. But she regretted that the front door opened into the bedroom. Caridad had neglected to straighten the tumble bedding that morning. Since Jorge had taken the bed, she now slept on blankets heaped on a foam pad. If she smoothed the layers out and covered it all with her mother's peach satin comforter, it didn't look too bad, especially in the gentle glow of her oil lamp. But under the harsh glare of the overhead fixture, the room looked as if it had been ransacked, with clothing and books strewn among blankets.

"Sorry for the mess," she told Seth. "I was in such a rush that I couldn't get much done." In truth, she'd been reading Flaubert's *Madame Bovary* while gnawing on the tough wedge of pizza. By noon, she was engrossed in the story—Emma Bovary, after losing Léon, encounters the dashing Rodolfe, who notices poor Emma "gaping after love like a carp on the kitchen table after water." Caridad then crawled under the comforter to devour several more pages, thinking Jorge should read the novel. Then maybe he would see it was not enough that Emma's husband, like Anna Karenina's, was not *that* bad—*what a standard!*—and hadn't Charles Bovary himself sought an ideal in Emma after his plain and shrewish first wife? But an unsophisticated reader like Jorge would surely find Emma Bovary as selfish and unlikable as Anna Karenina.

She'd read on and on, openmouthed and gasping carp-like herself as Emma grew reckless in her passion, risking more and more while Rodolfe withdrew in alarm. When Caridad glanced at her watch, she'd been shocked by how late it was. Still, she took the book into the bath with her, and then she'd scrambled to dress before Esperanza and Reynaldo picked her up for the wedding. Now the novel was lying facedown, pages splayed like wings of a bird shot down midflight, atop the jumbled bedding.

"It's usually not like this," she told Seth.

"It's fine," Seth said. "You should see my place."

They stepped into the kitchen, and Caridad flipped on the light. "Where's that?"

"I'm kind of staying with my folks now. It's not easy, you know, making it as a musician, so they're helping me out."

"Where do your parents live?"

"Brentwood."

"That's not too bad." Caridad imagined Felicia's voice braying in her ear: *Brentwood! Well, la-dee-fucking-dah!*

"Well, it's Brentwood. It's not a cool or happening place. Mostly old people live there."

Mostly rich people live there. Caridad collapsed the pizza box to fit it into the garbage.

Seth shrugged. "It's tough for musicians. You've got to make sacrifices."

Caridad nodded. It was hard for her to get by as a student, especially living alone. She'd never anticipated how difficult it would be to afford rent, utilities, and groceries on her work-study paycheck. Caridad worried that she would have to drop out and find a full-time job. Before the pizza, provided by Leland, she'd eaten saltines swiped from the campus cafeteria for dinner two nights in a row. The phone had been disconnected earlier that week, and she'd unplugged the empty refrigerator to save on electricity.

"Nothing's easy," she said. Picturing Brentwood's rolling lawns that led to columned edifices large enough to house entire neighborhoods in Calcutta or whole villages in the Congo, Caridad jammed the pizza box into the trash and offered Seth a glass of water.

In the morning Caridad woke to the dull clatter of crockery, the jangle of flatware. She turned on her side. The aroma of toasted bread wafted her way, and she sat upright. *Leland!* But an adenoidal falsetto—*ah, ha, ha, ha, stayin' alive, stayin' alive*—floated into the bedroom. She reached for her robe. Caridad shrugged it on and padded to the kitchen, where she found Seth fully dressed and peering into the oven.

"Good morning," she said.

"Hey, gorgeous." Seth slammed the oven shut and grinned at Caridad. His dark eyes were even more beguiling than they had been the day before, but his thick black moustache parted oddly in the middle when he smiled. Combined with his overbite, this made him look like an eager rabbit. He wagged a finger at Caridad. "You realize, young lady, that you have no food whatsoever in this house?"

At least she had her own place. "I've been kind of busy and—"

"Nah-*uh-uh*, no excuses—you have nothing to eat." Seth smiled, those dazzling eyes shining. "So I went out and picked up a few things for breakfast. I hope you like bagels and orange juice and coffee. I also got the Sunday paper . . ." He nattered on and on as he set out the food and the newspaper on the dinette table.

As they ate, Seth hummed and read aloud passages in the newspaper to her. He called her Mother Hubbard a few times, teasing her about the empty refrigerator. By the time they piled plates in the sink for washing, Caridad's temples pulsed in a warning way. She thought of Emma Bovary's unclouded glimpse of Léon, the lover who supplanted her husband: "Each smile," wrote Flaubert, "hid a yawn of boredom . . . each pleasure its own disgust . . ."

Seth stacked a last dish and turned to her. "So what do we want to do today?"

We? She knew what *she* wanted to do that day. Finish *Madame Bovary*, of course. If she were alone, she'd run a hot bath and soak in it while she read. Then she'd wash her hair and dry it in the sun, sipping tea brewed from the bag of chamomile she'd stashed in her purse at the reception. All the while, Caridad would savor the richness, the absolute luxury of solitude. No way to shut out the neighborhood noises— cars whooshing past, children's voices, barking dogs—but such sounds demanded nothing of her. After turning the last page, she'd flip back to the first page to start the novel over. She glanced toward the bedroom, where she'd left the book on the floor.

Seth traced her gaze and took her hand to lead her to the disheveled bedding. And, okay, the lovemaking was fine. Until their last days together, Caridad had enjoyed sex with Jorge, and she'd liked it more with Leland, who couldn't call her even if he wanted because her phone was disconnected. She pushed Leland from her thoughts while Seth was kissing her throat and making guttural sounds like an ardent pigeon. Caridad focused on Seth in a determined way. His urgency— like the morning's patter of compliments—flattered her. Still, Seth was uncomfortably bony, his moustache now redolent of coffee and onion bagels. His ivory-hued skin, though, was smooth to the touch, and Caridad's mind wandered to advertisement jargon: *silken, soft, supple.* Then she drew him into her with a low sigh.

They spent the rest of the morning strolling about Caridad's neighborhood. They walked as far as the park, more than a mile from the guesthouse. The day was dry and windy, and cool gusts whipped Caridad's hair into her face. Gritty dust devils spun near gutter grates, and banners in used-car lots on Laurel Canyon Boulevard billowed and snapped. Store windows were already festooned with Christmas displays of wrapped gifts on cottony tufts, the glass decorated with chalky images of candy canes, snowy trees, and images of Santa Claus.

"Isn't it strange how we fetishize snow?" she said. "It never snows here, so these displays invert the experience of snow. We on the outside have to look at representations of snow inside or on windows." If she'd told Jorge this, he would likely roll his eyes and say, "There she goes again, my Daydream Believer."

But Seth said, "I never thought about it before. That's pretty deep."

She smiled and took his hand. They passed a menswear shop, and Seth stopped to admire a blue dress shirt on a mannequin. Caridad found the print too loud for her taste, but she made a mental note of it, in case she'd ever have occasion to give him a gift.

After the park, no more than a swing set and slide in a wooded copse, they headed back to the guesthouse, and then Seth drove her to shop for more groceries. At the supermarket, Caridad filled a cart with fresh vegetables and fruits, bread, and cheeses. She tipped in rolls of paper towels and toilet paper, shampoo and dishwashing detergent. Not since living with Jorge had she tossed whatever she liked into a shopping basket. Her mind reeled with menu plans and recipes until she felt giddy, so preoccupied that she pretended not to notice when Seth dropped a toothbrush into the cart, along with a stick of deodorant.

When they returned to the guesthouse, Caridad pulled out her cookbooks to concoct vegetarian lasagna. She spent the late afternoon chopping vegetables and measuring ingredients, stirring sauce, and then layering noodles, cheese, and sauce in a casserole. Savoring the garlicky vapors, Caridad hardly registered Seth's talky presence in the close kitchen. After they ate and he settled in to stay for the night, she meant to mention that he might want to go home. But the hard truth was that as long as Seth stayed, she would have food to eat. The entire day, she hadn't had to endure the headachy listlessness, her nearly pornographic obsession with food, or that dull sense of panic caused by hunger, so Caridad didn't suggest that Seth return home that night or the next.

By the time Seth began hauling over trunk-loads of his belongings, including his bass guitar and stereo system from his parents' house, it was too late to protest without causing a tiresome conflict. Living with Seth meant Caridad wouldn't have to leave school to work full time or find a roommate to share the one-bedroom guesthouse with her. Why, Seth could be that roommate, and they would help one another: Seth by contributing to rent and household expenses, and Caridad by providing him a place to live apart from his parents. All would be fair and balanced—a mutually beneficial arrangement between adults. She discussed this with him, and Seth praised the sensibility of this plan. When the rent was due, he counted out half the amount in twenty-dollar bills, though Caridad wished he would have written her a check for this, instead of snapping each crisp bill into her palm.

A month after moving in, Seth planned a Saturday outing for them. He wouldn't tell Caridad where they were going, except to say that they'd be outdoors. They had to stop at his parents' house first to pick up his acoustic guitar, and Caridad steeled herself to endure a beach or park serenade. The December morning was chilly, so she pulled a hooded gray sweatshirt over a thermal top that she tucked into Levi's, and Seth dressed in a pair of blue-and-yellow plaid pants with a violet T-shirt bearing an antipollution slogan along with an applique of a craggy-faced Indian in a headdress, a solitary rhinestone-studded teardrop coursing down one weathered cheek.

Lately Caridad had tried to influence Seth's sense of style. Not out of possessiveness, but just as one roommate advising another. So far, she'd concentrated her efforts on persuading him to shed the ponytail, a look that emphasized his bulging forehead. But he claimed it identified him as a musician, a ponytail-wearing member of rock-band culture. That morning, she'd been so dumbstruck by Seth's loud pants and corny shirt that she'd blurted, "What the—"

"Eye-catching, isn't it?" he said. "Wait until you see where we're going, and you'll see why I need to stand out."

During the drive to Brentwood, Seth talked about his parents, weaving together strands of memory, longing, and family legend. While he spoke, Caridad considered *Madame Bovary* and how that narrative was put together—tragedy and absurdity, the stories within the novel inscribing the lives of Emma's father, Charles's mother, the ambitious pharmacist Monsieur Homais, and even the merchant Monsieur Lheureux, who extended credit to Emma, entangling her in debt. Caridad considered what these stories revealed about the characters and even about Flaubert. What did Seth's family stories say about him? Clearly, he admired his father, but his mother emerged less distinctly as he spoke.

Over the past weeks, Caridad learned that Seth was a twenty-five-year-old UCLA graduate who worked for his father selling wholesale gems to jewelers. At first he had been secretive about this, as if worried that Caridad, who wore no more adornment than a wristwatch, might expect him to lavish her with trinkets. Seth claimed to work well with his father, though sometimes he was disappointed about his commissions. Even so, he seemed to have plenty of money. He'd bragged to her that his new car was paid for outright—a gift from his father.

Before he'd begun selling precious stones, his father, Cyril Dunbar, had been a musician, too, a trumpet player in a jazz band. Cyril—who liked his sons to call him Cy—supported Seth and his older brother in their creative and spiritual pursuits. He'd even traveled to Southeast Asia with them for a Buddhist pilgrimage. They were all chanting Buddhists, the Nam-myoho-renge-kyo kind. The previous day, Seth had talked about assembling a shrine in the guesthouse, but Caridad, a lapsed Catholic, was uneasy about this. Now, speaking of his father and his spiritual support, Seth again mentioned installing a shrine. "It wouldn't have to be a big deal," he said. "Just a few brass cups, some incense holders."

"There's no room for that." Wasn't it enough that she was handing over a Saturday to him? She wasn't about to relinquish space for him to chant in the house on top of this.

"I'd put it in the towel closet and build shelves for towels in the bathroom."

"The bathroom's already too cramped."

"You're just being stubborn. It'd be such a small shrine you wouldn't even notice it."

"I like the towels where they are."

"My parents have a shrine," Seth said. "It doesn't hurt anything."

"That's their house. Not mine." Caridad gazed out the window at the other cars on the freeway, imagining that the many faces blurring past belonged to people on their way to places they really wanted to go.

When they arrived at Seth's family home, his mother Nancy, a slender white-haired woman with Seth's smoldering eyes, greeted them at the door. "So nice to meet you," Nancy said. "I always enjoy meeting Seth's girlfriends." She welcomed Caridad with a cool handshake and apologized for not offering refreshments. "It's Marta's day off," she explained as she led them into the house.

The living room struck Caridad as spacious beyond sense. The hardwood floor covered twice the area of Caridad's entire guesthouse. The walls were beige hued with a creamy trim at the wainscoting, and the blocky furniture was constructed of dark wood and upholstered with black leather. Despite the vastness of the room, the place felt close and overheated, emanating musty odors that Caridad associated with the elderly: Ben-Gay, mildew, and the acrid scent of dust burning in furnace vents. Seth led Caridad to the shrine at the end of a long hallway. There, Caridad beheld the shelves of brass bowls and handleless cups, the photograph of an emaciated man in a sagging dhoti atop one of these, and incense sticks sprouting like follicles from a bisque vessel.

"Nice," she said. The setup was not nearly as vibrant as her mother's altar for Our Lady of Guadalupe, with its turquoise and coral brightness, smoky copal, and votive flames guttering in beveled glass.

Seth turned to his mother. "Caridad doesn't want a shrine at our place."

Nancy issued a thin smile. "You should have a shrine if you want one."

"There's no space for it," Caridad said.

A door opened on one side of the hallway, and a red-faced man with crinkly gray hair partially encircling his bald head appeared at the threshold. "Seth," he said in a coarse, phlegm-thickened voice. "How's my boy?" He limped forward with a rolling gait.

After embracing his son, Cy glanced at Caridad. "How are you?" He spoke to her in a slow and amplified voice.

"I am fine," she said, also in a loud voice, in case *he* didn't hear well.

"Good, good!" Cy clasped Seth's elbow and led him into the room from which he'd emerged. "Excuse us, ladies. I want a private word with my son," he said before shutting the door behind them.

"Seth tells me you like to cook," Nancy said. "He's bragged about your lasagna."

Wary that Nancy would next ask about her aptitude for housecleaning, Caridad shrugged. "I just follow recipes." She gazed again at the shrine. The fine sifting of dust that coated the brass bowls suggested that Marta shared her indifference for the bland display. Muffled voices were audible from behind the closed door, but Caridad couldn't make out much until the old man uttered a distinct phrase: *jail bait*. This was followed by protestation from Seth. Her face hot and salty, Caridad stroked the cushion on a stool near the shrine.

"Of course, it's a lot of trouble for Seth to set up a shrine if he isn't going to be staying long," Nancy said.

Caridad looked into the woman's large glimmering eyes. "That's right."

"It's a shame Marta isn't here," Nancy told her. "You'd like her."

Seth and his father emerged from the side room, talking about plans for the next week: appointments to schedule and calls to make. Seth took Caridad upstairs to collect the guitar from his room. Before long, they tramped downstairs, ready to leave for their outing. Seth's mother invited them to return for dinner, saying she was sure she could fix something, though it wouldn't be much. Before Caridad could come up with an excuse, Seth accepted.

He and Caridad stepped out through the kitchen into the garage instead of using the front door because he needed a guitar case stored there. In the dimly lit space, they first had to squeeze past an enormous boat—a canvas-covered monstrosity that barely fit in the enclosed space—to reach the shelf that held the guitar case. Seth wiped this off and opened it to fit his guitar inside. Then he pushed a button in the wall to raise the garage door, and they stepped out into thin sunlight toward Seth's car in the driveway.

Once in the car, Seth said, "My parents seem to like you."

Caridad turned to gape at him.

"They do," he insisted. "Didn't they ask us to dinner?"

"What did your father say to you in that room?"

"It was just business stuff."

"Nothing about me?"

Seth gave a small shrug. "He thinks you look young. That's all."

"*Right.*" Caridad clicked on the car radio.

"How come *you* get to do that?" Seth's raised voice startled her. "Why do you get to sit in *my* car and turn on the radio without asking? What gives you the right when I can't even have a shrine in the place where I pay rent to live?"

Caridad switched the radio off, and they rode in silence until Seth parked the car in a lot near Barney's Beanery in West Hollywood. She hoped Seth's mood would shift with a warm meal. It was past one, and she looked forward to a bowl of chili on a frigid afternoon like this. But when they climbed out of the car, Seth opened the trunk to pull out his guitar case. "I'm going to sing for our soup," he said with a smile.

She trailed those clownish pants down the boulevard to a breezeway between two office buildings. The offices were closed now on the weekend, but the breezeway was filled with pedestrians on their way to shops and restaurants. When he was satisfied by a spot, Seth settled the guitar case on the pavement, flipped it open, and pulled out his guitar. *Sing for our soup?* Heat suffused Caridad's face, and her eyes stung. Shock and shame collided in her with such force that the ocean seemed to roar in her ears. Seth left the case open and placed a few dollars in it. Then he tightened and tested the strings before launching into "Blackbird."

Passersby hurried along without glancing at him. Caridad pulled her hoodie over her hair and inched toward a bus stop, hoping to be taken for a waiting passenger, connected only by mild curiosity to this street musician. Despite the chill, her cheeks continued burning and her armpits prickled. Caridad's gaze swept eateries and stores across the street. She examined her bare hands, reddening with the cold, and stared at the cars rushing past. When Seth looked her way, she smiled, but like a house in flames, she was engulfed in mortifying emotion.

He called it busking, but Seth was begging, and she was by his side. Face it—she was *with* him; together they petitioned strangers for money. She thought of her mother and sisters, envisioning the confusion and disbelief on their faces if they saw her like this. At last, the song ended, and no one had dropped as much as a coin into the case. *Please*, she silently implored him, *please stop*. But Seth strummed another chord, and his nasal voice rang out: "Teach . . . your children well. Their father's hell . . . did slowly go by. And feed . . . them on your dreams . . ."

"All of that sounds seriously fucked up," Felicia told her the next week at their mother's house. The three sisters had gathered to celebrate their mother's December 12 birthday by preparing enchiladas for her and presenting her with small gifts. Caridad had scraped together enough money to buy her a sugar-free cake. And now, after supper, Esperanza was giving their mother her "gift" of dyeing her gray hair black in the bathroom while Felicia and Caridad cleaned up the steamy, cumin-scented kitchen. The two sisters had shared a bottle of wine, which Esperanza and their mother could not drink. After two glasses, Caridad grew flushed and chatty. She told Felicia about Seth's singing for soup after describing his parents.

"Did you wind up going to eat at his folks' house that night?" Felicia asked while washing the dishes.

"I said I had a migraine."

"Who is this dipshit anyway?"

"He's this guy I met at Darlene's wedding."

"And yet you're living with him?"

"Once Jorge left, I couldn't afford the rent or pay the bills and—"

Felicia spun to face Caridad, soapy water dripping onto the floor. "Listen to yourself." She plunged her hands back into the dishwater and scraped at a saucepan. "We don't do this. We just don't."

"Do what?"

"Granted, Jorge is dumber than dirt, plus he's puro panzón, and *what* is up with that hillbilly beard? But you don't swap him out for someone just as shit-silly. If you don't have money, you do what I did when I wanted to go back to school and couldn't afford it. I moved back home. Problem solved, and Mama likes having me around to help her out . . ."

Caridad tuned out her sister as she enumerated the benefits of returning home, since *Felicia* was the main reason moving home would be impossible for her.

"But you let them talk smack on you," Felicia said now. "I don't get why you can't speak up and tell people to fuck off, with their boat and their beggar son—"

The phone rang, and Caridad dashed for the wall-mounted receiver. "Hello?"

"It's me, Seth. Listen, I'm with my folks, and there's something I should tell you."

Felicia shot her a curious look, and Caridad mouthed, *It's him.* She gripped the phone, convinced his parents had urged him to move back home. Relief and dread clashed in Caridad at this thought. While Seth the boyfriend was growing unendurable, she depended on Seth the roommate. If he returned home, how would she manage to pay next month's rent? How would she stay in school? Was he really *that* unendurable?

"It's that we're having steaks," Seth said.

"O-*kay.*"

Felicia crowded in to listen. Caridad tipped out the earpiece to let her hear.

"I thought I should be up-front about it since you're a vegetarian."

"What you eat doesn't matter to me."

Seth's father's phlegmy sputter and the low murmur of his mother's voice sounded in the background. "Hey, there's something else," Seth said. "I was telling my folks about your family and how they don't like me and—"

"It's not that." Caridad had insisted on coming by herself to her mother's, telling Seth it was too soon for her family to meet him. "I just wanted to give them more time."

"Anyway, my folks came up with a great idea to get them to accept me." Seth laughed. "I swear it's foolproof."

Felicia's eyes narrowed.

"What you should do, see, is tell them I'm black."

"*What?*" The phone nearly slipped from Caridad's grasp.

"If you tell them I'm black, then when they meet me and see that I'm not black, they'll be so relieved, they'll *have* to like me."

Felicia snatched the phone from Caridad. "Listen, asshole, what makes you think our family is as racist as you are?" Squawks emanated from the earpiece, but Felicia had pulled the phone away. "I'm her sister, not that it's any of your goddamn business." And she banged the receiver on the switch hook, hanging up. "Un-*fucking*-believable!"

At work on Monday, Caridad still winced when she recalled that phone call, and her face burned when she replayed her return to the guesthouse later that night to assure Seth that of course she had known he was joking. "I'm no racist," he'd said. "Think about it—if I was a racist, how could I be with you?" She shook off the memory and handed a library card to a faculty member's son, reciting the rules for using it by rote, but inflecting every other syllable to amuse him and to distract herself.

"The *library* card *comes* with *cer*tain *conditions* of *use*," she told the teenager, who grinned at her robotic-sounding speech. Something about being behind the front desk, issuing library cards and checking out books, transformed Caridad's normal reserve into something more outgoing, even performative. It was like being on stage, and the patrons were the audience. The library itself—its vast parquet floors, wooden desks, and modular furniture upholstered in bold primary colors—was like a secular place of worship to her, and Caridad, succumbing to this influence, cast herself in the role of jocular high priestess. Over winter break, most students abandoned the library, but Caridad asked to work as many hours as possible to earn much-needed money and to be free of Seth, at least for part of the day. He tended to make sales calls only while she was at work, and he'd stopped playing music at night, claiming he'd rather spend time with her.

Several minutes passed before the next patron, a boyish man with curly light brown hair, set a stack of well-worn hardcovers on the desk. As she slid book spines along the demagnetizer, Caridad noted the titles: *Candide*, *The Decameron*, *The Nibelungenlied*, *Don Quixote*, and *Sister Carrie*. She recognized all of his books but the last one from a course list. Caridad held a book's pocket card to her forehead like a talk-show fortune-teller. "I predict you will be taking Foreign Literature in Translation with Selcke next semester."

He nodded. His eyes were paler than his hair, nearly amber hued.

"How did I know?" Caridad glanced at the first name on the library card he'd handed her. Gray. Gray Kessler. Light brown hair, honey-colored eyes, suntanned face—he was really more golden than gray. "Now, how did I know that, Gray?"

"You must be in the class, too," he said, his voice high and hushed.

"Correct." Caridad ran the punch cards through the card reader, establishing a quick rhythm. "But this isn't on the reading list." She held up the last book, *Sister Carrie* by Theodore Dreiser.

"It's for Naturalism, Realism, and Capitalism in American Lit."

Caridad flipped through its pages. "This is me, you know."

Gray raised his sparse blond eyebrows. "You?"

"The title, it has my name in it—Carrie. Only my name's really Caridad."

"Caridad," Gray said, pronouncing it as she had.

She pushed the stack of books toward Gray. "They'll be due back in two weeks, but you can renew them unless there's a recall. Just renew and renew as often as you need to." She grimaced at the unintended rhyme.

Gray tapped his card on the counter, and Caridad thought he might ask her out for coffee, but he said, "I bet no one calls you Carrie."

"How do you know that?"

"Carrie is too easy to say." Gray swept up the armful of books and turned for the exit. As the turnstile clicked, Caridad noticed he'd left a book behind.

"Wait!" she'd called out to him. "You forgot something!" But he had vanished into the bright portico, and Caridad couldn't leave the desk to chase after him. She climbed on a nearby stool and pulled the volume into her lap. Now he would have to come back for *Sister Carrie*. She opened the novel to the first chapter, the brittle pages nearly translucent with age. She lifted it to her face for a sniff: dust and glue, traces of vanilla, and something earthy and sweet—the scent of mown grass? She stroked the print, raised like tight stitches embroidered in linen. "When Caroline Meeber boarded the afternoon train for Chicago . . ."

Somebody That You Used to Know

Leery about touching his stereo since his outburst in the car, Caridad waited for Seth to tune in to *Mystery Theater*. But he lingered over dinner, telling her again about his trip to India, the Buddhist pilgrimage with his father and brother. At first, Caridad, who had never been east of New Mexico, had been eager to hear about his travels. She'd read E. M. Forster's *A Passage to India* and nearly ached to visit those crowded cities, the hills, and the caves. But instead of describing the bountiful bowl of sky, busy bazaars, and pilgrims purifying themselves in the Ganges, Seth focused on the dysentery he'd contracted.

"I was so out of it," he said, "that I just curled up on a mat when I wasn't barfing up a lung or shitting water. Flies, *constant* flies swarming all over me." As he spoke, Caridad recalled a family trip to San Bernardino County—heat, flies, and car sickness. India, as Seth described it, sounded a lot like Barstow. Her bowl of lentil soup had grown tepid. Caridad trickled a spoonful of the lumpy brown broth back into the bowl, her appetite extinguished.

"Isn't it time for *Mystery Theater*?" Caridad rose to pour out her soup and rinse the bowl. Weeks ago, she would have slurped up every drop, but now that the refrigerator and cupboards were full, she rarely felt hungry. It was just as well. In the time that Seth had been living with her, her figure had filled out. She was tall enough to carry the added weight, but if she kept eating like a famine survivor, she would grow as plump as Esperanza. "Why don't you find the station while I clean up?" Caridad reached for his bowl.

He held on to it, and a small tug-of-war ensued. Taking this as playfulness, she grinned, but Seth said, "Can't you see I'm not done?" Caridad released the bowl.

"Some people don't gobble down meals in seconds," he said. "Some of us like to linger over our food, enjoying it with conversation in a civilized way."

"Oh." She continued standing by the table, unsure whether to sit down until he finished or to wait near the radio. Slow heat crept up her neck to pulse in her ears. *Just a roommate*, she reminded herself. Sometimes roommates were aggravating.

Seth spooned lentils into his mouth. "By the way," he said, his mouth full, "I've been meaning to ask you something."

"What's that?"

"Any idea why that jar of peanut butter I just bought is half gone?" He raised an eyebrow and narrowed his eyes, looking much like a silent-film sheikh who suspects treachery.

"No, I . . ." Caridad glanced at the cupboard, its scarred wood door and grubby knob. In truth, she *had* been eating his peanut butter, just a spoonful here and there, straight from the jar. Times like these, she almost missed Jorge, who never implied that she was uncivilized and wouldn't have begrudged her peanut butter. "I have no idea."

After paying for their first supermarket shopping spree, Seth had told her that he was sure she wanted to be autonomous in their relationship, so he'd suggested that they each buy their own food, in the spirit of roommates. At the time, she'd agreed. They now bought separate groceries, but she often wound up purchasing ingredients to prepare most of their evening meals. And he didn't compensate her at all for her time and trouble in making meals for him.

True, he paid his share of the rent and household bills, and he'd even covered the reconnection fee to have the telephone service restored. Seth also built a water-bed frame and bought a mattress for it, although he charged Caridad half the expense of this, along with an extra fifty dollars to cover his labor. And he never footed his share of initial deposits for utilities or for the rent, expenses he would certainly have incurred if he'd moved into a place on his own. Discussing money matters flustered Caridad, though, and since Seth's voice was louder and more insistent than hers, there was little chance of her achieving more than a quarrel if she mentioned any of this to him.

"That's strange," he said after a long pause. "Peanut butter doesn't just disappear. It doesn't evaporate, does it?"

She shook her head, staring at the cupboard as if her gaze could penetrate its scarred door. The telephone blurted a half-ring, and Caridad rushed for it, though there was no need to hurry. Fearing a call from Felicia, Seth rarely answered it. And in fact, it was her sister. Caridad covered the mouthpiece to tell Seth this. He glanced at his watch and shook his head, urging her to make the call short. She ignored him as she unspooled the plastic cord, taking the phone into the bathroom to talk to her sister in private.

While she and Felicia talked about Esperanza, covering Rey's latest bad behavior and speculating whether the baby—due in April—would have any effect on this, a loud crash shook the guesthouse. Caridad told Felicia to hold on while she checked on the noise. In the kitchen, a chair lay on its side and the front door was wide open. At the threshold, Caridad caught sight of Seth's car peeling into the street.

She shut the door, set the chair upright, and returned to the bathroom. Caridad picked up the phone. "You were right. He *is* an asshole, a total asshole."

"Then what does that make you?" Felicia asked.

"I know," Caridad said. "Believe me, I know." But was there even a word for what she had become? In Dreiser's novel, Sister Carrie was seen by the other characters as a loose woman, a prostitute of sorts, strategically moving from man to man to improve her circumstances. Readers these days might call Sister Carrie a victim, a powerless female in a patriarchal context. But Dreiser's heroine did not see herself this way, and Dreiser, cupping his chin with one long-fingered hand and wearing a stern but thoughtful expression on his face in the photo on the book jacket, seemed to concur: Carrie's situation—like Caridad's— was too complicated to sum up this way. She considered the books she loved most and how heroines in these were labeled one thing or another only by the shallowest of readers, in the way that Jorge found Anna Karenina, who gave up everything for love, "selfish."

She mulled this over as Felicia now explored the topic of Seth's assholishness in a thorough way, along with its implications for her sister's character, before hanging up. Then Caridad took a beer from a twelve-pack box that Seth had bought, though he rarely opened a bottle. She took it to the bedroom and turned on his radio to catch the last half of *Mystery Theater*. Caridad lit her oil lamp, casting a soft glow in the small bedroom, now dominated by the water bed and Seth's stereo equipment. And then she sat on the floor cross-legged, sipping beer, listening to the radio program, and enjoying the sound effects, from creaky doors to the soft hiss of rain. Before long, she was immersed in the story, holding her breath as a strangler crept undetected through a sleeping woman's house.

Seth returned to the guesthouse after ten, bearing a grocery sack. Since she was finished studying for the night, Caridad had just crawled into the water bed with *Sister Carrie*. The previous week, Gray returned for the book he'd left behind and asked her to have coffee with him during her break, so she checked out a second copy of the book to read on her own. "When a girl leaves her home at eighteen, she does one of two things," Caridad had read early on in the book. "Either she falls into saving hands and becomes better, or she rapidly assumes the cosmopolitan standard of virtue and becomes worse." Since then, she read the novel nightly as if it were medicine prescribed for a specific ailment. She now placed a marker in its pages and glanced up at Seth.

He smiled at her, his moustache parting above his prominent teeth. "I saw my folks," he said. From the bag, Seth pulled two holly-paper wrapped bundles, which he handed to Caridad. One was soft and pliant, like a deflated cushion, and the other, a flattish box. "Christmas presents for you." He pointed to the box. "That's from me, and the other is from my parents."

Since he was a Buddhist, Caridad hadn't expected to exchange holiday gifts with Seth, so she hadn't gotten him a thing, and it had never occurred to her to give his parents anything. Christmas was still a week away, though, so she still had time. Caridad's mind flashed on the blue shirt he'd admired in the menswear shop on Laurel Canyon.

"I had a long talk with my dad." With a sigh, Seth lowered himself onto the bed.

"About what?" She sniffed her breath for beer under the minty traces of toothpaste.

"Turns out, he sort of had a holiday gift for me, too." He gazed at Caridad, a rueful look on his narrow face. "He's offered to send me to law school."

Now that he lived with her, Seth admitted that he no longer enjoyed going out at night to play music, and he didn't have much inclination or aptitude for selling wholesale jewelry. He'd mentioned going to law school and specializing in contract law, creative copyrights, to stay connected to music in a practical way. "That's what you want, isn't it?" she said.

"Thing is—I'd have to move back home."

As if the window to a stuffy room had been flung open, unexpected possibility gusted in and Caridad drew a deep breath. "You should do it."

Seth touched her cheek with cool fingers. "You're really sweet." He leaned to twist off Caridad's oil lamp before flicking on the overhead fixture that cast glare on the pages of her book. "Look at you, reading in the dark like Abraham Lincoln. You're going to ruin your eyes like that, young lady." He reached into the grocery sack to pull out a small blue box labeled *Trojan-ENZ*. "*Hello*. What's this?"

"My stomach hurts." Caridad removed her glasses and placed them atop her book. She turned on her side, pulling the peach comforter over her shoulder. The grocery bag rattled, floorboards creaked, and Seth snapped off the light before stepping into the kitchen, creating sounds that echoed the radio play's effects, the intruder creeping about in the dark.

The next afternoon, Caridad stepped off the warm bus into a damp blast of frigid air. She buttoned her coat and jammed her fists in its pockets before heading to the bank. There, she withdrew forty dollars. Surely the shirt wouldn't cost more than half that and she would have money to buy her mother and sisters small gifts. She'd been meaning to buy a maternity blouse for Esperanza, but whenever she and Seth were near shops that sold such clothing, he'd wag a finger at her in a joking way, as if visiting such a store might give her ideas. Thinking of this as she trudged toward the menswear store, Caridad winced. That skimpy ponytail, the loud clothing, that wagging finger—how could Seth think she'd want a child with *him*? Felicia's words rang in her head: *Then what does that make you?*

In the empty menswear shop, the clerk, a wizened man wearing glasses atop the freckled dome of his head, approached her. As his gaze traveled from her high-top tennis shoes to her faded jeans to her pea coat, Caridad experienced a dizzying moment of acuity, as if she'd just wiped her eyeglasses clean. All she beheld took on an unfamiliar crispness and clarity. Though the store's fluorescent lighting flickered, the metallic racks and hanger hooks gleamed as sharply spangled as the buttons on the clerk's wool vest and the trio of straight pins in an ashtray near the cash register. Like her namesake, Sister Carrie, mistress to Drouet and then Hurstwood, Caridad perceived in this crystalline flash that though she hadn't much loved Jorge and had cared even less for Seth, she'd flown from one to the other, like a trapeze artist near the top of a striped tent, expecting to be caught and held until she was ready to leap again.

"May I help you?" the clerk asked.

Caridad was tempted to shake her head. No, he probably couldn't help her. But what would happen if she spoke her thoughts? *I need a gift for someone I don't like much, someone I'd be done with if I had more confidence or experience or even if I were a bit older.* What would this freckle-headed clerk—who had looked at her and through her and clearly doubted that she had any business in this store—say to that? Though curious what advice he might offer, she said, "That blue shirt in the window—how much is it?"

He scuttled to the display and reached for the tag inside a sleeve. "Thirty-two dollars."

Sunlight had blanched the front of the shirt, while the back was a deeper azure. "It's faded."

"Yes. But there are more on the rack—in all sizes. This is a medium."

"Will you sell this one for less because it's damaged?"

"Twenty dollars?"

She pulled a bill from her wallet. "Twenty, including tax?"

He nodded. With a groan, he climbed onto the platform to disrobe the mannequin.

Caridad arrived home before Seth and wrapped the shirt in gift paper. When she handed it to him, he said they should open their gifts that night. Caridad suggested they do this in the bedroom under the glow of the oil lamp, which she said would create more of a holiday mood, and which she hoped would be too dim to show the shirt's discoloration.

"You go first," Seth said. He handed her the soft gift from his parents.

Caridad peeled away the paper to uncover a flat square of brown-and-orange calico-printed fabric. She unfolded this, and strings and a neck loop spilled out. "An apron?"

"Pretty nice, huh?" Seth said. "My mom picked it out."

"Your mother gave me an *apron*?"

"Look, it has pockets."

"Great," Caridad said. "Pockets."

"Don't you like it? They didn't have to get you anything, you know."

"Can't wait to wear it." Caridad folded the apron and handed him her gift.

Seth tore open the paper. "Oh no." He unfurled the shirt. "It's the one I liked. I went into that shop once, and when I found out what it cost, I thought it was too much." He held it up to his chest, grinning. "Now I feel awful. I didn't actually *buy* you anything, but I think you'll like this." He handed her the box.

Caridad opened it to find a tambourine packed in Styrofoam. She lifted it out of the case. The metal jingles were tarnished and rusted, the membrane peppered with mold.

"It's actually my old tambourine," Seth told her. "I bought myself a new one, and I thought you'd want this. It still sounds fine." He took it from her and banged it a few times.

A smile stiffened on Caridad's face. "Nice," she said. An apron and a used tambourine. Now she hoped he'd notice the shirt's imperfection.

Seth stilled the tambourine. "You probably think I couldn't tell, but I saw how uncomfortable you were that day when I was busking near Barney's. It's got to be pretty awkward just standing around while I'm entertaining people. So I thought I could teach you some songs, and next time, you can join in, too."

"Thanks." Caridad smiled and kissed his cheek. Then she took the tambourine from Seth to wedge it back in its case. The percussive chinking was getting on her nerves. She folded up the wrapping paper. "I should call Esperanza," she said, "and see how she's doing."

"Just don't get any ideas." He grinned and wagged a finger at her.

Caridad laughed. "Trust me, I won't."

On the phone with Esperanza, Caridad described their Christmas gift exchange.

"Are you serious?" Esperanza said. "He gave you a moldy tambourine and an apron?"

"Well, to be fair, my gift for him was a half-faded shirt," Caridad said in a low voice, in case Seth were listening. "It was just like that O. Henry story, 'The Gift of the Magi,' but a screwed-up version, where the man and woman outdo each other by giving awful and unwanted presents. It's like 'The Gift of the Magi' from . . ."—not hell, because Caridad was sure that hell, if it existed, would at least be an interesting place—"Barstow."

In early January, Gray visited Caridad at the library and invited her to Thousand Oaks to try out the new ice-skating rink. Caridad, who'd enjoyed roller-skating as a child, accepted. A few days later, they headed north to Ventura County in Gray's battered compact car. "Sorry about the mess," he said when he picked her up after work. The backseat was crammed with boxes and books and clothing, and he had to remove a cast-iron skillet, a pair of antlers, and juggling pins from the passenger seat to clear it for her. "I'm kind of between things."

On the way to the rink, Gray explained that he was staying part of the time at a former professor's house, looking after her young sons, and living with his family in Thousand Oaks the rest of the time. His former professor had an unstable marriage. Her sometimes-estranged husband returned to the family when all was well, and he would look after the boys himself, making Gray's presence redundant. But when the couple fought and separated, the professor hired Gray to care for the children, providing him with room and board, along with paying him wages.

"Seems complicated," Caridad said.

"It can be."

"So that's your job? Taking care of children?"

"One of my jobs," Gray said. "I also work on campus, like you. I'm in photocopying service. I wheel this huge cart—you've probably seen it—around to departments, replacing toner and fixing the machines when they break down."

Caridad pictured him lugging the bulky copier cart from one end of the vast commuter campus to the other. "That sounds kind of horrible."

"True, but it's a work-study job, so I can't complain."

"I guess I was lucky to get the library."

"Really lucky."

Both unskilled on the ice, Caridad and Gray staggered about on skates that buckled at the ankles, often banging into the guardrail and colliding with one another. Black lights pulsed and disco songs blasted from wall speakers. More capable skaters bobbed to the music as they sailed around the rink. Early on, one of the rink attendants glided backward in Caridad's direction. As the skater sped toward her, Caridad let her feet fly out to land on her bottom, and then she scuttled crablike to avoid collision. Stiff-legged as a mummy, Gray inched toward her. Other skaters shot around them, flashing annoyed looks. "Interesting approach to the problem," Gray said when he reeled her to her feet. "Stop, drop, and scramble."

"Hey, it worked." She brushed ice from her pants and patted her behind. "I used to have a tailbone, some vertebrae back here."

"It'll grow back," Gray told her. "You'll get your spine back."

A herd of teenagers barreled past, toppling Caridad and Gray in their wake. They laughed so hard that it was impossible for them to stand. Caridad crawled to the guardrail, towing Gray along with her. There they got to their feet and wobbled forward on the ice again.

Later, while they waited to return the rented skates, Gray said, "I wish I didn't have to take you home."

"So don't." Shivering, she huffed into her cupped hands. The smell of sweaty socks, leather, and hot chocolate permeated the pinching cold.

Gray cupped her chilly fingers in his warm hands. "Do you like beer?"

"Are you kidding? I love beer."

"Peanuts?"

Caridad flashed on the depleted peanut-butter jar in the cabinet at home. "Apparently, I do."

"I have an idea," Gray said.

At the front desk, Caridad stood at Gray's side, holding a paper sack with a six-pack of Busch beer and a large bag of salted-in-the-shell peanuts, while he registered them for the night. The lobby was as clean and bright as a clinic. The linoleum floor gleamed under overhead panels of light, and potted palms with shiny fronds stood near racks of sightseeing pamphlets and luggage carts. The clerk, a woman with cat's-eye glasses, examined Gray's license. "Kessler," she said. "Aren't you Doug Kessler's son?"

Gray nodded.

"I know your family from church."

"Oh yeah?"

"I see them every Sunday—nice big family. Haven't seen you at Mass, though."

Gray shrugged.

The clerk handed over a key. "Tell your folks hello for me, will you? I'm Marion Shockley from Sacred Heart."

"I will."

In the elevator, Caridad turned to Gray. "Is it okay that she knows you?"

Gray raised his eyebrows. "Sure."

"What if she tells your parents?"

"Why would she? And it doesn't matter to me if she does."

"So your family's Catholic?" Caridad asked.

Gray nodded.

"What about you?"

"Me?" he said. "I'm not anything."

The elevator doors chimed, parting to open at the third floor. Their room was at the end of the long hallway. Gray keyed open the door and held it wide. "After you," he said.

She stepped into the small room with double beds, a dresser, and a television. "Ooh, television! Can we watch something?"

"But of course."

"Would you mind if we watched something stupid?" Caridad asked. "I'm ashamed to say it, but I love watching stupid things on television." Though he watched sports on it, Jorge had called television the "boob tube," and Seth referred to it as "the idiot box." Both seemed to believe watching TV robbed brain cells. Perhaps this posed a danger for them, but Caridad felt she had sufficient cerebral matter to gamble a few cells this way.

"The stupider the better." Gray turned, scanning the room. Caridad spied a paperback in his back pocket. "Ah, there's the ice bucket," he said.

"What are you reading?" She pointed at the book.

"What? Oh, *Naked Lunch*." He pulled out the worn and dog-eared copy and handed it to her. "It's my favorite book. I read it over and over."

"William S. Burroughs." Caridad flipped through the yellowed pages, many of these underlined in green ink. Indecipherable annotations marked margins on nearly every page.

"What's it about?"

"It's hard to say," Gray told her. "In a way, that's what I like about it, that I can't sum it up for you. I guess you could sort of say it's about this junkie, but it's really about more than that, much more than that. For me, it's the best book ever written." Gray released a relieved breath when Caridad returned the book to him, saying she'd have to pick up a copy to read.

"Now for stupid TV," she said. But before flipping on the set, Caridad glanced at the telephone on the nightstand. "I should make a quick call first." She planned to let Seth know she wouldn't be back that night. When Gray left to find the ice machine, Caridad picked up the receiver and dialed her home number. Inspired by Gray's unconcerned honesty with the hotel clerk, she decided to be truthful with Seth, who answered the phone almost instantly.

"It's me," she said. "I just want you to know I won't be home tonight."

"*Where are you?*" Seth's voice was so loud that Caridad had to hold the phone away from her ear. "*Who* are you with?"

"Gray," she said. "Gray Kessler, someone I met at school."

"You just *can't—after everything—*you *can't* do this to me."

"I'm not doing anything to you," Caridad said. "I'm only calling so you won't wait up."

"Listen to me, Caridad, *really* listen. You have to come home right now. Got it? Just come home, or tell me where you are and I'll pick you up."

"But I just told you I'm staying out tonight." She lowered herself onto one of the double beds. The quick call was taking longer than she'd thought.

"You realize I could legally *kill* you for what you're doing."

Caridad now wondered if Seth had any aptitude at all for a career in law. "I don't think it's ever legal to—"

"If you don't come right home, that's it, Caridad, and I mean it." His voice grew deeper, sharper. "You'll never see me again. Is that what you want?"

It kind of *was*, but Caridad said, "You do what you have to." And she hung up.

"Is everything okay?" Gray asked when he returned with the ice. He opened two beers and handed one to Caridad.

"That I don't know." Caridad doubted Seth had it in him to pack his things and clear out by morning. He'd more likely remain at the guesthouse to carp at her more when she returned. "I just discovered someone I know would make a terrible lawyer." While they sipped beer and cracked open peanuts, Caridad told Gray about the phone call.

Gray arranged the remaining beers in the ice bucket. "I'm no expert, but it does seem that killing a person, for any reason, is frowned upon by our legal system. Could be he's thinking of crimes of passion, but then he would have to be in France. Maybe back in the nineteenth century that defense might work." He scratched the stubble on his chin. "It would involve a cross-country and then a transatlantic flight—some time travel, of course—but I suppose anything's possible."

"He'll probably sort it all out in law school," Caridad said. She set her beer on the bed table and drew Gray close for a kiss. His warm face smelled sweetly sour, and his full lips tasted of beer and salt, like soft plums rinsed in a briny sea.

The next day, Gray drove her back to the guesthouse. Caridad spotted Seth's car parked alongside the curb as soon as they turned onto her street. "I knew it. He's still here."

Gray parked and yanked up the hand brake. "Want me to go in with you?"

She shook her head, nodded, and then shrugged.

Gray removed the key.

Caridad made no move to open the car door on her side. "This could be weird."

"I'm okay with weird." Gray climbed out of the car and she followed.

They shuffled toward the door, kicking leaves off the paved path to prolong the short walk. While she doubted Seth would physically harm her, Caridad expected him to make a scene; he might yell or even throw a chair over as he had when she talked on the phone with her sister. Her heart thudded in her throat, and she unlocked the door with shaking fingers. The bedroom was nearly as empty as it had been when she and Jorge first moved in—water bed, stereo equipment, Seth's clothing had all vanished—only the cinder blocks and her books, oil lamp, and peach comforter remained. Gray followed Caridad into the kitchen, where Seth sat at the table, staring into a cup of coffee. His bony face was sallow, grainy as a daguerreotype portrait. Shadows underscored his eyes and hollowed his thin cheeks; a blue vein pulsed on one side of his forehead, zigzagging like a lightning bolt above his temple.

"You've returned," Seth said in a flat voice. He glanced at Gray and then trained his gaze on Caridad.

"I'm Gray Kessler. You must be Seth."

"I see you've packed your things," Caridad said.

"You know, I really loved you." Seth's dark eyes thickened, and Caridad felt a pang. He turned to Gray. "I loved her. I was even going to marry her."

Annoyance flared in Caridad. "What makes you think I'd marry you?"

Seth lowered his head to the table, cradling it in his arms.

Unmoved, Caridad said, "Why do some men think that all women want is marriage? Why do they think that they are these great prizes that any woman should be thrilled to win?"

Gray shrugged. "Beats me."

Seth mumbled something she couldn't hear.

"What did he say?" Caridad asked Gray.

"No idea."

"I said you enjoy this." Seth raised his head. "Who do you think you are anyway? My mother's right—you have *no idea* who you are. You read all these books like they're written for you, like those authors are sending special messages to you. The books you love—they're not for you." He released a snort of laughter. "They never were for anyone like you."

"Excuse me," Gray said, "but what are you talking about?"

"Oh, you'll find out," Seth told him. "You'll find out all about the books and the know-it-all quotes she copies down, the little messages she writes in the margins. She'll shut you out with a book, trust me. She'll put it up like a wall." He turned to Caridad. "You just love doing that, don't you? Just like you love this three-ring circus."

"How is *this* a three-ring circus?" Caridad glanced about the kitchen—scarred table and chairs, open cupboards, half-empty shelves. She flashed on the image that she'd experienced in the menswear shop: a glimpse of herself at the summit of a striped tent, flying from one pair of hands to the next. Flying—or was she falling?

"Well," Gray said, "I suppose since there are three of us, and I *do* juggle—"

"It's all a circus to you, isn't it?" Seth said, likely casting himself as the sad, sad clown.

"That's just it. There is *no circus* with you!" Caridad's hands buzzed, twitching to overturn the table. She felt like a hot-faced child, ready to bare teeth and bite. "You promise to tell me about India, and instead you give me *Barstow*! A circus would at least be *interesting*." She drew a ragged breath, dropped her voice. "A circus might even be fun."

Seth and Gray drew back, wide-eyed with alarm.

Caridad, overwarm in the coat she still wore, longed for the rush of water on her skin. "I'm tired," she said. She couldn't bear another moment of this prolonged departure, Seth wringing what melodrama he could from it. "I'm going to take a shower."

Before she shut the bathroom door, Gray's low voice sounded from the kitchen. "So Caridad tells me you're a musician . . ."

In the days after Seth moved out, Caridad wavered before asking Gray to live with her. She wanted to be alone and not alone. By the end of January, she decided she enjoyed being with Gray more than she liked being on her own, and again, she needed help paying the rent. It took him less than an hour to unload his car. He found more cinder blocks, along with wood planks and plastic blue milk crates, out of which to fashion bookcases. He also had a small portable TV. Now his antlers and juggling pins were arranged on the top bookshelf near Caridad's wall hanging of the woman's torso in brick, and the television was atop a milk crate that held some of Gray's many record albums. Before it short-circuited, Caridad and Gray put the TV to much use, laughing over the stupidest programs they could find, from beach movies to beauty pageants, soap operas to sitcoms.

One of their favorites was a science-fiction serial called *Land of the Lost*, in which contemporary characters slipped through a wormhole to a prehistoric island where—curiously—the fur-clad cavemen somehow spoke slangy American English. Whenever the program aired, Caridad and Gray rushed to snap it on because the best part was the opening when the deep-voiced narrator would list the events that landed the characters in "the *Land of the Lost*." Caridad and Gray mocked that somber pronouncement, deepening their voices for mundane declarations. "It's *the toast of the toaster*," Caridad would proclaim when the bread popped up, or Gray would call out, "It's *the mail of the flap*," when the door flap clanked open in the morning, envelopes cascading to the floor.

Weeks after Seth had moved out, Caridad and Gray were enjoying a lazy Sunday afternoon, reading the paper and drinking coffee when someone rapped on the door. Caridad approached the threshold. "Who's there?" she called.

A sonorous voice—sounding much like the announcer for *Land of the Lost*—intoned, "*It's somebody that you used to know.*"

Caridad shot Gray a puzzled look. He glanced at her and shrugged. She turned the knob and cracked open the door. Seth, pink faced, stood on the doorstep. He'd snipped his ponytail and was wearing a denim shirt and jeans. An uncertain smile played on his thin face.

"Seth?"

Gray rose from the table and stepped beside her. "Hey, man, how's it going?"

"Great." His smile wavered, and he cleared his throat. "I've been busy, got some things going on."

"Have you applied to law school?" Caridad crossed her arms and planted herself in the doorway with Gray.

Seth renewed his moustache-splitting grin. "I'm chanting a lot, two, three times a day."

"Cool," Gray said, though Caridad doubted he knew what Seth meant.

All three smiled, nodding. A woman's voice rang out from a neighbor's yard: "Erica! Erica! *Erica!*" Another car whizzed by. Leaves near the curb swirled in its wake. The day was bright but windy. A gust swept into the guesthouse, rattling pages of the newspaper spread on the kitchen table.

"So, did you forget something?" Caridad hoped he would not ask for the jeweler's loupe he'd left behind. She liked having it handy when she needed a closer look at things.

Seth shook his head, glanced at his hands. His guitar calluses had vanished, his fingertips now smooth and pearly. "I just wanted to see you, and I thought you'd kind of like to know how I'm doing, since, well, we used to . . . since you used to know me."

Caridad withdrew from the threshold, pulling Gray along with her, to make space for shutting the door. "Right," she said. "Well, good seeing you." Though Seth may well have been somebody she used to know, he'd never bothered to know her at all. "Take care of yourself." She closed the door and leaned her back against it.

Gray's amber eyes danced with amusement.

Caridad dropped her voice to mimic Seth's. "*It's somebody that you used to know.*"

"From way back," Gray said, "in the *Land of the Lost.*"

They whooped and snorted, doubling over in mirth. Scraping sounds then issued from behind the closed door, Seth's shoes rasping on the doorstep. "Oh no," Caridad whispered, clapping a hand over her mouth.

"He had to have heard us," Gray said. "That's shitty."

The rest of the afternoon, they were quiet, even somber, as if they'd returned from a funeral service. But when Gray went out in the early evening to buy beer, he forgot the house key and had to knock to be let in. Though she was expecting him, Caridad nevertheless stepped to the threshold to say, "Who's there?"

"*It's somebody that you used to know,*" Gray said, and it was hilarious all over again.

While Caridad's Cuban landlords hardly approved of her living with three different men, as long as she paid the rent on time, there was not much they could do about this—apart from hissing "cualquiera" whenever she was in earshot. The elderly couple couldn't hurt her with name-calling. One morning at the end of February, though, when Caridad handed over the rent, the old lady told her that her son would be moving into the guesthouse. Caridad would have to vacate the rental in four weeks. On a walk that same afternoon, she and Gray found a yellow cottage only a few blocks away from the guesthouse. The owner was just planting a rental sign in the front yard. They were shown the house within minutes, and early the next week, they signed the lease agreement.

They began packing up the guesthouse the weekend before moving. Caridad worked in the kitchen, while Gray boxed books and knickknacks in the living room. When she pulled out a low drawer they rarely used, a peculiar odor—the sweetish putrescence of spoiled peaches—wafted out. The drawer held grocery bags and plastic cutlery from takeout meals. She yanked it out all the way to find the apron Seth's mother had given her, its brown-and-orange printed fabric wadded about the corpses of four newborn mice. Caridad reached into a top drawer for the jeweler's loupe that Seth had left behind. Through its magnifying lens, she beheld the tarry ossifying creatures—their furless flesh scored like an elephant's hide, their ears no more than nubs, and their eyes sealed slits.

Caridad dislodged the drawer altogether from the frame, and something thumped to the cabinet's base behind it. She reached in to grasp the flat and rigid body of a gray mouse, its flinty amber teeth bared. No doubt this was the mother to those naked newborns, crushed when she or Gray—or most likely Seth in a fit of anger—kicked the drawer shut. Their mewling too feeble to be detected, the tiny mice had perished without her. Caridad stroked the stiff fur with her fingertip. Then she bundled all five mice in the apron, making a pouch that she knotted shut with the strings—a shroud for burying the tiny creatures in the backyard.

Relevant Mortals

After checking it in and out again and again, with many renewals in between, and then finding a paperback edition at a yard sale, Caridad returned the library's copy of *Madame Bovary* with reluctance in late April. As she ran its punch card through the reader at the front desk, poor Emma and the dullard Charles flashed in her mind's eye as if they were aboard a ship pulling away from a dock where she stood waving. Emma, though sharply described by Flaubert, was less fixed in Caridad's imagination, but Charles appeared to her in a distinctive way. Le Docteur Bovary, as she pictured him, resembled Jorge, minus the beard. So when she glanced up at Jorge himself, now beardless and standing at the check-out desk, Caridad experienced a prickly sensation, as if she'd conjured his presence.

"Long time no see. How've you been?" The words sped out of Jorge's mouth, as if recited by rote. Clean-shaven, his pimply jowls bulged like a hamster's stuffed with seeds.

"Has Noah . . ." She patted her face. "Did he shave, too?"

"You think I can't do anything on my own?"

At this, Caridad knew that Noah had likewise razored off his beard. Jorge set a file sleeve on the desk. "I just need you to sign some stuff."

Caridad looked to see where Fakhri, the desk supervisor, might be lurking.

"You don't have to do it now," Jorge said. "Go over everything. Sign the places I marked and mail it to me in that stamped envelope I included."

She took the folder and slid it onto the shelf under the desk where she kept her purse and a copy of *Bullfinch's Mythology*. Then Caridad leaned toward Jorge. "How *are* you?"

"I met someone," he said, his lips barely moving. "It's serious, so I'll need to get those forms pretty quick."

Caridad drew back. "Okay."

Jorge's face softened, and he said, "How's your mom?"

"She's fine."

"I always liked her. She's cool people."

"She's fond of you, too," Caridad said. Mama still asked after Jorge, ever hopeful they might reconcile.

"And your sisters—how are they?"

"They're fine. In fact, I'm about to become an aunt. Esperanza's having labor induced this afternoon. After work, I'm heading straight to the hospital."

"What hospital? I'd like to send flowers or something."

"Manzanita Vista in Sylmar." Caridad smiled. How thoughtful Jorge could be. No wonder her mother missed him. "But she won't be checking in until four."

"Thanks for letting me know," he said. "Don't forget to sign that stuff, okay?" Jorge pivoted away from the desk. For a thickset man, he took long and swift steps toward the glass doors before disappearing into a flash of sunlight.

Gray was late picking her up after work. Squinting, Caridad stood near the temporary parking, an oblong paved area with metered slots. She checked her wristwatch as if this would speed up his arrival. A gaggle of Asian students wandered past, and two library coworkers—Kitty Fu and Phuoc Phong—lifted hands in greeting. Caridad waved back. They followed a fluffy dog, a gingery mutt being hectored by a pair of sparrows that dove at the dog, snatching at its fur. With each assault, the dog whipped around to snap at the birds.

"Birds steal dog feathers," Kitty Fu called to her.

"Fur," Caridad said. "It's called *fur*."

Kitty smiled. "See you later." Phuoc echoed this, and the group continued toward the bus stop. The dog spun as the sparrows swooped, baring teeth and barking now. The birds wheeled away before circling back to pluck more tufts when the dog continued trotting.

Gray would be interested in this. He would reach for the notebook he kept for scribbling observations in his tiny, unreadable scrawl. He might even construct a haiku with these bare ingredients. Anyone else would want to know the significance of this. Not Gray. He didn't care whether things had points or not. In his back pocket, he still kept *Naked Lunch*, a book Caridad found unreadable for its vagaries. Gray also enjoyed books that were sequential and clear, as long as these were in some way confounding. Since their world literature course, Voltaire's *Candide* had become a favorite of his, and he often quoted paradoxical observations from the novel. When things went awry, he'd say, "Private misfortunes make the public good, and so the more private misfortunes there are, the more all is well." Or he'd say, "If *this* is the best of all possible worlds, *what* are the others like?"

Gray appreciated things that were not what they seemed. "You're really not a nice person," he'd once told Caridad. "Your voice is quiet and your touch is gentle, but you're not that nice at all. I like that." Caridad, who considered niceness a bland affliction, had beamed at this. He liked that she wore a stained baseball cap of his when they worked together in the yard, and he would sometimes call her "Daddy," a nickname derived from the last syllable of her name. Gray claimed that balanced people had both masculine and feminine energy, and he said she had good masculine energy.

Once when Caridad awoke from a nap, dazed and dream-bleary, she'd mumbled, "I love you more than ten thousand cans of mushroom soup poured all over the rug." And Gray, amber eyes gleaming, had opened his notebook to record her words. No, Gray was not like other people, and this was probably why he was late. He'd likely stopped on the way to write in his notebook or to collect something strange that had been set out as trash. Maybe he'd lost track of time. Gray wasn't good with time.

Luckily, she had Bullfinch to keep her company. Caridad opened the book to where she'd left off: Juno discovering Jupiter in the company of an exquisite heifer. Caridad struggled to imagine this striking cow. All cattle—though limpid eyed and velvety muzzled—were rather plain and blocky. She was envisioning a tawny bovine with glossy lashes, though, when Gray's car rumbled curbside. "Hey, baby," he said through the opened window. "Need a ride?"

"That depends." She closed her book. "Where you headed, big boy?"

Gray swung open the passenger-side door and Caridad slid in. He kissed her wetly. "You'll never guess what I found in the Dumpster behind Woolworth's."

Jupiter or Jove doubled as Zeus, and Juno, a.k.a. Hera, was his wife. Venus was the Roman version of Aphrodite, and Cupid became Eros for the Greeks. In the hospital's waiting area with Gray, Esperanza's friends, and Felicia, Caridad longed for index cards to keep track of the many gods. She should also make cards for the Titans and non-Titans, as well as the demigods, beasts, and numerous relevant mortals that kept cropping up. It was not enough to highlight the names; there were too many of these for that, and telling Gray the myths proved useless. His recollection was so poor that strolling down Memory Lane for him would be like wandering about on some strange planet. Now he sat among Esperanza's friends—Delfina, Viviana, and Raven—as they recounted childbirth experiences.

Esperanza's friends were telling where they were when their water broke, what they said when begging for anesthesia, and how they coped in the aftermath of the inevitable episiotomy. "Donut pillows," Raven was saying, and Delfina added, "Hemorrhoid cream." These women liked him. Even Felicia had to admit Gray wasn't that bad. He now winced as Viviana complained that her milk didn't come in for four days. "The third day, my chi-chis were like boulders, and they *hurt*. I'm talking killer-*diller* pain."

Caridad glanced from Gray to Felicia, who was seated on a turquoise vinyl chair, a stack of papers on her lap. Felicia, now a student teacher, was marking work by fifth graders with a purple pen. Their mother, Esperanza's birthing coach, was in the delivery room. Who knew where Reynaldo was? He'd claimed that being present for the birth might ruin marital relations for him, but Esperanza explained to her sisters that the sight of blood caused him to faint.

Caridad was squinting at Felicia's marks on a paper, hoping these were not too brutal, when commotion at the door drew her attention. Jorge and Geraldine barged in to the waiting room, trailed by Noah, who had, as she'd suspected, shaved off his rust-colored beard, revealing a pale nub of chin. Caridad blinked and shook her head as if to clear her vision of the unexpected and unwanted interlopers.

"Where is she?" Geraldine asked Caridad. The large woman wore aqua scrubs. A gauze mask dangled from her neck. Braless as usual, her pendulous breasts hung over her stomach, calling to mind the netted sacks that held volleyballs in Caridad's gym class.

"Who?" The atmosphere tightened, filling Caridad's ears with pressure. Esperanza's friends went mute, their eyes round, and Gray drew knees to his chest. Felicia, though, stood and strode forth, papers sailing to the floor. She clenched the purple pen in one fist like a blade.

"Esperanza," Geraldine said. "She said I could assist with the birth."

Standing on either side of her, Noah and Jorge glanced about, examining furniture, framed prints, and plastic potted plants, as if fascinated by the room's décor.

Felicia stepped closer to Geraldine, causing her to backpedal. "You're full of shit," she said, lifting Geraldine's bangs with a huff of breath.

Geraldine's face pinkened. "I have training as a birth coach. I'm taking courses in reproductive science at West Valley Occupational—"

"But that's animal husbandry," Caridad said. She'd seen brochures for the program at Geraldine's. "My sister's not *livestock*."

Felicia shoved Geraldine's shoulders, rocking her back another step. "Get out before I throw you out."

"That's assault," Geraldine said. "I could have you arrested, but I'll let it go if—"

Advancing, Felicia backed Geraldine toward the door.

"These premises," Noah began, "are open to the public—"

Caridad turned to Jorge. "*This* is what you do?"

Esperanza's friends rose to converge on the intruders, chorusing Felicia: "Go on! Get out!" Gray watched, wearing a stricken expression.

A security guard, a monolithic Samoan who'd earlier helped Caridad and Gray with directions, now appeared in the corridor. "What's going on?"

"These people," Felicia said, "are leaving."

Geraldine opened her mouth, but Noah tugged her arm. Jorge had already stepped over the threshold, his rounded back receding into the corridor.

"I'll take you to the exit," the guard said. "It's easy to lose your way. This place is a maze." Jorge, Noah, and Geraldine trailed after the guard. Felicia, hands on hips, stood at the threshold, watching to make sure they departed.

As soon as they'd all settled back into their seats, Caridad's mother shuffled through the door, wearing—like Geraldine—aqua scrubs. Her face shone with perspiration, as if she had been the one to give birth. "It's a girl," she said. "I have a granddaughter."

"*Uh*-oh," Caridad blurted out. Reynaldo had been counting on a son. Planning to call the baby Reynaldo Jr., he and Esperanza hadn't even considered a girl's name.

Felicia shot her a sharp look. "Is Espie okay? Is the baby okay?"

"Everyone's fine." Mama turned to Caridad. "She wants to see *you*, m'ija."

"What about *me*?" Felicia said. "When do *I* get to see the baby?"

Mama patted Felicia's arm. "You're next."

"Dah-Dah." Esperanza grabbed Caridad's hand, pulling her close. The briny odor of blood penetrated the room's sharp astringent smell. The light was off, the shades drawn. Esperanza's face shone, blanched as a hothouse orchid. "They're bringing the baby in a bit, and I want you to hold her first." Her tongue traced her cracked lips.

"Can I get you water?"

Esperanza's eyes flickered with impatience. "Listen, Dah-Dah, this is important. I want you to hold her. You're going to be the god-mother. If anything happens—"

"*Me?*"

"You know Mama's not well, and Felicia . . . Felicia's too hard. It has to be you, Dah-Dah. If anything happens, I want you—"

"Nothing's going to happen." Caridad drew back, but Esperanza's fingers bit into her palm.

"I want you. Not Mama, not Felicia." Her voice dropped to a harsh whisper. "*And not Reynaldo.*"

"Sure, of course." With a free hand, Caridad stroked her sister's matted hair.

Esperanza licked her lips again. "What will we name her?"

"Minerva," Caridad said in a flash, "for the goddess of wisdom."

"Minerva, I like that."

Later, while her sister rested, Caridad held the snugly bundled infant in her arms as she stood before the window. The small face was the color of turkey wattle with puffy seams for eyes. An island of hair, a single black tuft, crowned her lumpy head. She smelled of cooked carrots and stewing beef. Her grotesqueness was startling. Still, Caridad beamed at Esperanza as if the creature she'd produced was not too monstrous. The baby's appalling face, in fact, compelled Caridad's gaze. Brakes shrieked on the street below. Horns blared. But Caridad could not look away from her exquisitely hideous niece. "Minerva," she said. "Minerva."

Weeks later, while Caridad stood at the Laurel Canyon kiosk worrying that she'd missed the Vanowen bus, she envisioned herself speaking to someone neutral, say a psychiatrist or a judge. She would say it all started in bed that morning and then tell how she'd gathered a hank of her boyfriend's hair to tug it back, ponytail style. "You'd make a pretty girl," she said, and he'd replied, "Funny you should mention that . . ." No, no, no. Caridad peered down the smog-shrouded boulevard. It started long before that, with blouses hung inside out, with inexpert gouges in her blushing powder, with beige dribs—foundation cream?—speckling the bathroom sink. It began with missing pantyhose. It really started with the wig.

Caridad stepped off the curb for a broader view of the hazy intersection. At last, a rectangular form shimmered in the distance. The bus loomed near, so densely thronged with passengers that Caridad worried the driver wouldn't stop. But brakes keening, it sailed alongside the curb, wheezing a noxious gust in her face.

Caridad climbed aboard, clanked quarters into the coin box. The haggard driver's gray eyes were filmy and vacant, giving him the look of an exasperated Tiresias about to impart some appalling truth about her destiny.

She wedged past many standing passengers. The bus lurched, and Caridad staggered. She grabbed an overhead strap near a double seat occupied by a bubble-haired brunette whose purse occupied the cushion beside her. Did the woman not notice all the travelers tethered to hand-straps, standing for the duration of their ride? The brunette wore a red smock with a convenience store's insignia on it, and her hair was teased and sprayed to a lackluster finish, like the preserved pelt of a deceased pet. Caridad dropped her gaze to the woman's jetbead clutch—a stingy little bag. The brunette smoothed her hair. Caridad flashed on the bewigged Styrofoam head she'd found in the closet, a faceless ovoid also wearing lusterless brown hair. Everything should have started with that cap of synthetic hair, if only she'd known how to interpret it. Gray kept so many odd things in the closet that it was hard to tell what each object meant.

He had several shelves filled with objects he intended to render one day, such as a cow's femur, coconut shells, carapaces of oversized insects, rusted horseshoes, a mannequin's hand, a stringless ukulele, a canister of buttons, a limp carrot that bifurcated in a way that suggested legs leisurely crossed at the ankles. She'd assumed he planned to sketch the wig, though it and the Styrofoam head were the only objects in his collection that were not furred with dust. That, along with the odd-turned clothing and missing hosiery, should have prompted her to ask a few shrewd questions.

Now the brunette reached for the beaded bag, and Caridad prepared to sink into the seat. But the woman just opened it to fish out a tube of lipstick.

"Excuse me," Caridad said. "Your purse is taking up a whole seat."

"Yeah, so?" the brunette said.

"If you hold it in your lap, someone else could sit down."

"What if I want to sit by myself?"

"What about . . . *common* courtesy?" Caridad hadn't expected the woman to argue for her selfishness. How indefensible was that?

"What about minding your own business?"

Quaking, Caridad was preparing to embrace this suggestion, when someone else spoke up. "Move that thing." The voice was a thin tenor, clearly masculine. It was the Library Rat, now standing behind her.

Caridad divided up fellow bus passengers into two categories: those who irritated her due to noisiness or hygiene and those she didn't mind much. Though Caridad privately dubbed him the Library Rat, he easily fell into the latter category. He wore his blond hair greased back, baring his rodent face—narrow nose, pink-rimmed eyes, longish yellowed teeth, and recessed chin. Reading one book or another, he often rode the bus with Caridad in the morning. He'd exit at the Vanowen Branch Library, which they were soon to approach.

"Mind *your* own business," Selfish Brunette called over her shoulder.

The pull-cord buzzed, and the Library Rat stepped closer. He was scrawnier than Caridad had thought, but paunchy under his worn white T-shirt.

The woman snatched up her purse. "Satisfied?"

As the bus hauled to a stop, Caridad tumbled into the seat. The Library Rat exited from the middle door. From the window, she watched him march, book in hand, toward the library as if following orders to report for duty.

Of course, since the first bus was delayed, she missed her transfer on Reseda Boulevard, the bus that would deliver her to campus. Its funnel cloud of exhaust spumed a few blocks up ahead. She would again be late for Greek and Roman Mythology. The professor—an ex-military something or other—used a sign-in sheet for attendance. When she was late, Caridad had to approach him after class to ask humbly for the roll sheet. Each time, he'd been uncharmed by her soft voice and shy smile. Last week, the professor had sarcastically asked if she'd had trouble finding a parking space again. Remembering this, Caridad winced. But at least now, while she waited for another bus, she could replay what Gray had told her that morning in bed.

"I like to dress up," he'd said, after she told him he would make a pretty girl.

"You *do*?" Bafflement descended on her like a stage curtain that she had to struggle out from under. To her knowledge, Gray didn't own a tie, let alone a suit. "When?"

"When you're not home."

Caridad pictured him donning a top hat and tuxedo. She added white gloves and patent-leather shoes with spats, superimposing his wiry frame in a ballroom with crystal chandeliers. "*Why?*"

Face aflame, he'd shrugged. "It relaxes me."

A beige Volkswagen Beetle pulled to the kiosk on Reseda. The driver pushed open the passenger-side door. "Hey," he called. "Need a lift?"

Caridad glimpsed the familiar moustache—a furry mass with curled-up tips—worn by Max, a middle-aged man who was in her classical drama seminar. Though tempted, she hesitated. Max wore an aftershave so powerful, it filled the classroom like mustard gas.

"Come on. It's no trouble."

Caridad slipped into the bucket seat and pulled the door shut. This was like diving headlong into a cinder-block wall of that scent. She sneezed three times.

Max handed her a box of tissues. "My car makes people sneeze," he said.

Up close, she could see he was older than she'd thought, and he was amateurishly tattooed about the neck. Max, she now learned, was an embittered veteran, now "philosophically, morally, spiritually, and psychologically" opposed to the war in which he'd served. As he drove, he released a steady flow of passionate but dull political diatribe. This freed Caridad to consider how she'd not kept secrets from Gray—nor disturbed *his clothing* when he wasn't home—the rest of the way to campus.

In the parking lot, Max asked when her last class ended. "I could give you a lift home."

Caridad embarked on her usual list of polite excuses: She had her campus job that afternoon, she might stop to see a friend, she had to pick up some groceries, and—

"You do know that the RTD is going on strike at noon today, right?"

See, Caridad wanted to say to Gray, this is what happens when you can't afford a daily newspaper, when you don't replace a busted television set. Since his car broke down, he'd been getting around well enough on his ten-speed bike, but what about Caridad—bikeless and with less than five dollars stuffed in the pocket of her Levi's?

"Yeah, the bus drivers are walking out to protest the fat-cat bosses in city government, the bastards that exploit the hell out of them."

"But that's *impossible*," Caridad said, referring not to the exploitation of laborers, which she, the daughter of a cafeteria worker, accepted as a given. Instead, she was responding generally to the challenges of living without access to critical information like this and specifically to the problem of getting home without the bus.

Max shrugged. "So are you going to need a lift?"

Caridad shook her head and thanked him anyway, partly because she hoped he was wrong about the strike—maybe his political leanings clouded his perceptions—but mostly because she couldn't inhale another molecule of that offensive aftershave. The roof of her mouth itched and her eyes stung from it. She trudged away from Max, gulping in great scent-free draughts.

Seated in a neatly arrayed sea of desks, Caridad was transfixed by the boyish neck before her, longing to touch the pale skin, the summit of knobby spine. Caridad imagined stroking that velvety hairline, palming the smooth band of warm flesh beneath it, and her hands tingled with desire. The boy flicked fingers over his neck as if he felt her gaze insect-crawling on him. Caridad looked away, letting her mind loft like a beach ball at a concert while the professor spoke from the lectern. *My boyfriend likes to dress up*, she thought. *Gray likes to dress up.*

How long had it taken her to catch on to what he was saying that morning? Gray must have thought her thick as paste. She had to have him spell it out. And she'd always considered herself not only liberal-minded, but even "out there" with her ideas about open relationships and her laissez-faire attitude toward Ernie, her body-building neighbor with his ever-rotating phalanx of young boyfriends. Gray's admission shocked her, but to her credit, Caridad's default reaction to being confounded was silence that she hoped might be taken for thoughtfulness. But when she finally understood Gray, she'd been shut down by this news, all thoughts snowed-out like images on the TV screen when it shorted-circuited. Reflexive courtesy then replaced thought, prompting her to say the opposite of what she felt. "I *see*," she'd told Gray. Then Caridad had glanced at her wristwatch. "Wow, it's getting late." She was tempted to add, in a joking way, "My, how time flies when talk turns to transvestitism," but this seemed off, so she'd said, "I should shower."

Queasiness lodged in her stomach while she showered, as if she'd eaten a cake of soap like the one with which she was lathering herself. She whisked between shame for this unexpected narrowness of mind and compassion for Gray, who'd trusted her with what had to be a hard truth. And what did this confession mean? Did he plan to enlist her when he relaxed in this way? Would they then become best girlfriends? Or would they be more like lesbian lovers? She pictured Gray's hopeful face, trying to read it for clues as she rinsed and dried off. When she'd returned to the bedroom, towel-wrapped and dripping, Gray had fallen back asleep. Or was he pretending? She'd dressed and slipped out of the house in silence.

Now Caridad gazed at the tender neck before her—such a vulnerable thing. She imagined flowing ringlets in place of his short hair, a capped-sleeve blouse instead of the T-shirt. Was this preoccupation hijacking her hearing, too, or did the professor just say something about cross-dressing? She focused on the precise man up front. He wore a self-amused look on his face, his usual expression when discussing the randy behavior of various gods.

"Thetis," he was saying, "learned from an oracle that Achilles would die young and glorious if he joined Agamemnon in Troy, or else he would grow old in obscurity."

Caridad scribbled in her notebook: *Who again is Thetis?*

"So she disguised her son as a woman." The professor leered at the students, a twinkle in his eyes, and Caridad crossed out her question. Of course, Thetis was Achilles's mother—she knew *that*—and she wondered about Gray's mother, a frugal woman who clipped coupons and shopped at yard sales and thrift stores. Had she dressed him in his older sister's clothing when he was young to save money?

"Thus, Achilles," the professor continued, "is, as mentioned, the first-known cross-dresser. Thetis's trick nearly worked, too, if not for Odysseus, who revealed the disguise, forcing Achilles to enlist in the army against Troy." The professor shuffled his notes, straightening pages to insert them in his binder. "More on the Trojan War and Achilles in the assigned reading, and next time we meet—a quizzie!"

The cruelly understated euphemism unleashed groans in the classroom. These quizzies—demanding detailed knowledge of gods and goddesses, demigods, and that extensive cast of relevant mortals—were tougher than Caridad's climatology exams, wherein she only had to remember cloud types and weather patterns. Plus, Caridad had stupidly opted to take this course the same semester she was enrolled in classical drama. She often confused Odysseus with Oedipus and Agamemnon with Antigone. After the first quizzie, she'd muttered under her breath, "If these are his quizzies, I'd hate to see his testes." The guy with the attractive neck had honked with laughter at this. And now, while she was jamming her notebook into her bag, he turned to ask her to have coffee with him. But Caridad had two more classes and a shift at the library. More polite excuses, though she regretted these. That tempting neck—she would touch it one day.

The late edition of the *Los Angeles Times* in the Periodical Reading Room bore a headline announcing the bus strike at noon. After her shift at the library, Caridad borrowed her supervisor's phone in a recessed office to call her mother for a ride home. With any luck, Mama would answer, and she wouldn't have to speak to Felicia, who was still bitter that Esperanza had asked Caridad to be the baby's godmother, and who made no secret of the fact that she considered her youngest sister to be A) lacking in morals for leaving her husband to live with two different men, and B) after the baby's christening party, at which Caridad drank a considerable amount of wine, something of an alcoholic.

"What's up?" Felicia asked after Caridad's tentative greeting.

"Is Mama home?"

"She has Weight Watchers today. Why? What do you need?"

"Nothing, I guess. It's just that I'm a little stranded—ha, ha, ha." Since the baptism, Caridad relayed problems to Felicia as if these were self-deprecating jokes. "RTD went on strike, and—oops!—no buses. I have no way to get home." She emitted a chuckling sound.

"It's almost rush hour. You have any idea how long that would take? You *do* know Mama has cataracts?"

"I just sort of hoped—"

"She's not your fucking chauffeur," Felicia said.

"I know that."

"Where are you anyway? Happy hour at some bar? You could ask the bartender to call a cab for you or get one of your male floozies to drive you home."

"I'm not at a bar." Caridad lowered her voice, so Caleb, her supervisor, wouldn't overhear her as he pecked at a keyboard nearby. He'd stopped typing and appeared to be going over his work, but Caridad sensed suction from his ears as he listened in. "I'm on campus."

"Well, don't expect me to pick you up. I have Open House tonight, which you would know if you ever bothered listening to—"

"*Look*, Felicia," she said, ready to release the hot burst of anger filling her lungs, but she caught Caleb's eye and exhaled in a measured way as if cooling a cup of coffee. "It's fine. I'll call a cab. Thanks." Caridad recradled the phone. One day she would break herself of the habit of thanking the people she yearned to slap.

Caleb, a Russian literature major who wore his long frizzy hair in a ponytail, now sipped from his samovar and inclined his lean torso toward her, his neck and head curved like the top of a question mark.

"Family! What can you do?" Caridad laughed again and yanked up her book bag for a quick getaway. But the bag's strap caught under the rolling wheel of Caleb's desk chair, resulting in an awkward struggle.

Then Caleb cleared his throat. "Happy families are all alike; each unhappy family is unhappy in its own way." He paused, arched a brow. "That's Tolstoy, *Anna Karenina*."

Caridad pursed her lips and nodded. "*Thanks*."

As she loped down Reseda Boulevard, Caridad's conscience pricked her for not remembering about her mother's eyes. Lucky thing her mother didn't answer the phone because Mama would have driven to the Valley despite being unable to see. "Ni modo," she would have said. "Cataracts, so what?" If need be, Mama would ride a motorcycle into Hades to collect her youngest daughter. She was the kind of mother who longed for an opportunity to do something like that for any of her daughters. Crossing at Nordhoff, Caridad envisioned Mama exchanging housecoat and slippers for a fringed leather vest and boots, gunning a Harley past Cerberus and leaving the hound choking in a black cloud of exhaust as she gained momentum to vault over the River Styx. Smiling at this, Caridad leapt to the curb when a wood-paneled station wagon slowed alongside her.

The driver tooted the horn. Caridad stopped and glanced in the open passenger-side window. A middle-aged man, bald on top, with a monkish corona of rust-colored hair, summoned her with a wave. "Hey, where you headed?" he called out in a falsetto drawl. "I can give you a ride." He was pudgy with a jaundiced complexion, a butterscotch pudding of a man. Caridad gazed out at Reseda Boulevard, the expanse of it. Heat shimmered on the pavement, creating iridescent puddles in the distance, reflective pools that would vanish with her approach only to reappear several yards ahead.

Caridad cupped her eyes against the sun. "Going as far as Vanowen?"

"I sure am." He pushed open the passenger door.

She glanced right and left before stepping off the curb and ducking into the car. They traveled a few blocks in companionable conversation, Caridad complaining about the bus strike, when he interrupted to ask if she had a boyfriend. That's when she noticed it, bobbing like an elongated pink balloon in his lap. He stroked this with his free hand like a pet. Despite the stomach-turning surprise of it, she couldn't help but marvel at his sleight of hand, the magician's trick of whipping it out undetected.

"My boyfriend's an ex-con. He's sort of jealous and violent." Caridad stared at the streaked windshield while discreetly fumbling for the door handle with her right hand. She'd read that kidnappers remove the inner handle and lock release on passenger-side doors. "He follows me everywhere."

"You're funny." The man jiggled and tugged at his penis. "I'm . . . *ahh* . . . I'm not going to hurt you." As he slowed the car for a red light, Caridad's knuckles at last brushed the smooth chrome latch. She grabbed her book bag and swung open the door, bolting when the car came to a stop.

Caridad raced for the entrance to the nearest building and heaved open the heavy glass door to a mint-green bank, a familiar landmark for its digital marquee that displayed the time and temperature, along with interest rates. Caridad slipped inside the dark lobby. A gray-haired man in a khaki uniform approached her, his shoes click-clacking on the parquet floor. "We're closed for renovation," he told Caridad. "I'm locking up after the carpenters." He reopened the door, ushering her out.

Caridad nodded, panting to catch her breath.

"What's wrong?" he asked.

"A man . . ." Caridad faltered, not wanting to tell this grandfatherly guard about that long, bobbing balloon. "This man scared me."

"Is he following you?" The guard looked past her, searching the street.

She shook her head. "I just got scared."

He asked if she'd be okay, and Caridad nodded before stepping over the threshold and emerging from the dim lobby back into the sun's glare, the hot and noisy boulevard streaming with cars, trucks, but not a single bus. The guard closed the door behind her, and Caridad surveyed the street—no trace of the paneled station wagon. She peered down the boulevard, the many blocks ahead. The perverted man hadn't driven her more than a few blocks! Why, oh, why couldn't he have waited at least until Sherman Way to whip out his thing?

Her feet, in huaraches, pulsed with pain, blisters stinging where skin chafed against the stiff leather weave, especially at the heels. After several minutes of power walking, her calves burned and the leg she'd broken throbbed in such a way that she listed to one side to favor it, causing her hips to ache. Her lungs burned, and she was simultaneously thirsty beyond belief while experiencing an urgent need to pee. She reached Vanowen, but she was several blocks from Van Nuys, the halfway point to her bus stop on Laurel Canyon. With her forearm, Caridad swiped sweat from her brow and plodded on.

A car cruised to the curb, honking. Caridad kept up her pace, not even bothering to look. During her long trek, many horns blared, men catcalled from cars, and some made pumping jerk-off gestures to get her attention. *What is wrong with you?* she wanted to ask them. Wearing jeans and a loose cotton blouse while walking in broad daylight, Caridad attracted the same lewd attention that she'd draw if she wore a G-string and pasties while pole dancing in a topless bar. She thought of Artemis and Actaeon, how the huntress turned the voyeur into prey, chased and devoured by his own dogs for gazing at the goddess after she bathed.

"Hey, where you headed?" A familiar voice, high and reedy— where had she heard it before?—called out to her from the car at the curb that slowed to keep pace with her. She hazarded a sidelong glance. The Library Rat leaned out the passenger-side window of a white sedan, waving her over.

Caridad stopped short. "I know you," she said.

The Library Rat was drunk, and so was his friend, sloppily steering the large car. They urged Caridad to drink one of the bottled wine coolers sloshing about in an ice chest on the backseat beside her. But the sweet stench of these filled the car, sickening her. She refused, thirsty though she was. The driver, with slicked-back yellow hair like the Library Rat and a great pillow of a gut, kept saying he needed to get "some box." Though Caridad wasn't exactly sure what that meant, she suspected it had to do with sex. The Library Rat told him to shut his trap. Beneath the sticky stink of wine coolers, the car smelled of sweat, gasoline, and cigarettes.

"I just need me some box." The driver ran fingers through his oily hair. "I'll be okay once I get some box."

"Shut your face," the Library Rat said.

"Where are your books?" Caridad asked.

The Library Rat turned in his seat to gape at her. "What books?"

"You always have books with you," Caridad said, "on the bus."

"What bus?"

Caridad surveyed his small eyes and sharp nose, those long yellow teeth. Doubt crept up her spine, and she glanced at the door on her side. The handle and lock release had been removed, a trio of ragged-edged sockets in place of the handle, and a gap like a neat round bullet hole marked where the lock had been. "But I thought . . ."

"Look, we got plenty of drinks and smokes. How 'bout we party at your place?"

The driver moaned. "I need me some *box*."

Something louder than the ocean filled Caridad's ears. This was more like a turbine, a mind-scraping roar obliterating all other sounds and making her feel she would have to shout to be heard. Still, she kept her voice steady as she directed them to her street. The driver pulled into a parking space in front of Ernie's stucco house. The two swung open their doors, and the driver unlatched the back door. As soon as Caridad hopped out, they crowded her. "I hope my boyfriend's not here," she said. "He has a bad temper. You better wait while I check."

"I don't think so," the slighter man told her. "We're coming with you."

Caridad shrugged. "Suit yourselves."

She opened the gate and stepped into the shady yard that held an array of potted ferns with long curling fronds, along with blooming red rose and peach-blossomed hibiscus bushes. The grass still damp from watering gave her reason to stamp her shoes on the concrete step. A dog yapped inside, and within seconds, the door yawned wide. The Herculean mass of Ernie's densely muscled body appeared in the frame. He held Baby, his Chihuahua, in his arms, and he grinned at Caridad before he noticed the men behind her. She stood on tiptoes to kiss his cheek and whisper, "Help me get rid of these two."

He handed her the tiny dog and swept Caridad inside his house. "What the hell you want?" Ernie stepped outside, shutting the door after her. Once inside Ernie's air-cooled and well-insulated house, Caridad barely made out their raised voices. Baby trembled, whimpering in her arms. In a few moments, Ernie reopened the door and entered. "Damn." He took Baby from her. "Where'd you find those bitches?"

"Long story," Caridad told him, but after using the bathroom and gulping down a glass of iced tea, she relayed most of it.

"I'm going to say what I told you before: You need to buy a car."

Caridad swirled the ice cubes in her glass. "If only I could afford one."

"Get a loan." Ernie set down his glass of tea. "You're not helpless, you know, and you're not stupid, so stop acting like you're both."

After Ernie made sure the white car was gone, Caridad stepped through the gate adjoining their yards. She'd forgotten her key, so she rapped under the decorative window in the front door. Through the beveled glass, she glimpsed her long mauve skirt and pink blouse sailing near. Caridad drew in a sharp breath. It was as if her clothes had become animated or another version of her, a doppelgänger, now approached. The bolt scraped, and the door swung wide. A narrow face caked with foundation cream greeted her with a bright waxy smile. Beneath this, Caridad spied Gray's familiar honey-colored eyes, small nose, and lean cheeks. "*Gray?*" she said, inflecting his name not because she didn't recognize him, but because she was slow to take in this transformation.

"I'm Leslie," Gray said in a voice so high-pitched that in different circumstances, it would have triggered laughter instead of causing Caridad's eyelids to prickle. "Gray's not here, but please come in. He's told me all about you, and I've been looking forward to meeting you."

Caridad's swollen feet balanced on the raised chrome strip that sealed the bottom of the door shut. She teetered, shifting her weight from her throbbing toes to her blistered heels, taking measure of Leslie from the floor up—patent-leather pumps, shaved legs encased in panty hose, flowing skirt, diaphanous blouse, foundation cream and powder, false eyelashes, penciled-on eyebrows, and that brown cap of synthetic hair, slightly askew. What would happen if she flat-out refused to take that next step? Then Caridad slid from the tracking and kicked off her shoes. With the syrupy deliberateness that spooled out her actions in dreams whenever she had the sense of performing the same motions before and again and always, Caridad reached to tug the dull-haired wig, to straighten the thing on Leslie's head.

Do Not Duplicate

Caridad's head thumped and thwacked. Was it the Danes or the Norwegians who compared hangovers to carpenters in the forehead? It was as if she hosted a crew of construction workers, all hammering, sawing, drilling, and shouting abrupt curses in her head. Despite this, an odd thrill surged in her as she passed a rack of bicycles near the library's entrance. Unsure why excitement flooded her, Caridad continued across the sunny portico to start her morning shift, glancing again at the row of bikes. One ten-speed stood out for a white carton affixed to its back tire frame. A label on the box bore a trio of chocolate disks, one halved to display its pale green filling. Lettering above this read *Junior Mints*. On this muggy morning in early June, the image suggested refreshment but not much else to jump-start the giddiness that briefly hushed the raucous builders in her head.

As she entered the library, Caridad remembered that she would submit her application this day for promotion to stacks supervisor. *That* must be the source of her anticipation. The job would require her to have a car to close the library at night, and when interviewed, she planned to say she was buying one. After work, she and Gray would see a man about a used Chevrolet Impala advertised in the *Penny Saver*. Caridad now made her way toward the circulation desk, mindful to smile at the supervisor. Eye contact, she told herself as she strode through the inner office, greeting coworkers on her way to the assignment sheet posted in back. There, she found her name and beside that her hourly task: discharging. This meant she would remain in the back room, sorting returned books. *Perfect.* There was no better job when enduring a hangover than the undemanding chore of organizing returned books.

Usually student workers were paired up for discharging, but no name appeared next to hers on the assignment sheet. Even better—she would work alone. There were only a few tubs of books to be sorted. After finishing these, she'd sneak to her locker for *Lady Chatterley's Lover*. She'd devoured the novel—as if in a fever—over the weekend and was now rereading it, pausing to pen notes in the margins and to write favorite quotes in the notebook Gray had given her. "Patience! Patience!" she now told herself, having copied this down last night. "The world is a vast and ghastly intricacy of mechanism, and one has to be very wary, not to get mangled by it." It didn't exactly apply, but the general truth of it appealed to her.

As she distributed books among the sorting tables, a dolly stacked with plastic tubs wheeled into the work space. These were filled with texts collected from depositories around campus. Daniel Marsden, a stacks supervisor who'd just transferred to the main library from the Technical Sciences Annex, appeared behind the tall column of tubs that he carefully settled near the tables. Daniel was a philosophy major with a disproportionately large and handsome head set atop a short and stocky body. He had dark hair and thick eyebrows, along with a flattish nose and brown eyes fringed with dense black lashes. Over a T-shirt that stated "Plato was a bore," he wore a blue-and-gray Pendleton flannel that draped over his loose khakis. A tough guy's moustache and connecting goatee framed his full mouth, but his café-con-leche cheeks were as bare and smooth as a child's.

Caridad knew him well enough to dislike him in a vague way. Female coworkers gossiped about his live-in girlfriend—who wore wrinkled clothing and had straggly hair—as if her dorkiness somehow made him available to them. Only Kitty Fu claimed that he was "one mean maternal fucker," and Caridad was inclined to agree. She'd taken an art class with him, and since then, apart from giving her a withering look when she'd once smiled at him, Daniel ignored Caridad whenever they encountered one another on campus.

After becoming a supervisor, though, Daniel had grown more talkative. In fact, these days at work, he often argued philosophical ideas with staff members. Caridad hoped he would not provoke a dispute with her just to sharpen his debating skills. She was in no mood for that. One of Gray's favorite quotes from *Candide* now surfaced in her thoughts: "Let us work without theorizing . . . 'tis the only way to make life endurable." Together, they hefted tubs off the dolly and distributed sun-warmed books onto the sorting tables in silence. Caridad's headache dulled over the course of the hour. Though they'd started with gusto, the carpenters in her forehead grew sluggish as the morning dragged on. These were lazy laborers who knocked off early, the clamor in her head usually subsiding by noon. In the meantime, she developed such a powerful thirst that she could barely swallow. After they unloaded the last tub, Caridad excused herself to lap water from a fountain in the lobby.

Daniel dropped his gaze, issuing a contemptuous look, but he said nothing. When she returned, he was staring into a thick medical text as if striking a pose. Wordlessly, Caridad began arranging the sorted books for placement on nearby bookshelves.

Daniel cleared his throat. "My father is a doctor, did you know?"

Caridad shook her head. She continued shuffling books into order.

"He's half Filipino and half British. That's where the Marsden comes from, the British. He practices medicine in San Clemente. My mother is German-Irish from Minnesota, a farm girl. But I'm Puerto Rican." He snapped the text shut and plunked it into a bin designated for books to be returned to the Technical Sciences Annex. "They're not really my parents. See, I was adopted, along with my two sisters."

Caridad turned away to arrange books on the wall shelves, and Daniel took up an armload of texts from the tables. In the work area's horseshoe configuration, he began sorting the A-B call number books in a shelving area opposite to where she worked among the Hs. Their backs to each other, Daniel started telling Caridad about his child-hood, his adoption, and the people who'd raised him, his voice as flat and relentless as if he were reading aloud from an uninspiring text.

His earliest memory, he told her, was witnessing his biological father strike his mother with a hammer. Welfare workers discovered him and his two younger sisters in a tenement apartment, abandoned by both parents, alcoholics who'd left them on their own for days. Daniel and his sisters, no more than toddlers, had distended bellies from malnutrition. All three were infested with parasitic worms and head lice. Initially, his adoptive parents had only wanted one child, a playmate for their only son, but they'd been moved by the trio of deserted siblings and decided to adopt them all. "It was an impulse they'd regret," Daniel said, before telling Caridad he'd been institutionalized for mental illness at fifteen after he'd threatened to kill his adoptive family. Afterward he was released into foster care and sent to a boys' home, where he lived until starting college. He told her how both his sisters, turned out of the home in their early teens, were now prostitutes, working out of massage parlors.

Such a narrative would compel sympathy in almost anyone, but this story struck Caridad as unbelievable. As Daniel spoke, Caridad flashed on Marsha Lowenstein, another student worker with whom she'd sorted books. Marsha chattered nonstop, making one outlandish claim after another. She'd confided witnessing an assassination attempt on the pope, saying she was now in the witness protection program. She'd insisted that her brother had been born with a dog's face and had to have plastic surgery to correct the problem. Marsha swore she'd once enabled an alien spacecraft to land in a Kmart parking lot by signaling it with a flashlight. Though Daniel's story was far more credible than Marsha's whoppers, Caridad wondered what it was about the sorting area—maybe the word "discharging"?—that prompted people to unleash such tales.

When Daniel stepped out to update assignments, Caridad cast an irritated glance at his retreating back, a flash of blue-and-gray flannel. Moments later, she checked the sheet for her next task. Discharging—*again?* Caridad slipped away to gulp more water. She returned to find Daniel back in the sorting area and braced herself for more of the same. He picked up where he'd left off, filling in details related to his adoptive parents' preferential treatment of their biological son and introducing a new chapter on abuses he'd endured in foster homes. As Daniel spoke, they loaded books onto "book trucks," the narrow carts with shelves that they used for returning books to the stacks. The second hour ended, and Caridad set out of the library for her break.

She'd sit on the portico and silence her humming head while enjoying her book. As she scoped the sun-bleached benches for an isolated spot, she caught sight of that now-familiar blue-and-gray flash of flannel. Daniel approached Caridad as if he'd followed her out of the library. He was on his way to class, he said, but he looked forward to talking to her again soon. Daniel pointed at her book. "What are you reading?"

"*Lady Chatterley's Lover*," she said.

He waggled his eyebrows as if she'd said something suggestive.

"It's for a *class*—Modern British Literature."

"You're so serious." Daniel smiled to show he was joking with her. "Okay," he said after a pause. "See you later." He pivoted away, striding for the bike rack, where he crouched to unlock the ten-speed bearing the Junior Mints box in back. Of course, this was his bike. Weeks ago, Caridad had glimpsed him clamping it to the rack.

As Caridad and Gray stepped off the bus to meet the man selling the Impala, the setting sun flamed like a blood orange and the sky bloomed pink and gold, calling to mind the gilt-edged holy cards depicting ascension into heaven. In such peach-soft radiance, Caridad believed ugliness impossible, a notion dispelled as soon as she saw the rusted gray sedan with a jaundiced interior, along with its owner, a thickset man with a lumpy vein-scribbled face, at the gas station where they'd arranged to meet. The car reeked of hard-boiled eggs and foot funk, with underlying traces of ant spray. As they waited for the car's owner to climb into the backseat, Gray whispered, "What do you think?"

"*Très* stenchy." She fanned fingers under her nose.

Gray sniffed. "Eau de sulfur et sweaty socks."

"A little morphine in the air," Caridad quoted Lawrence. "It would be wonderfully refreshing for everyone."

The owner settled in back with a groan. He slammed the door, and Gray churned the engine. It started up at once and glided from the curb.

"See how nice she drives," the man said.

Gray drove about two blocks before signaling to turn right, and the man leaned forward to say, "One thing I should tell you—"

With a mind-mangling blast, the horn sounded—startling pedestrians on the street—as the Impala veered right. It blared without stopping until the car straightened out of the turn.

"A little problem, see," the owner said. "She tends to squawk a bit when you turn right. Mechanic told me it's a quick fix, just a few dollars to replace a part. But tell you what—I'll knock fifty off the asking price, so you can take care of it."

"Just fifty?" Caridad said.

The man sighed. "Best I can do. Listen, I got to get back. Another guy wants to look at her today, and my nephew's been bugging me to buy this sweet old bucket. Now I don't like to do business with family, but oh well . . ."

At a red light, Caridad and Gray traded looks: a silent consultation. He winced, but she gave him an imploring look, a wordless reminder of her application for promotion. "We'll take it," Gray said when they returned to the gas station. He counted out several bills into the owner's palm in exchange for the car's title and an extra key.

"We saved fifty dollars," Gray said after the man loped off for the bus stop.

"And now we have a car."

They climbed back into the malodorous car, and Gray restarted the engine. "If this is the best of all possible Impalas," he said, "I wonder what the others are like."

"Things cannot be otherwise than they are," Caridad said, completing the quotation. "As all things are created for some end, they must be created for the best end."

Gray nodded. "We just need to get home without turning right."

"Or we can wave when the horn goes off." She raised a palm and shifted her cupped hand right and left. "We can pretend we're greeting people we know."

"It's not exactly a friendly toot, though. It's more like a foghorn."

"We'll figure it out," Caridad said, though she was scheduled to take the licensing test first thing in the morning, too early to have the problem fixed. "We always figure things out." Since it would cost so little to repair the car, they decided to go out to dinner at an all-you-can-eat smorgasbord only a few left turns away, and afterward, they took a few more lefts to a liquor store, where they bought a case of beer. On the way home, Caridad said, "Now we can finally take those empty cans to recycling."

Carless, they'd managed just about everything on foot or with public transportation, from grocery shopping to trips to the coin laundry. But they couldn't haul cans to the recycling plant in Van Nuys on the bus. They'd likely earn more than ten dollars for the several bags of these that were stored in the backyard toolshed.

By making only left turns, they traced an odd boxlike route that led them into unfamiliar neighborhoods. They lowered the windows and a sultry early evening breeze swept in to flush out the car's noxious smell. They cruised through a neighborhood of stucco houses with sweetly junky yards. Residents decorated their homes with flamingoes, gnomes, cupids, and jockeys. Lifelike plaster deer, a doe and two fawns, stood in one lawn, and another displayed a cement fountain shaped like a fish spouting water from its mouth. Gray fumbled with the radio's dials to find a station that played a staticky early recording. "Whoa, it's Depression-era!" He turned up the volume. *You are my sunshine my only sunshine. You make me happy when skies are gray . . .*

"Cool." Caridad stared out the window as the kitschy yards and small houses gave way to more familiar sights—graffiti-scrawled apartment buildings and then the housing projects. A huddle of khaki-clad men in wife-beaters gathered on the sidewalk, talking and drinking beer. A tattooed tough, sporting a moustache and goatee like Daniel Marsden's, glowered at Caridad as they drove past.

But now you've left me, wailed the singer on the radio, *to love another, and you have shattered all my dreams . . .*

"We're going to get lost." Gray clicked on the right-turn signal. "I have to turn."

"Not here," Caridad said.

But if you leave me to love another, you'll regret it all someday . . .

Gray waited a few blocks to turn. The horn blasted, setting off car alarms and howling dogs. "You really think you'll be okay in this for the test tomorrow?"

"Sure," Caridad said. "It's not a *car* test. It's a *driver's* test, right?"

But in the morning, Caridad, again hungover and headachy, was much less sure about this. How would she complete the test without having to turn right? What if the examiner thought that she was inexplicably hitting the horn at each turn? When Caridad and Gray climbed into the car that morning, it smelled worse than before, as if the odors had gathered strength overnight. Brewery foulness added to the usual stench. This would not impress the examiner, who might gag as she had, and then deduct points for being sickened by the stink.

As Gray pulled away from the curb, clanking sounds emanated from the backseat. "What's that?" Caridad asked.

Gray shrugged. "Just the cans."

"The *cans*?"

"I loaded them up while you were showering. We can take them in after your test. The recycling place is just a few lefts—"

"Wait. Let me get this straight . . ." Caridad glanced over her shoulder at bulging garbage bags in the back. "You put beer cans in the backseat—"

"They wouldn't all fit in the trunk."

"—on the day I'm taking the *driver's license test*?"

"The recycling place is really close to the DMV. It just makes sense—"

"No, it really does *not*. None of this makes sense. This nasty-smelling car, the honking, and now *beer cans* in the backseat." She squinted at his profile. Clots of foundation cream clung to his hairline—traces of Leslie from last night. "*You* don't make any sense to me at all."

A week later, Caridad pulled the Impala into the campus parking lot, the horn bellowing when she turned to thread the car into a narrow space. She waved at a group of startled black students, who smiled and waved back as they emerged from a nearby van. Caridad set the emergency brake and withdrew the key with a heavy sigh. While she had adjusted to the convenience of having a car, she couldn't get used to the horn or to her own poor driving skills. Just now, she'd parked so close to the car on her left that she had to scoot to the passenger side to climb out. It amazed her now more than ever that she'd earned a license.

Of course, she'd aced the written part. Caridad enjoyed such exams, but passing the practical test—what with that right-turn blast of the horn, the beer cans rolling around on the backseat, and the stop sign at which she failed to brake—was nothing short of freakish. At the time, she had been sure she'd failed, despite the bald examiner's smiling assurances. "Anyone can miss a stop sign," he'd said after she plowed through an intersection without pausing, and when the tie on one of the garbage bags came loose and beer cans cascaded onto the floorboard in back, he'd commended her for recycling. After the horn blared the first time she turned right, he said, "I once had a car like this." Kicking back loose cans that rolled under his seat, the examiner made only a few notes on the form affixed to his clipboard. When Caridad finally parked the car (a yard from the curb), he'd pumped her hand in congratulations and pressed into her palm a tag of paper with his phone number on it.

Now she pulled her book bag from the backseat and locked the doors. As she hiked toward the library, she shook out her long hair and flapped her loose gray cardigan to release the car's odor from it. Today was the day she would be interviewed for the supervisor's position.

Once in the library, Caridad passed as usual through the gauntlet of student workers and staff members, smiling and greeting all—eye contact, eye contact, eye contact. When she reached the assignment podium hoping to find the interview penciled in for the first hour, Caridad couldn't find her name at all. She stepped aside so others could read their assignments. After her coworkers dispersed, she lingered near the podium for a few awkward moments until Daniel Marsden appeared.

"I'm not on the—"

"I know," he said. "We need to talk." From his pocket, Daniel produced a Stacks Reading Log, an index card tallying errors in the bookcases that student workers "read" to make sure books were in order. This one designated a range of ML call numbers, which consisted of thin and tightly packed musical scores that had razored Caridad's cuticles when pulled out one by one in order for her to read the call numbers. She'd initialed that she'd read six bookcases.

"I checked your reading," Daniel said.

Caridad's cheeks flamed, the ocean thundering inside her. Stacks supervisors randomly read a few shelves in the middle or at the end of sections student workers reported reading. They kept records of the errors they found and used these to evaluate job performance. She recalled a stuffy afternoon during midterms, when she'd sat on a short stool, resting her forehead against a shelf's edge and dozing for the hour instead of reading the narrow texts.

"Those books were a mess. Your error rate's going to skyrocket if I report this."

Caridad nodded.

"With stats like that, you won't get an interview," he told her, "*unless* you go up to read that section now." Daniel handed her the card.

"Daniel . . ." she said. "Thanks."

"I've checked your sections before. They're always perfect. What happened?"

Where to begin—those blade-thin musical scores, the overheated stacks, her exhaustion at exam time? Caridad opened her mouth and then closed it. She shrugged.

Daniel's thuggish face softened. "It's not like you."

She pocketed the card and turned toward a door leading to an emergency-exit staircase. Maybe people would forget they'd seen her arrive if she didn't sashay past the front desk to take the elevator up to the stacks. Caridad jogged up the corrugated aluminum steps, each footstep a hollow echo in the dank stairwell.

A bright bubble of elation rose in Caridad when Wade Wamble, director of library circulation, phoned her at home a few days later to tell her she'd earned the promotion. She experienced a rare rush of glee. No question, she'd been a flawed wife, and lately she'd become a negligent sister and daughter. Maybe she was meant to be a career woman, rising toward distinction at work—Queen of the Library one day. Whatever the outcome, the news thrilled her just for the extra money she'd be earning. But she kept her tone calm as she thanked Wade for the call. Then she hung up and performed a breathless dance, comprised of high kicks and arm flinging, while wishing Gray would return so she could share the news with him.

After catching her breath, Caridad called her mother to tell her. But Felicia, as usual, answered. "What's up?"

"*Oh*," Caridad said. "It's nothing. I . . . Is Mama there?"

"She's at the doctor's with Esperanza."

"What's wrong?"

"Nothing—it's the baby's six-week checkup, which you would know if you ever bothered to call anyone."

"I'm calling now." Caridad's eyes darted about the disheveled living room—beer cans and cups on the coffee table, clothes humped on the couch, shoes scattered about the floor, books and loose paper everywhere—as if searching the mess for an excuse, or an escape.

"Just curious, but when *was* the last time you saw the baby?"

"I have classes and work—"

"Forget Mimi," Felicia said, using the nickname she'd given their niece. "She's too young to care, but what about Esperanza? Have you even *called* her lately?"

Caridad shook her head. Gray pulled open the front door, and she waved, mouthing Felicia's name. He flashed a sympathetic smile on his way into the kitchen. The refrigerator sucked open, cans rattling, and whooshed shut.

"If you bothered to call," Felicia said, "you'd know she's not doing too great."

"What's going on?" Caridad asked.

"You're the damned godmother, and you can't even take the time to—"

"What's wrong with Esperanza?" A nerve in Caridad's right eyelid began twitching.

"Get off your ass and go see her if you really want to know how she's doing."

"Fine!" Caridad slammed down the phone.

Gray emerged from the kitchen, bearing two cans of beer.

Caridad took one, popped it open, and gulped. "I just made the mistake of trying to call my mother."

"Mistake?"

"Yeah, I got Felicia instead, and I just wanted to tell her . . ." Caridad, remembering the reason for her call, grinned at Gray. "And I want to tell you, too . . ." She paused here for effect. "*I got the job.*"

Gray set down his beer and reached to embrace Caridad. "Congratulations!" He pulled back to beam at her. "We have to celebrate."

"That'd be nice." Glee again lofted in Caridad. "Maybe we can order a pizza?"

Gray shook his head. "No, no, *no*—not good enough. I'm think we should go out."

"Out to dinner?"

"Not just out to dinner, but *out* out."

"Where?"

"Like maybe a nightclub or a bar, something like that." Gray flushed. He busied himself sorting through the jumble on the coffee table. "I think I'm ready, don't you?"

Caridad cocked her head. "Ready?"

"Yeah, I've had lots of practice." He finally met her gaze, his amber eyes wide and shining. "Don't you think I'm ready to go out?"

The beer in her hand chilled her fingers, stiffening them as it spread and raising gooseflesh on her arms and shoulders.

"I mean, as Leslie," Gray said.

Caridad pasted on a wide smile. "Sure."

That evening Gray perched on the closed toilet seat in their small bathroom, a towel draped around his shoulders, while Caridad bound his hair in a nylon cap. Lately, he'd been more interested in dressing up as

Leslie at night than in going to bed with Caridad. It had been weeks, maybe more than a month since he'd touched her. Caridad considered this as she daubed foundation cream and dusted powder on his freshly shaven cheeks. Then she stretched the wig over his scalp. She outlined his eyes with kohl, brushed mascara on his quivering lashes, and smoothed ruby gloss over his lips. He examined himself in the bathroom mirror. His face grew bonier, elongated in an equine way, and his Adam's apple seemed to protrude more when he was bewigged and made-up, so Caridad wound a pink scarf, a gauzy length of raw silk, around his neck. He slipped on a pair of heels, and *wah-la*—Leslie appeared.

They chose a small bar in a strip mall with a grim storefront entrance, an uninviting place where they hoped Caridad would not be carded. Leslie pulled open the battered door to the thick effluvia of beer and cigarette smoke. Inside, half a dozen men wearing faded jeans, T-shirts, and baseball caps sat among the shadowy booths or at the bar. Caridad and Gray climbed onto stools and ordered beer on tap from the white-haired bartender in dark glasses. He didn't give Caridad a second look, much less ask to see her ID. She and Gray sipped beer while talking in hushed voices about nothing in particular, like extras on a movie set hired to fill in a scene. After they ordered a second round, a man in a red ball cap, a long coppery ponytail snaking down his back, sat beside Caridad. "I like your girlfriend," he said, his voice a gritty whisper. Then he spoke over her to Leslie. "That's a great look, real convincing."

Leslie gaped at Caridad. The bartender brought their mugs of beer, and the man turned again to Caridad. "You helped, I bet."

Leslie tugged Caridad's sleeve. "We better go."

She shook her head, wanting to finish her drink.

Leslie leaned toward her. "We really need to go."

The man in the red cap glanced from Caridad to Gray. "Hey, don't freak out. I been to the Queen Mary over on Ventura. I know what's what."

Caridad tilted her mug, draining her beer.

"Come on," Leslie said.

"Let him go," the man told her. "I'll give you a ride."

Caridad lowered her mug onto the bar. Muzzy-headed, she glanced from Leslie's lean horsey face to the man in the cap. His skin was mottled and pouched, his nose mashed, one ear puffy with scar tissue. Under a thick matting of rust-colored hair, tattooed serpents crawled up his muscle-corded arms. He looked like an old boxer, someone who could get rough.

"Stay," he said. "I'll treat you good."

Was this how Mellors, the gamekeeper, first appeared to Lady Chatterley? Crude and gruff, but tempting in a dangerous way? Caridad dropped a hand onto the man's forearm, her fingers tightening as if to measure the furry mass. "Will you?"

He raised a bristly eyebrow, nodded.

"I'm leaving." Leslie set a bill on the bar and lunged for the door.

Caridad raised her mug again, swallowed its foamy dregs, and slowly lowered it back onto the bar as if it were a game piece she'd deliberated about positioning. Then she stood to trail after the fluttering tips of Leslie's bright scarf, that unfurling cloud of pink silk.

On Monday, her first day as stacks supervisor, Caleb filled Caridad's cupped palms with a chinking jumble of keys. Some were round bowed, others squared, all had ridged blades with irregular teeth, and a few were etched with a warning: *Do Not Duplicate*. He then tossed her a lanyard keychain before explaining what each key opened. Staff members opened and closed the library, but student supervisors kept keys to the electric cart, book depositories, service elevator, supply closets, and panels covering the escalator's on/off switches, as well as a master key to the study carrels. Caridad barely listened to this rambling list, so taken was she with the heft and chime of these many keys.

That afternoon, Caridad steered the electric cart through campus to collect returned books from depositories. Daniel Marsden bounced on the bench seat beside her as the cart bumped over the library lawn. He directed her to the various drop boxes and helped her transfer books within these into plastic tubs. Next, they loaded the heavy tubs into the back of the cart. Since he'd just undergone the same instruction when he transferred from Technical Sciences, Daniel provided most of her training. After his unexpected kindness about the musical scores, Caridad didn't mind his company, but she would have preferred being trained by Caleb, whose quotations from Russian literature she sometimes enjoyed.

As they rode, Daniel talked about Beryl, his live-in girlfriend, bragging about their relationship and how they never quarreled—instead they "questioned" one another when conflict arose. Such questioning smacked of interrogation to Caridad, but she made no comment. Now, as the cart puttered across campus, Daniel explained how Beryl, a former art major like himself, had not switched to philosophy just because he had, but because it was the right thing to do. They had questioned each other rigorously about this, until Beryl, too, surrendered "the pretenses of art for the honesty of ideas."

The afternoon sun burned away the morning's haze, bearing down on the electric cart. Caridad wore jeans and a long-sleeved green shirt that Gray had thrown in a dryer set on high heat. The gauzy fabric had shrunk, now constricting about Caridad's shoulders and bust. The shirt's buttonholes stretched, causing the pearly heart-shaped buttons to pop open. From time to time, she fingered these to make sure they were fastened, discreetly buttoning up when the shirt gaped open. With attention divided between maneuvering the cart and the tight shirt, Caridad was too distracted to put together the alarmed faces of students at a nearby picnic table—faces clearly reflected in the rearview mirror—with the fact that she was steering the cart straight at them in reverse.

When the students dove away from the picnic table, abandoning food and drinks—and Daniel shouted, "Stop!"—Caridad at last made this connection. Too late. The cart slammed into the table, launching it into a pillar. Caridad stomped the brake, and Daniel's forehead collided with the visor. They leapt out to help students gather their belongings. The electric cart had struck the table with its rubber bumper, so it was undamaged, but the stacked tubs inside had toppled with the impact. When Daniel opened the back door, books avalanched out.

They had to empty the cart and refill and restack the tubs before continuing on to the last depository stop. As she drove toward this, Caridad stroked her shirt front and was mortified by the warm touch of bare flesh. All the buttons undone! A towering tsunami of shame shot skyward before crashing inside her. She struggled to fasten the shirt with her left hand.

"You should steer with both hands." Daniel's voice sounded labored, his breathing a bit ragged. "And pay more attention when you drive."

At the last drop box, he refused to get out of the cart to help her. "You need to do this one on your own." His tone was agitated.

"Sometimes you won't have anyone with you. You have to be able to empty the drop boxes by yourself."

When she went around back to extract an empty tub from the cart, Caridad refastened the buttons and tugged on the gauzy fabric, stretching it so it would give instead of popping open. Then she unloaded the books and hoisted the heavy tub into the cart before climbing back into the driver's seat. As she drove, Daniel continued telling her about Beryl and the paper she was writing on Wittgenstein, his flat voice *pip-pip-pipping* like a jar-trapped wasp.

At the library, Daniel ambled alongside Caridad as she struggled to balance the dolly stacked with tubs, rolling it into the discharging area. Again, they unloaded books onto the sorting tables. Daniel grew silent while they worked, but after the tubs were empty, he turned to Caridad. "Do you know you make these chirping noises when you're working?"

She shook her head.

"You do." He cast a downward glance. "And, um, your shirt is open."

"Damn it!" Eyes stinging, Caridad clutched her shirtfront. Her glasses fogged as she blinked back hot tears. She was blindly fastening the buttons when she felt unexpected pressure at her waist. Daniel's arms encircled her, and next, his soft lips covered hers. Warmth radiated from the pit of her stomach, tightening in her lungs and throat. She wrenched away, and Daniel gasped like a swimmer surfacing for air. Caridad released a nervous laugh as if he'd told a joke she didn't really find funny but was polite enough to acknowledge all the same.

"Caridad, I . . ."

She bent to button her shirt.

"I had to do that. I've been thinking about it all day—you have no idea."

Caridad pushed the odd-shaped buttons through their ragged holes. Why so many? Why so useless?

"Look." Daniel pointed to where she'd skipped one.

"I hate this shirt!"

"Come with me." Daniel led her to the recessed stairway, the emergency exit. Once inside the stairwell, he sat on a step and guided Caridad to sit beside him on the cool corrugated aluminum. He reached for her shirtfront. Instead of fastening the buttons, he pulled it open.

"I don't hate this shirt. It's the best shirt ever," he said. "It is."

There, on the steps, they unbuckled and unzipped—removing only what was necessary for Daniel to lunge into her, saying, "Oh, oh, oh." Like Constance with Mellors in the woods, Caridad yielded, blooming like a seaflower, tentacles unfurling to draw him deeper. She pulled him closer and quicker until she lost herself, her urgency fading to slow pulse-beats of pleasure that rippled one into another. Daniel moaned. Then he collapsed onto her, bumping his nose on her collarbone. They clung to each other, now aware of muffled voices sounding from the assignment desk, student workers milling about, talking and laughing. Caridad and Daniel pulled apart to tug on clothing. "I'll head up to the second floor and come down the escalator," he whispered. "Wait a few minutes, go up, and take the elevator."

His footfalls bounced up the stairs while she remained on the hard step, hugging her knees to her chest. No, it was probably not a good idea to have intercourse at work during her first week as a library supervisor. Even so, Caridad had a hard time stirring up regret. She'd always believed that any imaginative person could enjoy a rich sex life. Rare were the times when she couldn't "finish"—as D. H. Lawrence would put this—no matter who her partner might be, and she only failed at this when she'd had too much to drink. This time, though, it was as if she'd been drugged or hypnotized, certainly stupefied from that first embrace. She could no more resist Daniel than she could have refused water on that morning when her throat burned with thirst. Caridad now stood on quaking legs and smoothed her shirt. She glanced down at the buttons, that pearly trail of hearts. How long would they hold this time?

Moscow, Odessa, Saint Petersburg

Beryl, Beryl, Beryl—the name looped in her mind as Gray drove them to the party, repeating like an incantation invoked to distract her from apprehension. Still, Caridad expected that meeting Daniel's girlfriend would sting like static shock. Daniel had said that since Gray planned to attend Caleb's Labor Day party, he would bring Beryl, so as soon as she entered Caleb's ranch-style rental, Caridad began searching for her to avoid being startled by the encounter. The threshold led to a hallway with a small parlor on one side and a dining room on the other. Though ceiling fans whirred, the crowded house felt close and steamy. Shiny-faced coworkers milled about, holding Solo cups of beer and paper plates with chips and nuts. Caridad and Gray followed the corridor toward the living room, where Caleb told them they could exit the sliding glass door to find a keg on the patio.

They navigated through clusters of talking and laughing guests, voices amplified to counter Bruce Springsteen's voice—*Tramps like us, baby, we were born to run!*—blasting from unseen speakers. She and Gray made their way past wall-mounted travel posters depicting spired buildings, domes, and minarets in Moscow, Odessa, and Saint Petersburg, Caridad scanning faces as they went. Once in the crowded living room, Caridad perched on tiptoes to peer over others, and she at last spied Beryl, sitting beside Daniel on a tangerine-colored couch and wearing khakis like his with a T-shirt that read *Thus Spake Zarathustra*.

All summer long, Caridad and Daniel had ferreted out storage closets, unused stairwells, even the rare book room on Saturday before the library opened. A permanent bruise mottled Caridad's tailbone like a blurry tattoo, and her knees were often abraded, scabby from coarse industrial carpeting. On evenings when Beryl worked, Caridad would drive her smelly car to Daniel's apartment during her dinner break for the comparative luxury of his lumpy bed. These days Caridad's skin prickled, tingling in the shower, and a persistent hunger gnawed at her. But food odors disgusted her, as they had in the early days with Jorge. She craved meat, though, and broke her habit of vegetarianism to eat chicken and fish. Even so, her face grew gaunt, making her eyes appear enlarged, darker, and shinier, glimmering in a craven way.

Her gaze swiftly edited out Daniel seated at Beryl's right—the despairing look on his face—and the orange cushion to the left of her. She yearned to sketch Beryl's sharp foxlike features, her brown eyes, and nimbus of frizzy wheat-gold hair. With a pointillist's precision, she'd daub the freckles spattering Beryl's pale skin. Then the room wobbled and spun like a whirligig. Her stomach empty, Caridad nearly swooned, wavering on her long legs. Overhead fans chopped the dusky sunlight pouring through the glass door into glittery filaments. Voices and music flattened into a monkish chant. Gray, chatting with Phuoc Phong, hadn't noticed that she'd stopped short. He stumbled into her, catching her before her knees buckled and breaking her vertiginous trance.

Gray joked about his clumsiness. Phuoc and Caridad laughed, and Beryl caught her eye and smiled. So *this* was Beryl of the many artifacts in Daniel's apartment: the brush threaded with golden hairs, the scuffed leather clogs in the closet, the hardcover copy of *The French Lieutenant's Woman* on the nightstand, the pillow perfumed with hair oil. As if at last encountering the inhabitant of a museum home she'd often toured, Caridad longed to sit by Beryl's side and speak to her. Perhaps intuiting this, Beryl patted the bright cushion beside her. Caridad staggered forward and sank into the corduroy lap of the couch. Gray gave her a curious look and then offered to bring her beer.

She nodded at him and turned to Beryl. "You must be Beryl. I'm—"

"I know." Beryl's voice rang out high and clear as a precocious child's.

Daniel fixed his gaze on the hardwood floor, wearing the expression of someone awaiting sentencing. He'd claimed that he and Beryl had questioned each other intensely about his involvement with

Caridad. He'd said that Beryl had become emotional before accepting the reasonableness of his actions. "I had to explain it over and over," he'd told Caridad. "Since my relationship with her is so great, of course I'd want another like it." Only his experience with Caridad in the hidden places they'd discovered on campus was nothing like what he felt with Beryl—or so he'd also admitted. He didn't enjoy "questioning" or debating Caridad, who was not easy to persuade, especially when Daniel suggested she leave Gray to move in with him and Beryl—an idea Caridad refused with a simple, "No." Frustrated that she gave no reasons for him to counter, Daniel would say that she was illogical, impossible to reason with. He'd said, "How can you argue with 'no'?" And Caridad told him, "You can't."

Gray returned from the patio, bearing two cups of beer. Like Beryl, he also knew about Caridad and Daniel. She'd confided in him when he was costumed as Leslie and they were gossiping about boyfriends. Gray, as Leslie, couldn't break role to react much, but the next morning, he told Caridad that learning this had hurt him, and they talked about it. In the end, Gray supposed that his cross-dressing must be at least as confounding to Caridad as her relationship with Daniel was for him. "At *least*," she'd said.

Gray handed Caridad a cup of beer and sat on the arm of the couch. A rock anthem filled the room, and Gray grimaced. "It's your favorite," he told Caridad, as Queen's "We Are the Champions" spooled from the speakers.

"*Right*." Caridad often complained about the song's simplistic lyrics.

"Oh, you like this song, too?" Beryl clasped Caridad's hand, her stubby fingers warm and moist. "It's my favorite, too!"

Daniel leaned out, nodding to verify this. "She really does love it."

Caridad sipped the flat beer, its foulness souring her tongue. "I actually *don't* like this song. Gray was being sarcastic."

"But *why* not?" Beryl's fluffy head drooped, a wilting dandelion.

Gray drew breath, likely preparing to quote William S. Burroughs or to make some confounding comparison. "It's like cantaloupe," he might say, "firmly fleshed but icky with seeds inside."

To prevent this, Caridad said, "The lyrics aren't great and the music's dull."

"Very dull," said Gray, who liked songs with abrupt beats, surprising melodies, and onomatopoeic lyrics, musicians ranging from Captain Beefheart to Philip Glass.

Daniel regarded him with hooded eyes.

Beryl grew quiet, listening to the song. Then she said, "What's wrong with the lyrics?"

"Cliché." Caridad burped silently and set the cup on the floor. The warm beer tasted the way she imagined suds used for bathing dogs might taste, like flea dip. "Listen to it. 'No bed of roses,' 'fame and fortune,' 'paid my dues,' 'no pleasure cruise'—there's hardly an original phrase in the entire thing."

Beryl mouthed the lyrics along with the vocalist.

"Is it just me," Gray said, "or is this beer disgusting?"

Caridad grinned at his setup for a joke they often shared. "It's *you*. *You're* disgusting!"

They both laughed. Gray beamed, his ears pinkening with pleasure. Caridad squeezed his knee. "But so is the beer."

"I don't see what's wrong with the song," Daniel said.

"You have to listen to it," Beryl told him. "Really listen."

Caridad willed Beryl not to surrender a song she loved this easily.

Beryl squinted, knitting her sparse eyebrows. "The lyrics *are* pretty predictable. It's one cliché after another."

"But you love this song," Daniel told her. "You're always singing it when you're puttering around cooking and cleaning up."

Beryl shrugged. "I just never thought about it before—the lyrics, all the cliché."

"It's still got a great message," Daniel said.

Caridad considered the hardship of his early life and how a song like this suggested triumph, even vindication, over those who'd hurt him. This might have been *his* favorite song, not Beryl's.

"It *does* have a good message," Beryl said. "You're right about that—absolutely." She cast Caridad a look and smiled. "I just wish it weren't filled with cliché."

"Cliché works in some songs." Maybe she could maneuver Beryl into changing her opinion again. While Caridad admired Beryl's slender androgynous form, her sweet vixen face, and her unruly curls, disappointment now sharpened her gaze. No surprise Daniel enjoyed interrogating and debating Beryl, who groped to say whatever she thought a person might want to hear. And no wonder when they were alone, he couldn't keep his hands off Caridad's full breasts and generous backside.

"You can have your cake and eat it, too," Gray said, looking at Daniel.

Daniel started, his eyes widening. "Excuse me?"

"'You can have your cake and eat it, too.' It's Bob Dylan, from 'Lay Lady Lay.'"

"*That's* a great use of cliché," Caridad said.

"I love 'Lay Lady Lay,'" Beryl said. "I really love *that* song!"

After a few awkward moments more, Caridad and Gray excused themselves to find something to eat. Gray was soon waylaid by Patty, the fines clerk, who had a question about her copier, and Caridad continued threading her way to the kitchen. There, she found tiny Kitty Fu near the refrigerator, quarreling with Kayode, a massive exchange student from Nigeria who worked in the Technical Sciences Annex. Kayode so dwarfed Kitty that coming upon them was like encountering an elf bickering with a giant. They hushed in Caridad's presence, the atmosphere between them taut as razor wire.

"I tell you I need more time," Kayode said, and he strode into the hall.

Caridad poured her beer into the sink below a curtainless window. On the ledge stood a Russian nesting doll with a grim expression on its pink-cheeked face. "What was that about?"

But Kitty compressed her lips, shook her head. "I saw you with the Daniels."

"The Daniels?" Caridad reached for the matryoshka and struggled to pry it open.

Kitty took the doll and twisted it. "Watch out for those two."

"Since we're giving advice . . ." Caridad lifted her chin toward the doorway where Kayode's shadow still hovered. "You should be careful, too."

"Always careful, very careful." Kitty handed Caridad the doll and slipped past her, leaving the kitchen.

Caridad palmed the matryoshka, stroking the smooth wood and admiring its varnished sheen, the vivid yellow and green of the peasant dress and scarlet babushka scarf—but what a harsh look on that rosy face! She shook it. A hollow rattle emanated. Caridad separated the halves loosened by Kitty, expecting to find a smaller doll nested within. Instead, a brown nut—an acorn—bounced onto the floor. She crouched to scoop it up and replaced it inside the doll. She screwed its halves together and set it back on the ledge. As Caridad exited the kitchen to find Gray, she imagined the doll's stern face leering after her.

In early November, Caridad invited Daniel to the cottage for lunch while Gray was working. She'd planned to roast a red pepper and puree it with fresh tomatoes and basil for a soup that she'd serve with chicken salad. But that morning, she overslept. So profound was her sleep and so strangely inveigling were her dreams that Caridad didn't hear Gray leave for campus. When she finally woke near noon, she remembered only wisps of these. In one, she'd received a complimentary piglet at a hotel. When checking out, Caridad realized she'd left the pig in her room. A bellman offered to retrieve it while she waited outside, but somehow, the piglet launched itself from the bellman's arms, flying out a window and into Caridad's arms below.

Now her skull felt as if it had shrunk, clamping her brain like a tight helmet. Her head throbbed with pressure, a familiar drumbeat usually remedied by caffeine. But they'd run out of coffee, so she brewed a cup of Earl Grey instead, even though the bitter tea sometimes upset her stomach. Of course, there was no time for preparing soup and chicken salad. She'd barely have time to make the bed and shower before Daniel arrived. As Caridad sipped from her steamy mug, she peered into the cupboards and refrigerator. She'd heat a can of tomato soup and grill cheese sandwiches for lunch. That would have to do.

After they ate, Daniel praised the canned soup and sandwiches as if Caridad had spent the morning cooking for him. Then he wandered through the living room, duly admiring her brick wall hanging of the female torso, but he was drawn to Gray's two field paintings—one a deep emerald and the other an indigo-covered canvas, both teeming with smoky swirls. They hung on the walls like below-deck portals to seas aboil with ghostly serpents and twisting wraiths. "These are amazing," he said. When she told him Gray had painted the canvases, Daniel's face darkened, as if he'd stepped into a shadow.

In bed after lovemaking, Caridad mentioned that she'd planned to put together a better lunch, and Daniel said, "What was wrong with what we had? I said I liked it."

Overwarm, Caridad rolled out of bed to retrieve the rotating fan from the front room. She set it before the open window, plugged it in, and set the dial for the blades to issue a soft undulating breeze. Daniel caught her wrist, reeled her back into bed. "I liked the lunch, and I like this, too."

In his embrace, Caridad smiled. "My, you're easy to please."

His arms stiffened, muscles knotting against her skin.

"What is it?" she said. "What's wrong?"

He pushed away from her. "Why would you say that?"

"What did I say?" Caridad raised herself on an elbow.

Eyes closed, his face became a stone mask. "How can you say I'm easy to please?"

"It's nothing. I didn't mean it as a *blanket* statement." Absurdly, her gaze traveled to the covers bundled at their feet.

"You think I'm easily satisfied? That I'd settle for anything?"

"Really, it was just something to say."

He threw off the sheet and sat up to face her, his lusterless eyes black as bullet holes. "Why do you have to say anything?" Daniel pulled on his briefs.

"I was joking." Caridad's palms grew chilly, her mouth dry.

He rose to stand at the side of the bed, his bare chest thrust out and his hands balled into fists. "Don't you *ever* tell me what I am."

Caridad licked her lips. "But I was only—"

"Shut the fuck up." In two strides, Daniel reached the fan and lifted it from the floor, yanking the plug out. Then he heaved it against the wall. The fan exploded, gouging a crater in the plaster and tumbling to the floor in pieces. "*No one* tells me what I am." He snatched up his clothes, stomped out of the room.

In bed, Caridad clutched the blanket about her, without knowing how or when she'd pulled it up. She stared at the broken fan—its dust-pitted blades stilled, the mesh guard fragmented into jigsaw pieces. Her ears pulsed, straining for muffled sounds from the front room. Moments later, heavy footsteps shook the floorboards. Daniel, now dressed, loomed again at her side. "For the record," he said. "I am *not* easy to please. I'm not completely satisfied by Beryl, *obviously*, though she's at least loyal to me, and I'm not *at all* satisfied by a fucking whore like you."

"You should leave." Caridad kept her voice low. Detachment now supplanted the panic that had been rising in her. She'd collected herself while he was dressing, converting her confusion and alarm into an artificial and—she hoped—infuriating calm.

"Oh, I'm leaving, and I'm *never* coming back."

Caridad, still gazing at the shards of the broken fan, nodded.

"You hear me?" Daniel drew nearer. "I never want to see you again. Think you can tell me what I am? You fuck him, you fuck me, and who knows who else. What gives you the right to put me in some box with a label on it?" He lifted an arc of the fan's mesh screen and hurled this at the wall. It grazed the windowsill before clattering to the carpet.

Motionless, Caridad met his eyes before glancing at her wristwatch.

Daniel drew his face to hers, working his mouth this way and that. Caridad thought he might strike her, but she neither startled nor flinched when he spit full in her face. She just blinked and then wiped her face with the blanket. Now she raised her wrist to look at her watch. He stomped from the room, his footfalls pounding through the house until the front door opened and slammed shut. Caridad rushed into the bathroom and sank to her knees before the toilet. Hot sour vomit—*that awful tea!*—erupted into the bowl's rusted base.

Days later, in Modern British Literature, Caridad couldn't pay attention to what the professor, a middle-aged man with a smartly trimmed beard, was saying about *Lady Chatterley's Lover*. She hadn't read the book since spring, so it was as distant in her memory as the first time Daniel kissed her. Both seemed a lifetime ago. Lately she hadn't read anything that absorbed her in the way that Chekhov, Shakespeare, Flaubert, Dreiser, or even the Greek myths had. Maybe she was just tired, too much work and too little sleep. That was no doubt why she'd gotten sick. Now, in the classroom, Caridad's eyes smarted with fatigue. To keep alert, she drew pictures in the margins of her notepaper—teeth, mostly molars and canines, but also full sets of dentures. When she grew bored with these, she sketched a plump piglet, a cartoonish rendering. To its rounded sides, she added a pair of feathered wings.

Pleased with the drawing, she glanced up at the professor as if she expected him to admire it, too. But he was reading from the novel in his rich baritone: "Logic might be unanswerable because it was so absolutely wrong." Caridad sat up straight. The rightness of this sentence resonated, rippling in her like sound waves from a tuning fork. She flipped to the book's opening, where the quote appears, when Constance listens to her husband's fatuous friends argue about women and the human heart—matters beyond their comprehension.

Wasn't what Lawrence mocked in those men the same audacious act he attempted in telling Constance Chatterley's story?

Others in the seminar room now slapped their books shut and rustled notepaper, chairs scraping as they pushed away from their desks. Caridad collected her things. She was scheduled to work in ten minutes. Though she rose slowly, her head spun and she nearly fell back into the seat. Knowing it was Daniel's day off kept her from calling in sick again and going home. Caridad hadn't seen him since he'd broken the fan and spit in her face nearly a week ago. She'd been sick with the flu after his visit and hadn't returned to campus until today. During this time, he'd phoned and phoned, but she refused to pick up the receiver. At first Gray would answer, telling Daniel she didn't want to speak to him. They then began unplugging the phone, reconnecting it only when they needed to make a call.

Last in the stream of students exiting the classroom, Caridad trudged out the door, and as if conjured by dread, Daniel popped like a fist into view. He stood waiting for her in the noisy corridor. Heart juddering, Caridad backpedaled. She bumped her backside on the closed door and reached behind, feeling for the knob.

"You must hate me," he said in a quiet voice. With eyes dark and soft as brushed velvet, Daniel's expression recalled for her the neglect and abuse he'd suffered as a child. "I don't blame you. The other day at your house—something came over me. It wasn't me. I swear it wasn't." His eyes welled.

Horrified that he might weep or rage, Caridad scanned the crowded hallway for a familiar face, someone to signal to her side.

"Just give me a chance to explain. That's all I want." Passersby lowered their voices, casting curious looks at him. "If you still hate me, fine, I swear I'll never bother you again. But first give me a few minutes, please."

Though sorry for him, she shook her head. "I have to work."

"Can I see you during your break?"

Her head bobbled—an indecisive tic, more yes than no.

An astonished grin lit his face. "You don't know what this means to me."

"I have to go." Caridad turned to join the students hurrying from the building. Once outside, she loosened her grip on the book bag that she'd been holding to her chest like a shield. Ahead on the paved path to the library, she spotted Marsha Lowenstein's chestnut-brown ponytail bouncing alongside the familiar violet head scarf worn by Fakhri Zarin, the desk supervisor. Caridad quickened her pace. "Fakhri, Marsha, *wait*—wait for me!"

The two girls glanced back, halting on the path until Caridad reached them, winded and dizzy. She clutched Fakhri's elbow to steady herself while she caught her breath.

"Are you okay?" Fakhri said.

"I've been sick, but I'm better now."

"I had triple pneumonia last year," Marsha said. "I spent ten weeks in an iron lung."

Fakhri cast her eyes skyward before turning to Caridad. "Are you working today?"

"Until closing."

"Good." Fakhri twined her arm with Caridad's, an affectionate gesture that disguised the support her solid body lent. "Me too."

"We were talking about those girls who were raped, the ones in the news," Marsha said. "I was telling Fakhri that I think my cousin's the rapist."

"What nonsense." Fakhri braced Caridad's back as they walked.

"No, really, I think it's him. He fits the profile perfectly. He has all the—what do you call them?—the symptoms. He's white and he's male." Marsha counted off her cousin's suspicious traits on her fingers. "He doesn't have any friends."

Caridad's breathing slowed, but she still clung to Fakhri's arm.

"Such foolishness," Fakhri said.

"It's true. He's pure evil. You can see it in his eyes. Plus, he keeps a jump rope in the trunk of his car. No one knows *why*."

"Perhaps he skips rope," said Fakhri. "I skip rope for exercise, and I have not assaulted anyone . . . *yet*."

Caridad laughed.

"I just know it's him, and I hope he gets arrested soon. Those poor girls!"

"Those *poor* girls should not have been walking about alone at night." Fakhri's tone sharpened.

They approached the library's basement entrance, and Caridad reached for the door handle, stepping away to catch the flinty look on Fakhri's face.

"What about the schoolgirl?" Marsha asked. "A little girl on her way home in broad daylight."

Fakhri sighed. "This would never happen in my country."

"I think it could happen anywhere," Marsha said. They followed the long corridor, stopping at the elevator.

"Women should not be out alone." Fakhri pushed the button marked *Up*. "They are only safe in the company of others or in the home."

The elevator dinged, its doors parted, and they boarded it to ascend to the main floor. No one said a word, until it chimed again and the doors reopened. Marsha, the known liar, spoke as they approached the circulation desk. "That's not true. What about Kitty?" she said. "Kitty was home when—"

"*Kitty?*" Caridad stopped short. "What happened to Kitty?"

"She was attacked in her apartment," Marsha told her. "She's in the hospital."

Caridad turned to Fakhri.

"She's actually out of the hospital now," Fakhri said. "It was Kayode. He owed her money, and when she let him in to pay her, he beat her up instead."

"Oh no," Caridad said. "Is anyone with her?"

Fakhri shrugged. "Her roommate, I suppose. Her parents are flying her back to Taiwan."

At the circulation offices, they separated: Fakhri headed to the front desk, Marsha wandered toward the assignment podium in back, and Caridad, thinking of Kitty Fu, stowed her bag and grabbed the supervisor's clipboard before crossing the lobby to the escalator. She pictured Kayode towering over Kitty at Caleb's party, the giant and the elf. She'd call Kitty during her break and visit her after work. On the way to Kitty's apartment, she would stop at the supermarket to pick up a pineapple. Kitty loved pineapple. Not that it would help, but it was something sweetly fragranced, something of heft to hold and hand over to Kitty.

Caridad preferred the escalator over the elevator that warned student workers of her presence by chiming at each floor. Caleb, whom she was relieving, had already made the next hour's assignments, so she went upstairs to assess the shelving to be done and check on who was doing what. She'd start on the fourth level and working her way down. Minutes later, still thinking of Kitty Fu as she rounded the corridor on the third floor, she was jolted again by the sight of Daniel, seated this time in an armchair near a long window. He stood and approached her. "I have to show you something." His voice was husky. "Please. It's important."

Last year, Caridad was summoned from shelving by Gretel, the stacks supervisor then, to the second-floor ladies' room. Gretel had discovered a fetus in one of the stalls, a bulbous-headed knot of tissue curled at the bloody base of the porcelain bowl. She'd asked Caridad to bar entrance to the restroom while Gretel called the campus police. Maybe Daniel had likewise made some disturbing discovery. She followed him to the study carrels—a series of doors with two-foot square windows at eye level. He pulled out his master key and unlocked one of these before flipping on the light switch, gesturing for Caridad to enter. She stepped inside the empty cubicle, his familiar muskiness—sweat and hair oil and mentholated soap—enveloping her. "What is it?"

He closed the door, locked it, and snapped off the light. "Nobody can see anything from the outside when there's no light."

"So—"

Daniel drew her close. His moustache brushed her lips, and then his warm mouth covered hers. Caridad had imagined a time like this while she was at home sick in bed, and she'd envisioned herself pushing him away and stalking off without a backward glance. But now while he was pressing his groin into hers, her body buzzed with yearning. She folded into his arms, and they sank to the cool linoleum floor of that dark study carrel, where nobody could see anything from the outside without light.

During her break, Caridad hurried to the nearby administration building, with its bank of pay phones in the lobby. These offered more privacy than the office line in the library. She chinked in coins and dialed the familiar number. It rang and rang. Finally, Kitty's roommate answered. Kitty, she said, was gone. She'd taken a shuttle to the airport that morning.

A few weeks later, Caridad was ill again. She'd vomited during the night and woke feeling overheated and weak. If not for the fever and the first spotty traces of menstrual blood, Caridad might have thought she was pregnant. She and Gray begged off Thanksgiving dinner with her mother and sisters. They stayed home and ate canned chicken soup with crackers instead. That Saturday morning, she called the library to say she was too ill to work the closing shift that day. Caleb agreed to cover it for her, and Caridad unplugged the phone before climbing back into bed. At noon, she was awakened by pounding at the front door. Gray had left for campus, so she staggered to the entryway and peered through the beveled glass. Felicia and Esperanza, Mimi in her arms, stood on the front step. Caridad pulled the door wide.

Felicia stepped over the threshold, followed by Esperanza and the baby, whose dark hair was growing in thick and curly. Mimi wore pink overalls that showed off her plump arms and legs. At the sight of Caridad, Esperanza gasped. "Dah-Dah, what's *wrong*?"

"You look like shit," Felicia told her. "Or worse than that—more like the shit of shit."

"I'm sick. I have the flu."

Esperanza wheeled away. "I'll wait in the car. I don't want Mimi catching anything. Sorry, Dah-Dah. Hope you get better," she called over her shoulder. Her heels clattered on the pavement, and the car door chunked open and slammed shut.

"What the fuck?" Felicia said. "You're sick and you don't tell anybody?"

"If you'd called first, I would have told you."

"*Hmm*—wonder why we didn't think of that?" Felicia strode to the telephone. She lifted its unplugged cord and waggled the jack end at Caridad. "Wait a minute. We *did* call. We've called and called, and *weirdly*, we never seem to get through."

"I disconnected it to get some rest."

"Really? Because we haven't been able to get through for days, and Mama is freaking out. She made us drive over to make sure you're still alive."

"I've been busy and then I got sick."

"Have you seen a doctor?"

Caridad shook her head.

"There's something fucked-up going on here." Felicia plugged in the phone and leveled an accusing stare at Caridad. "Where's Gray?"

"Work."

Felicia surveyed Caridad's rumpled pajamas and sleep-swollen face. "You do look worse than shit. If I didn't have those two with me, I'd drive you to the doctor myself. Swear you'll make Gray take you when he gets back."

"I will." With this new bout, Caridad feared some serious illness, something rare and incurable, maybe sexually transmitted, though it felt more like being poisoned at intervals—allowed to recover and then cruelly re-dosed all over again. She had an appointment at the student health clinic for that afternoon.

"Keep your damn phone plugged in and call Mama," Felicia told her. "And get your ass to the doctor, or I'm coming back here to kick it all the way there myself." She stalked off without closing the door behind her.

Once plugged back in, the phone blurted a half tone, and then it rang fully—one, two, three times. Caridad swung the door shut before lifting the receiver. Daniel's flat voice filled her ear. This was why she'd disconnected the phone—that ceaseless voice droning on and on, listing reasons why Caridad should leave Gray, retelling childhood memories, or else explaining abstract philosophical arguments. She couldn't abide it, especially not now. After the interlude in the study carrel, Daniel had grown even more expansive with her, while Caridad had become withdrawn and impatient, a thin blue flame of fury flaring in her when she recalled the afternoon he'd broken the fan and spat in her face.

"I'm sick," she said. "I can't talk now." She re-cradled the phone, pulled the cord from the jack, and stumbled back into bed.

When Gray woke her hours later, Caridad felt so rested and well that she was sure she didn't need to go to the clinic. But Gray, who rarely pushed for anything, insisted on taking her. At the clinic, as she expected, her temperature was normal. Blood pressure, eyes, ears, nose, and throat—everything was fine, except that she'd lost a few pounds. The nurse-practitioner drew blood and collected a urine specimen for the lab, and she advised Caridad to avoid spicy foods that might be causing indigestion.

"What a waste of time," Caridad told Gray as they drove home. "I told you I feel fine." The car's stench, though, turned her stomach within minutes.

"If it's nothing," Gray said, "it's good to know it's nothing."

"If you say so." Caridad closed her eyes, concentrating to control waves of nausea rolling over her. After a few miles, she said, "Pull over, Gray. Pull over as soon as you can."

At home, her stomach settled, and Caridad was again infused with a feeling of well-being. She was even hungry. Gray suggested they go out for pizza. But Caridad hesitated. She didn't want to climb back into that noxious-smelling car. "Let's walk then," Gray said. "There's a place just a couple blocks from here. You okay to walk?"

"Sure," said Caridad. Fresh air and some exercise would be just right.

As the sun flamed into the horizon, Caridad and Gray strolled side streets toward the boulevard, talking all the way to the pizzeria, where they ordered a thick-crust pie with just cheese. Gray drank beer, but Caridad sipped ginger ale. When they headed home, the sun had set, though it was still warm. Fragments of mica sparkled under the streetlights, and cars whizzed past, snatches of radio music blaring through their open windows. Sprinklers misted lawns, releasing the sweet scent of grass and damp earth. On impulse, Caridad pulled Gray close and kissed him deeply. She threw an arm over his shoulder, and he held her about the waist while they walked. They both waved at Ernie, who was wearing a turquoise shirt and shiny black slacks as he watered his rose bushes before heading out for the evening.

Inside, the house smelled of stale air, the living room close and stuffy. They hadn't yet replaced the broken fan. Gray raised windows, first in the front room and then in the bedroom. As Caridad headed to the kitchen for a glass of water, a fist hammered on the front door. She glanced at the unplugged phone. Of course, she'd forgotten to call her mother. Leery of driving at night, Mama had no doubt dispatched Felicia to check on her again. "I'll get it," Caridad called to Gray. Without snapping on the porch light, she twisted the knob, and the door thrust open, banging into her forehead and shoulder.

Daniel burst into the living room, his face dark with wrath. "I saw you out there. I watched you walking with him, all over him, like you just fucked each other." His voice thundered in her ears. "You said you were sick, you lying cunt."

He crowded closer, backing her into a corner of the room. Caridad's pulse ripped, blood thumping in her ears. With a quick sigh of torn fabric, Daniel's fingernails slit her blouse and zinged her flesh. Then he gripped her arms, pushed her against the wall. Again, he spit full in her face, splotching her glasses. In the periphery, Gray stood paralyzed, motionless as a wax figure in the hallway. Daniel hauled back, and Caridad, heart thrashing, glimpsed a flesh-toned flash. A hot white blast and she plummeted, falling through the carpet and the floorboards, down and down and down a black-walled well. She marveled at finding such a thing under the house, wondering at its endless depth, the beautiful soundlessness that promised to last forever.

—

A coarse coppery odor—seawater and iron rust—filled her nostrils, and Caridad glanced up at a bristly knob. Without her glasses, she squinted to focus: A chin? Gray's chin? Caridad opened her mouth to speak, but her lips had stiffened as if coated with dried paint. Caridad looked about; she was outstretched on the living room floor, her head cradled in Gray's lap.

"Are you okay?" he said over and over, his words pounding her temples.

"Stop saying that." Caridad fingered her upper lip and chin—sticky and numb, rubbery as a mask.

Two massive policemen appeared at the threshold, the door standing wide open. One rapped on the doorframe. Gray told them to come in. He daubed Caridad's face with a damp washcloth, pulled a hoodie over her torn shirt, and zipped it up. Then he hauled her to her feet. The officers entered the cottage, stiff leather belts and holsters creaking as they moved. Their deep voices caused Caridad's face to throb. She let Gray, who had called them, answer their many questions, nodding only when necessary. One scratched notes into a small pad while Gray spoke, and when they were done asking about what had happened, the pad clapped shut, and they told Gray to take her to an ER.

As they were all leaving, Daniel returned to the cottage. His bike skittered to a stop on the loose gravel in the driveway. At the sight of his rueful face, Caridad turned away to gaze over the garden wall at Ernie's rose bushes, the leaves shiny under the yellow porch light and the blooms drained of color in that same jaundiced glow. If she looked at Daniel, Caridad would be sorry for him, sorrier for him than for herself, and then she would be lost. Worse than a busted face, this was what he had taken from her: compassion. While an officer rattled off Miranda rights, Caridad trembled as if demented by cold. Handcuffs jangled, car doors clicked open and slammed shut, and the engine roared. After the squad car peeled away, Gray took her to a nearby hospital, where she was photographed and x-rayed, her nostrils plugged with gauze and her nose taped. Hours later, Gray drove them back home, where Caridad, fully dressed and still shivering, fell into bed.

A few days later, Caridad, who could again reconnect the phone while Daniel was locked up, got a call from Caleb. At first, he asked how she was doing, and then he got to his point. He urged her to drop charges against Daniel, stunning Caridad into silence. Her nose had shifted right of center, and eggplant-colored bruises raccoon-ringed both her eyes. The one time she ventured to the store, people gaped, children pointed, and a toddler burst into tears at the Technicolor spectacle of her damaged face. The checker asked if she'd been in a car accident, and Caridad nodded. A door slamming, a dog barking, a book falling—sudden sounds hammered her so that her eyes pooled. She couldn't smile, couldn't smell anything but blood. Yet Caleb was telling her to let it go. He told her that Daniel had contracted conjunctivitis in jail.

"Pink eye," Caridad said.

"What's that?"

"Pink eye," she repeated. "He has pink eye."

Caleb cleared his throat, deepened his voice. "The medic said it was conjunctivitis."

"Conjunctivitis is called pink eye."

"I didn't know—"

"He has pink eye."

"Okay," Caleb said.

"Say it, will you?"

"I don't see why—"

"*Say it.*"

"He has pink eye." Caleb said. "Daniel has pink eye."

"It's what teenage girls get when they share eye makeup," Caridad told him. "They stay home from school for a day, put in drops, and it clears right up."

"I didn't *mean* anything by it."

"Do you know what my eyes look like?"

"Look, I'm really sorry about what happened. They told me to call to see if you'd drop charges, so Daniel can be released. He's locked up with all kinds of rough types, he's scared, and now he's got this infection. Can't you just let it go?"

Caridad hung up.

Wade Wamble phoned the next day to arrange a meeting with Caridad later in the week at Caleb's house, likely to spare her the embarrassment of appearing on campus with her broken-looking face, but also to prevent others from seeing what Daniel had done to her. Caridad had no desire to show up at the library plainly wearing the evidence of her bad judgment. Daniel would say that he didn't know what he was doing, or he might blame the hard circumstances of his early life. She couldn't shrug off responsibility like that. "How could you let this happen?" Felicia said when she saw her sister's battered face. Caridad didn't know how she'd let it happen; she only knew that she somehow had. This disturbed her more than her sister's angry tears.

On Friday afternoon, Wade, Caleb, the library director, and the co-director, along with the supervisor from the Technical Sciences Annex—all men—met with Caridad in Caleb's living room. Caleb had arranged dinette chairs in a circle; the men were already seated there when Caridad arrived. She took the single remaining chair. One by one, they all insisted that dropping the charges would be the first step in putting this trouble behind her. Finally, the library director, a sandy-haired man with a droopy moustache, cleared his throat. The other men gazed at him expectantly. He was the overseer of both libraries, a youthful-looking man in his forties who biked to work and played Frisbee with students on the library lawn during breaks. Twenty-year-old Gretel, the former stacks supervisor, had left her job at the library to move in with him after he'd separated from his wife.

"If you don't drop charges, we'll have to report this incident in your personnel file." The silky blond hairs over his upper lip fluttered when he spoke.

A breeze lofted through the sliding glass door, ruffling its sheer curtain and rippling the posters tacked to the walls. Moscow, Odessa, Saint Petersburg—places she'd never been, places she was sure she would never see. Caridad's eyelids prickled. She had no idea what all this meant. It sounded damning and irreversible, like the fact of her broken nose—something that might prevent her from graduating or being recommended for other jobs. It didn't matter to these men that her face still throbbed, that her glasses had been shattered and she had no money for a new pair, let alone to pay the staggering ER bill. It made not a fleck of difference to any of them that these days she inhaled the sorrow of lost ships, their hulls entombed beneath the sea, briny rust stinging her nostrils with each whiff of crusted blood.

The director spoke again. "You want to put this trouble behind you."

The breeze died away and the room grew so silent that Caridad's eyes clicked when she blinked. "Yes," she said at last. "Yes, I do."

Positive. In the chilly examining room a week later, relief surged in Caridad. More good news! That morning she'd met with the visiting writer, an award-winning poet who was teaching a small workshop to select students in the spring semester. Caridad had worked up the nerve to apply, submitting a poem she had written while her face was healing. The bruising had faded to amber-ridged blue mottling, so she wore dark aviator glasses—borrowed from Gray's closet of found objects—to meet with the poet, a kind-faced woman with gray curls piled like metal shavings atop her head. She admitted Caridad to the workshop, praising her poem. "Your sonnet 'The Blow' resonated with me," she said. "It will be a long time before I forget the last image, those rusted ships on the ocean floor. I look forward to working with you." She'd risen to shake Caridad's hand.

Now her test results were positive—so no deadly malady, no poisoning. "That's great," Caridad told the unsmiling nurse at the clinic. "I was worried I had something serious."

"This *is* serious," the nurse said. "You're pregnant. It's very serious."

"*What?*" Caridad's heart thumped thickly. "But you said the results were positive."

"Positive for pregnancy." The nurse scanned the opened file. "You must have had some idea."

Caridad shook her head. She was often irregular, usually late, but these past weeks, she'd had no clue because she had been bleeding each month, glad for the convenience of a light flow instead of worried by it.

The nurse adopted a matter-of-fact tone as she spoke. Her thin lips pleated with plosives and parted for fricatives, the tip of her tongue peeking between teeth with sibilant sounds. She issued a stream of syllables that Caridad could not stack sensibly in her head, though she stared at the woman's face, nodding now and again. The nurse handed her a prescription for prenatal vitamins. Caridad pulled her book bag's strap over one shoulder and glanced at her watch. She had less than ten minutes to start her library shift. Caridad rushed out of the clinic and hurried across campus, her head crackling with static.

They'd both been warned by the library director to have no contact or communication with one another. Despite this, Caridad's phone still rang and rang. She'd taken to unplugging it again. And the first time she returned to work, Daniel startled her by appearing in the discharging area. She flinched when he tossed something at her. Then he vanished. She scooped up what he'd thrown—a balled-up note. In it he wrote that he had to see her, that he had to talk to her. Caridad stuffed it in her pocket, intending to take it to the director, to ask for a transfer to the Technical Sciences Annex. But as long as Daniel knew where to find her, nothing would change.

Caridad climbed the concrete steps to the library's portico, her bag banging against her side. Last semester Caridad had written a paper on women's reproductive rights, in which she argued for choice, meaning abortion, of course. Since they are always the bearers and usually the caretakers of children, she'd reasoned, women should determine whether or not and when to have babies. But then she had been thinking of other women, other babies.

She glanced at the row of bikes secured to a rack near the entrance, and there it was, the white Junior Mints box. A spasm of dread clamped her stomach. She flew back down the stairs and bolted across the lawn for the tall edifice nearby, an obelisk comprised of smoky reflective windows—the administration building, with its bank of pay phones on the first floor. She shut herself in one of the booths and fished change from her pocket. Then she dialed the number to the library. Caridad waited and waited, reminding herself to breathe, until she heard a voice on the line. "I need to see you," she said. "I'm in Admin, near the phones."

She hung up and paced the lobby's shiny floor. A clerk at the fee window called out to her, wanting to know if she was okay. Caridad nodded, trying to smile. At last, she saw him through the glass door. He cut across the lawn, taking long strides to save time. She rummaged in her bag, pawing through books, notes, and pens for the cool metal, the rounded and sharp-angled bows and blades notched with jagged teeth.

When he reached the door, Caridad pulled it wide. "I have to move," she said. "I'm leaving tonight."

"What about school?" Behind wire-framed glasses, Caleb's blue eyes softened. "What about the library?"

"I quit. I'm not coming back." Caridad then poured the jangle of keys into the warm bowl of his hands.

Rust and Stardust

Baby on her hip, Caridad swung open the kitchen door. A rare deluge obscured the yard, raindrops darkening the orange trees, freighting branches, and plopping from leaves. Runnels of mud sluiced over the brick footpath, submerging the welcome mat. Since midnight, rain had been pounding the North Hollywood rental where Caridad was living with Gray in late summer 1978, waking her with an insistent sizzle that thickened into thumping. Hours later, the rainfall undulated, quicksilver drapes of it rippling with each gust. A cannon boom of thunder rattled the walls. In her arms, Miles cried out. Caridad banged the swollen door shut and lugged him into the yellow-walled bedroom, where she found Gray near the closet, fingering the sleeve of her new blouse—a seashell-printed fabric—a birthday gift from her mother.

Caridad coughed. He dropped the sleeve and spun to face her.

"It's not letting up," she said.

"Are you going to work?" Gray winked at Miles, who thrust dimpled arms out to him.

Caridad kissed the baby's cheek and handed him to Gray. "I have to." She kneaded the small of her back. At fourteen months, Miles spoke a few words, and he crawled about in a swift and sure way like a windup toy, but he was a late walker—he'd so far shown little interest in taking his first steps.

"Bike." Miles jabbed a finger at the door. "Bike!" Most Saturdays, Gray strapped Miles into the baby seat affixed to his ten-speed, and they'd ride to the park while Caridad worked.

"Not today, honey boy," he told Miles. "It's wet outside. Let's play in your little house instead." Gray had found a large cardboard box in a Dumpster, and he'd covered the outside of it with blue contact paper. He'd cut a door and windows to make a playhouse for Miles. Gray was nimble enough to crawl into it with him. But when Caridad crouched within its corrugated walls, the tight space constricted her, tightening her lungs and filling her ears with pressure.

Miles squinted, his mouth pursed. Then he bobbed his head, saying, "'Kay." Gray swung him up onto his shoulders, and Miles shrieked with laughter.

Caridad reached to stroke Gray's jawline, her fingertips grazing stubble. Working outdoors had sun-bleached Gray's hair, infusing his cheeks and the small wedge of his nose with the color of a ripened apricot. His eyes had also darkened, now a shade closer to maple syrup than honey. "Are you growing a beard?" she asked.

He looked away. "Just forgot to shave."

"I like you with a beard."

Gray withdrew from her touch and galloped toward the back room, neighing as Miles tugged on tufts of his hair like reins.

Caridad gazed about the bedroom, taking in the daffodil-colored walls. The bed was still a tumble. Gray's mother, a saleswoman at Sears, used her employee discount to purchase its indigo comforter. This now formed a cozy hillock in the center of the bed, along with a smaller turquoise blanket belonging to Miles. Though a crib stood in one corner of the room, Miles usually slept with Gray and Caridad. He'd doze off on his own, but near midnight he'd awaken, whimpering until Gray or Caridad roused to change him and bring him to their bed. Near the bed a three-legged stool served as her nightstand, holding her oil lamp and a borrowed novel, Nabokov's *Lolita*, spine up and splayed open where she'd left off reading it the night before. The upside-down crate on Gray's side contained a notebook, a few pens, and a thick stack of magazines — *Vogue*, *Cosmopolitan*, *Glamour*.

In another corner of the room stood a wood-burning stove installed by the Loudermilks, their landlords who'd touted this as an attraction instead of admitting that the house had no heating system. "Your very own wood-burning stove," Rusty Loudermilk had said when he and his wife first led Gray and Caridad through the rental. He'd pointed at the wrought-iron contraption as if it were a valuable sculpture. "Who else," asked his wife Helga, "do you know who has such a thing?" Gray and Caridad had exchanged puzzled looks. In winter, they struggled to keep wood on hand for stoking its flames, though the Loudermilks provided planks torn from the barn they were dismantling in the side yard, and the stove took time to heat a room as large as this. But when it glowed like a crucible in the dark, the grate was as magnificent as a roaring dragon's maw.

The rental wasn't built as a dwelling, they'd learned after signing the lease nearly two years ago. It had been a citrus orchard office. Intended for seasonal occupancy, the structure lacked air conditioning as well as heating. There were, though, phone jacks in every room, even the bathroom. "You can plug in a phone wherever you want," Rusty bragged. "You can even make a call in the bathtub." The phone jacks had seemed more a plus than the wood-burning stove. The last house they'd rented, the yellow cottage next door to Ernie's place, had only one jack—not that this was the reason they'd hurriedly moved out when Caridad quit school. "Who else," added Helga, "do you know who has phone jacks in every room?" Caridad and Gray traded another glance.

Over time, the sunless living room with its dark paneled walls depressed Caridad, despite the olive-green pleather sofa they'd purchased with Gray's mother's store discount, so they spent most of their time in the kitchen or in the spacious bedroom. The brick-colored linoleum floors accumulated dirt from the woodpile no matter how often they swept. To save money, they had a wall-mounted phone installed in the kitchen with a short cord that tethered callers near the sink. They never used the many phone jacks.

Soon after Caridad and Gray moved in, the Loudermilks began chopping down the orange trees while dismantling the barn. Since it was a large orchard and only the two of them worked at it, this took time. Still, they'd managed to remove more than half the trees. After earning rent on the place to raise money for building, the Loudermilks planned to raze the orchard office, to replace it with a Swiss chalet-style horror. Almost every weekend, the robust couple worked on the property, arriving early with their daughter Bettina, a blond kindergartener with skin so lucent that her veins were visible, her complexion blue-tinged like skim milk. Silent Bettina wafted about like a vapor, spooking Caridad when she'd appear nearby, a sudden glowing apparition. Today's rain meant there would be no Loudermilks, no ghost child sightings. Bad weather would keep them away.

Caridad surveyed the bedroom again, deciding whether or not to tidy up before preparing for her shift at the bookstore. Miles's and Gray's voices echoed from the back room. Her gaze returned to the tangled nest of bedding, her soft pillow beckoning to her, near the novel that she was now rereading. Days ago, Caridad had devoured the book in great greedy gulps, and at the last page, she regretted not lingering over the dazzling prose. "Love at first sight," she murmured to herself, quoting Nabokov, "at last sight, at ever and ever sight." As she pored over it again, Caridad savored its intricacies of language, deft turns of plot, the ebb and flow of sympathy and revulsion for Humbert Humbert. This read, a deeper vein of feeling opened in Caridad for orphaned Lolita, who sobbed herself to sleep each night of that first North American odyssey.

Laughter rang from the next room. Caridad would crawl back into bed with the book, but first, she stepped to the closet, grit rasping the soles of her feet. She clutched the makeshift curtains — two orange batik bedspreads printed with headdress-wearing elephants — and yanked them shut, obscuring the rack of clothing, the seashell blouse. "No Loudermilks," she said in a low voice, "and no Leslie. *Please.*" The decorative elephants trembled in her wake, the tusked beasts still quivering when she climbed back into bed.

How was it that Gray, an imaginative man of depth and complexity, became such a dull cliché of a woman? With face caked in foundation cream, lips waxy with color, and synthetic hair styled in yesteryear's flippy 'do, Leslie was far more caricature than character, her breathy falsetto more Minnie Mouse than Marilyn Monroe. And those outfits! High heels, pantyhose, skirts, gauzy scarves, and ruffle-trimmed blouses spritzed with perfume — all this to wear in a converted orchard office with a wood-burning stove and an ever-gritty floor?

"Seriously," Caridad would say, "why bother?" She'd point at her own long hair knotted into a messy bun, her T-shirt and cutoffs. "It's kind of casual around here."

But Leslie would say, "Let's talk about boyfriends." And she'd pull her chair to the table and light a cigarette.

Boyfriends? Caridad and her sisters never ponied up to talk boyfriends or even husbands. Felicia would roll her eyes and Esperanza would crack up if anyone opened a conversation this way, and if the subject came up spontaneously, it would unleash a barrage of complaint, especially from Esperanza. Instead, they usually talked about other people. Who said what to whom and who was acting like an asshole and who was being a stupid martyr and who would be a total fool for getting together with that chorizo sin huevos. *Human* behavior fascinated them, not boyfriends or husbands specifically. Leslie, though, only wanted to discuss her make-believe romances, all involving boyfriends with forgettable one-syllable names like Bob or Joe. Every one of whom, Leslie claimed, was madly in love with her. They were all big silly dopes who just wouldn't leave her alone.

"Why don't you ever date someone named Iggy?" Caridad asked Leslie that Saturday night after she returned from work, the bedroom door shut with a towel wadded underneath to keep out cigarette smoke. The weather prevented a Loudermilk visit, as Caridad hoped, but Leslie appeared soon after Miles fell asleep. "That's at least an original-sounding name."

"Iggy? What kind of name is that?"

"Short for something," Caridad said. "Ignatius, Ignacio—"

"Why would anyone date an Iggy?"

Hot-faced, Caridad glanced at her hands, the nails bitten so far down that her fingertips bulged into blanched bulbs.

"Besides I'm in love with Bill. He's the sweetest thing on earth." Leslie drew on her cigarette and exhaled, waving the blue-gray spumes toward the open door.

The rain had stopped hours ago, and the night was starless, damp, and dark. Under the cigarette smoke and Shalimar, the bittersweet breath of the vestigial citrus orchard wafted into the kitchen. *Phantom fumes*, thought Caridad, *haunting us like persistent memories*. She gulped a bitter mouthful of wine and set her tumbler on the table. "You know something, *Leslie*? I don't always talk about it, but I have a husband I love." Caridad searched Leslie's face, fixing on her maple-colored eyes. "And you know what? I love him most when he's just being *himself*."

Leslie recoiled, as if slapped. Her fingers flew up to pat her stiff hair. "Well, I bet he loves you, too, just like Bill loves me. Did I tell you that Bill's in construction? He gets all sweaty at work, so I have to tell him, 'Now, go take a shower before you kiss me!' And he's such a big sweet goof that—"

"*Stop*." Caridad raised a hand. "Just stop, stop, *stop*. That is *not* how it goes."

Leslie's eyes thickened, inky pupils subsuming the irises. A deeper voice sounded from the vivid gash of her mouth. "I can do better."

Caridad shook her head. "Really, you have no idea how—"

"Let me try again," Leslie said. "Please."

With a smacking sound, Caridad peeled bare thighs from the dinette chair, rising to pad to the refrigerator. Her face warm and buzzing, she yanked it open to pull out a spouted carton. "We don't have much wine left," she said. By the time she got off work, Caridad would be quaking, shivering even on warm summer evenings like this. After her first glass of wine, she grew still and calm. "We need more."

"I'll go." Leslie's voice was again high-pitched and fluty. "If you'll just let me . . . I mean, we can keep going, right? We can chat more—when I get back?"

A motor churned and fans whirred, issuing a chilly gust. "*Chat*," Caridad said, as if pronouncing an unfamiliar word. She touched a fingertip to the refrigerator door, nudging it just enough so the suction would draw it shut.

Weekdays, Caridad looked after her niece Mimi, along with Miles. Her sister worked mornings as a medical aide in Northridge and took classes in the afternoons to become a registered nurse. The next day was Labor Day, a holiday for the nursing school, so Esperanza offered to take both children to the zoo when she finished her early shift at the hospital.

Before Esperanza arrived with Mimi that morning, Caridad hoisted Miles into his high chair and served him a bowl of yogurt sprinkled with muesli. The baby, just learning to use a spoon, spilled more food than he managed to get in his mouth. While he ate, Caridad lifted the receiver from the wall phone. She dialed a number. A sleepy voice answered, and Caridad said, "Sorry if I woke you . . . Listen, my sister's taking Miles and Mimi to the zoo this afternoon. Want me to . . . Sure, about one?"

Within minutes, Esperanza's car rumbled into the drive, gravel crunching under its tires. The car idled while Esperanza, dressed in aqua scrubs, bustled into the orchard office with Mimi in one arm and a duffel bag in the other. "I'm late." She kissed Mimi and set her down in the kitchen. "I'll see you after lunch."

Mimi scrambled into her aunt's arms for an embrace. Caridad lifted and spun her around the kitchen. "Bye," Esperanza called over her shoulder.

Miles waved his goopy spoon. "Buh-bye."

Caridad released Mimi, who approached Miles. "Eat, Miles, eat. Look," she pointed to a dollop of yogurt that had fallen on the tray. "You missed that. Get it. With the spoon, use the spoon." She stood by the high chair, coaching him while Caridad washed breakfast dishes.

When Miles later settled for a midmorning nap, Caridad prepared lunch with Mimi's help. The toddler stood on a chair and rinsed grapes in the sink. She gazed out the kitchen window. "Why the sky?" Mimi asked. Almost as soon as she could speak, she began asking her aunt such questions and listening in grave silence to Caridad's answers.

"Good question." Caridad dredged up what she could recall from that long-ago climatology class. "The sky is cupped over us. Like this." She took a bowl from the dish rack and inverted it on the counter. "It's what we can see of outer space." Caridad pointed overhead. "It's like the ceiling."

Mimi nodded. "Why blue?"

"It's blue because when there aren't too many clouds, the molecules—these little bitty bits too tiny to see—throw out more blue light from the sun than any other color. When the sun sets, the light that's tossed out is mostly red."

"Bitty bits?" Mimi squinted, crinkling her nose, as if straining to see molecules.

While Caridad was astounded by the depth of feeling she had for Miles, she connected more to her niece, especially in moments like this, when Mimi favored her with an intensity of attention that no one else bestowed on Caridad, attention missed like a phantom limb when her niece was away from her. Mimi would follow Caridad about, imitating her expressions and parroting her speech. With long dark curls and pink cheeks, Mimi even looked more like Caridad than Miles did. Miles was olive-skinned and flat-nosed, with such straight black hair that Caridad perceived little of herself, and no trace at all of Gray, in the baby. And while Miles would chew on their covers and crumple pages, Mimi cherished books, the stories in them. Over the months that she cared for her niece, Caridad had read Mimi many of her childhood favorites—*The Wonderful Wizard of Oz, Alice's Adventures in*

Wonderland, and *The Secret Garden*, adopting what she considered a convincing burr for the moor-dwellers.

Mimi now cocked her head, still gazing out the window. "Why the sun?"

Nash, in bed beside her, reeked of the fistful of vitamins he took each morning and of sweat. The water was turned off in his bungalow apartment to correct a plumbing problem, so he couldn't shower or flush the toilet, he'd explained to Caridad when she arrived, apologizing for the odors. She minded the odors much less than she minded the shelf of Monarch Notes near his bed. When she'd studied literature in college, Caridad had had no idea such things existed.

Nash worked as a pharmaceutical assistant in a drugstore and was taking evening classes to become a high school English teacher. Maybe he didn't have much time to read. Naked now on his bed, Caridad *click-click-clicked* a fingernail over the stapled spines of his many Monarch Notes: *The Sound and the Fury, Vanity Fair, The Adventures of Huckleberry Finn, Silas Marner, Moby-Dick, For Whom the Bell Tolls, Bleak House*. From examining these, Caridad learned his full name—Ignacio Quiñones. He'd printed it with the unselfconscious pride of ownership on the front of each booklet.

Nash nuzzled the back of her neck, telling her of the dream he had that night. It was much like other dreams he'd described to her. These involved Gray's disappearance or death, events that would clear the way for him to live with Caridad. As Nash spoke, she envisioned him packing his Monarch Notes in a carton for moving into the converted orchard office.

"So his car breaks down near this off-ramp." His breath was warm in Caridad's ear, redolent of ascorbic acid and cod-liver oil. This scenario required little imagination of him. Their used green Fiat, bought to replace the now-extinct Impala, was a catastrophe on wheels, notorious for stalling out and stranding them all over the Valley.

"And you and Miles are at home, so he's alone," Nash continued. "And the car just sort of dies, so he's all puzzled. Like, what's happening? He rolls the window down and sticks his head all the way out. And this semi comes barreling along, right near the shoulder, and—"

Caridad turned to cup his mouth with her palm, saying, "Don't." Nash might think her squeamish, disturbed by the graphic details of his dream. But it was the idea of losing Gray that upset her. Such dreams offended her in the way they would if they involved her mother or sisters. "I don't want to hear this."

Nash clasped her hand, placed it over his bare chest. "I hate that we can't be together because of him. I can't stand how selfish he is, how he treats you." A knot of bronze skin between his eyebrows bulged when he knitted these. His deep-set eyes darkened. Nash would no doubt make a dedicated and conscientious high school teacher, the type to volunteer at athletic events, chaperone dances, and moderate extracurricular clubs. And he would be dumbfounded, deeply wounded by the betrayals—tacks on his seat, tires punctured, even accusations of sexual advances—that would surely assail him.

Caridad had no clue why Nash thought Gray mistreated her or that he was selfish. Though distracted, even absent-minded, Gray, who did more than his share of the childcare and housekeeping on top of working full time, was the opposite of selfish. Caridad hadn't said much about Gray to Nash, apart from mentioning that he had a few troubling habits. At thirty, Nash was eight years older than Caridad and three years older than Gray, yet he still clung to simple convictions—like the belief that couples who were intimate were somehow obliged to plan a future together and that husbands whose wives were unfaithful must be so cruel that they deserved not only cuckolding but also dismemberment and death.

"Can we not talk about this?" Caridad glanced again at the Monarch Notes. The authors should publish another set, a few handy booklets to explain more complicated relationships for people like Nash.

The phone on the nightstand rang, and he snatched up the receiver. "Hello? . . . Hey, man," he said. "What's up?"

So as not to eavesdrop on his conversation, Caridad reached for the radio that had been playing softly on the shelf beneath the Monarch Notes. She turned the dial, raising the volume a notch for "Jumpin' Jack Flash."

Nash cupped the receiver. "Shush. Turn that off. He's calling from the station."

Caridad narrowed eyes at him before flicking the dial. She flashed on Seth's outburst years ago in his car. What was it with these two and the radio? In this case, Nash bragged about having friends on the police force, cops who played handball with him. Did he think that his officer friend would send out a squad car and a drug-sniffing dog because he'd heard rock music playing in the background?

Gray never shushed her.

Caridad rose out of bed and plucked her panties from the floor, wondering if the butterfly silhouetted on Monarch Notes signified freedom from thinking too hard about things. She dressed, slipped on one sandal and reached under the bed for the other.

Nash hung up the phone. "Sorry about that."

She shrugged.

He stood and stepped into his boxers.

Where was that other sandal? Caridad lifted the quilt. Her fingers scrabbled over the beige shag carpet, feeling for the leather straps. Her fingertips grazed a slick surface. She crouched beside the bed and peered under. A Polaroid photograph. Caridad palmed the picture, tilted it toward the light to see the image of a girl's bare torso: thin shoulders, waifish neck, and no more of a face than its pointy chin. The girl's breasts were pink-tipped buds like those of the pubescent nymphets, the girleens that Humbert Humbert lusted after in *Lolita*. Caridad's scalp tightened, an ocean pounding the shore in her head.

"What've you got there?" Nash said, now pulling on pants.

"A picture." Dizzy with dread, she set one hand on the floor to brace herself and lifted the photo with the other.

"Dana."

"What?"

"That's Dana," he said. "I told you about Dana."

Weeks ago, Nash mentioned that his last long-term relationship ended a year ago when his then-girlfriend Dana completed dental hygienist school, found a job, and moved into her own place. "The *woman* you lived with," Caridad said, "is this girl? She looks twelve."

"Fourteen."

"*Fourteen?*"

"She was around fourteen when she moved in."

Hot-faced, she gawked at Nash. He'd lent her Nabokov's book, said it was his favorite.

"I know it sounds off," he said, "but she was a handful for her parents. I'm talking really wild—drinking, drugs, shoplifting, you name it." Nash shrugged on his shirt, fastened it with slow care, one button after another. "I was tutoring her to bring up her grades, and—I don't know—she just sort of took to me. She listened, you know, cooperated and all that."

"*Cooperated?*"

He waved this off. "You know what I mean. Anyways . . . we sort of fell in love, you know, and her folks were, like, great, *you* handle her, so she moved in with me."

Caridad shook her head as if to dislodge insects in it. "You fell in love?"

"Hey," he said, searching her face. "It was nothing like what we have."

"You think I'm jealous? You think *that's* the problem?"

"Maybe you don't get it, then. Yeah, okay. On the surface, it looks bad. It's not exactly something I'd put on a résumé, especially not for a teaching job, but it's also not anything I would ever deny. Look, her parents didn't want her, so for Dana, it was me or the street. And, hey, I got that kid through high school. I put her through technical college. I even helped her find an apartment, gave her money for first and last." Nash's eyes shone, his face set in an aggrieved expression.

Caridad scanned that row of narrow red spines, the staples glinting in them, searching these for notes on *Lolita*. Such notes should have explained the novel for him, telling how it implicates instead of rationalizing the narrator's obsession. Nash really *did* need help with his reading comprehension skills. Or else . . . *she* could be wrong. That idea about Monarch Notes for people who couldn't understand complicated things—maybe *she* was the one who needed them. "The other woman," she said, "the one you lived with before Dana, how old was she?"

Nash turned away, jammed on his loafers. "I'm not telling you."

Caridad set the photo on his bed. "Why did you leave out her face?"

Nash released an exasperated breath. He pointed under the bookshelf. "There's your shoe," he said. "You left your purse in the kitchen. I guess you won't want to leave anything behind."

She shook her head and slipped on the sandal without looking up.

Minutes later, Caridad pulled into the driveway alongside the van owned by the metal-refinishing company that employed Gray. Dave Wong, his work partner, usually drove this home. The two of them must have taken a break or knocked off early to have a beer at the house. She slid out of the ticking car into sunshine so bright, the sky pulsed with white heat. A fresh crop of dandelions dotted the lawn, now strangled by snaky cords of crabgrass. She and Gray should pull weeds while the soil was still damp and pliant. Though the Loudermilks chopped down fruit trees and tore apart the barn, they did nothing to improve the yard.

"I'm in here," Gray called through the open door. He stood in the living room, still wearing his navy painter's pants and light blue T-shirt with its red-and-white company logo.

"Where's Dave?" Caridad asked

"Sick. I had to take him home."

"*Sick* sick or sick?"

"Sick." Gray mimed tipping a bottle to his lips.

Caridad nodded, catching a whiff of her skin—traces of vitamins, Nash's hair oil, and, unmistakably, the sweaty musk of sex. "Hmm," she said. "That's not good."

Gray shook his head. Both he and Caridad worried that Dave's drinking would jeopardize the job for Gray more quickly than he would manage on his own through distractibility and a slapdash approach to physical work. "I called in, though, said he had food poisoning. Supervisor told me to drive him home and keep the truck overnight."

"Whew! It's hotter than blazes," she said. "I need a shower."

"Wait," Gray said. "I have a surprise for you."

Caridad shrank back. Though it had been months since he'd touched her, she feared he'd embrace her. Instead Gray stepped aside to reveal a TV tray laden with crackers, cubes of cheese, and slices of apple. "Voilà!" he said. "I even have two bottles of Cold Duck chilling."

"Champagne!" Caridad's mouth flooded. "But what are we celebrating?"

"This." Gray handed her a thin bound volume that he pulled from the back waistband of his pants. "Check out the table of contents."

A monochromatic photo of a hand holding a rusted bucket was displayed on the cover, and below that image appeared the words *Points and Lines*. It was an issue of the university's literary journal. She opened it and flipped to the table of contents. She was stunned to find her name listed and across from that the title of a poem she'd written, "The Bluest Clown." It was a series of verses about Mimi drifting off to sleep—her moist brow, the translucency of her fluttering eyelids, the way she puckered and released her coral lips as if suckling while she slept. Then the poem shifted, describing the toddler being drawn, even seduced into the gaudy circus of her unconscious by a sky-colored fool.

"But how . . . ?" Caridad had been distressed by the downturn the poem had taken, the easy way it veered toward darkness, that leering buffoon in an azure fright wig. Though written for Mimi, it was something Caridad could never read to her niece, not even when she was grown—a love lyric that devolved into a dystopian lament. "I *know* I threw this away."

Gray nodded, beaming. "I found it in the trash, typed it up, and sent it in."

"Why can't you *ever* leave trash alone?"

His face folded. "Aren't you happy it's published?" Gray snatched the journal, opened it to her poem. "Look, *look* at this. First place," he read. "Your poem won first place, best in the magazine. Isn't that great?"

"I guess." Though it *was* kind of nice, Caridad didn't ever want to read the thing again. Her face heated up just thinking of it. "I wasn't done with it."

"You *threw* it away." Gray pulled out his billfold and extracted a folded slip of pale green paper. "And here, look at this." It was a check for fifty dollars. "It's your prize money. Look at the date. It was written months ago, when the poem was first accepted. I've been waiting all this time to surprise you with this. I can't believe you're not thrilled."

"It is a surprise." Caridad smiled, pleasure rising like a bright balloon in her. "A poem of mine—published. The money's nice, too."

"You bet it is," Gray said. "We should celebrate."

"I'll just have a quick shower, change—"

"Oh, and I called Esperanza." While Gray uncorked and poured the champagne, he told Caridad that he'd asked her sister to keep Miles overnight and to bring him in the morning with Mimi. "So, maybe . . . we can go out tonight."

Caridad paused in the doorway, staring down at that weirdly patterned linoleum, each square imprinted with a mandala design comprised of pinprick-sized indentations, each of which trapped dust and grit. Under that fine sifting and in the shadowy room, the flooring was oxblood—not brick red, the same shade as the wall hanging she'd constructed for her studio art class. Oxblood—she envisioned a great beast lowing, a blade glinting at its muscle-corded throat. "I guess we could."

"Just an idea. We'll see what we feel like later."

Caridad shuffled toward the bathroom. The scraping of her sandals on the linoleum sounded like well-worn sandpaper on splintered wood.

Early on, the night promised to be hard to remember and worse to forget, constituting what Nabokov called "the insolent logic of nightmare" even before molecules began casting about more red light than blue. After two shared bottles of champagne, followed by tumblers of boxed Chablis, impressions and images for Caridad were already fragmenting into kaleidoscopic shards—both remembered and imagined—while they were still at home. By the time Caridad rested her forehead against the cool mirror hours later in the restroom at Dante's, she had trouble arranging these mosaic pieces in a recognizable pattern before rejoining the blur of faces in the dark and noisy club.

Though she couldn't say when Leslie first appeared that evening, Caridad envisioned her at the dining table, deep in a monologue about her boyfriends. Caridad had interrupted this by flouncing off to the bedroom. She'd returned with a stack of fashion magazines that she'd slapped on the tabletop. "Think I could be a model?" Caridad asked, flipping through the pages and pointing at the hollow-cheeked images. "I could be her or her or her."

Leslie shook her head.

"But I'm pretty, aren't I?" Caridad's voice sounded petulant, grating in own ears. "I can be like that, can't I?"

"You're too fleshy to model," Leslie said, "too much bust and hip. And, honey, you're too old to start now." Then Leslie steered the conversation back to boyfriends, her crimson lips flashing, the blouse with seashells tucked into a blue skirt of Caridad's.

Later, they'd climbed into the car and driven out—god knows how—to the nightclub, but Caridad had no recollection of this. What else? What else? *Shoes*—something about shoes. Caridad's feet were bare and sticky on the damp floor of the restroom. She cupped a hand over her mouth, heartbroken that she'd lost her shoes. Another fragment flashed: Leslie, in a shadowy corner booth with a boozy man in a bowling shirt. The drunk had accosted Caridad first, weaving before her with a lit cigarette in one hand, the tip flickering like a firefly in the dim bar. He'd asked to be introduced to her friend.

When she hesitated, he winked. "I get it. I know the score, see."

Now Caridad squeezed her eyes shut. She'd left the two of them in the booth—gobbling at each other like greedy fish. Caridad wheeled away from the mirror, yanked the stall door open, and crouched before the toilet. She heaved until her stomach churned up no more than bile, her throat raw as a gash.

The outer door banged open, and music and laughter gusted in, followed by the hollow *pock-pock-pock* of heels.

Leslie? Caridad flushed the toilet, wiped her mouth, and rose to exit the stall.

Before her stood a large woman, a brassy blond monument in a fringed green shift, her small eyes outlined in kohl, her bowed lips tinted cherry red. A vast sequined bag, shimmery as a mermaid's tail, dangled from one meaty shoulder. "Sweetie, you okay?" she asked, her voice deep.

"My husband . . ."

"Your husband out there?" The big gal raised a penciled-in eyebrow. "You want me to get your husband for you?"

Caridad shook her head. "I need to, I just . . ."

"What, honey? You been sick?" the blond asked. "Can I get you anything?"

"Phone? I need to call someone."

"There's a pay phone just outside the door there. You got change?"

Lips quirking, Caridad shrugged. No shoes. No purse.

The blond opened her handbag and fished out a worn leather pouch. "I got some."

Caridad held out her palm, and the woman dropped coins into it.

The blond behemoth smiled, baring a row of small teeth. "Splash some water on your face, darling. Makes a world of difference. Trust me, it does." She sidestepped Caridad and slipped into the stall, graceful despite her girth. "Gum, sweetie?" she called out. "I may have a stick or two in my bag."

No more than ten minutes, he'd promised. Caridad said she'd wait outside, so she pushed through the crowded bar. Blinkered by hanks of sodden hair, she fixed her gaze on the glowing exit sign. She soon heaved the door open and stepped out. After the rain, the street was slick as vinyl. Rainbow-ringed puddles glimmered under the amber glow of streetlights. Dampness sharpened the stench of trash bins nearby, along with the acrid odor of urine. "I shall be dumped where the weed decays," lamented Humbert Humbert. "And the rest is rust and stardust." Footsteps and voices faded in and out, tires hissed past. No one bothered Caridad as she waited on the damp and warm pavement, not far from the club's red-lacquered door.

After rinsing her mouth and hair, Caridad had glimpsed her face in the restroom mirror. Swollen and mascara-smeared, her eyes stood out against her ashen face as if she'd again been slugged. A wine stain, dark as blood, spattered the front of her skirt. Her hair, frizzed by moisture, now cast an umbra on the pavement in the shape of an explosion. "Our imagination flies—we are its shadow on the earth," she said aloud, quoting Nabokov. A trio of emaciated women, miniskirted and tottering on stiletto heels, glanced at her and looked away as they hurried past. A car rolled near, its tires misting her bare legs. The driver's side window scrolled down. "I got here as soon as I could," Nash said. He took in her smudged eyes and stained skirt, and his coppery face tightened. "Damn, what did he do to you?"

Caridad picked her way to the passenger side, and Nash reached to push open the door. She slid in.

"Where are your shoes?"

Her chin wobbled. She clamped her jaw, but a thick tear rolled down her nose to plop on her bare thigh. She rubbed it away and drew in a shuddery breath.

Nash jutted a thumb at the red door. "Is he still in there?"

"Sort of, but not really . . ."

"I can't stand to see you like this. I swear to god, I can't." He swung the car in an arc and nosed it into a parking space facing the club's entrance. Then he released the trunk latch and opened his door. He bounded behind the car, and muffled thumps sounded from the trunk before he slammed it shut. Nash returned to the car bearing a tire iron and a wadded sweatshirt that he tossed to her. "Put this on."

Caridad nested the sweatshirt in her lap, stroking it like a pet rabbit.

Nash ran a hand along the tire iron. "When he comes out, boy, I tell you." He released a low whistle. "He's not going to know—no, sir—not going to know what hit him." Nash stared at the red door, his face knotted like a fist. He'd examined their photos mounted with magnets on their refrigerator, taking measure of Gray in these. Now Nash seemed sure he would know Caridad's husband as soon as he stepped out of the club.

"Just take me home," she said. "*Please.*"

"Not yet."

Wine and weariness threatened to flatten her. Caridad wadded the sweatshirt against the car window and leaned on it. Nash could watch that chipped red door all night and he would never recognize Gray, bewigged and costumed as Leslie. Caridad's eyes burned, her eyelids fluttered shut. Another image flashed: Miles—his mouth gaping in confusion, his arms outstretched, windmilling as he fell backward into a vortex, a deep and churning column of smoky shadows. Caridad lunged to catch him, jerking with such force that she banged a knee on the glove box.

Nash turned to her. "You okay?"

Alert now, Caridad raised her head. "Look," she said in a low voice. "Take me home now, or I'm getting out. I'll *walk.*"

Nash tossed the tire iron on the backseat and then churned the engine. The car surged over the drive, and Caridad again thought of Miles—and Mimi. *Why the sun? Why the sky?* She gazed at Nash's sharp profile. *Why this guy? Or that?* Caridad shifted in the seat so she was sitting upright. She flexed her arms as if bracing to absorb the weight of both children. Then she glanced back at the nightclub's entrance, the battered red door that remained shut.

Portrait of a Family

By the end of March, the Loudermilks had chopped down all the orange trees. Without shade, the sun-scorched lawn grew pale as straw. Tree stumps like broken teeth were now corralled within temporary fencing installed to protect building materials that would soon be arriving. All that remained of the barn was a crumbly concrete slab and rusted rebar that twisted out of it like insect appendages. Still, on mild days, Caridad would set her manual typewriter outside on a charred picnic table. Here, while she composed a paper or poem, Mimi and Miles would play with the squat peg people—a chef, a farmer, a nurse, a fireman—and their toy homes that Gray's mother had bought for Miles at garage sales. Almost two, Miles walked ably on his short, well-muscled legs. Unlike many toddlers, he was not willful or demanding of attention, nor was he inclined to run off, climbing and jumping from things. Instead, he preferred manipulating the stubby "people dolls," playing with Mimi.

One warm Friday afternoon, Gray—after finishing his shift—joined them in the yard with his Super 8 camera, a plastic crate containing his moviemaking paraphernalia, and a tall can of Budweiser. Lately, he'd been making stop-action films, all of them involving Baby Beans, one of Mimi's dolls. The last of these, "Baby Beans Climbs the Slide," was so similar to the one that preceded it, "Baby Beans Goes Up a Tree," that Caridad didn't see the point to a sequel. Gray's films were herky-jerky "anti-epics," as he called them. All of them began with the Styrofoam pellet–filled doll stuttering up an incline and ended with Baby Beans's pink plastic face leering down at viewers from some zenith perch before vanishing from sight in the last frame. Caridad appreciated the craftsmanship in Gray's films but was troubled when she speculated on autobiographical influences in his work.

Now he affixed wads of tape on the doll's hands and feet so these would adhere to the fence for a new anti-epic called "Baby Beans's Great Escape." Gray shot frame after frame of the doll inching up the fence, intermittently sipping beer from the can nearby. Shoot, sip, sigh, and shift the doll's position, replacing the tape if needed, shoot, sip, sigh, shift—Gray developed a rhythm to his process. As he filmed Baby Beans and the children played with "people dolls," Caridad struggled to find a way into her paper, wondering if there could be anything more obstructive to ideas than the contented industry of others. She was taking a course in realism and naturalism at a community college because it offered transfer credit and Gray already owned many of the required books, though not the one she was writing about. She'd had to buy her secondhand copy of Henry James's *The Portrait of a Lady*, which was now propped open on the blackened tabletop before her.

Caridad's throat tightened each time Gray sipped beer. She typed: *In Henry James's novel, it is evident that . . .* But what exactly *is* evident in the novel? And why bother mentioning this if it is evident? Shoot, sip, sigh, and shift. Caridad ran her tongue over her teeth. She'd not tasted beer or wine since last summer, the night she lost her shoes and called Nash to drive her home. (She hadn't seen Nash again either.) For nearly seven months, she'd been sober—that much, she thought, *is* evident, though not at all relevant for her paper. These days, she climbed into bed soon after settling Miles down for the night. If he was tired, Gray would join her. But most nights, she read alone while Gray watched television or sometimes smoked in the kitchen as Leslie. On Saturday nights, Leslie would go out to Dante's or the Queen Mary. Almost every day, Caridad would wake before dawn, clearheaded and refreshed. She'd huddle under a quilt in the lamp-lit living room with a mug of coffee and a book, reading until Miles woke up.

She still quaked sometimes, but not from craving wine. Instead she'd tremble when yawning, shaking long after the yawn subsided, as if at the same time torpid and terrified. She thought of Lady Chatterley, whose tremors signaled frustrated sexual longing. Isabel, in *The Portrait of a Lady*, quivered, too, but Henry James presented this to suggest his heroine's anticipation of new places. Caridad picked up the book and glanced at a phrase she'd marked in the book: "the sin of self-esteem." In the margin, she'd printed *Is this sin?* The transgression was supposed to be Isabel's problem—hubris, the false pride that encouraged a woman of her milieu to imagine an unfettered life of travel and discovery. Pride was the flaw that marred the portrait of a lady. She twisted the roller to type the phrase as a title at the top of the page.

Unlike Chekhov, Flaubert, Tolstoy, Dreiser, and Nabokov, Henry James was not that lovable to Caridad. Bald-headed and cloaked in shadows, his domed face glared at her from the book's jacket, eyes narrowed as if he were about to complain. His prose was dense and unyielding. Isabel emerged an infuriating heroine, flirtatious but headstrong—naïve beyond belief to succumb to Osmond's scheming charm. For Caridad, the novel argued against providing bold and bright women the resources to live life on their own terms, suggesting they would, like Isabel, squander these on ruthless and controlling men. Night after night, Caridad forced herself through the pages, and still she hadn't finished the book.

A small shadow flashed in the periphery, and Mimi appeared at her side. Glad for the interruption, Caridad turned to her niece with a smile.

"What is today?" Mimi's eyes were wide, her expression solemn.

"It's Friday," Caridad told her, dreading what would come next.

"Mommy's not picking me up today."

"No, your daddy's coming for you." Caridad kept her tone light. Mimi had only recently stopped hiding in the house when her father collected her on Fridays, the day that Esperanza worked a split shift at the hospital—four hours before and after her classes.

"I don't like Fridays."

"I know." Caridad didn't like them either. Over time, Reynaldo had lost whatever attractiveness he'd once possessed. He'd grayed and put on weight in his early thirties, especially in his midsection and buttocks, giving him the look of a grizzled boar. He was brusque with Mimi, often exasperated by her reluctance to leave her aunt's house.

Mimi's dark eyes filled.

Caridad pulled her niece onto her lap. She held Mimi close, rocking her.

"Mimi," Miles called out, his voice husky and insistent. "Come here. We need you."

The little girl clambered down. "I got to go play now."

Her brother-in-law in mind, Caridad removed her glasses and pinched the skin between her eyebrows, forestalling a headache. Already, an engine roared into the long drive. Moments later, a car door clicked open and slammed shut. It was too early for Reynaldo. Caridad and Gray exchanged curious looks before the gate swung open. A gray-suited man with close-cropped black hair strutted into the yard. There was something familiar in the way he held himself, in his confident stride. Without her glasses, Caridad couldn't tell much more about him. Mimi took a few tentative steps toward the stranger. "You're *not* my daddy," she said.

Gray set his camera in the crate and grabbed up the beer can as if to have it handy for chucking. "What are *you* doing here?"

Caridad slipped on her glasses. With a heart-squeezing jolt, she recognized the gray-suited visitor—*Daniel.*

"I was in the neighborhood." He grinned at Gray, turned to Caridad. "So I thought I'd stop by. Lately I've been visiting old friends, just to catch up on things."

The way crystal chimes before an earthquake, agitation in Caridad vibrated out, tremors rippling like sound waves from her core. She squinted through smudged lenses. Daniel, and yet *not* Daniel—this was a revised and edited version of him. Coiffed hair, stylish sunglasses, and well-cut suit, he approached Gray, one stiff arm extended for a handshake.

Mimi pointed at Daniel. "He's not Daddy."

Caridad rose from the picnic table, backed toward the kitchen door. "Miles, Mimi," she said. "Come inside for your snack."

Miles groaned, but he trudged from behind the burnt picnic table to join his mother and Mimi at the threshold. When Daniel caught sight of Miles, he winced. Caridad shepherded the children inside, and through the open door, she heard Daniel ask Gray, "Those your kids?"

She couldn't make out Gray's answer. While she spread peanut butter on saltines for Miles and Mimi, Caridad strained to overhear the conversation between Daniel and Gray in the yard. The children grew silent, as if they, too, were eavesdropping.

"I've been driving around, seeing people," Daniel said. "I just bought a new car, so I'm breaking it in."

"How did you find us?"

"The phone book."

The cracker in her hand snapped. When Caridad married Gray, she had taken his name. In the directory, their number was listed under his name alone.

"So, you came to see *me*?" Gray said.

"Say, is that your car out in the drive? The green one? What kind is that?"

"A Fiat."

"Want to have a look at my car?" Daniel asked.

Their voices faded, growing inaudible. The gate whined open and banged shut.

After a few minutes, Gray bustled indoors, lugging his crate of moviemaking equipment and bringing the warm smell of beer and sweat into the kitchen.

Caridad searched his sun-flushed face. "Is he gone?"

He nodded and carried the crate into the back room. Gray then returned and tossed a small rectangle of purple plastic on the table. "You left this in the car." It was the name tag Caridad wore at work. In bold cursive letters, it bore the bookstore's logo. "It was face up on the dashboard." Gray hoisted Miles out of his chair and lifted him over his head. He gazed up at the toddler's laughing face. "Daddy's boy, Daddy's boy, who's my Daddy's boy?"

"Me! Me!" shouted Miles.

"Mimi, that's my name," Mimi told Caridad in an undertone. "But I'm not a daddy's boy. I'm a girl, and I don't like daddies, do you?"

"They're like anyone, I guess." Caridad's father, out of work and no doubt overwhelmed by his fast-growing family, had disappeared, deserting her mother and two older sisters before Caridad was born. When she was a young girl, Caridad imagined he'd been struck on the head, that he was a wandering amnesiac with no idea about the family he'd left behind. She'd fantasized that he'd recover his memory and return to them, envisioning herself meeting him for the first time in countless scenarios—a bakery, a bank, a museum, a church. But as a teenager, she'd overheard her aunts gossiping about another wife and sons, his job as a factory foreman in Juárez. "Some are good," she told Mimi. "Some could be better."

At the bookstore on Saturday afternoon, Dora, the manager, handed Caridad a list of tasks before leashing her two Siberian huskies, sluggish dogs that slept in the stock room while she worked. Appalled by the length of this list, Caridad drew breath to speak. But the manager slipped out the back door with her dogs, her bright red braid no more than an afterimage flashing in the shadowy room. Caridad shook her head, cursing Dora under her breath.

The door chime sounded from the front of the store. At the two-toned *bing-bong*, Caridad's heart vaulted to her throat. Now that he likely knew where she worked, she feared Daniel would appear. And since she worked alone that afternoon, Caridad couldn't hide out in the back room. She stepped out onto the sales floor. In relief at the sound of unfamiliar voices, Caridad strode up front to find a man with a little girl. "Can I help you?"

"Go on, honey pie," the man said. "Ask the nice librarian."

Caridad flashed an encouraging smile. No point in correcting him. People often confused bookstore clerks with librarians. On the phone and in the store, customers so routinely requested reference information from staff that Dora kept an almanac and a two-volume encyclopedia set near the register.

The man nudged the child forward. The little girl, blond and blushing, squirmed out of his grasp and hid behind his legs.

"My daughter wants *Goodnight Moon*," he said. "We don't know who wrote it, and everything seems to be arranged by the authors' last names." He indicated shelves of hardcover fiction, as if he expected to find the picture book among novels by James Clavell, Stephen King, and Colleen McCullough.

Caridad led them to the children's section. The man limped after her, his daughter clinging to one leg. She handed him the book, thinking it babyish for a child who looked to be about Mimi's age. The man sank to the parquet floor to sit cross-legged with the child in his lap. He opened the book and began reading it in a loud voice. He grinned up at Caridad as if enlisting her as his audience.

But the phone rang. Caridad slipped behind the sales counter to answer it. "Periwinkle Books," she said. "How may I help you?"

A reedy voice strained through the earpiece. The caller was an elderly man, his voice creaky as a bad saw on green wood.

"I beg your pardon," she said.

Amplifying, the oldster tried again. "I *said* do you have your drawers deliciously low?"

Caridad now and again received obscene calls at the store, but never one from someone as ancient as this caller sounded. Was there no cut-off age for perversion? Caridad would deal with this the same way she handled all others. "Please hold." She pressed a button that pulsed with red light, while Muzak streamed into the caller's ear. Caridad took her list to the display window to rearrange best sellers. She'd just finished with hardback fiction when the phone rang again. Caridad returned to the register area to answer it.

The nasty old man again—he'd hung up to redial the store. "Well, have you or haven't you got your drawers deliciously low?"

"Listen, sir," Caridad said, "this isn't—"

"It's my daughter's idea," he told her.

"Your *daughter's* idea?"

The caller chuckled. "You see, I crave sweet things."

"Sir, I hope you know I can report—"

"Problem is," he continued. "I'm borderline diabetic, so she ordered the book for me. I just want to know if it's come in. My name is Wilkes, Chester Wilkes."

Caridad scanned the shelf of special orders. Shame furnace-blasted her face when she spotted a book tagged for Wilkes: *Deliciously Low* by Yuri Dross.

"One moment, sir."

"Now, don't you dare—"

Caridad pressed the hold button. Its ruby eye blinked just once before she snatched up the receiver again. "How may I help you?" she said, affecting a British accent.

"I've called twice already." Impatience sharpened the caller's voice. "Some gal put me on hold for so long I had to call back. Now, do you or don't you have Yuri Dross's *Deliciously Low* for Chester Wilkes?"

"We do, indeed! That title is on hold for you at the register."

"Okay then," he said. "I'm coming by to pick it up."

"Very good, sir, we're open until six today," Caridad said. "Please accept my apologies for the delay. We have a new girl here—rather slow, I'm afraid."

"Listen here, I don't want to get anyone in trouble. I just want my book."

"It is ready and waiting for you, sir. Cheerio!" Caridad hung up the phone.

The blond child stood before the register, twisting her pudgy hands together. "Got more books with bunnies?"

"I'm about to open a box of books with bunnies and chicks and lambs," Caridad told her. "Give me a minute to bring it out." As she made her way to the back room, the door chimed again. Once more, Caridad's heart shot to her throat. Still, she lugged the large box of Easter books to the children's section, peering over it to see who had entered. It was just the Pilot, a thirty-something Lebanese man who enjoyed thrillers. He visited the store weekly to stock up on paperbacks, and he would often invite Caridad or her coworker Lisa to join him in the cockpit of the chartered plane he flew. Though he had shown them photos of the small aircraft, Caridad and Lisa, put off by the word "cockpit," refused these invitations.

The chime sounded several times more as customers came and went throughout the afternoon. Caridad's heart no longer leapt at the electronic *bing-bong*. Instead, she grew busy with customers, phone calls, her many tasks. At seven-thirty, Caridad bolted the back door, expecting to feel relieved and invigorated as she usually did at the end of a shift. Instead, a heavy mantle of lethargy freighted her as she closed the store. After dimming the lights, Caridad slipped her purple badge into her purse and shuffled to the entrance, where she glimpsed a young woman timorously approaching in the dark. "Stupid mousy thing," she snapped, knowing her voice would not carry beyond the heavy glass door. "Can't you see we're fucking closed?" Her focus sharpened, and Caridad realized the late-arriving customer was just her own image reflected in the darkened glass. That tentative step was her walk, the fearful expression issued from her face. Caridad let herself out and locked the store.

While Caridad was at work, the Loudermilks had stopped by. Rusty told Gray that he and Helga had been approached by a film production company on the lookout for demolition sites. If they'd allow a film crew to stage an explosion in the rental, the filmmakers would cover the costs for razing the structure and removing all debris, in addition to paying the Loudermilks four thousand dollars. Rusty offered to split this with Gray and Caridad, provided they could move out in one month instead of two, to accommodate the production schedule.

"That's a nice nest egg," Gray said when they sat down to supper that night.

Caridad had barbecued a chicken with skewered vegetables on the hibachi, and while the chunks of zucchini, mushroom, and green pepper had roasted nicely, the chicken had charred. Her hands and hair reeked of charcoal smoke.

"We could move just about anywhere we want. There's no reason we have to stay here." Gray often complained to Caridad about living in the city—the traffic, the smog, the crowding. He wanted to live in the mountains where the air was crisp and clear. He'd found a warped and rusted Colorado license plate in a Dumpster, and taking this as a sign, he'd nailed it above the front door. "Just think—in six months, we could be learning to ski."

"Ski!" echoed Miles. "What's that?"

"It's riding over snow on long wooden slats." Caridad held her hands out, flat and parallel to each other. She swerved these over the tabletop. "Swish, swush, swish."

"There's a place called Trinidad that would be perfect for us."

"Trinidad? Why there?" *Trinidad, Trinity*—Caridad flashed on fragments of the catechism she'd learned as a young girl: The Father, the Son, and the Holy Ghost.

"It's nestled in the foothills of the Rocky Mountains," Gray said, as if reciting from a tourism pamphlet, "between Santa Fe and Denver. It's got a pretty interesting history. Bat Masterson was the law out there at one time, and Wyatt Earp and Doc Holliday holed up in Trinidad after the shootout at the O.K. Corral."

"Really?"

Gray nodded. "Earp took off the next day, but Doc remained. Arizona tried to extradite him for the O.K. Corral thing, but Bat Masterson had him arrested on trumped-up charges, so Doc wouldn't be sent back to face the gallows."

"What's that?" asked Miles.

"A bad punishment," Gray told him.

Miles knitted his brow. "Like time out?"

"A really, really long time out," Caridad said.

Later that night, Gray climbed into bed beside Caridad, who was reading Henry James under the amber glow of her oil lamp. Before he reached for a fashion magazine, Gray talked to her again about moving, describing what their lives might be like in Colorado, with the mountains, the crystalline streams, the vast blue sky. "Don't you see?" he said. "This is our chance to be whatever we want to be, wherever we want. Most people never have a chance like this."

Drowsily, Caridad pictured the three of them under the clear Colorado sky. Gray could repair intricate machinery—a job that tapped his skills for meticulous work—instead of cleaning metallic surfaces in buildings as he did now. He'd wear a shirt with his name machine-stitched on the breast pocket. He could grow a beard, and Caridad would weave her hair into a thick braid that dipped toward her buttocks. She'd let herself fill out, widening in the hips and bust, and wear calico skirts and hiking boots. She would bake bread each week and hang laundry to flap outdoors in the thin, sweet-smelling air. She pictured Miles playing in a field of wild flowers, his eyes shiny, his mouth opening to speak: *Mimi, come here. We need you.*

Caridad jerked upright in bed. "We *can't.*"

"Why not?"

"Mimi," Caridad said. "We can't leave Mimi."

"Mimi's not our child," Gray whispered. "She has a perfectly good mother and a father. She'll be starting preschool soon and then kindergarten. Trust me—she'll be fine without us."

Caridad shook her head. Maybe Mimi was resilient enough for this, but how would *she* manage without Mimi? "And what about my mother?" she said. "Her health's not going to improve as she gets older. She'll need me nearby. And my sisters—I can't leave them."

"But that's what people do," Gray told her, his tone gentle. "They grow up and leave. They move where they want to live. They lead their own lives."

Caridad gazed at the open book before her. Early in the novel, Isabel Archer was avid for the adventure of travel. She leapt at the chance to visit an estranged aunt in England without a second thought about the sisters she'd left behind. And Isabel soon departed for Florence, then Rome and Bellagio, leaving disappointed suitors in her wake. How disgusted Isabel would be with Caridad's unwillingness to move just a few states away.

"At least, think about it," Gray said.

Caridad shrugged, staring at the printed pages without taking in a single word. Then she marked her place in the book, set it aside, and huffed out the oil lamp's flame.

—

Over the next week, Caridad was infused with brisk energy at the bookstore. When she and Gray moved, they'd likely have to pay more rent than the Loudermilks charged for the orchard office. Caridad hoped to gain an extra shift, maybe even a promotion and a raise. The following Saturday, Caridad asked to speak to Dora before she vanished with her large dogs, planning to make a case for more hours as a start.

Leashes in hand, Dora stood with her dogs at the back door.

"I was just wondering," Caridad began, "I mean—I'm doing okay, right? At work?"

Dora's freckled face wore a bemused expression. "No one's thinking any bad thoughts about you." Her tone suggested no one was thinking about Caridad at all. And before she could get another word out, Dora pushed open the door and rushed out, dogs trailing in her wake.

Again Caridad issued a soft stream of curses as she made her way to the front of the store. Dora barely took notice of her staff, except to criticize their work, and she was impatient with customers. The woman had no business working with people. Dora ought to run a kennel, not manage a retail store. Caridad was sure she could do a better job than Dora, and she wondered how much managers—salaried employees with benefits—were paid.

The door chimed when the Pilot entered the store. Caridad waved, and he grinned at her. He would usually select his books before approaching the register to chat. After several minutes, the Pilot made his way to the counter with an armload of paperbacks.

"What do you do with these after you read them?" Caridad imagined the walls of his apartment lined with shelves of paperbacks.

"I donate them to prisons."

"How kind of you," Caridad said, though she wondered if books about murder and mayhem made the best reading material for the incarcerated.

The Pilot shrugged. "Say, are you free this weekend?" He wore a hopeful look on his tanned face. With his well-shaped eyebrows, large eyes, and glossy moustache, he was the kind of man who should have no trouble attracting women. If only he didn't use the word that triggered for Caridad the image of a penis-filled chasm. "I'm flying to Denver on Saturday. Maybe you could take a ride in my cockpit."

Caridad shook her head. "I can't." She keyed in the sale and began bagging the books. "But tell me something. Do you often fly to Colorado?"

"Denver, Telluride, Aspen—"

"Have you ever been to Trinidad?"

The Pilot nodded. "Perry Stokes Airport in Trinidad—I get chartered there some."

"Really?" Caridad said. "What's Trinidad like?"

His moustache twitched. "It's not a good thing to talk about with a lady."

Caridad considered Isabel Archer and smiled at the idea of being a lady. The Pilot could be courtly, even prim, despite his passion for pulp fiction. "You can tell me," she said. "I have a friend who wants to move there."

"How can I say this?" The Pilot handed Caridad his credit card. "The people there are not always what they seem to be."

"Meaning?"

"In Trinidad, you might meet a woman who is maybe not a woman."

Caridad's face grew warm. "It's a place for—"

"Operations," the Pilot told her. "That's what Trinidad is known for—gender reassignment surgery. I fly lots of passengers out there for that. It's strange to me, not my thing, but it takes all kinds, right?"

She tore off his receipt, placed it atop his books, and slid the bag toward him. "Thanks for telling me." Caridad kept her tone light, though she was anxious to usher him out, to call Gray to release the hot blast of fury scorching the back of her throat.

"Tell me." The Pilot gathered up his books. "When will you take a ride in my cockpit?"

"Honestly, I'm really not a cockpit kind of person."

He issued a two-fingered salute before leaving the store.

As she reached for the phone, Caridad glimpsed one of the Pilot's paperbacks near the register; she'd neglected to put it in his bag. The door chime sounded, and Caridad reached for the book, but it slipped from her grasp and plummeted to the floor. She ducked behind the counter to retrieve it, and when she stood, Caridad gasped at the sight of Daniel standing before her. "What are you doing here?" she asked, surprising herself with the sharpness of her tone.

"I've missed you, Caridad." His voice was soft and low.

"I can't talk," Caridad told him. "I'm working."

The chime sounded again. A middle-aged woman stepped into the store with a teenaged boy in tow. The boy clutched a sheet of notepaper. The woman grabbed this from him and handed it to Caridad. "Summer reading list," she said. Caridad scurried into the stacks to pull books from the shelves with shaking hands. A small wave of customers entered the store, and after ringing up the woman's sale, she helped them, too. Following this burst of busyness, the store emptied, and Daniel again approached the register to speak to her as she processed special orders.

He remained in the store for the last hour of her shift, telling Caridad how he'd changed. He no longer enjoyed arguing, he said, and he'd given up philosophy after earning his degree to become a sales representative for an office machine company. Daniel gestured at the navy blue suit he wore, as if offering it in evidence of his transformation. The suit became him—what an apt phrase. The suit became Daniel, and Daniel became the suit. Its sharp lines elongated his compact form, rendering his large head more proportional to his body. After telling her about himself, Daniel asked about her, his voice low and urgent, as if he deeply wanted to know how she was.

It had been such a long time since anyone but Mimi had shown any curiosity in her that Caridad was tempted to tell him about moving, about Colorado, about Gray—though this would be a mistake. So she asked about Beryl instead, expecting to hear of her enthusiasm for Daniel's transformation. Beryl was probably in the parking lot, waiting in the car.

He examined a display of bookmarks, slowly spinning the revolving rack. "I'm not with Beryl anymore."

"What happened?"

Daniel grimaced. "I want to be honest, *really* honest, with you because I care about you." He explained that when Caridad left school, Beryl had at first been cheerful and affectionate, presenting him with small gifts and treating him to movies and baseball games. At a Dodgers game with her one afternoon, he'd had the physical sensation of being crushed, as if a tremendous weight was bearing down on him, squeezing his lungs so he couldn't breathe. Alarmed, Beryl asked what was wrong. "You know what I told her?" Daniel said.

Caridad shook her head.

"I said, 'I miss her.' That's all I had to say, and the pressure lifted. I could breathe again, really fill my lungs." Daniel flashed Caridad a rueful smile. "Beryl didn't say anything. She just gave me this look. A few weeks later, she moved out. We said we'd always be friends, but I haven't seen her since the day she left."

"Have you tried to find her?"

"No."

"What other old friends have you looked up?"

"None, really—just you."

At closing time, Caridad told Daniel he had to leave.

"I've taken up so much of your time that I should probably buy something." Daniel strode to the business section, where he picked out a book titled *Getting to Yes*.

Caridad rang up the sale and took his check.

"Your little boy," Daniel said, "is he—"

"You'd better go."

"Can I see you again?"

"That's not a good idea."

"At least, you didn't say no." Daniel held up the book to display its title before heading out of the store.

Caridad wrote the Pilot's name on a slip of paper and tucked this between the pages of the paperback he'd left behind. Then she hurried up front to lock the door. This time she recognized her reflected image, though the bounce in her step was as unfamiliar as the brightness in her face, flame-bright in the darkened glass.

Since Caridad had no time to call Gray from the store, she planned to wait until after Miles was in bed to confront him about Trinidad. That evening, Miles refused to eat his supper. He was cranky and fitful. Caridad palmed his warm forehead and then took his temperature. It was only a few degrees above normal, so she held off giving him baby aspirin. Caridad bathed him and tucked him in bed earlier than usual. After reading to him, Caridad sat by Miles's side, stroking his hair until his slow breathing thickened into snoring.

She tiptoed into the kitchen, where she found Gray washing dishes. "He's asleep."

Gray dropped a plate into the sudsy water. "You startled me."

"I need to talk to you about something." She sat at the table.

He fished out the plate. "What is it?"

"No, I mean, when you're done there. We need to sit down and talk."

"Sure." He twisted on the tap to rinse the plate. As Caridad watched his swift movements, wistfulness twisted in her. Why couldn't he always be like this, in his denim work shirt, gray sweatpants, and gym shoes? She even felt fondness for his oily, unwashed hair, and especially for his whiskery face. Why wasn't it enough for him to be this comfortable-looking, easygoing man?

He wiped his hands on the dish towel and turned to her. "What's up?"

"Sit with me," she told him.

Gray scooted into a seat facing hers. Working in the sun had seamed his forehead and leathered his neck. He wasn't yet thirty, but silvery strands threaded the curls at his temples. His eyes, though darker, were still avid as a child's. "Okay?"

"Trinidad," she said, "sex-change operations—why didn't you tell me?"

He dropped his gaze. "I didn't think you'd go for it."

"So . . . your plan was—*what*? To move us there, hoping I wouldn't pick up on all the transsexuals, and what then? One day you'd check into a clinic or whatever and just come home as Leslie from there on out—was I not supposed to notice *that* either? What about Miles?"

"Miles is too young to—"

"But Miles knows *you*. He loves you as Gray. Leslie is someone else altogether. He will lose the father he knows, the one he loves."

Gray picked up the salt and pepper shakers—miniature ceramic chefs, scavenged by his mother from a yard sale—and he held these to face each other in the way Miles handled his people dolls.

"And I've got to tell you, losing Gray for Leslie is not a good deal for me either. There are probably lots of men who'd make really great women. Isn't that the point—to explore emotional depth, to add dimension to the self? But you're already a complicated person. You're a creative and sensitive man who becomes a silly and shallow woman."

"You just don't like Leslie," Gray said.

"Why should I? She shows up, and I lose you. I don't like *that* at all."

Gray looked up at her, his eyes thickening. "Everything can't be for you. I can't live my life just to please you. Before you know it, I will have lived half my life pretending to be someone I'm not. Do you have any idea what that's like?"

Caridad shook her head.

Gray gazed at the pink-cheeked shakers in his hands as if addressing them. "I've worked all this time at a shitty job I hate. I help in the house, and I take care of Miles, even though . . ."

Caridad's throat tightened.

"That doesn't matter," Gray said. "Really, I don't care. I love you both. I'm sorry I wasn't honest about Trinidad. I wasn't trying to trick you. I guess I hoped we'd get there and things would change, that you'd love me enough to accept me the way I'm meant to be."

"But you never touch me."

"After the surgery, things can change."

Caridad shook her head. "But I'm not—"

"You never know."

"I *know*," Caridad said. "In the same way you know you want to be a woman, I'm sure I want to be with a man."

"So? What happens now?"

Caridad shrugged, staring along with Gray at the grinning shakers in his hands. The clock above the stove clicked when the minute hand shifted, and Caridad imagined she could hear the flow of blood through her veins, the whisper of waves rolling over fine sand.

Then a howl rent the quiet kitchen. The shakers clattered onto the tabletop, and Gray and Caridad bolted to the bedroom. Half awake, Miles wailed, thrashing about in his small bed. Gray gathered him in his arms while Caridad hurried to phone the pediatrician. The nurse on call told her to keep Miles cool and hydrated and *not* to give him children's aspirin. Instead he should have a small dose of liquid acetaminophen. While Gray stayed with Miles, who had settled some, Caridad drove to an all-night drugstore for the medicine. When she returned, Miles had fallen back asleep. She and Gray debated waking him for a dose. He slept so deeply that they decided not to disturb him.

Before tiptoeing out of the bedroom with Caridad, Gray grabbed a coral skirt and ruffled blouse from the closet, along with a pair of heels.

"*Unbelievable*," Caridad said. "You're going *out?*"

"I'm meeting someone. I'd already made plans." Gray brushed past her on his way to the bathroom.

In the middle of the night, Caridad was jostled from her sleep. She opened her eyes to Leslie's chalky face. "What's going on?"

"Miles is worse," Leslie said in Gray's voice. "He's burning up."

Caridad lunged to Miles's bedside. He was twisting and turning, flopping in the sheets like a fish trapped in a net. "Turn on the light," Caridad said.

Under the glow from the overhead fixture, Miles's cheeks were rash-red, though the skin around his lips was blanched as if bleached. His eyes were half-open and unfocused. Miles muttered about people dolls and Mimi before opening his eyes wide and clearly calling out, "Daddy! Daddy!" But when Leslie reached for him, he flung his head back. Miles's chest bucked, his arms and legs jerking. His eyes rolled, the irises walling in his lids. A terrible rattle emanated from his throat. Pinkish foam filled his mouth, trickling to his chin.

"Oh god, he can't breathe," Gray said.

Caridad gulped back the panic rising in her like floodwaters. "We've got to take him to the hospital." She swaddled Miles in his blanket. "Go start the car. I'll carry him out." As she hurried through the yard, holding her son close, Miles's rigid body grew limp in her arms. She kissed the damp and salty crown of his head. "You're going to be okay," she whispered to him. "You *have* to be okay."

When they pulled up to the emergency room entrance, Caridad sprang out of the passenger seat with Miles. "I'll wait in the car," Gray said.

"*What?* You're not coming in?"

"I can't." He gestured at the coral skirt and blouse he still wore. "Not like this."

"Go home and change, damn it! Then come right back." Caridad banged the car door shut with one hip and turned to bear Miles, now breathing evenly, into the buzzing fluorescent glare of the emergency room.

When Gray returned, Caridad was seated in a plastic scoop chair, Miles sleeping in her arms. She waited along with nearly a dozen other people whose faces were washed-out, ghoulish-looking under the tubed lighting overhead. *The undead,* thought Caridad. They were all silent and listless, except for a raw-faced blond, an emaciated woman in a grubby tank top and cut-off jeans, who begged the admitting nurse for pain-killers. "Come on," she said, her voice harsh and gritty. "I'm fucking dying here. I'm in pain. Can't you see?" Gray gaped at her as he made his way to the vacant seat near Caridad's.

Caridad glanced at her watch. She'd been waiting with Miles for almost an hour. "What took you so long?"

Though his cheeks were rubbed pink, foundation cream clotted his hairline and his hair was sweat-flattened, plastered by the wig into a crimped cap of curls. He held up the book from her bedside, as if retrieving this had detained him. Gray tucked the novel between her hip and the seat. He extended his arms and reached for Miles. "Here, let me take him."

She handed her son over and flexed her arms.

"He seems better," Gray said. He stroked Miles's hair. "He's cooler now."

Caridad set the book in her lap; its pages fell open. Gray didn't know she'd finished it that night, gaping in disbelief when Isabel chose to go back to Osmond rather than to start anew with Caspar, who'd loved her all along. Maybe Isabel would turn around, or one day she would return to him from Rome. Caridad's eyes slid down the page, fixing on a random phrase: "To read between the lines was easier than to follow the text." She snapped the book shut.

The ruddy blond pounded on the admitting desk with her fists. "Come on," she said, "come on! What's *wrong* with you? Can't you see I'm dying here?"

The receptionist glanced at her, stifling a yawn.

"What are we going to do, Gray?"

He rocked Miles in his arms. "First, we'll find out what the doctor says—"

"I *know* that," she said. "I meant after this—what will *we* do?"

"We're going to have to move pretty soon. Maybe we can stay with my mother, if we don't find a place right away."

"What about your plans?" Caridad said, thinking again of Henry James, whom she still did not love, but who had once written: "Three things in human life are important—the first is to be kind; the second is to be kind; and the third is to be kind." "Don't you want to move to Trinidad?"

He glanced at her over Miles's head, his eyes brightening. "More than anything."

"Then that's what you should do."

"Really?" Gray's voice rose. "We'd move there?"

Caridad shook her head. "Not we—*you*. You should take the

money from the Loudermilks, that nest egg—all of it—and use it to move, to become who you're meant to be."

"And leave you? I don't think I can live without you, without Miles."

"This way, at least you'll have the chance to find out," Caridad said.

He took her hand, squeezed it. "You'd let me do that?"

"I'm not *letting* you do anything. It's what you want, what you need, and for us, something has to change . . . because *this* isn't working—not for me, not for you—is it?"

Gray dropped his gaze, shook his head.

"Aren't you human? Don't you have any kind of heart?" The blond fell to her knees and clasped her hands together. "Look, *look* at me. I'm fucking *begging* you!"

A tense and tired-looking Filipina wearing aqua scrubs and holding a clipboard shuffled into the waiting area. "Kessler, Miles Kessler, the doctor will see you now."

Redundancy Reports

To open the refrigerator: a simple, self-evident act. Like raising a window or flipping on a light, it was the type of gesture that went unquestioned, unnoticed when Caridad lived in the converted orchard office with Gray. But here in Mama's kitchen on a Saturday morning in early September, sunlight streaming through windows to illuminate, even clarify, Caridad's movement, Felicia nevertheless had to ask, "What do you think you're doing?"

"What's it look like I'm doing?" Caridad shut and pulled the door wide again to demonstrate. At her side, two-year-old Miles gazed with her at the chilly contents: dewy jug of Borden skim milk, clouded Tupperware containers, egg carton, Imperial margarine, Miracle Whip, the pink squadron of Tab cans arrayed on the shelf above the vegetable crisper.

Felicia arched a brow. "*Why?*"

"Do I need to give you a reason?"

"You need to *have* a reason. You can't just keep opening the fridge and letting all the cold air out for the hell of it. Some of us actually pay the electricity bill around here."

Caridad slammed the refrigerator door shut. Jars and bottles chinked against one another with the force of this. Miles squinted up at her, and she took his hand, tugged him toward the kitchen door that led outside. "Come on, buddy. Let's walk over to the little market. We'll get some animal crackers."

"You know, you really shouldn't give him so many sweets."

Caridad stopped short, her pulse throbbing in her ears. "Felicia."

"*What?*" Felicia flung the word down like a gauntlet.

Miles's gaze darted from his mother to his aunt and back again.

"Nothing," Caridad reached for her bag, a gray pouch with a long strap looped on the back of a chair. "Let's go, son."

"Wait, Mama," Miles said. "I need *my* purse." He dashed to Caridad's childhood bedroom, the room they now shared.

Felicia snorted, and it was Caridad's turn to cast out a terse, "*What?*"

Her sister shrugged, but when Miles reappeared in the doorway bearing a yellow patent-leather clutch with pink applique daisies, she said, "Boys don't carry purses."

Baffled, Miles glanced at the bright handbag he held. This was the vinyl purse he had begged for the last time he and Caridad visited a toy store. In it, he kept the purse's accessories that had been packaged with it—plastic compact, lipstick, and comb—along with Bee-Bee, a small doll with a plastic face pinched into a permanent scowl.

Miles's lips twitched, ready to smile or frown, as soon as he figured out if his aunt was teasing or scolding him.

Mama scuttled into the kitchen, her slippers rasping over the linoleum. She glanced from Caridad to Miles, noting the purses. "Where's everybody going?"

"We're going to the store, 'Buela," Miles said, "for a snack."

"Don't we have food here?" Mama heaved the refrigerator door wide. Mist rolled from the shelves as she surveyed their contents. "We have cheese and yogurt . . ." She slid out the drawer to the produce bin. "There are apples, carrots, even celery. How about some grapes, m'ijo?"

"Felicia doesn't want us to open the refrigerator," Caridad said.

Her sister shook her head. "That's not what I—"

"But how can you see what's inside," Mama said, "without opening it?"

"I'm just trying to save energy."

"Tía says boys don't carry purses," Miles added.

Mama looked down at Miles, clutching his yellow purse. "Well, no se." She smiled at her grandson. "But you have a very beautiful purse. I have always wanted a purse just like that, so bright and yellow, like a splash of sunshine. Oh, it's so shiny!"

"Want to know what's inside, 'Buela?"

"Tell me, m'ijo."

Miles crooked his index finger, summoning her closer. Mama leaned toward him, leaving the refrigerator door ajar. Fans whirred within to replace the escaping cold. Caridad shot her sister a sharp look.

Felicia wheeled away, strode out of the kitchen.

"I got Bee-Bee in here," Miles whispered. He opened the clutch, so his grandmother could peek inside.

Mama pointed at the doll. "Pee in a pot."

Caridad was puzzled for a moment, but then she said, "You mean pea in a *pod*?"

"I wish I had thought of that," Mama said, "a purse to hold my babies, so they'd always be together and none of them would ever get lost."

Beaming, Miles nodded at his grandmother.

That afternoon, Caridad drove along Burbank Boulevard, her silver Honda Civic gliding past Balboa Park and its nature preserve toward her store in Encino. The quiet hum of the engine and the traces of the new upholstery scent that lingered months after she'd bought it filled her with the unfamiliar pride of ownership. Most of all, she appreciated its reliability. Unlike the Fiat, the Honda neither stranded her nor died out while idling at red lights. The compact car had been more expensive than she'd hoped—she'd be paying for it for the next five years—but Caridad needed dependable transportation for work and to get Miles to daycare on weekdays.

Car payments, insurance, those trips to emergency rooms, and the battery of tests before Miles was prescribed an effective anticonvulsant—medical expenses from the time before she had benefits—prevented Caridad from moving into her own place with Miles. But now that she was a salaried bookstore manager, Caridad was finally paying off debt and saving money. She'd also begun contributing toward household expenses, even if this was not sufficient (in Felicia's opinion) to cover electricity. She had hoped to save enough for her and Miles to move out of Mama's house a year from when she moved in. The morning's irritation now fading, Caridad wished she had more compassion for her sister, who'd understandably chafed at the adjustments, the sacrifices she'd had to make when Caridad and Miles moved into Mama's house.

Big-bellied geese sailed up over the park, pulling skyward all at once, expanding and contracting their wings in unison like synchronized swimmers. The airborne birds then reversed direction while maintaining a tight formation. At a stoplight, Caridad rolled down her window to watch the geese, marveling at such collective purpose. Their sleek bodies now formed a chevron comprised of precise check marks against thick frothy clouds. If creatures with thumb-sized brains could coordinate with one another to execute such a pattern, why couldn't she and Felicia spend more than few minutes together without friction?

A horn blasted behind her. The signal had flashed green. After Balboa Park, traffic on Burbank Boulevard grew denser, so Caridad focused on driving. Though she'd improved, she was still far from an accomplished driver. Caridad scooted the seat so close to the dashboard that she hunched over the steering wheel, nearly hugging it to her chest while peering tensely through windshield. She drove just under the speed limit, often tapping the brakes. Other cars swerved around her, angry-faced drivers glaring, sometimes flipping her off or shouting obscenities as they passed. Her store loomed just a few blocks ahead on the left. The neon sign was unlit during the daylight, but the store's name in its trademark script—Periwinkle Books—appeared at the top of the strip mall's marquee. This was Caridad's second store to manage, voluminous in contrast to the tiny shop she ran in North Hollywood for a few months after Dora quit. Periwinkle Encino was the shopping center's anchor store, and it housed the regional manager's office.

Caridad pulled into the parking lot, wondering if Alvin and Val—her assistant managers—had set up the Halloween display and whether they had gotten all the received books shelved. She doubted it. Alvin would, of course, have an excuse for not doing his work. With a smirk on his handsome face, he'd insinuate that Caridad was somehow to blame. "Oh, you wanted me to *shelve* the receiving, but I'm sure you told me to *receive* the shelving," he'd said when she'd given him verbal instructions. "I wondered about that because it looked like everything had already been received, so I didn't have anything to do, and I was kind of bored actually." After that, he'd misplaced the to-do list she'd written out for him, complaining that she should have put it where it wouldn't get lost. When she taped her instructions up in the back room, he claimed a breeze had snatched the list off the wall and whooshed it out into the busy street. "I would have been hit by a car if I'd have chased after it," he'd told her, his tone aggrieved. Alibi Al, Caridad privately called him.

Still, he was an improvement over Val, a pasty-faced woman who wandered the store like a baffled spirit. Though often in the store even when not scheduled for work, ghostlike Val never accomplished much, as if she lacked the substance to do more than drift about and moan. When Caridad pointed out her lack of productivity, Val's long nose quivered and her mild eyes filled with tears. Caridad had inherited both assistants from the woman who'd run the store before becoming a regional manager in the Midwest. If her predecessor had earned a promotion despite being freighted with such incompetents, Caridad felt challenged to do the same. Still, she wished she could fire them both, and she spent many satisfying moments imagining this. "In different ways, you are both worthless and annoying. Therefore, I must let you go," she'd say. "Good-bye and good luck."

Apart from Alvin and Val, Caridad's staff wasn't entirely incapable. Her receiving clerk, a sulky British girl who wore grubby neon-green ski pants, worked steadily, if mutely, to absorb all shipments into inventory. The salesclerks on the floor appeared sane and hygienic. But last week, Vera, the regional manager, who usually left hiring up to Caridad, had been impressed with a walk-in applicant, a former lawyer named Walt, who'd turned up on Caridad's day off. Vera had hired him on the spot. As Caridad completed the new-hire paperwork, she wondered what kind of lawyer settles for a minimum-wage job as a salesclerk. Upon meeting Walt, Caridad had her answer: the babbling and paranoid kind—with sweaty palms, facial tics, and spittle that flew from his lips as he raved about conspiracies and cover-ups. Now Caridad would have to let him go. "Clearly," she'd begin, "this job is beneath your level of education and experience."

Despite steeling herself to deal with shenanigans from Alibi Al and Val and to terminate the former lawyer, Caridad was infused with energy as she parked her car. Invigorated, she strode past the yogurt shop, the gym, the fondue restaurant, and the Assertiveness Training Institute. She often regretted that her store was near such a place; customers often stopped at the bookstore after sessions at the Institute, eager to try out their newfound pushiness. Her step grew brisker as she approached the entrance to Periwinkle Encino, her store, the anchor, "the jewel," as Vera often said, "in the crown of the region." Though this metaphor strained her imagination, Caridad *was* proud of the place and thrilled to step over the threshold, sounding the chime that sent clerks scurrying when they glimpsed her entering the store.

This particular Saturday afternoon, Vera swooped up front to greet Caridad, towing a suit-wearing man in her wake. He was as tall as a basketball player, though too thin and gangly for any kind of sport. In fact, he seemed disjointed, comprised of mismatched body parts. His smallish bald head sported large ears, oversized hands flopped at the ends of his thin wrists, and his long neck and head preceded his torso as he loped giraffe-like behind Vera. The regional manager wore a pink floral-print dress with a full skirt, a matching fabric-covered belt cinching her waist. In coral lipstick and pearl earrings, Vera looked nearly attractive, despite her spiky white-blond hair, pebbly eyes, and toothy grin.

"*There* you are," Vera said, as if she'd caught Caridad hiding in the store. She turned to the tall man. "This is the store manager, Caridad Kessler. Caridad, this is Eric Heinz, our VP of marketing and sales."

"Pleased to meet you," Caridad said.

He grasped her hand, squeezed it once. "Likewise."

"Eric's here to see how we're doing with the shelving markers."

Caridad flashed on the plastic brackets she and her staff had jammed onto the edges of various shelves, snapping these on by banging them into place with thick dictionaries or Bibles. The shelf brackets labeled sections already indicated by bookcase signs and placards hanging from the ceiling. Again and again, the damn things had to be pried off with a screwdriver, also smacked repeatedly, and then—*bam, bam, bam*—reinstalled whenever book volume shifted and sections expanded or contracted to accommodate this.

The VP stooped to peer into Caridad's eyes. "What kind of impact," he said, "do you think the shelving markers will have on customers?"

"Well," Caridad began, thinking A) none whatsoever and B) what a stupid question. "That's hard to say."

Eric Heinz emitted an abrupt honk of laughter. He clapped her on the back. "Wise woman here," he told Vera. "Keeps her cards close to the vest."

"We're heading out to lunch at the Melting Pot," Vera told Caridad. "Care to join us?"

"Thank you, but I've already eaten." Caridad had lunched with her before. Vera always requested separate checks, and the fondue restaurant was too pricey for Caridad. "Nice meeting you," she told Eric Heinz. "Enjoy your lunch."

As soon as Vera and the VP stepped out the door, Alvin sprang out, bearing the store's ledger, as if he'd been skulking behind bookcases, waiting to ambush Caridad the moment Vera, whom he feared, had gone. "That guy," he said, without preamble, "the one you've been seeing—remember he bought all those books a few weeks ago?"

"Yes?" Caridad covertly admired Alvin's glacial blue eyes, his high cheekbones and full lips, the single obsidian curl arranged on his forehead like an upside-down question mark.

Alvin produced a small rectangle of paper from the ledger. "His check bounced." His dewy complexion glowed, his arctic eyes gleaming. He waved the check in her face. "Insufficient funds!"

Shouldn't attractiveness make life easier for people? Caridad thought of Alvin and then of Felicia. Shouldn't the good-looking be less inclined to meanness?

"Do you have a picture of him for posting in the 'deadbeat gallery'?" Alvin asked.

"Have you called to collect? It's probably just an oversight."

"Doesn't matter!" Alvin grinned. "Store policy—we've got to post his mug. I'm going to redeposit this first thing Monday. If it's flagged again, he'll pay double overdraft fines. At the bank where my wife works, that's twenty bucks a pop."

Caridad groaned. "I'll cover the check. Just give me a minute to get settled in back." She turned for the stock room. Near the true crime section, Walt's breathy voice lofted over the stacks, rambling about JFK, the CIA, and the mafia. She glanced down the aisle. An elderly woman was backing away from the former attorney, an uneasy look on her face. Caridad turned to Alvin, who was trailing her with the ledger. An expression of malice had transformed his face into a cruel mask, a look Caridad had grown accustomed to seeing on him. "Oh, and send that ex-lawyer to the back room," she said. "I need to talk to him."

Caridad waited only a few minutes for Walt in her makeshift desk area, a corner of the long receiving counter that held a fluorescent table lamp, an adding machine, legal pads, and a jar of pens. She sat on a wheeled rotating stool at this "desk" where she balanced the books, completed paperwork, and interviewed job applicants. With Walt's wary approach, inspiration struck, and she told him that some men in dark suits had come to the store asking about him. Ashen-faced, Walt resigned at once. Caridad issued his final check and sent him on his way, planning to complete the paperwork later.

During her dinner break, Caridad perched on the spinning stool and folded Walt's redundancy report into an envelope. *Letting people go is really not so bad*, she thought. She tossed the envelope into the outgoing mail basket and opened the coverless paperback, a "stripped" copy of *Tess of the d'Urbervilles* by Thomas Hardy that she'd pulled from the recycling bin. At first glance, she'd been intrigued by the novel's structure with subheadings that transmitted the narrative: "The Maiden," "Maiden No More," "The Rally," "The Consequence," "The Woman Pays," "The Convert," and "Fulfillment." Why, the first five sections could be the story of her life. But a few nights ago, Caridad had blinked back hot tears as Tess christened her baby, naming him Sorrow, just before his death: "So passed away Sorrow, the Undesired." At this, she'd put the book aside to check on Miles. Relieved by his deep breathing, she'd kissed his warm forehead. Isabel Archer in *The Portrait of a Lady* had also lost her child. How handily Hardy and James disposed of infants borne to their heroines! As if raising a child, even on the page, proved beyond their creative faculties, or else these great authors were intent on denying Isabel and Tess even a sliver of satisfaction: no pleasure in sex and no joy in motherhood. What punishers they were! Caridad couldn't bear to imagine losing her child.

"I could never let *him* go," she murmured. Caridad found her place in the book and read until the regional manager cracked open the door connecting the back room to her office to poke her head in.

"I know it's your break," Vera said, "but if you've got a minute, something's come up."

Caridad marked her place in the novel and followed Vera into the adjacent room, a real office with a true desk and a blotter, on top of which the matching belt to her pink dress was now snake-coiled next to a box of tissues.

Vera flopped onto her chair, a padded ergonomic thing that swiveled, rolled, and even reclined. "I had to get rid of Sully today."

"What happened?" Caridad pictured Barb Sullivan, the frumpy woman who managed Periwinkle Studio City, banished from the Studio City store in the way Tess was cast off by Alec d'Urberville. Her nickname—Sully—was sadly apt. Sullen was how Barb came across if one did not know her story: her high school teacher husband whom she had nursed through colorectal cancer and who, after going into remission, began sleeping with his students. Sully had caught him in their bed with a tenth grader, and now he was serving time for statutory rape. For last year's white elephant gift exchange, Sully had drawn Caridad's name, and at the holiday party, she'd given Caridad an envelope stuffed with strange confetti: Barb's wedding portrait scissored into tiny bits.

"After lunch," Vera said, "I took Eric to her store, and the place was a dump." She snorted, wearing a look on her face that was both indignant and defensive. "There were magazines on racks that should have been returned weeks ago. She had a beach-reading display in the window, for Christ's sake! And it's nearly October! Sully never even bothered to install the shelf brackets. They were still in the shipping box. "

"She's been kind of overwhelmed since her assistant quit," Caridad said.

"That assistant was running the whole show. Sully does nothing." Vera pantomimed tearing out her spiky hair. "Still, I would have finessed things with Eric. I would have told him about her husband and whatnot, but she got all pissy when he asked about the brackets. She actually said they were 'a bunch of useless crap.'"

Caridad nodded. The brackets *were* a bunch of useless crap.

"No way could I finesse that." Vera's eyes shone and her nose reddened. "I really had no choice." She plucked a tissue from the box nearby and honked into it. "So here's the thing. I need a manager to take over that store and cut costs so Studio City shows some kind of profit."

Caridad placed a finger over her lips, suppressing the joyful yip rising in her throat. She would unload Alibi Al or Val, maybe even both since Periwinkle Studio City needed a manager and an assistant. "So, Alvin?"

"Are you insane?" Vera's small eyes bulged in disbelief. "I wouldn't trust that little turd to run a lemonade stand."

"Then who—"

"I bet *you* could whip that place into shape."

"But Studio City does half this store's volume." Caridad knew well that managers' salaries were based on sales in their stores. "I can't afford to take a cut in pay."

Vera shook her head. "You don't get it. I want you to run *both* stores. You'd be a dual-store manager, first in the region. It's not a pay cut. In fact, you'd get a pretty big bump, making just about what Sully earned on top of your salary at this store. Interested?"

Though she understood that earning "just about what" Barb Sullivan made would be the part of the cost cutting that Vera intended for the smaller store, Caridad performed quick calculations. How much would she need to move out with Miles before the year's end? She stared as if transfixed by that coiled pink belt. Its fabric-covered buckle made a squarish snake's head, the silver prong its unforked tongue. "I might be," she said.

"Books," Daniel told her that night, "are really nothing."

This struck Caridad as absurd, especially since he'd just kited a check for a stack of "nothing." When he made such declarations, Daniel reminded her of Miles, who would throw out his arms and cry, "The moon is a balloon!" Or, "Leaves are letters from the trees!" Daniel even looked like Miles in this moment, and Caridad was often moved by his impulse to define the world that had shaped him in harsh ways as a child. But irritation over the bad check now trumped that tenderness.

After Gray moved to Colorado, Daniel began visiting her at the bookstore when she worked evenings. Lonely and flattered by his attention, Caridad warmed toward him over several weeks, and one night in June, he persuaded her to follow him home. By the time she transferred to the Encino store, she had the habit of stopping by his apartment on Saturday nights when Miles was asleep at her mother's house. Over the past few months, intimacy made them closer and more comfortable with one another, and Daniel grew so relaxed and confident in her company that he again became voluble and persistent in pushing his views.

He now picked up the book that had fallen out of her bag when she'd tossed it on a chair near the door in his apartment. "A novel is less than dust. Don't you see?" Daniel held up the coverless paperback. "Soon books will be like those prehistoric etchings found in caves. A handful of archaeologists might get excited about them, but most people won't give a damn. Machines are the future. Copiers, fax machines, computers are just the start. Technology is the next phase in human evolution. That's what will last until the end of civilization."

Though Caridad had just shrugged off her sweater, she reached to pull it back on, to leave and perhaps not return. But then the week would drag on, the routine of bookstore and home, home and bookstore. By Saturday, her flesh, the very epidermis and nerve endings at the surface of this tingled, aching for touch. *Skin hunger*—a craving she experienced as powerfully as thirst—propelled her to drive through dark streets to this apartment week after week, where she could slip between Daniel's cool sheets to satisfy her longing, if only for a short while.

Caridad set her sweater aside. "By the way," she said, "your check bounced—the one you wrote to the store last time. I used all the cash I had to cover it."

"I didn't ask you to do that."

"Alvin was ready to redeposit it. You would have been charged bank fees twice."

"So what? It's just money—checks, bank notes—just slips of paper used for getting stuff," Daniel said. "In the future, we won't even have that. We'll be able to type in codes on a keyboard to get what we want." He pointed to his computer.

Nearly every time she visited, some new possession appeared in his apartment. In the dining area, a stereo system with sleek speakers stood near barbells arrayed on a rack, neglected now and furred with dust. Against one wall, an oversized television loomed, in front of which modular taupe cubes were stacked to form seats. A glass-top coffee table stood before these.

On the walls, Daniel, having resurrected his desire to paint, had hung his own canvases. These were mostly blank expanses, in Caridad's estimation, though they were impressively large. "Gesso on Gesso," he'd told her when she'd asked about the work. "It's a series. That's One, Two, and over there, behind the artificial palm, that's Three." Caridad moved from one to the next, studying each. The second was more interesting than the first for a wispy cobweb connecting it to the ceiling, and the third was most interesting for the shadows cast on it by the plastic palm. Caridad had struggled for a tactful response to the work. "No one," she'd finally said, "could have painted these but you."

"It's all imaginary," Daniel told her now. "Money, books, even art—none of it is real, or, I should say, none of it will be real in the future, so why should it matter now?" He sank into a seat before the coffee table and gathered the envelopes scattered on it. "Know what these are?"

"Your mail?"

"Bills, all bills—MasterCard, Sears, Neiman-Marcus, Texaco." He ripped one open, then another and another, reading from their contents randomly. "Please remit, second notice, final notice, remit, remit, late penalty, and on and on. None of this means a thing to me because it isn't real, so why should I care about a bounced check? What are they going to do? Come after me? I'll make a big sale before then, get a huge commission, and pay everything off."

"What about the late fees?" Caridad asked. "What about interest? You'll wind up paying more for things than they're worth."

"I can always declare bankruptcy." Daniel clasped his hands together behind his head and leaned back, his legs outstretched and crossed at the ankles. "It's just money. Like I said, it's not real."

"It's real to me. You bounced that check in my store. I paid to cover it."

"Doesn't matter." He shook his head. "None of it."

At first, Caridad wanted to believe he had changed almost as much as he longed to convince her of this. He was her son's father. Maybe they might be together one day—a family. But this hope, like his commitment to change, had been all but forgotten, set aside like the dusty barbells. Daniel now reminded her of Alec d'Urberville proclaiming his newfound faith to Tess, whom he had raped and impregnated at the start of Hardy's novel. "You, and those like you," Tess had told Alec, "take your fill of pleasure on earth by making the life of such as me bitter and black with sorrow . . ."

"In the future," Daniel continued, "everything will be different. Nothing we have now, nothing we want now will be the same." He spoke in a smug way, as if he alone had such foresight.

She stood, pulled on her sweater, and shouldered her bag.

Daniel sat upright, eyebrows raised, his eyes wide. "What are you doing?"

"I'm leaving," Caridad said.

"You can't leave. You just got here."

"I have to go."

Daniel's face darkened, his eyes grew dull. "You *can't.*" He rose to block her path to the door, but when he spoke again, he softened his tone. "Are you upset because I said nothing we care about will matter in the future, that nothing is real?"

Caridad sidestepped him.

He caught her, reeled her close. "You're real. You and me—*we're* real. We'll always be real. I want to be with you. All the time. *That's* real."

"You can't say what's real and what isn't," she said. "You can't tell me what matters and what doesn't."

"So you just get up and leave and that's it?" Daniel's voice was low. "Like I don't know about Miles?"

His body radiated heat, a sour feral odor. She jerked away.

Daniel clasped her arm. "You think I couldn't prove it with a paternity test and sue you for visitation, even custody?" His fingers tightened, digging into her wrist.

The modular pieces, the monolithic television, the glass table, and the blanched canvases on the walls now swerved, rising and sinking like carousel horses. Caridad's former coworker Lisa was undergoing a bitter divorce in which her estranged husband was fighting for full custody of their daughter. ("These days," Lisa had complained, "fathers usually get whatever they want from the judges who are— guess what?—*men*, and a lot of them divorced, too.") Caridad took in Daniel's Oxford shirt, his cashmere pullover, his wool slacks, and his leather loafers. She glanced down at her faded work pants and scuffed gym shoes, noting these differences the way a judge might. Still, she struggled to wrench free.

"You're not going anywhere." Daniel grabbed her handbag, yanking it. The purse upended, spilling its contents. Caridad dropped to her knees to gather what had fallen out. The paperback novel landed near Daniel's feet. He scooped it up.

Caridad's dizzying dread flared into rage. "*Give that back.*"

"*Now* I have your attention." Daniel held open the book while she jammed wallet, tissues, pens, and receipts into her purse. "Your precious book here—you really believe there's something in this for *you*?" He flipped through the pages. "All the underlining, and what's this? Little notes—'violation, buried Sorrow, remember this, never forgive and never forget.'" His eyes bore into hers. "This is about *me*, isn't it?"

Caridad snorted. "Not everything is about you."

Daniel turned the book over, revealing a sketch of Hardy on the final page. "Oh, so I'm not all that, but this old bald guy, this *dead* guy is? Like he has some great message for you?"

"He does," she said.

"Oh yeah?" He cocked his head, a sarcastic smile on his face. "What's that?"

"People *don't* change. They just get sicker and sadder and *older*, and then they die."

As if deranged, Daniel began plucking out the book's pages, shredding these into small bits that drifted like snowflakes onto Caridad's head and shoulders. "Now what does he say, huh? What's the great message now?"

Caridad, still crouching, inched for the door. Daniel reeled her up by her hair, and when she was standing, scalp aflame, he trapped her in his arms. She writhed and twisted, kicking and elbowing him. He laced his fingers at the back of her neck, his thumbs on her throat. His grip tightened, cutting off her voice, her breath. Caridad made herself go limp. Her muscles loosened, her legs folded. She closed her eyes as if unconscious, and Daniel released her to the floor. Through the shadowy mesh of her lashes, she spied him striding toward the window and cranking the blinds shut. Caridad grabbed her bag, shot to her feet, and burst out the door. Footfalls bounced behind her, but she was already charging through the courtyard when Daniel pounded down the steps behind her. He was shouting, calling her back even as she slammed into her small car. With quaking fingers, she churned on the ignition and zoomed out of the parking lot, whooshing past Daniel, a hollow-eyed blur in the periphery.

As she sped toward the freeway, she approached a police station near the park. She nearly pulled over to file charges and have him arrested, but remembering her broken nose, that endless night, and its useless aftermath, Caridad accelerated toward the on-ramp, silently blessing Felicia's neurotic insistence on paying for an unlisted phone number. Daniel would have no way to find her. In minutes, she merged onto the freeway, thinking of the book she'd left behind and imagining how the story might turn out. Tess, of course, would marry good Angel Clare in "Fullfillment," and Alec d'Urberville would live out his wretched life in despair.

By Monday, Caridad welcomed the routine of work. Daniel, likely worried that she'd have him arrested, wouldn't dare confront her at the store. Since the paperwork to process her promotion would take several days, the week passed like most others, but for one unexpected encounter. On Thursday, she experienced what the deejay on the oldies station called a "blast from the past" when Noah—Jorge's best friend—wandered into the bookstore. Caridad noticed him at the same time he saw her, otherwise she would have slipped into the back room and waited until he left the store. Noah had gained weight and regrown his rust-colored beard, now streaked with silver, and his eyes were more recessed in his thickened face. Bearing a cash drawer to the back room, Caridad acknowledged him with a nod.

"Do you work *here* now?" Noah asked.

She bobbed her head again and issued a tight smile. "How're you?"

"I am well," he said.

"How's Geraldine?"

Noah averted his eyes from the cash drawer, as if Caridad were holding a platter of fresh dung. "Geraldine is also well. She's completed the program and now works as a veterinary nurse-practitioner at West Valley Agricultural."

Caridad pictured Noah's wife wearing a lab coat while jamming together the sex organs of farm animals. "And Jorge—how's he?"

"I must say, since you split up, his work has really flourished." Noah cast her a sidelong glance. "For one thing, he's stopped thinking small. No more clay pots, cookie jars, and the like. Now he's making ten-foot installations, tremendous things." He waved toward the magazine racks. "Any day now, I expect to see his work featured in *Artforum*."

"That's nice."

"And you?" Noah fixed Caridad with an accusing look. "Have you worked here since finishing your degree? When did you graduate again?"

Caridad's cheeks stung. "I actually got a little sidetracked."

"A *little* sidetracked." Noah laughed. "One is either sidetracked or not."

"Yes, well, I have to get back to work, but it's good to see you. Give my best to Geraldine and Jorge," she said, sure that Noah could barely wait to give them her very worst: the spiteful lowdown on how she had dropped out and was now working in retail. She might as well be tending fowl or milking cows like Tess of the d'Urbervilles. "My life," as Tess told the privileged Angel Clare, "looks as if it had been wasted for want of chances . . . I feel what a nothing I am."

"I will be sure to do so." Noah made his way toward the travel books as if to underscore that he was going places, while she was not. Caridad longed to call after his dumpy, round-shouldered back: *I'm about to become a dual-store manager—the first in the region! And my car is nearly new!* But this temptation struck Caridad as more pathetic than raking out chicken coops. She slunk to the back of the store, holding the cash tray against her midsection like a cigarette girl, a bit player in a black-and-white film, the coins chinking with each step.

On Saturday night, Caridad closed the store with Alibi Al. Since he'd learned of her promotion to dual-store manager, Alvin didn't bother to conceal his contempt. He'd ignored the full cart of new books to shelve and spent much of his shift erecting an architecturally startling display of Stephen King's *The Dead Zone*—a table arranged with helical spires twisting around one another, an intricate arrangement sure to domino-topple the first time a customer reached for a book. Clearly, Alvin had read the recent issue of the company newsletter, in which regional managers named their three favorite titles. Vera had listed *The Dead Zone*, *The Dead Zone*, and *The Dead Zone* as her trio of best-loved books. "There," he told Caridad when he'd finished. "Make sure to take all the credit when Vera sees this."

At the register, Caridad shook her head. "She wouldn't believe me. No one could have built that but you."

"True." He folded the step stool he'd been using.

The phone on the counter blurted a half-ring, and then a full ring sounded, followed by another. "Leave it," she told Alvin. "We're closed."

When she turned to unlock a cash drawer, Alvin barreled past her to snatch up the receiver. "Periwinkle Books," he said. "How may I help you?" He went silent as a flat voice buzzed from the receiver. "Yes, she's right here. Hold on." Alvin cupped the mouthpiece. "We're not supposed to take personal calls on the *business* line."

"Then hang up."

Alvin stubbornly held out the phone to her.

Caridad reached around him to press the switch hook.

"Well, excuse me." Alvin's face paled, but his voice was haughty. "I forgot that your word is god's law now—"

"Alvin, you can go," Caridad said, "and after I count down the drawers, I'll fill out your redundancy report. Or you can stop talking, cash out your drawer, and count it down in back."

Wordlessly, he closed down his register, yanked out the drawer, and stomped off.

The phone rang again and again. Neither she nor Alvin answered it, though Caridad lifted it to hang up once more, and then she left the receiver off the hook. Over the past week, she'd thought of the many bills littering Daniel's glass coffee table. Despite the contrast between his new suits and her worn work clothes, Caridad had money in the bank, but more than that, she had her mother, her sisters, and Gray. She had resources he lacked. If Daniel fought her for custody of Miles, she would win with these—she *had* to win.

Just before she turned out the lights and exited the store for the night, Caridad replaced the receiver on its base. As she locked the door from outside, the phone began ringing once more—a strident but muffled sound from where she stood, like the insistent cry of a solitary bird, shrieking and shrieking from some faraway place.

When Caridad returned home, she found Felicia in the kitchen, filling the teakettle. Though it was nearly eleven, her sister was still dressed in Levi's and a sweatshirt, even wearing the chanclas she usually kicked off the moment she stepped indoors. "Ah," Felicia said, "look who's here. The weekly rendezvous canceled, I presume."

Caridad hung her purse on a chair. "What are you talking about?"

"Every Saturday night, you're out until one or two in the morning. You think I haven't noticed?" Felicia's lovely face looked haggard. "I know you have something going on. I only hope it's not with that motherfucker who broke your face. You've *got* to be smarter than that."

"It doesn't matter." Caridad said, stunned that Felicia had not flung this in her face when they bickered. "It's over now."

"You and Espie must have some tag-team arrangement. It's like you take turns tormenting me. Now, apparently, it's her turn."

"What's going on?"

Felicia twisted off the tap and set the kettle on a burner. "It's like a chemical spill between her and Reynaldo. It's fucking toxic over there—total hell for Mimi. *That's* what I was trying to tell her tonight. She got all bent out of shape and said I should leave. As usual, whenever I try to help you two out, I get my head bitten off. No one wants to listen to me."

Caridad reached for her sister's shoulder, stiff as Sheetrock under her palm. "I know."

—

That night Caridad dreamed of riding in a car driven by a dead man named Thomas. He was an older man, a white man in his fifties or sixties. He wore a crisp dress shirt, a checked tie, and a gray tweed blazer. His head was egg-shaped, neatly balanced above his starched collar. Short wavy hair receded from his forehead, dark brown but grizzled about the ears. His face was smooth; his black eyes deep set, embedded in folds of flesh under bristly brows; and his straight nose broadened at the nostrils, just above a thick handlebar moustache. She knew him and she didn't. He had the look of a sensitive, even delicate, man, but Caridad was sure he was once hardy. Though his dress and moustache signaled a much earlier era, Thomas had just died. Eyes open, he gazed off into the middle distance as if absorbed in lonesome thoughts.

Caridad was in the passenger seat beside him on her way to get ice cream for Miles. The car slowed, drifting from lane to lane. That's when she noticed the deceased driver, but she didn't panic. Instead, Caridad treated this as a practical problem: How does one go for ice cream in a car driven by a dead man? She nudged his foot off the gas pedal and clasped the steering wheel when a faraway bomb detonated with a muffled boom, a percussive blast that was followed by another and another: *Bam, bam, bam.*

She jackknifed to sit upright, fully awake. Miles snored softly in his bed nearby; the room was otherwise cloaked in shadowy silence. Then an explosive bang shook the walls, and Caridad jumped. The banging continued. She kicked off bedding and rushed to the kitchen. Someone was pounding on the back door. The overhead light snapped on, and Felicia, in a bathrobe, appeared at the threshold, making her way toward the entry. "What the hell?" Before Caridad could stop her, Felicia pulled the door wide.

Esperanza burst in, bearing a sleeping Mimi over one shoulder. "What took you so long?" she whispered. "I knocked and knocked like forever."

Caridad took her niece from Esperanza to settle her in bed with Miles, her sisters' low voices emanating from the kitchen.

"What happened?" Felicia asked.

"I did it," Esperanza said. "I finally did it, and I'm never going back. I swear, not ever."

Mimi groaned as Caridad lowered her into the bed beside Miles, who'd curled toward the wall. She tugged the blanket out from under Mimi to cover her. Caridad tucked her in, and the little girl released a long sigh. It stirred the air, whooshing like a wing stroke in the still and darkened room.

Damage of Isolation

———

One early morning in June, Caridad woke to a harsh and howling wind that batted a tree's branch against the window to the bedroom she now shared with Miles and Mimi. The leafy limb whipped the paned glass until the lashing sound worked into tags of her dream. In it, she was goaded on in the way a horse is driven by a whip flicking in earshot. Moments later, Mimi shot up in bed, howling. Caridad whisked her niece out of the top bunk—before Miles woke—and into her own bed to comfort her. Soon, the tense bundle of Mimi's body softened, her breathing slowed, and she drifted back to sleep. Just as Caridad was dozing, Mimi shrieked again, this time waking Miles.

Caridad shepherded both children into the kitchen and settled them at the table. Soundlessly, she pulled a saucepan from a cupboard and eased open the refrigerator for the milk. As she poured milk into the pan, Mimi's kitten Smoky skittered underfoot. The little black cat wove between her ankles, purring and then mewing loudly, and Felicia appeared in the threshold, a cranky look on her face. "What's going on?"

"Nothing." Caridad lit the stove and settled the pot on it. "Go back to bed."

"Oh, *right*." Felicia cinched the belt to her robe. "I'll be sure to do that while you're in here banging around."

Caridad shrugged. "Suit yourself."

Esperanza shared a bedroom with Felicia as she had when they were younger, and bunk beds had been installed in Caridad's room for Miles and Mimi. The books Caridad read at bedtime these days were illustrated tales that involved talking animals, elves, or fairies, before lights were turned off so the children could sleep. Caridad hadn't opened a novel since finishing *Tess of the d'Urbervilles* months ago. Now she barely remembered the details in it. After Daniel had destroyed her stripped copy, she'd borrowed another from the library to read the ending, and she'd been bitter with disappointment at how Tess was punished. *That* she remembered. It also seemed ages ago since she'd last seen Daniel—a hollow-eyed blur in the periphery as she'd sped away from his apartment. Apart from occasional calls to the store late on Saturday nights—calls she suspected were from him and never answered—Caridad hadn't heard from him again. But weeks ago, she'd run into Caleb at a gas station near campus, and he'd told her that Daniel had lost his sales job. He was working at the library again.

"There were *pirates* under my bed," Mimi now told Miles.

Miles gasped. "*When?*"

"It was just a dream." Caridad stirred the milk, sweet steam wafting from the pot. "We don't have pirates here." She glanced at Felicia's sour-looking face, the snaky strands of hair that trailed past her shoulders. *A witch, perhaps, but no pirates.*

Nightmares had awakened Mimi before, but usually Caridad calmed her without disturbing Miles. Despite these, Mimi appeared untroubled, even pleased with her new living arrangement. When they first moved into Mama's house, Esperanza had explained to Mimi that though she and her father both loved her very much, they could no longer live together. She encouraged Mimi to ask questions and talk about her feelings. Mimi had only one question: "Can we get a kitten?" Reynaldo despised cats and would not allow one in their house. Esperanza drove Mimi and Miles to the animal shelter on her next day off, and there they'd picked out Smoky.

Miles, not quite two at the time, had adjusted well to Gray's departure, though he missed him. Unlike Reynaldo, Gray, after introducing himself as Leslie and explaining as best she could the transformation she was undergoing, called Miles often and sent him pictures and letters from Colorado, along with small gifts when she could. Reynaldo, though at first outraged and obsessive about calling Esperanza, now rarely phoned, and when he did, it had to do with financial matters. He'd speak to Mimi only after Esperanza reminded him to say hello to her, and he had yet to take advantage of the visitation he was granted during the separation. While Esperanza was relieved that Reynaldo wouldn't fight her for custody, she worried his indifference would hurt Mimi.

Smoky extended her forepaws to stand upright against Caridad's leg, yowling. Felicia sighed and reached into a shelf under the sink. She rattled kibble into the cat's dish. "Put more milk in the pot," Felicia said. "I may as well have some, too."

Later, at the Encino bookstore, Caridad released a yawn so wide her jaw popped. Then she yawned again and again as she unpacked the boxes in which the computerized registers had arrived. After assembling these, she'd hurry to Studio City to install that store's system. She spread the hardware and cords on the counter before poring over pages of poorly translated directions printed in pale green ink. At the top of the first page of these appeared this warning: *Do Not Immersion in Water. To Avoid Damage of Isolation!* Caridad now read the instructions aloud, hoping this would make them clearer. "Insert the masculine blue wires into her female outlet jack circle and modem will branch into drive easy here." *Blue wires?* Only black and brown cords had been provided. Caridad was reexamining the ends of these non-blue cords for an insert that looked as if it might fit in the modem's outlet when Val popped into the back room to tell her there was a problem up front.

Caridad tossed the wires on the counter. She trailed Val, wishing she had scheduled someone more competent to cover the sales floor while she struggled with the system in back. Val led Caridad to confront a stocky towheaded man standing before a stack of books on the sales counter. His pinkish skin was blotched and crusty with silvery patches like fish scales. Small rectangular glasses perched low on his upturned nose.

"How can I help you?" Caridad asked.

He pointed at Val. "She refuses to take my check."

"He doesn't have his license," Val said. "We can't accept checks without a photo ID."

"Look, my office is down the block. I just dashed over for a few books, grabbed my checkbook, but left my wallet in my desk. Surely you can make an exception this one time."

"I'm *so* sorry," Val said.

The man snorted. "I'll bet."

"If your office is nearby," Caridad said, "why don't you go for your wallet? We'll hold your books for you."

He shook his head with such force that flakes of patchy skin sifted onto the countertop as if his face were shedding itself. "Of all the senseless, idiotic . . . Christ, I'm in here all the time. You've taken my checks for years. Everyone knows me."

Caridad, certain she would have remembered such a man, squinted at him in doubt.

Val turned to her. "*I've* never seen him before."

"You're supposed to be the store manager," he said. "Use your brain, will you? Take the check. Sell some books. Isn't that your damn job?"

Caridad clenched her jaw. Exhaustion, frustration, and now hunger—since she skipped lunch to install the system—pinched off all patience. Not trusting herself to speak, she shook her head.

"Fine." He snatched his check off the counter. "This isn't the end of it. I can promise you that." The man whirled away and flounced out of the store.

Later that day, Caridad, after setting up the new computers in Encino, arrived at the Studio City store to repeat the task. The incoherent instructions were printed in faded orange ink this time, so she was glad she'd brought along the more readable directions from Encino. She unpacked the boxes and rummaged through the Styrofoam blocks and pellets, unable to find the necessary wiring. She was double-checking shipping cartons when the phone trilled on the sales floor. The clerk up front buzzed her to pick up in back. "Periwinkle Books," she said. "How may I help you?"

"It's me." Vera's voice blasted through the earpiece. "Just what the hell happened while I was at lunch?"

"I set up the computers, though the instructions are awful. Now I'm putting together the Studio City system, but I can't find the cables," Caridad said. "Why? What's going on?"

"A customer called corporate—says he's a regular and you refused to sell him books."

"Oh, *that*." Caridad nested the phone between her jaw and collarbone. While she shook out the many boxes in which the hardware had been shipped, she explained what had happened. "I put the books on hold for him."

"Listen to me." Vera spoke with slow purpose, as if addressing a dimwitted child. "You're coming back here to pick up those books right now, and you're delivering them to the customer."

"But I'm in the middle of—"

"And get this, will you? You're not going to charge him one penny. Do you hear me? You're marking those books down to zero. Then you'll apologize and promise it will *never* happen again."

"I can't," Caridad said. "I have to pick up my son at day care by six." In truth, Esperanza had already collected Miles more than an hour ago, but she hoped the excuse would exempt her from the humiliating errand.

"Honestly, I don't give a shit about your day-care issues," Vera told her. "After you deliver the books, get your ass back to Studio City to finish with those computers. All systems need to be operational by midnight. I hope I'm being clear as fucking crystal."

The phone clicked. The dial tone buzzed like an insect in Caridad's ear.

After dropping off the books to the complaining customer, Caridad cruised along Burbank Boulevard from Encino back to Studio City. She drove slowly, glancing at the darkened offices, restaurants, and shops. The people who worked in these places were likely on their way home or already enjoying an evening meal. Between her two stores, Caridad often put in fifty- to sixty-hour work weeks. She earned enough so that she could afford a place of her own, but if she moved out of her mother's house, who would look after Miles when she worked evenings and weekends? Before leaving the bookstore, Caridad had called Esperanza, asking her to bathe Miles after supper and to put him to bed. She drove past a flower shop, café, real estate office, camera store, bakery—all of them vacant and locked up. Darkened plate-glass windows mirrored the street and Caridad's car streaking past like a silvery fish.

Earlier, the complaining customer had led Caridad into his spacious office where a vast ebony desk stood before a throne-like leather chair. His nameplate read *Philip T. Jefferson, Esquire*. Embossed business cards, arrayed in an onyx tray, indicated that he specialized in personal injury/workers' compensation law. A snippet from a hectoring TV commercial rang in Caridad's head: *If you've been injured at work, don't delay! Call Jefferson and Meyers right away!* As he sidestepped her, a roseate bald spot flashed at least an inch below her nose. Short but dense, he outweighed her, though Caridad could probably take him in a fair fight. In an unfair one, she'd brain him with the books and whip around to kick his buttocks while he reeled from the first blow. Pleased by this thought, Caridad gazed about. Between glass-encased bookshelves, the mauve walls were decorated with framed certificates and many photos of racehorses. The scaly man sank into the leather chair and gestured for Caridad to take the seat across from his desk. Holding the books to her chest, she shook her head.

"Maybe," Philip T. Jefferson, Esquire, said, "this will teach you a little something about the lost art of customer service." He produced the check he'd written earlier that day. "Here."

Caridad approached the desk to deposit the books. "I don't want your money." She waved away the check and glanced about the office again—leather furniture, black desk, glass-encased bookshelves, and those many framed photos of horses, some of these wearing floral wreaths. She thought of Miles, his face dewy, his hair damp and smelling of shampoo after a bath. Then she pictured the modem, hard drive, and monitor she'd set out on the receiving counter—the system she had to assemble without wiring before she could go home. Caridad had swallowed hard, cleared her throat. "I don't need anything from you."

The setting sun lit the boulevard with a flaming glow of infinite wattage; the effect was radiantly, even gloriously, blinding. A dicey driver in perfect visibility, Caridad lowered the visor and hunched closer to the steering wheel. Periwinkle Studio City would be closed by the time she arrived, and Caridad could put together the computer system undistracted by customers. A strip mall appeared a few blocks ahead with two lit stores, one of these an Electronics Plus. She flicked on the blinker and turned into the parking lot. Broken glass glinted in the spaces before the electronics store, so she parked in front of a nearby beauty salon. Caridad glanced in at an olive-skinned redhead who was sweeping the salon's floor. The pink-smocked woman looked up at her in a beckoning way. How Caridad would love to have her hair washed and cut, the warm touch of hands on her scalp, the ticklish snip of scissors, and a soft brush whisking the nape of her neck. But she'd trudged past the salon, as if drawn like a moth to the neighboring store's glaring signage, neon script that read *Electronics Plus Equals Customer Service Plus*.

The store was manned by a solitary clerk with pale green eyes and thick black hair. He looked to be the same age as the college students Caridad hired at the bookstore as temporary help over the holidays. In a white shirt, narrow tie, and black slacks, he was overdressed for selling electronic equipment. "I'm about to close up," he called out, his voice garbled in a way that Caridad associated with the profoundly deaf. When she approached the desk, she spied flesh-toned hearing aids embedded in his ears.

"I really need some help," she said in a loud voice.

He watched her lips. "What is it?"

She explained about the missing wires, the system she had to install, and she showed him the instructions she'd brought along.

"I know what you need," he said in his mangled way. "First, let me lock up." He hurried to the glass door in front and twisted the bolt. Then he switched off the neon sign and the fluorescent lighting overhead, leaving a desk lamp lit at the counter. He summoned her to join him at a display of cords and wires along the back wall. He pulled various plastic-wrapped packages down, saying, "You'll need this, one of these, and probably this." His forearms, visible under the dress shirt's rolled-up sleeves, were well muscled and densely furred with black hair; his hands were large but deft. In the darkened store, Caridad drew near to take the packages he offered. A warm clove scent emanated from his skin, and when his finger brushed her wrist, static sparked, zinging like a rubber band snapped against her skin.

"I think this is everything you need."

Caridad nodded.

"Once you have the right wires, it's pretty easy." He looked into her eyes. "Are you okay?"

Her throat tightened, and her eyes filled. He was the first kind person to speak to her since she'd left the house that morning. "I'm sorry to keep you like this at closing," she said.

"It's okay." His green eyes glimmered, his teeth flashed when he smiled.

Caridad's pulse stuttered, her flesh prickling as if thousands of bubbles were bursting pleasurably over her arms and face. On a whim, she perched on the tips of her toes—because he was much taller than she—to kiss him full on the mouth. He flinched in surprise, but his arms encircled her waist. She drew his hips toward hers. A current flooded her, thrumming in her throat and ears until her head swarmed with longing.

He pulled back to say, "My name's Carl." His breathing now as ragged as her own, he kissed her again.

"Can we go in there?" Caridad pointed to a door marked *Employees Only*.

Carl took her hand and led her through the back door. In a stock room similar to those in the bookstores, Carl layered collapsed boxes on the concrete floor. His white shirt strained across his broad back as he piled the cardboard. *I should go*, Caridad told herself. *The computers!* But when he lowered himself to sit cross-legged on the flattened boxes and grinned up at her, she sank into his arms without speaking. On the cardboard nest, he stroked her long hair until static sparked again. Caridad pulled off her sweater and unhitched her bra. Carl quickly unbuttoned his shirt and shrugged it off. He unbelted his slacks and slid out of them and his boxers at the same time. Then he reached for his wallet and pulled a condom from it.

"Do you do this often?" Caridad asked.

"Not really. Not ever." He held up the wrapped condom. "I've had this a *long* time."

She wriggled out of her pants and pulled him close. Her hands shook, her legs quivered. His touch was tentative, as if his body were asking of hers: *Is this good? What about now? Do you like this? This?* Yes, she wanted to tell him. Yes, and don't stop. "Okay," Carl said in her ear as if she'd spoken aloud—and maybe she had. "But I have to go slow or I won't last." And in this way, he didn't stop, not after the first, second, or third time for her, not until long after she'd lost track.

When they pulled apart, Carl glanced at his watch. He said he'd missed an awards banquet he was supposed to attend. "Anyways," he said with another grin.

"Were you getting an award?" Caridad asked. Surely, he deserved one.

"Not me. My brother," he said. "I have a twin brother who plays football."

"College football?"

He shook his head and mumbled something that sounded like "night school."

"*Night* school?" echoed Caridad. Did night schools have football teams?

"No, not night school," he said. "*High* school—he plays football in high school."

That familiar ocean churned in Caridad's head. "You're in high school?"

"I'm a senior."

"How old are you?"

"Eighteen." He smiled again and asked her to tell him her name.

"Caridad."

"Calidad?" he said, pronouncing her name so it sounded like the Spanish word for "quality."

Not even close, thought Caridad, but she said, "That's right." She gathered her clothes and began dressing.

"Do you have to go?"

"I do."

After they were dressed, he rang up the sale. She paid for the purchase, and he kissed her again. Though he said he didn't do well on the phone, Carl jotted his number and work schedule on the back of her receipt. "Will I see you again?" He was just eighteen, still in high school, and she was in her mid-twenties, a mother, and dual-store manager.

She looked deep into those jade-colored eyes, certain she would never see him again. "Of course," she said.

Still quaking with pleasant aftershocks, she wobbled toward her car. She stopped in front of the hair salon and glanced back at Carl, who was watching her through the window. Caridad raised a hand and smiled. Inside the salon, the redhead, now mopping the floor, caught sight of this and waved back.

Less than two blocks from the Studio City bookstore, Caridad stopped at a red light, debating whether or not to pull into the drive-thru hamburger stand just ahead. The smoky scent of charred beef wafted into the car. Her mouth flooded, her stomach moaned. Now ravenous, she felt like an animal, instinct driven and lacking in self-control. *What kind of woman am I?* Caridad wondered. Nothing like Isabel Archer, resigned to a loveless marriage out of stubborn virtue, and not at all like Hardy's Tess, who'd unsuccessfully spurned Alec d'Urberville. Perhaps she was more like Carrie Meeber, bedding men to make her way in the world, though Dreiser neglected to mention her physical desires. And while mythological gods were a randy lot, the immortal or mortal females of character were not all that lustful. No way would Antigone, for example, fornicate with a high-school kid in an Electronics Plus.

Was this the longest red light in the world, or what?

Maybe she was like Madame Bovary, though Caridad cared little for the fineries that proved nearly as irresistible to Emma as her lovers, and she couldn't imagine ever swallowing arsenic. Caridad also lacked the melancholic determination to throw herself under a train like Anna Karenina. Why did passionate women so often take their lives to relieve their suffering? Why so much suffering? Even Lady Chatterley put up with way too much before leaving her impotent, narcissistic, and controlling husband to wait for the groundskeeper, who, though sexy, was likewise bossy. Could Caridad be a superannuated Lolita? Poor Dolores Haze was passed like a preteen blow-up doll from one middle-aged pedophile to another before she matured—grew pregnant, plain, and bespectacled—and married a deaf young man. Wasn't he named Carl, too? Caridad felt for her wallet to find the receipt where he'd written his schedule. At last, the signal flashed green. She lifted her foot from the brake to press the gas pedal.

Cause and effect. Caridad would later marvel how doing so little could undo so much. "The works and days of hands," a poet said. Visions and revisions. The intricate tapestry of a life so far. A pattern sometimes picked apart but rewoven until a design issued. A foot lifted from one pedal and lowered onto another, nearly as small a thing as tugging a loose thread. And all of it unraveled. Tires shrieked, metal crunched, glass splintered. The skunky stench of scorched rubber bloomed in a dark obliterating cloud. Fissures fractured concrete, and again the earth gaped wide. The dank well opened once more, and Caridad tumbled down and down and down, into the dark and silent abyss.

Was it minutes, hours, or days later, when sound, as if asking permission to enter, first rapped at her brain? Tap, tap, tap, beeping, whirring, then the whisper of fabric parting, and somewhere in the background, the persistent *brr-ring, brr-ring, brr-ring* of an unanswered telephone.

"Periwinkle Books." Caridad raised her head and was bludgeoned by a blinding flash—something arctic white but searing, sharp as a burning blade. Fire *and* ice? She sank back, clenching her eyes shut.

Footfalls and voices: "She said something."

"Stay with us, honey. Come on now."

Voiceless, Caridad moved her lips. *How may I help you?*

When she woke again, slats of sunshine striped an aquamarine blanket on which hands shaped much like her own rested. But these hands were too still and waxen, too disconnected and strange to be hers. One wrist was taped, transparent tubes secured to the veins. Caridad doubted she could impel movement of these fingers. Then, with a flicker of thought, a thumb twitched. The glowing bands of light stung her eyes. "Turn it off," she said.

"Turn what off?" A girlish voice rang out. Then a stiff-faced woman with amber eyes and rubied lips sharpened into focus. Glass-bead earrings, intricate things dangling like miniature chandeliers from long-lobed ears. Frothy pink chiffon spun like cotton candy under the sharp chin.

"*Leslie?*"

The bright mouth curved into a smile. Leslie lifted one of those pale hands and cupped it warmly. "You're awake."

Window, white walls, aluminum cabinets and sink, narrow bed, its curtain-shrouded neighbor nearby, a swing-arm tray holding a sweating plastic pitcher—ochre, a color she abhorred—a clean and well-lighted place. "What happened?" Caridad said.

"You had a car accident—a pretty bad one," Leslie told her.

"Miles! How's Miles?"

"He's fine. He wasn't in the car with you."

"Where is he?"

"He's at your mother's with Esperanza and Mimi. I flew in as soon as Felicia called."

Dark guilt gathered, massing into a shadowy cloud—the conviction that she'd done something terrible, something she couldn't even remember now. "Was it my fault? Was anyone hurt? Or killed?"

Leslie shook her head. "No, honey, it wasn't your fault. It was a busload of tourists from Malaysia. The driver ran a red light and hit your car. No one else was seriously injured."

"Malaysia?" What did tourists from Malaysia have against her? "What about my car?"

"It's totaled."

"Oh." Caridad closed her eyes. Light flamed through her lids—a harsh scarlet glow. Her temples throbbed.

"Felicia's here. She's been waiting to see you."

"Not now." Caridad shook her head, detonating a sickening series of small blasts in her brain. "Can you turn it off?"

"Turn what off, honey? What do you want me to turn off?"

"The light—will you please just shut it off?" She compelled those hand-shaped things to tug the aqua blanket over her head as Leslie closed the blinds.

Later, Caridad drew the covers from her face. A black-robed figure wafted toward her. Her eyes traveled up the dark broadcloth toward a small upright rectangle of white at the collar and beyond that to an oddly familiar face, a hank of sun-bleached hair spilling into his eyes. "Leland?" she said. "Leland McWhorter?" He nodded, issuing a long-dimpled grin, and he tucked something into her hands. Caridad's fingers skimmed pebbly leather, embossed print, pages—a book.

"The New Testament," he said. "The Book of Revelation—have you read it?"

Caridad shook her head, and he was gone.

Mama then entered the room, bearing a steaming Styrofoam cup. "You're awake, m'ija?" she said. "Do you want something to drink? Some tea?"

Caridad shook her head. "Did you see that man?"

"Where?"

"A priest—did you see him in the hallway?"

"I didn't see anyone," Mama said. "It's late. The visiting hours are over. They only let me stay because Esperanza knows the nurses here from school."

"That's strange because I just *saw* him."

Mama shrugged. "If you want to know something strange, it's that lady over there." She jutted her chin to indicate the curtain-shrouded bed across the room.

"There's someone there?" Caridad whispered.

Mama nodded. "She sleeps a lot, like you. But I've seen her, and she is the spit and image of Imelda Marcos, tu sabes, from the Philippines."

"*Spitting* image." Caridad yawned, her eyelids now fluttering shut again.

"And her husband," Mama continued, "is exactly Ferdinand Marcos. He wears those puffy riding pants with boots." She sipped her tea. "Maybe that was him you saw."

Felicia and Esperanza appeared at her bedside in the morning. They came to relieve Mama, who'd spent the night with her, dozing upright in the visitor's chair, while Caridad faded in and out, lofting about in a twilight sleep. That morning, Esperanza, like a fairy-tale prince, woke Caridad with a peck on her cheek. The narcotic fog finally lifted, and she snapped her eyes open to glimpse her sister's round face, withdrawing after the moist smack of her lips.

"How are you?"

"I don't know." Caridad lifted her shoulders to shrug, but these felt strapped into a harness, a spiked chain-metal thing, a medieval torture device that pinned her to the hospital bed, piercing her with mind-blanking pain when she tried to move. Her eyes filled and she bit her lower lip to keep from crying out.

Dimples dented Esperanza's full cheeks. "You're going to be fine. I know it probably doesn't seem like it now, but little by little, you're going to feel better and better." Her tone was upbeat in a practiced way that troubled Caridad. She jockeyed for a look over Esperanza's shoulder.

Felicia's blanched face bobbed like a balloon in the background. "I knew this would happen. I knew it when you bought that car. You're a shitty driver." Felicia's voice broke. "You're the worst ever."

Esperanza shook her head. "It wasn't even her fault."

"I *am* awful at driving," Caridad said.

"You're just trying to make me cry." Felicia rushed out of the room.

Esperanza drew nearer. "Can I get you anything?"

Under the odor of antiseptic soap, Caridad whiffed cinnamon and nutmeg, the cloying fragrance of pumpkin pie. "What's that smell?"

Esperanza stepped around to the nightstand beside the bed. "It's potpourri with a get-well card." She lifted the card and opened it. "It's from Vera. Do you want me to read it?"

"Go ahead."

She showed Caridad the card: a pigtailed girl propped in bed with a thermometer in her mouth. "'Hope you feel better . . .'" Esperanza read before opening to the inside flap. "'Real soon.' *Hmm* . . . Here's what she wrote inside: 'Caridad, I'm sorry to hear about the accident you had on your way home from work. Everyone at Periwinkle Books sends warm wishes for a speedy recovery. Vera.'" Esperanza gave Caridad a puzzled look. "Didn't you ask me to put Miles to bed because you had to work late? I didn't know you were heading home."

"I wasn't."

Esperanza bit her lower lip in a pensive way. "But Vera seems to think—"

"She *knew*. I don't know why she says I was on my way home."

"I do," Esperanza said. "Liability, that's why." At the hospital where she worked, Esperanza sometimes dealt with workers' compensation and personal injury claims. "Don't you see? If she can make you think you were injured outside of working hours, the company is off the hook. You need a lawyer, Dah-Dah, a mean one, right away."

What was his name, the flaky-skinned lawyer? It would come to her. "I think I know someone with high standards for customer service, and he's a real ass."

Esperanza held up the scented sachet. "What do you want me to do with this?"

The potpourri was Vera's all-purpose gift, presented for holidays, birthdays, and anniversaries. Once, when Miles had strep throat, Vera gave Caridad a pouch for him, as if it were just the thing for a sick little boy. "Throw it away, will you? Take it out first, though. I can't stand that smell."

Esperanza pinched the sachet's drawstring and held it at arm's length as if grasping a rodent by the tail. "Anything else you need?"

"Miles! I want to see Miles and Mimi."

"Sorry, no kids allowed on this floor. If I worked here, I could sneak them in. But think about it, Dah-Dah. Don't you want to wait until you're better before they see you?"

Caridad gasped. "Do I look *that* bad?"

"No, not to me, of course not, not at all, but it might be upsetting—"

"How badly am I hurt?" Caridad winced, remembering how long it took her fractured leg to mend, those awful crutches. "Is anything broken?"

"No broken bones, I swear." Esperanza dangled the mesh pouch. "Let me throw this junk out. I'll be right back and tell you everything I know, okay?"

Caridad nodded, palpating her tender face. "Bring me a mirror, will you?"

As Esperanza turned to leave, she stumbled and caught herself on the bed frame. "What's this?" She stooped for the obstacle that tripped her. "A book?"

"I must've dropped it." Caridad took the black leather-bound book from Esperanza.

"You're reading a prayer book?"

"Someone gave it to me last night."

"Was that creepy priest here?" Esperanza clicked her tongue. "Big guy, wearing a polka-dotted clown suit with red Bozo hair?"

Caridad flashed on Leland's long-dimpled grin. "He didn't look like a clown. What's his name?"

"He calls himself Father Clown from Get-Well Town. He hangs around hospitals, handing out these books or little teddy bears. I wish he'd given you a bear instead."

"I'd prefer a novel." Caridad set the leather-bound book aside. "But a bear would have been nice."

When Esperanza returned, she had a file sleeve tucked under one arm and a paperback in her other hand. "I found this for you. *Moll Flanders*—have you read it before?"

"No, I haven't." Caridad reached for the book. "Thanks."

Esperanza closed the door before sitting down and opening the file sleeve. "I'm not supposed to have this, but I know the girl at the desk from nursing school."

"What is it?"

"Your chart." Esperanza flipped the file open and rifled its pages. "Okay, here goes . . ."

Caridad couldn't understand much of what Esperanza read. The pain-killer haze settled over her again. What did it mean that she had subluxation and increased laxity in the spine? The hematoma on her left femur, okay, a bruise on the bone—she got that. But Caridad couldn't tell a C2 from a C3, and she had no idea what posterior longitudinal ligament involvement meant. She watched the pupils of her sister's brown eyes tracking as she read.

Finally, she interrupted Esperanza. "I'm kind of fading. Could you sum things up?"

Esperanza flipped through the remaining pages, scanning these. "They'll probably release you in a few days, but you could have nerve damage and back problems, along with some pain."

"For how long?"

"That depends . . ."

"What's the worst it could be?" Caridad wriggled her shoulders and was again pierced by that searing flash. "Will it last for the rest of my life?"

"It doesn't have to be that way," Esperanza said. "There are clinical trials, treatments, and therapies. You're young and healthy—"

"Did you bring a mirror?"

Esperanza fixed her eyes on the file in her lap. "Couldn't find one." She was nearly as bad as Felicia at dissembling.

"That's okay," said Caridad, who—unlike her sisters—had a knack for telling lies. "I'm sure I'll be fine."

The Voice of the Sea

Gerard Hochner's eyes glimmered, his cheeks flamed. His mouth was a blur, his lips barely keeping pace with the rapid flow of his speech. Angry Young Man, Caridad called him privately, AYM, for short. She'd taken Victorian literature with him in the fall semester, so she was used to his outbursts, though they'd alarmed her at first. While angry and male, Gerard was no younger than Caridad, but his penchant for animated argument made him seem adolescent, even childish to her. She imagined herself hauling Gerard out of his seat and removing him to a quiet place until he grew calm. Though she'd never struck Miles, Caridad now pictured herself turning Angry Young Man over her knee to smack the flat bottom of his saggy jeans.

She glanced at the wall clock mounted over the shelves of books written by faculty members at the university where, after finishing her undergraduate studies with the help of summer coursework, she now worked toward a master of arts degree in English literature. The room was cramped and windowless. An oblong table and black vinyl chairs took up so much space that students had to squeeze in, jostling past one another to claim seats. According to the clock's sallow face, the seminar would end in ten minutes, yet Angry Young Man seemed nowhere near to winding up. Directly across the table from Gerard, the professor, a mild man with sandy hair and wire-rimmed glasses, tilted his chair back against the wall, his eyes half closed and small puffy hands folded over his vast stomach.

Caridad swallowed a yawn. After she decorated the date—January 24, 1983—at the top of her notes with vines, leaves, and blossoms, her gaze flitted about the classroom, alighting like a winged insect on the others seated around the scarred table, one by one. To the right of Angry Young Man was Hilda Swan, an angular blond known for vague and baffling utterances. Next to Hilda perched Linda Burke, a plump brunette in her fifties who'd returned to college after her children were grown. Beside Linda, Lance Chu hunkered over his notes. Lance, an Asian studies scholar, rarely spoke, though he made much racket unwrapping granola bars at the start of each session. Appreciative of self-imposed silence, Caridad claimed a seat close to Lance's. To her right was the professor, followed by the high school teachers, a trio of exhausted-looking and apologetic women who were taking the seminar for continuing education credit. Near the teachers—whom he treated in a courtly manner that amused them—sat Harrison McCann, a former actor in his late thirties, a lantern-jawed man with light brown hair and twinkling turquoise eyes. McCann, as Caridad thought of him, usually performed the role of enforcer, settling questions of authority in the sleepy professor's favor with his deep voice.

"So it's no wonder the book was critically condemned and banned," AYM's tone pitched toward crescendo, filling Caridad with hope that his diatribe would soon end. "What the character does to resolve her conflict is unconscionable, even immoral. Never mind her infidelity—as a mother of young children, she has *no right* to take her life."

They were discussing *The Awakening* by Kate Chopin, a book that reignited Caridad's passion for novels, the ardor that had dimmed while she recovered from the car accident. Though Caridad's policy was to tune out Gerard Hochner, his criticism of Edna Pontellier offended her in the way it would if he'd insulted her sisters.

"So," the professor said, "a woman with children forfeits choices over her own life?"

Gerard dipped his head in a decisive way. "Certain choices, yes."

McCann wore a pensive look on his jut-jawed face. Linda Burke smiled and nodded at Gerard in an encouraging way. Two of the schoolteachers were slyly grading papers in their laps. The third was dozing, though her book was propped to hide her face.

Caridad drew breath to speak, but Lance beat her to it, ending weeks of elective muteness to say, "That is such bullshit."

Gerard drove his fingers through his hair. He blinked rapidly, his lashes fluttering like frantic moths. "Bullshit? *Bullshit?* How is it bullshit to denounce a woman for deserting her children, leaving them to deal with the fact that she chose death over them?" Spittle misted the dull tabletop.

Caridad wondered if Gerard's mother had been neglectful, absent, or even suicidal. Could this be the reason for his many outbursts? She reconsidered what she'd planned to say, which would have only echoed Lance's observation. Instead, she asked, "What about men?" She thought of her father who'd vanished before she was born. "Shouldn't men who have children also forfeit the right to abandon them?"

Angry Young Man sank back in his seat, shaking his head. "Men are different," he said. "Mothers hold the key to the child's sense of self."

Caridad cocked her head, squinted at him.

"Especially back then," he said, "in Chopin's time—she should have known better than to write such a book, as if it's okay for a mother of two little kids to up and drown herself, just because she can't do whatever she feels like doing, just because society's a little strict. Again and again in the novel, she makes bad decisions."

Caridad was tired of this complaint about fictional characters. It often issued from the most unsophisticated readers. "Would we have this novel," she said, "would we have any novels if characters always made good choices?"

"That's right," Lance said. "What kind of story would that be? She was a good wife and a good mother. The end." He flipped through the pages. "What if she were just like the other women on Grand Isle?" Lance began reading a passage: "They were women who idolized their children, worshipped their husbands, and esteemed it a holy privilege to efface themselves as individuals and grow wings as ministering angels." He slapped the book shut. "Would we be at all interested in a story about such women—women who aren't even interested in themselves?"

"Okay, I know it wasn't easy for women back then," Gerard said, "but men had it tough, too. I mean, come on, what was so bad about her husband in the first place?"

McCann cleared his throat. "In fact, Léonce allows her a good deal of freedom and—"

"*Allows* her?" Lance said.

Papers rattled in the two schoolteachers' laps, and the third awakened with a gasp. Hilda Swan tensed and leaned forward, preparing to speak.

"Look," Gerard said, "I'm not saying anything antifeminist. In fact, I'm saying women are far too important. Mothers are too crucial to put their own desires before the welfare of their children."

Linda Burke took up her pen, scribbled in her notebook.

Lance snorted. The schoolteacher who had been napping now shook her head and raised a hand before saying, "I'm *sorry* but I have to disagree—"

"Now, wait a minute." McCann spread his thick fingers as if to ward off dissent in a physical way. "Gerard might have a point here."

"Are you kidding me?" Having broken his silence, Lance appeared eager to make up for lost time.

Hilda nodded as if in self-agreement. "On a metaphysical level," she said in her high, fluty voice, "especially from a Buddhist point of view, Edna's suicide can be seen as an attempt to grasp the essence of her being—an act of heroism." Hilda opened her book to a marked page. "In fact, Edna Pontellier says this outright: 'I would give up the unessential; I would give my money, I would give my life for my children; but I wouldn't give myself.'"

Caridad drew back, astonished that this made sense.

With Hilda's unexpected coherence, sparks ignited, flames caught, and the discussion combusted into a bonfire of conflict. Gerard ridiculed Hilda's statement, another schoolteacher begged his pardon before repudiating his ridicule, Harrison said he respected her opinion but they would just have to agree to disagree on this, Linda Burke *oohed*, and Lance stated that anyone who wanted to commit suicide—regardless of race, class, religion, or gender—should have the right to do so. A contented smile bloomed on the professor's face. Caridad shifted in her seat to relieve pressure on her spine and bumped the rubber-tipped cane that hooked on the back of her chair. It was a heavy length of dark wood, a cumbersome, geriatric-looking thing that she needed to negotiate the vast commuter college on foot. She snatched at it. But the cane swayed out of reach and clattered to the floor, startling the others into silence.

In the kitchen of her three-bedroom rental in Reseda, Caridad sautéed celery, onions, and bell peppers for jambalaya. Chicken breasts cooled in the lukewarm broth she would later reheat to boil the rice. The apartment filled with a pungent aroma that would please Miles when he arrived home with Leslie. Jambalaya was his favorite meal, so she made it often. On weekdays when Caridad had afternoon seminars, Esperanza would pick up Miles and Mimi from school and bring them to Mama's, where Leslie would later collect Miles after finishing work at the same Encino law office that handled Caridad's workers' compensation case. Who'd have thought that the scaly Philip T. Jefferson, Esquire, would wind up being the one to help her more than anyone else after the accident?

Phil, as she now called him, did know a thing or two about customer service, and as she'd expected, he was a fierce litigator. Just over two and a half years ago, he'd gotten her a settlement from Periwinkle Books that enabled her to finish her bachelor's degree and pursue graduate education. Phil had argued that Caridad, due to on-the-job injuries, could no longer perform the physical work of bookstore management and so she had to retrain for a career in academia. On top of this, Phil, after meeting Leslie, had been intrigued by her gender reassignment. He admired the courage and determination this took, so when his receptionist retired, Phil hired Leslie to replace her.

The phone rang just as Caridad added minced garlic to the sauté. She turned off the burner, steeling herself for another call from Vera, who, like a telemarketer, used to phone near suppertime. But the regional manager hadn't called since Caridad had mentioned this to Phil. Before then, Vera had phoned sporadically to ask how she was doing since the accident. Though not liable for damages covered by the other driver's insurance, Periwinkle Books was responsible for workers' compensation. Caridad's tuition, books, and transportation to and from the university, as well as a monthly check for living expenses, were paid by the bookstore's parent company, a conglomeration of specialty and department stores. "Corporate," as Vera called it, no doubt encouraged her to uncover reasons for disqualifying Caridad from receiving benefits.

The first time Vera phoned, Caridad had been caught off guard, as if given a pop quiz for which she hadn't prepared. When Vera asked how she was, Caridad had just said, "Not that good." The next time, she had her medical report ready by the phone.

"I have hyperreflexia in the patellar tendon," she'd told Vera, "and cervical spine flexion at sixty degrees, when fifty is normal. I've lost close to around sixty percent of my strength in both hands. Overall, I've had loss of motion, intense muscle spasms, and very limited movement of my neck with pain. I also have headaches and—"

"I just called to see how you're doing. I don't want to take up your time."

"Wait, what about my x-rays? I haven't even gotten to the vertebrae."

"Okay, bye now," Vera had said before hanging up. Still, she'd called again and again, as if she expected someone else to answer the phone and let slip that Caridad was off playing tennis professionally or teaching high-impact aerobics.

Caridad wiped her hands on a dish towel and hurried to the living room to answer the phone. "Hello?" she said into the mouthpiece, her tone more confrontational than friendly.

"Good evening, I'm calling for Caridad Kessler." The deep masculine voice called to mind a radio or television announcer.

Suspecting a telemarketer, Caridad kept quiet, her hand hovering over the switch hook.

"Hello?" The voice wavered. "Is anyone there?"

"Who is this?" Perhaps Vera had enlisted another person to make her snooping calls. Caridad flipped open the medical report and cleared her throat.

"This is Harrison."

"Harrison?"

"Harrison McCann—from Turn-of-the-Century U.S. Lit."

How had she failed to connect his name to that distinctive voice? "Yes, of course, how are you?"

"I am well. Thank you." His tone was again confident, tracking smoothly like a record after a skip. "I got your number from Hilda Swan. I hope that's okay."

"Sure." Caridad closed her medical file and searched around for her book bag, expecting him to ask about her seminar notes.

"I'm calling to invite you to have dinner with me on Saturday night."

"Oh?" Caridad's heart plunged. *Harrison McCann?* Caridad scanned her memory for flirtatious comments he might have made to indicate interest in her, but what came to mind was the first day of the seminar. During introductions, McCann had barked at Lance for opening a granola bar while he was explaining his decision to give up acting for academia. She should say, "No! Absolutely not!" Caridad glimpsed her cane, hooked to the back of a dinette chair like the petrified neck of an ebony swan with a mean little head. She gripped the phone with both hands. *This* was the kind of person she now attracted? A bluff and blustery failed actor? "Listen, I'm in the middle of something right now. Can I call you back?"

Harrison gave her his number. She jotted it down on the file sleeve at hand. Then he wished her a good evening, and they hung up. Caridad limped back to the kitchen and relit the burner under the skillet, adding tomatoes, broth, rice, and spices to the sautéed garlic, peppers, and onions, which had gone a bit soft. Even so, her eyes stung as if the onion were freshly chopped. She stirred the vegetable broth and shifted her weight from one leg to the other to alleviate pressure in her hips and lower back, a throbbing sensation as regular as a pulse beat.

During dinner, Miles chattered about the pet rabbit a classmate had brought to school and told Caridad and Leslie about a fire-safety lesson. "Stop, drop, and roll." Miles ate his favorite meal with gusto, but Leslie raked the mound of rice and chicken from one side of her plate to the other before saying she might save it to take for lunch the next day. After the dishes were washed, they played a few hands of Uno, and Leslie, still preoccupied, had to be reminded to take her turn. When Miles was in bed, Caridad asked Leslie if she might want to watch a rerun of *Columbo* with her. Leslie flushed and shook her head.

"What's going on?" Caridad asked.

"Something strange happened at work." Over time, Leslie had given up the hyper-girly mannerisms and the high-pitched voice that irritated Caridad. She had grown her hair out, a thick curly mane. She no longer wore the stiff wig nor plastered her face with makeup. As Caridad had predicted years ago when gathering that hank of hair into a ponytail, Gray ultimately did make a pretty girl. Apart from becoming more natural looking, after her surgery, Leslie had transformed from a man intent on passing as a woman into a human being who happened to be a woman, someone Caridad liked and trusted. More than roommates, or even friends, she and Leslie now forged a close bond, sharing responsibility for Miles in much the same way as they had when Leslie was Gray.

"What was it?"

Leslie shrugged and gave Caridad a shy smile. "Phil asked me to go to Florida with him for his brother's wedding."

Caridad drew a sharp breath. Leslie sometimes lunched with Phil, and once in a while, they went to foreign films together. But such an invitation crossed professional boundaries. "Tell him no," she said. "Tell him it's a mistake to get involved with the person you work for. If you want, *I'll* talk to him for you. He should know better than — "

"I'm tired, and I've got a headache." Leslie pinched the bridge of her nose. "I'm going to bed." She made her way to her room and clicked the door shut behind her.

Alone in the living room, Caridad gathered up the Uno cards and replaced them in their box. She turned on the television. *Columbo* had been preempted by a basketball game going into overtime. Caridad changed the channel to a situation comedy with a hectoring laugh track. She flipped to another channel, then another. More and more rollicking hilarity sounded from the set. She snapped it off. Caridad approached the door to Leslie's room to peer under the door for a strand of light. There was none. She slunk into the kitchen and opened the refrigerator to eat a few spoonfuls of jambalaya, but the lukewarm rice made her queasy, so she put it away and wandered back into the living room. She pawed through her book bag for Chopin's novel, planning to review the passages she'd quote in her seminar paper.

She sank into an armchair and opened the book, turning pages until an underlined paragraph caught her eye: "The voice of the sea is seductive; never ceasing, whispering, clearing, murmuring, inviting the soul to wander for a spell in the abysses of solitude; to lose itself in mazes of inward contemplation. The voice of the sea speaks to the soul. The touch of the sea is sensuous, enfolding the body in its soft, close embrace." In the margin, Caridad had written *Tempting*. She set the book down and wrapped arms around herself. What was it like to succumb to the voice of the sea? Had it been like falling into a dreamless sleep? Was it the end of pain? Caridad stretched her spine to ease her cramped back. Did the sea enfold Edna like a soothing embrace, masking that last moment of utter isolation? *We are born and die alone*, thought Caridad.

Yet, in the meantime, everyone seemed to have someone. Felicia now dated a jazz musician, a drummer from Panama who was much older than she, mature enough to be bemused instead of offended by her outbursts. Reynaldo, after joining Alcoholics Anonymous, had

been baptized into an evangelical Christian church. He was now strug-
gling to win back Esperanza. They still lived apart, but nearly every
Saturday, Reynaldo took them on family outings, and on Sundays,
they went with him to church. Even Mama had started playing cards
in the evenings with Mr. Nevelson, a retired neighbor. And now Leslie
would go to Florida with Phil for his brother's wedding. You don't
bring a transsexual to a family wedding unless you mean business.
Caridad returned to the kitchen and poured herself a glass of water to
swallow down the familiar thickness forming in her throat. Soon she
stood before the telephone, dialing the number she'd penned on the
file sleeve of her medical report.

Glad the women's dressing room was empty, Caridad tugged up the
back of the black one-piece swimsuit Felicia had lent her. It was long
in the torso but tight at the bust and saggy around her midsection and
buttocks. She supposed she could drape a towel around her sarong-
style and fasten it with the locker key's pin. She'd remove the towel
just before slipping into the pool. Caridad leaned her cane against the
back of the locker and hung her Levi's on a hook to obscure the thing.
She banged the metal door shut, locked it, and pinned the towel at her
waist. Caridad drew breath to pull her stomach in, her lungs aching
from the chlorinated steam. Girlish voices bounced off the dank walls
and wet cement floor, and she froze.

Two coeds in bikinis sauntered into the changing room. How easily they moved, their hips rolling with each rhythmic step. One opened
a nearby locker and the other smiled at Caridad. She nodded in return.
Hot and humiliating anger flared in her chest. She blamed Harrison for
this. He was the one to insist on the outing and to invite Miles to go
with them to the university pool. Now he and Miles, already wearing
swim trunks, were waiting for her in the pool. Harrison had no doubt
gawped at these two as they emerged from the water to sashay, hips
swinging, toward the changing room.

"Swimming is the best therapy for joint and back pain," he'd said
after Caridad explained about the car accident during their first date a
few weeks earlier at an Italian restaurant.

Caridad had nodded. This was what her physical therapist had
said. Neither seemed to consider the self-consciousness she'd feel at a
public pool or the fact that she could not swim a stroke. The latter had

been the reason she'd given Harrison that night for not taking advantage of the therapeutic benefits of swimming.

His turquoise eyes had bulged in disbelief. "Are you joking?" Harrison told Caridad he'd been swimming since he was three. He had been on swim teams from elementary school into high school. In fact, Harrison had first entered college on a swimming scholarship, and he'd worked as a swimming instructor and lifeguard for a few years after that. Harrison promised to teach her to swim, claiming he could teach *anyone* to swim.

Now, as Caridad emerged from the changing room, Harrison was already showing Miles how to float on his back. Both of them were so absorbed in the lesson that they took no notice of her until she was standing in the chilly water nearby. "Oh, hi, darling," Harrison said.

Caridad winced. She disliked the casual way he used endearments with her.

"Look, Mommy!" Miles stood chin deep in the pool and then leaned back to resume floating. "The water holds me up."

"I see." Caridad smiled at him. Though Harrison often irked her, she appreciated his interest in Miles. He'd also won over Leslie, now Caridad's litmus test for potential friends. When she explained about Leslie's sex change, Harrison had, like Phil, expressed admiration for the courage this took. He met Leslie soon after that first date, and when they discovered shared interests in music and film, they formed a liking for one another.

When wet, Harrison's brown hair was much thinner on top than she'd thought, and there was no way to ignore the thick matting of prematurely blanched hair—white as shredded coconut—that covered his large chest. Caridad glanced away and patted the chilly water with her palms, imagining herself gliding along the marked lanes like the swimmers nearby. Harrison manipulated her son's arms to teach him the backstroke, and she grinned in his direction, averting her eyes from the dense polar fur that spread from the hollow of his neck, past his navel, and into the waistband of his black trunks.

One Saturday weeks later, when Miles was spending the night at Mama's and Leslie had gone with Phil to Santa Barbara, Caridad invited Harrison over for supper. She planned to try out a ratatouille recipe. It was the type of determinedly nutritious dish that Leslie and Miles would refuse to eat. Harrison, a big man, would consume just about anything she set before him. "I eat like a horse," he often told her.

Though she paid close attention to the recipe, she must have mismeasured the ingredients or used tomatoes that were off because the ratatouille tasted odd to her—bland and bitter. Even so, Harrison ate every bit she served and then served himself a second heaping plate. She'd also bought a bottle of red wine and even drank a glass with dinner. Harrison enjoyed wine. In the weeks they'd been going out together, Caridad ended her long abstinence, sipping a glass with him now and then.

After dinner, they watched a videotape of *Das Boot* together on the couch. Though the film was long and focused on the tedium and terror experienced by the crew of a cramped vessel, Caridad was mesmerized. But before it ended, Harrison drew Caridad into his arms and began kissing her deeply, his pointy tongue darting into her mouth as she peeked around his head to catch glimpses of the movie. They'd kissed many times before and even discussed becoming intimate or, as Harrison liked to say, "being committed in an intimate relationship." While Caridad had nothing against casual sex, this was how Harrison wanted things to be: committed and intimate. He insisted they wait until they were ready for this, but Caridad suspected her limp—that awful cane!—made her unappealing to him.

Harrison switched off the television. His kisses trailed down her throat to her clavicle. His fingers fumbled unbuttoning her blouse and unhitching her bra. Then his tongue flicked over her nipples. He raised his head and looked into her eyes. "Do you think we're ready?" His words sounded histrionic, as if uttered in a soap opera just before organ chords sounded to signal a commercial break. "Are we ready to be committed?"

Committed? The word for consigning the insane to institutions—was she ready for this? "I mean," Harrison said, "do you feel ready to be intimate with me?"

Caridad nodded, and Harrison stunned her by gathering her in his arms as if she were a small child. He lifted her off the couch and carried her into her bedroom. There he settled her on the bed and tugged off her clothing, kissing and tonguing her skin as he went. Harrison shed his slacks and briefs. He slipped on a condom before easing his large body over hers. Caridad pulled him toward her, drew a deep breath, tensing to meet his pressure with her own, and then, and then . . .

Something loose and damp as turkey gizzards flapped against her inner thigh.

"Oh *god*." Harrison rolled away from her. "I'm sorry, darling."

"What's wrong?"

"Sometimes I have . . . trouble." He sighed. "You're so beautiful, you know that? It scares me. I start worrying that I won't be able to satisfy you, and then, well . . ." He glanced down at his flaccid member, the condom shriveling like a discarded snakeskin as his penis retreated into its snowy pubic nest. "It turns out I *can't*."

"It's okay." Moved by his mortified expression, Caridad stroked his face. "Really, it is."

"Do you mind if we just maybe sleep? Would it be okay if I stay the night?"

"Of course." Caridad rose to wash the dishes, turn out the lights, and lock the front door. When she returned to her room, Harrison was under the sheet, spread-eagle on his back, taking up much of the bed and snoring. His face wore an open and trusting look, and as she gazed at him, Caridad supposed this was what he had been like as a child—a mild and tender boy, despite his great size. He'd told her he was often challenged to fight when he was younger because he was large, but this never went well for him. Harrison had no desire to hurt others. He was no fighter. *No lover either*. She suppressed that unkind thought, wondering instead what happened to the crew aboard das boot.

Caridad slept in fits that night, clinging to the edge of the mattress so she wouldn't fall off. She had troubling dreams—fragmented images of raw poultry and moldy mushrooms in the snow. At daybreak, she woke to a warm pressure against her backside, then a string of soft kisses at the nape of her neck. "Good morning, darling," Harrison whispered in her ear. Then he turned her over and dove under the covers to lap at her crotch like an eager sheepdog. When he emerged, red-faced and panting, he said, "I think it'll work this time, if I get on top."

He sheathed himself with another condom and entered her tentatively before plowing with industry. Chilly drops of sweat plopped from his face onto her shoulders. Harrison began snorting, then bellowing. Caridad flashed on a documentary film she'd seen about water buffalos. In it, a bull, wild-eyed and frenziedly tupping a cow, had lowed in the same way. She grew distracted by an image of those mud-slicked beasts locked in earsplitting collision until the cow shot out a hind leg, kicking spasmodically. Harrison's cries soon subsided into

wheezing grunts. As he quieted, Caridad fixed her thoughts in a determined way on Carl—his clove-scented flesh, his sure and silent movements that matched her own—and she shuddered with brief pleasure
just before Harrison softened and slipped out.

That Sunday morning at dawn, while he perspired atop her, she
had at last become intimate with Harrison. Caridad supposed this
meant she should be committed, too.

One early afternoon in late spring, while Miles was at school, Caridad
and Harrison made plans to trade end-of-term essays at her apartment. They had just finished lunch, and Harrison was washing the
dishes while she looked over his paper. After cleaning up, Harrison
would join her at the table to go over her essay. Caridad frowned at
the pages before her, her face growing warm as she read. Like her,
Harrison had written about *The Awakening*, but his thesis repeated
Gerard Hochner's fatuous argument. She warned herself not to criticize this. Changing his main point would require him to rewrite all
twenty pages, an impossibility since the paper was due the next day.
And the essay, as it should, expressed *his* opinion of the novel. She
glanced into the kitchen at his broad back as he wiped the counters.
However asinine these were, Caridad had no business pushing him to
alter his ideas.

But why open the paper with a personal anecdote about competitive swimming? Was it necessary to mention his athletic scholarship?
And why end that first paragraph with a hanging quotation from a
vitriolic review in *Public Opinion*—"We are well-satisfied when [Edna
Pontellier] deliberately swims out to her death in the waters of the
gulf"? Was he trying to provoke her by concurring with that wrong-
headed reviewer? Surely Harrison knew how she revered Chopin's
novel. Had he not noticed how she'd begun piling her thick hair atop
her head in the style worn by the author on the book's jacket? Eyes
narrowed, Caridad continued reading Harrison's scornful diatribe
against the novel until a misspelling snagged her attention. She chuckled at it. There were many such errors, but this one achieved the humor
Harrison aimed for with his sarcastic criticism.

He hurried to her side, grinning. "What is it, darling?"

"Malpheasants." She pointed at the word. "What are mal*pheas-
ants*? Extra-foul fowl?"

Harrison's face fell. "That's a typo." He called his misspellings "typos," as if to blame them on his errant typewriter. He took the pencil from her, crossed out the word, and scribbled another above it.

"Mal*peasants*?" Caridad said. "So . . . bad rustic folks, evil *peons*?"

"Big deal. You know I can't spell. Hemingway and Fitzgerald couldn't spell."

But they could write.

"I'm glad you're going over it for me," Harrison said, "to catch little things like that."

"I see." Caridad took the pencil for him. She printed *malfeasance* in the margin.

"Mea culpa," he said in a tone of exaggerated contrition. "Mea *maxima* culpa."

Caridad winced.

"That came out wrong. Look, I'm grateful that you're reading my paper and correcting my stupid mistakes. I'm sorry I snapped at you. When you laughed, I thought you were enjoying my paper. It *is* witty in places, isn't it?"

Picturing a brace of wicked game birds, Caridad nodded. She wouldn't mention the odd anecdotal opening, the hanging quotation, the faulty argumentation. Like many graduate students, Harrison no doubt believed taking potshots at enduring works of literature somehow established his ascendancy as a scholar. Caridad should at least question him about his ideas and encourage him to think them through, but it was growing late. They would have to pick up Miles soon. Harrison would have to take her since she still didn't drive and had no car. So Caridad returned to where she left off reading, continuing to circle misspelled words and to correct the punctuation. She focused her attention on catching the little things.

"Your ideas are very clear," Caridad told Harrison. "There's no mistaking your position."

"Thank you, darling." He smiled and sank into the seat across from her. He reached for another pencil and took up the pages she'd written.

More and more these days, Caridad found herself silencing an inner skeptic, even though Harrison sometimes said things that compromised his credibility. The introduction to his paper reminded her of his insistence that he'd once qualified for the Olympic swim team. When Caridad pressed him for details—what events, what year, and how he'd trained and qualified for this—Harrison grew vague and then irritable, claiming he didn't like talking about it. He also told a few suspected whoppers related to his experiences as an actor. In one of the most outlandish of these, he said Farrah Fawcett had pursued him so relentlessly on the set of a TV show they'd both appeared in that he'd had to ask the director to intervene. When Caridad saw a video of the episode—Farrah, the ravishing young star, and Harrison, a walk-on baddie gunned down in under a minute of screen time—she had to wonder if he might be delusional.

Truthful or not, Harrison also told Caridad what she wanted to hear. He loved her writing, he said, and he admired how she could read an entire novel in the time it took him to slog through the first few chapters. Harrison was convinced of her culinary genius, though given his appetite, that didn't count as high praise. He often told her how beautiful she was, how sex with her was the best he'd ever had, making her ashamed that she couldn't say the same of him. But the intimacy between them did improve, though Caridad often wished for earplugs. She learned to finish quickly in the wake of his water-buffalo throes. But not wanting to alarm Miles and Leslie, she refused to let Harrison spend the night when they were home.

Everybody still had somebody else. The Panamanian drummer proposed to Felicia. Without a word of complaint, she accepted the engagement ring he'd offered her—his deceased mother's opal set in gold filigree. Esperanza and Reynaldo, who, after years of separation, had never gotten around to filing for divorce, began talking about living together again. A few months ago, they started seeing a marriage counselor together. Unasked, Mr. Nevelson had varnished the porch to Mama's duplex, a puzzling gesture that was discussed at length by Caridad and her sisters. Lately Leslie and Phil spent most weekends together at his large house in Topanga Canyon. On campus, Caridad caught sight of Daniel, who again worked at the university library, holding hands with a long-haired coed. Even Miles had a crush on another kindergartner, a little girl whose parents invited Miles along for picnics at the park. And now Caridad had Harrison, whose turquoise eyes sparkled, his prognathous face softening at the sight of her with an expression of longing, a look that was a lot like love.

Sitting across the table from her, Harrison again wore that tender look. "Brilliant," he said. "Your introduction is absolutely compelling."

Caridad beamed at him and gazed down at his paper. She circled an incomprehensible sentence fragment. In the margin, she printed a neat question mark.

Harrison took Caridad to poetry readings and wine bistros, to small ethnic restaurants where he ordered pungent and spicy dishes for Caridad that she'd never even heard of before, let alone tasted. He invited her to attend cocktail parties with him in the Hollywood Hills, where the other guests were fascinated by her cane, as if it were something she donned for distinction like a velvet cape. His friends were minor actors, stunt people, producers' assistants, makeup artists, and others who worked in the periphery of filmmaking. His closest friend, Athena, a thirtyish redhead, awed Caridad because she had published an autobiographical novel. When they met at a poetry reading, Athena had been chewing on an onyx cigarette holder, eyeing Caridad. Then she turned to Harrison to say, "No fair, Harry! When you told me you were dating a Hispanic woman from the Valley, I expected big hair, long earrings, and spandex." Athena leaned to air-kiss Caridad's cheeks. "You don't drive a Camaro, do you?" Baffled, Caridad shook her head.

True to his promise, Harrison taught Caridad to swim—freestyle, breaststroke, backstroke, and sidestroke. Nearly every weekday, she would head for the university pool to swim laps in the tepid aquamarine water. Sometimes Harrison accompanied her, and on weekends, they often brought Miles to the pool, but Caridad preferred swimming on her own. Knifing her long body through the water, reaching and pulling, had strengthened her back and neck, just as Harrison had predicted. Her latest x-rays showed such marked change in her spinal alignment that the physical therapist gave her a high-five at their last appointment. It wouldn't be long, her doctor said, before Caridad would be able to walk without a cane.

Stroking and flutter-kicking the length of the lanes over and over again, Caridad often thought of Edna Pontellier. "A feeling of exultation overtook her, as if some power of significant import had been given to her to control the working of her body and her soul," Chopin wrote. "She grew daring and reckless, overestimating her strength. She wanted to swim far out, where no woman had swum before." Exquisite and sentient Edna darted through the waves toward her death, while

Caridad trained like an amateur athlete, swimming lap after lap to build strength and mobility. But now and then, she imagined, as Edna had in her last moments, hearing an unseen barking dog, dragging its heavy chain, and Caridad knew that she and Edna Pontellier both plunged through water to outdistance that shackled hound.

The Reserve

Openmouthed, Miles gaped through the plane's portal. Cars, trucks, houses, and office buildings below shrunk into Monopoly-sized pieces before disintegrating into pixilated bits as the plane climbed skyward. Neither he nor Caridad had flown before. She, too, gazed in amazement as the dots below converged, forming a patchwork of subdivisions and fields overlaid by a grid of streets and highways before being swallowed up by a dense meringue of clouds that—*whuff*—blanked out the window. After this, Miles turned his attention to the sliding shutter. He lowered it, darkening their bank of seats, and lifted it, flashing frothy brightness. He shut and raised the shutter again, as if expecting the clouds to vanish.

"Okay," Harrison said from the aisle seat. "That's enough."

Caridad, in the middle, cupped her son's hand to hold it still.

Harrison pinched his nostrils shut and gulped, his Adam's apple bobbing. He stretched his neck, turned his jaw this way and that. Flying, he'd told Caridad, bothered him. The pressure in his ears and dehydration caused his head to hurt, and she suspected the wine he drank the previous evening contributed to his discomfort. Harrison had suggested that she and Miles spend the night at his place since he lived closer to the airport. After Miles fell asleep in the spare room, Harrison, after finishing two bottles of Pinot Noir, flopped into bed, snoring within minutes. Caridad, anxious about the flight, struggled to sleep through his raucous snorts and wheezes. Harrison's parents, who lived just outside Greenville, South Carolina, had bought the roundtrip tickets, so he, Caridad, and Miles could spend the Christmas holiday with their family. The plane tickets cost more than Caridad had earned in a month as a dual-store manager, and all three were stamped *Nonrefundable*.

Relieved that they'd been on time for the flight, Caridad relaxed when she slipped into her middle seat on the plane, while Harrison sank into a headachy gloom. She stole a glance at him as he massaged his temples. He'd put on weight in the several months they'd been together. At six-foot-three, he carried bulk better than most, but now his midsection pulled his burgundy shirt taut, buttons straining their holes. His turquoise eyes had sunk into his thickening face, and his brown hair had grown gray and shaggy.

Harrison now leaned out to scan the aisle, likely seeking the refreshment cart they'd seen trundle past earlier. Tenderness stirred in Caridad. She knew him well and could guess what he was thinking. He longed for treats of all kinds, but especially food and wine. After gaining slow confidence as a lover, he craved Caridad these days, too. Weeks ago, he announced that he'd thrown out his store of pornographic magazines, declaring, "I don't need them anymore," as if he expected praise for this. But Caridad, who had had no idea he'd owned such things, felt freighted by this news, as if presented with something cumbersome and unwieldy—the gift of a boulder, say, to have and to hold.

Caridad drew her hands into her lap. Her skin was dry, even raspy. She pinched at a cuticle. Harrison could be coarse in the way he talked about sex. "How about a blow job?" he'd say. Or "Want a muff dive?" He'd frame his desire as the impulse to satisfy her, as if she were anything but exasperated when he'd slip under the sheets to lap at her in an aimless way, as if what followed did not demand the full force of her imagination and willed deafness in order for her to achieve a stingy sliver of pleasure. Caridad glanced at Harrison again. He'd closed his eyes, his shiny forehead rippling with tension. Poor Harrison. She could try harder. Apart from the sex, there was no reason not to love him. Even if unreciprocated, his desire showed attraction to her despite her limp and the cane she still used now and again. He'd often praise Caridad, a single mother finishing graduate school while recovering from a serious accident. "Only you," he'd say, "can do what you do." Though it sounded like an advertising jingle, his words infused Caridad with pride, even *hope*. Being with Harrison was like gazing in a magic mirror that reflected radiance and invincibility—an image of her as a dazzling Wonder Woman, instead of a graduate student in her late twenties, a disabled Latina without work and with a young child to raise, which was—of course—what she really was.

Caridad pulled out her copy of *Moll Flanders*, the novel given to her in the hospital by Esperanza. Its pages were soft-edged with wear by the previous reader, who, like her, had underlined passages and made margin notes, but in purple ink. Just after the accident, Caridad had lacked the focus to follow Defoe's antiquated language. The capricious capitalization irked her, but after a seminar in pre-1800 English literature in which the professor often alluded to the novel, and after learning the book's full title, which did not appear in her copy—*The Fortunes and Misfortunes of the Famous Moll Flanders, &c. Who was Born in Newgate, and during a Life of continu'd Variety for Threescore Years, besides her Childhood, was Twelve Year a Whore, five times a Wife (whereof once to her own Brother), Twelve Year a Thief, Eight Year a Transported Felon in Virginia, at last grew Rich, liv'd Honest, and died a Penitent. Written from her own Memorandums*—Caridad, intrigued, brought the novel along to read during this trip.

She found her place, a page where the wielder of the purple pen had underscored this passage: ". . . Women had lost the Privilege of saying No, that it was a Favour now for a Woman to have THE QUESTION ask'd, and if any young Lady had so much Arrogance as to Counterfeit a Negative, she never had the Opportunity given her of denying twice; much less of Recovering that false Step, and accepting what she had but seem'd to decline: The Men had such Choice every where, that the Case of the Women was very unhappy; for they seem'd to Ply at every Door, and if the Man was by great Chance refus'd at one House, he was sure to be receiv'd at the next."

Miles now discovered the refreshment tray. He turned the notch to lower it and then lifted it back up. He glanced at Harrison, who—eyes still closed—sat motionless, as if dozing, and Miles let the tray down again. He was pushing it up once more when Harrison turned to Caridad. "Jesus Christ—do *something*, will you?"

Harrison's parents met them at Hartsfield Atlanta International Airport, nearly a three-hour drive from their home in South Carolina. At baggage claim, Caridad recognized his mother at once from the photos she'd seen. Gayle, a stout woman with gray hair styled in a blunt Dutch cut, waddled toward Harrison, her arms outstretched. She wore gym shoes, navy stretch pants, and a hooded windbreaker over a pink T-shirt. Hal, Harrison's father, followed her, listing to one side and leaning on a cane much like Caridad's as he approached. He wore round rimless glasses that fogged after he hugged his son. He then fumbled for a kerchief and honked into it.

Caridad shook Hal's plump spotted hand, but Gayle reeled her in for a lilac-scented embrace. "I'm just thrilled to meet you!" She buried Caridad's face in her slippery nylon windbreaker. "Harrison talks about you *all* the time. And this must be Miles." She swooped to pull him into her arms. "My, what a dear, dear boy you are!" Harrison, after greeting his parents, stood apart from their group, deep in the throng of passengers waiting for the luggage to appear on the carousel. Caridad and Miles answered Gayle's questions about the flight, making awkward small talk until their bags were at last disgorged onto the conveyor belt.

During the drive to Greenville, Miles soon fell asleep. Hal steered their massive white Lincoln with Gayle beside him in the front seat and Caridad, Harrison, and Miles in the back. Caridad continued chatting with Gayle while gazing out the window at unfamiliar landscapes along the interstate—many russet-colored fields, herds of cows, great hairy spirals of hay, and dilapidated barns interspersed with billboards advertising shops, fast-food restaurants, and hotels. After several minutes, Gayle produced a stack of books on cookery and local history. She handed these to Caridad in the back. "Harrison tells me you're a fast reader."

Did Gayle expect a demonstration now—proof of her rapid reading skills? Caridad glanced at Harrison, but he stared out the window on his side. With Miles stretched out between them, his warm head nested in her lap, Caridad maneuvered the heavy stack to the floorboard. "Reading in the car gives me motion sickness," she said.

"Well, maybe later, then," Gayle said. "It amazes me that speed-readers take in any of the content. That Evelyn Wood business seems a sham to me. I think books should be lingered over, savored, and enjoyed."

As if in response to this, Harrison began loudly listing Caridad's accomplishments: her high grades on papers, her scholarship, her publications in the university's literary journal. Caridad gaped at Harrison as if he'd been filled with the Holy Spirit and had commenced speaking in tongues. She shook her head, silently imploring him to stop, which he did when he ran out of things to say.

"I love to read," Gayle said, "but I'm very slow."

Caridad was unsure how to reply to this. "Oh?"

"I started a novel by Flannery O'Connor this summer, and I still haven't finished it. Something called *Smart Blood* or *Blood Knowledge*. I forget."

"*Wise Blood*," Caridad said.

"No, that's not it. It's very peculiar—not at all nice, if you know what I mean—and O'Connor's supposed to be this great Southern writer. In my opinion, she doesn't hold a candle to Margaret Mitchell, the woman who wrote *Gone with the Wind*. Have you read that?"

"Not yet."

Gayle turned to face the backseat, her jowly face crimped in astonishment. "Oh, you have to read it. You really do. I'll lend you my copy to read while you're here."

"Thank you, but I brought a book to read."

"What's it about?" asked Gayle.

Caridad drew breath to recite the full title. "It's *The Fortunes and Misfortunes of Moll Flanders, the—*"

"How nice," Gayle said. She then launched into a long monologue to explain why she and Hal had relocated to the South. Harrison's family had lived in Michigan until Hal retired, selling the auto-parts distributorship he'd inherited from his father-in-law and moving to South Carolina over ten years ago. Gayle described their adjustment, the "culture shock" they experienced in the South. She discussed Southern cooking, Civil War reenactments, the proliferation of kudzu, the heat, and slower pace of life. Hal grunted assent while he drove, tossing back occasional comments to his son. But Harrison leaned against the window and closed his eyes, feigning sleep.

After a few hours, Hal steered off the interstate for a highway that delivered them to the gated community on Lake Keowee where they lived. A carved wooden placard was suspended over the latticed entrance. *The Reserve*, it read. Hal nosed the Lincoln toward a booth, where they were cleared by a security guard before the gate lifted. Then Hal drove around the lake to the family home. Birch trees, loblollies, and pines scrolled past the car windows, and a lacy mist rose from the lake's emerald water. The stately edifices that appeared when they left the main road had nautical names: Mizzenmast, Bowsprit, Topsides, and Coxswain. Tucked behind these, the McCann family home—Sextant—was grander than any dwelling Caridad had ever entered as a guest, including the oversized home that belonged to Seth's parents. Stepping over the threshold was, for Caridad, like slipping into the glossy pages of a women's magazine.

While Harrison unloaded and unpacked their luggage and his mother heated food prepared by her "helper," Hal gave Caridad and Miles a tour of the three-story house. He led them through the hunter-green-and-burgundy study, the sandstone living room, the sea-foam bathrooms, and the Laura Ashley bedrooms, some with canopied beds and gauzy mosquito netting. On the main floor, a Christmas tree, tall enough to decorate a shopping mall, stood near the fireplace, winking with blue and white lights. Uncountable porcelain ornaments and shiny indigo bows decorated its great branches. Dazed, Miles tagged after Caridad, an anxious look on his face, as if he feared getting lost in the vast house.

Before supper, Harrison mixed martinis, and his mother concocted a Shirley Temple for Miles. Caridad had never tasted a martini before. Its bitter tang delighted her. Over dinner, Harrison remained withdrawn and uncommunicative, so Caridad raked her travel-weary brain for topics to engage his parents—especially Hal, who'd also grown silent—and she and Miles fielded Gayle's questions about their lives in California. She learned that Harrison's brothers and sister would arrive the next day and hoped for some conversational relief from them.

Hours later, Miles was settled in a bedroom on the top floor. Caridad sat at his bedside, reading to him until he fell asleep. When she returned to the main floor, she discovered Harrison had already gone to bed. She wished Gayle and Hal a good night before descending the stairs to the basement guest bedroom. There she found Harrison naked atop the bed. The silvery hair matting his chest glinted under the glow of a nearby lamp as he read an issue of the *New Yorker*.

She closed the door behind her, and he glanced up. "There you are, darling," he said. He tossed the magazine to the floor and opened his arms, reaching for her. "Care to spend some time with a cunning linguist?" All traces of aloofness had vanished from his face. The ceiling creaked with footsteps, and muffled voices sounded as Hal and Gayle entered their bedroom directly overhead. The profound silence in the cavernous house intensified the merest sounds.

"It's been a long day," Caridad said. "I'm exhausted."

Harrison patted the bed beside him. "I bet I can make you feel all better."

She pointed to the ceiling. "If we can hear them, then—"

"I'll be quiet as a mouse. You'll see."

Caridad was relieved his gloom had finally lifted. Maybe he'd suffered from the flight more than she'd realized, or else seeing his parents—no doubt older and feebler than he'd expected—saddened and frustrated him. Still, she shook her head. "I don't want to. I really don't."

He stood and lifted her off her feet, the way he had the first time they'd spent the night together. Caridad tensed. "Put me down," she hissed.

Harrison laughed. "So you want to play?" He tossed her on the bed and grabbed her up again by the waistband of her Levi's. He unzipped her jeans and yanked them to her knees, then caught her wrists as she struggled to pull free, pinning her down and laughing. "I like to play, too." The ceiling ceased creaking, and the voices overhead grew silent. Apprehension penetrated the beams, the drywall, the plaster. Caridad sensed the older couple straining to listen. She could cry out, kick, or even bite him when he loomed near, but her resistance excited Harrison. He *wanted* his parents to hear him take her. Caridad swallowed the panic wadding in her throat, willing away her tension. "Wait," she whispered. She sat up to undo buttons on the blouse she did not want torn.

Caridad imagined herself a spirit, floating vapor-like from her body and passing through Harrison's to loft out the screened window and into the deep South Carolina night. She would twist beyond the moss-bearded trees and over the sparkling lake—up and up and up into the tilted smile of the moon. And then she was back on the bed, squeezing her eyes shut and biting her lower lip. The canopied frame knocked into the wall over and over and over. *Hurry up*, she silently begged him. Caridad opened her eyes to glimpse his sweat-slickened face, his empty eyes. How easily he could crush her. Her lungs tightened. She drew sharp and shallow breaths. Taking this as arousal, Harrison bellowed, his voice exploding in her ears. When he at last withdrew, she turned away, her crotch burning. He reached to stroke her backside. "That was incredible," Harrison said. "I always say it, but *that* was really, really—"

"You promised you'd be quiet," Caridad said in a low voice.

"I tried, I swear I did."

"Your parents—"

"Who cares about them?"

"I do," she said.

"Probably gave them a thrill."

Caridad turned to gape at him.

"Don't pretend you didn't like that," Harrison said. "I heard you gasping like a sweet little guppy. You're such a shy and funny thing."

Caridad drew breath to speak. She would tell him she didn't find stabbing pain or mortification the least bit erotic. She'd admit she hadn't climaxed and tell him it hardly mattered since orgasms with him were such tiny, ticklish things—skittish as sparrows she had to coax into grasping range. Caridad would say this was *not* lovemaking. She'd say this was . . . But what was it? Hadn't she undone her blouse and parted her legs? She didn't know—couldn't say—what it was. She wouldn't say—not for years. Harrison now beamed at her, his expression as expectant as a child's on Christmas Eve, which it would be in a few hours' time. A snippet of the purple pen–marked passage in the novel resounded in her thoughts, issuing in a soft Cockney accent, the way she imagined Moll Flanders might speak: *I found the Women had lost the Privilege of saying No* . . . Caridad exhaled slowly and reached to flip off the light.

"Talk to me, darling. I love hearing your voice before I fall asleep." He snuggled close. "Tell me what you're thinking."

Instead, Caridad framed the question that had been forming in her thoughts since arriving at his parents' house. "Your family is so wealthy. How do they live like this?"

Harrison paused to consider this, and when he spoke, his voice was forceful. "My father works very hard."

In the dark, Caridad envisioned her mother rising before dawn to pull on her nylon jumper and hairnet and then driving to the elementary school where she stirred up great vats of pancake batter, cauldrons of oatmeal, and industrial-sized skillets of eggs for the children with breakfast vouchers. She flashed on Esperanza racing through the hospital in rubber-soled shoes, sometimes working ten- and twelve-hour shifts. Caridad pictured Felicia grading papers at the kitchen table after the others had gone to bed. She saw their small rental house with an alley—a graffiti-scrawled cinder-block wall lined with battered garbage cans—for a backyard.

His father, she thought, *works very hard.*

In the morning, Caridad woke to find Miles dressed and standing at her bedside. She was glad she'd risen after Harrison had fallen asleep to put on a nightgown. Caridad now glanced over her shoulder to make sure that Harrison, still nude, was at least under the bedcovers.

"Is it wake-up time?" Miles whispered.

"Sure, honey. Did you have a good night?"

"I can't remember because I was asleep."

"Makes sense," Caridad said. "Wait for me quietly on the stairs while I get ready. Then we can go up together."

Miles padded toward the door. Caridad gathered clothes and slipped into the bathroom. She dressed, washed her face, and brushed her hair before tying it into a neat knot at the back of her head. After last night's racket, no way would she appear before Harrison's parents this morning looking like a disheveled slattern. Though she dreaded facing them, she hurried to keep Miles from waiting. He was probably hungry and eager to explore the lake as Hal had promised they would. When she was ready, they ascended the stairs to the main floor and wandered into the kitchen where they found Harrison's mother, aproned and pouring batter into a muffin tin.

"Good morning," Miles called out.

Gayle jumped. "*Ooh!* Good morning! I didn't hear you come in. You were quiet as a mouse." She looked away, her cheeks pinkening. "Did you two sleep well?"

Miles nodded.

"How about you?" Caridad asked.

"Hal had a bad night." Gayle wiped her hands on a dish towel and opened the oven door. "He's still resting. But if you give me a minute to put these in the oven, young man, I'll take you to see the lake."

"Can Mommy come, too?"

"She could, but it would be better if she's stays here in case the buzzer goes off." Gayle placed the tin in the oven, closed it, and set the timer.

Caridad glanced about the kitchen. "I can set the table or—"

"Relax, have some coffee. Just take the muffins out when they're done." Gayle removed her apron and toddled with Miles toward the front door. "Let's go see if we find any geese or ducks. Maybe we'll see some deer or rabbits."

"Do they bite?"

Gayle laughed. "Oh no, they won't come close enough for that."

They disappeared into the recesses of the house. Soon the front door yawned open and clicked shut. After she poured herself some coffee, Caridad approached the vast Christmas tree. She broke off a needle, sniffed its piney crispness. The tree was real, but it had to have been professionally decorated. Caridad gazed at the gifts piled on its red velvet skirt. Many of these had tags bearing Miles's name. As she turned from the tree, she accidentally kicked a gift off the skirt. Caridad reached to set it back.

"No peeking now." Hal's voice startled her.

Heat flooded Caridad's face. "I was admiring the tree and—"

"Curiosity killed the caribou," he said. Hal was wearing a red plaid bathrobe and blue-and-white striped pajamas. "Isn't that how the saying goes?"

Caridad replaced the present under the tree. "Caribou can be very curious I've heard."

"Oh, they're noisy buggers," Hal said. "*Nosy*, I mean, nosy buggers."

Caridad's face flamed anew. "I am so sorry—"

"My own fault for not taking my hearing aid out." Hal limped to the kitchen, and Caridad trailed after him. He leaned his cane against the sink counter to pour himself a cup of coffee. "Where's Harrison?"

"Still sleeping, I suppose."

Hal peered at her over the tops of his bifocal lenses and spoke in a low voice. "One thing *I'm* curious about." His dark eyes were shiny crescents, his short lashes dusted with sleep. "What is it you want?"

Caridad, who had leaned in to listen, now pulled back. "Excuse me?"

Footsteps sounded from the basement stairwell, deliberate and plodding sounds that Caridad recognized as Harrison's when he was in a "Lennie" mood. Though he hadn't acted in years, Harrison regretted that he'd never had the opportunity to play Lennie Small, the oxlike and slow-witted ranch hand in Steinbeck's *Of Mice and Men*, a role he claimed was made for him. Harrison sometimes adopted Lennie's mannerisms, from his vacant expression to his heavy, cumbersome gait while speaking lines from the play.

Not Lennie again, thought Caridad as she held the old man's gaze. "What do you mean?"

Harrison burst into the kitchen, his face slack-jawed and eyes agog, unfocused. "How ya doin'?"

"Well, look who's here. Hiya, Lennie," Hal said to his son before turning back to Caridad. "We have cornflakes, yogurt, and fruit. I could whip up some pancakes or scrambled eggs. Just tell me what you want?"

Caridad pointed at the oven. "I think Gayle's baking muffins."

"Where's George?" Harrison's speech was loose and garbled to mimic Lennie's. "George says we could live offa the fatta the lan'."

Harrison's brothers and their girlfriends had driven down from Michigan, arriving at midday along with his sister Maxine, who traveled from North Carolina. At suppertime, the ten of them filled the long table in the dining room. The table itself was crowded with place settings, serving platters, carafes of wine, long and glowing red tapers, and a cornucopia centerpiece—the horn-shaped basket disgorging tangerines, apples, and cranberries along with various nuts in their shells. Miles's dark eyes shone large and liquid in the candlelight. In the presence of so many strangers, he grew quiet and watchful. The McCanns celebrated Christmas Eve, while Christmas Day was spent eating leftovers and watching college football games. Gayle's "helper," a silent and furious-looking black woman named Mrs. Greaves, had prepared and then served a country ham—"a Smithfield," Gayle bragged—with a sweet potato soufflé, collard greens, macaroni and cheese, black-eyed peas, and cornbread to introduce Caridad and Miles to an authentic Southern meal.

At the head of the table sat Hal, his jowls clean-shaven and his sparse hair oiled and raked over the pink ruin of his scalp. To his right was Clark, the brother closest in age to Harrison. Clark, Harrison told Caridad, had been injured years ago while hunting, and now he was unable to work. He was a dour, dark-haired man with thick horn-rimmed glasses. Clark's girlfriend Daphne, seated beside him, supported Harrison's brother by working as an editor of a small-town newspaper. With her auburn pageboy and full cheeks, she looked like she could be related to Gayle, a cousin or niece. Next to Daphne, Matthew—Harrison's youngest brother—sat with his girlfriend,

Brandy, a freckled blond who looked young enough to be in high school. Gayle took the chair across the table from her husband, and her daughter Maxine was next to her followed by Miles, Caridad, and Harrison, whose chair was to the left of his father's.

With a look at Matthew and Brandy, Caridad performed quick calculations. Harrison, the oldest of the McCann children, was thirty-eight. He and his siblings, as Gayle had mentioned earlier, were all two years apart, so Clark would be thirty-six, Maxine around thirty-four, and Matthew close to thirty-two. He was nearly twice Brandy's age. Earlier, Caridad learned that he coached soccer at the high school Brandy had attended and that she had moved in with him during the last months of her senior year. Caridad remembered Carl with a pang and had no right to a high ground here. Matthew, with his thick dark hair and boyish face, looked younger than he was. Even so, he seemed more like Brandy's father than her lover.

Harrison and his brothers were tall men. In fact, Harrison, at six-foot-three, was the shortest and heaviest of the three. The McCann brothers all ate like machines, an unbroken sequence of fork to plate to mouth that called to mind coal being shoveled into a steam engine.

"My boys," Gayle said, "have big appetites."

Maxine turned sideways and winked at Caridad. Harrison's sister was a regional manager in retail like Caridad's former boss Vera, but Maxine worked for a music store chain. Maxine was as tall as Caridad and had a pixie cut that drew attention to her small-featured face, her almond eyes and bowed lips. Since arriving that afternoon, she cast Caridad so many conspiratorial looks and winks that Caridad wondered if Maxine had a facial tic. "They eat like horses," Maxine said now in her flat Michigan accent.

"I know *I* eat like a horse." Harrison jutted a thumb at Caridad. "Ask her."

Miles regarded Harrison's large belly. "Do you eat *horses*?"

Hal barked with laughter.

"I might," Harrison said, "if I was hungry enough."

"Tell me, Hal," Daphne said. "When did you propose to Gayle?" Daphne glanced at Clark, who continued loading food into his mouth. Since their arrival, Daphne had made many references to marriage, cornering Caridad at one point to tell her she hoped she and Clark would soon wed. "The thing is, I want to have a baby before it's too late," she'd said as if to persuade Caridad of this.

"Didn't you propose around Christmastime?" Daphne asked.

"Propose? *Propose?*" the old man sputtered as he reached for his wine glass. He'd nearly emptied the carafe at his side. The McCanns had downed several martinis before dinner, and the table had been set with no fewer than four crystal decanters filled with a "late harvest" Riesling. "I never proposed. She asked me!"

Across the table, Gayle's cheeks crimsoned. Harrison had told Caridad that his parents had married when his mother became pregnant with him. When they'd met, Hal was on furlough from the army—in which he served as a medic—during World War II. Inspired by aiding the wounded, he had made plans to reenlist after the war was over in order to become an army surgeon. But on a visit to a buddy's hometown, he'd met Gayle, his friend's sister. He dated her until he returned overseas. A few months later, he had a letter from Gayle telling him she was expecting. When Hal returned to the States, they were married, and instead of starting medical school, he moved to Michigan to work in his father-in-law's auto-parts distributorship.

"That's not true," Gayle said now.

"It was her idea." Hal nodded at Daphne. "I wanted to be a doctor."

Daphne grinned. "So there's a tradition for this in the family, the woman proposing marriage to the man?"

"Forget it." Clark sopped red-eye gravy with a wedge of corn-bread before stuffing it in his mouth.

Caridad, after being lectured at length on sidearms by Clark that afternoon, thought he should consider himself bizarrely lucky that anyone would be willing spend ten minutes, let alone a lifetime, with him.

Hal sloshed wine on the tablecloth. "I never proposed to anyone in my life."

"Gayle," Brandy said, "did you know that Matt got Teacher of the Month in November?" Her vowels were broad and flat like Maxine's.

"That's wonderful!" Gayle beamed at her youngest son. "I'm so proud of you."

"Bunch of deadbeats at my school," Matt said. "It's not like there's much competition."

Caridad studied Matt while he spoke, amazed that a soccer coach who'd taken one of his students as a live-in lover had been recognized as outstanding in the teaching profession, if only for the month of

November. Matt turned the topic to his school's production of *Little Shop of Horrors*, which he called amateur on every level.

"Sure could have used your help, bro." He grinned at Harrison.

In the presence of his siblings, especially Matt, who struggled for his oldest brother's approval, Harrison had become more expansive. "Sounds like they're rank amateurs."

"Whew, boy." Matthew fanned his face. "Some ranker than others."

Hal snorted and honked with laughter until he wheezed and grew violet in the face. He fumbled for his stemmed glass, toppling it.

"No more wine for Daddy," Gayle said to Harrison, who removed his father's glass and the carafe from the old man's reach while Clark blotted the spill with his napkin.

"Killjoy," Hal said to his wife. "That's what you are." He slammed the flat of his hand on the table, loosening a chestnut from the cornucopia. It rolled out and wobbled across the tablecloth to chink against Caridad's plate.

"So what time is the first game tomorrow?" Brandy asked.

Caridad glanced at Harrison, who was tonguing scraps of food from his teeth, while Clark discussed the scheduled games, key players, and statistics. She snatched the chestnut and slipped it back into the horn-shaped basket, burying it deep.

"Did you know that married men live longer than single men?" Daphne said. "It's true. We just did a piece on this in our paper."

Maxine cast Caridad yet another mugging look and a wink.

"What did I *just* say?" Clark said.

Miles glanced from one person to the next. Far from bored by the adult conversation, he seemed so absorbed that when the fierce Mrs. Greaves collected plates and Harrison suggested they go to the living room to open gifts, his face folded in disappointment.

"All this talk of proposals and marriage," Harrison said once they were all seated on the plush furniture near the tree, "makes me think that maybe I should go first."

Something bulky plummeted past Caridad's rib cage to crash at the pit of her stomach, as if some internal elevator car had been severed from its cables. *No,* she thought. *Oh no!*

Harrison produced a velveteen box from the pocket of his khakis. His family whooshed silent as he approached Caridad, who was sitting on an ottoman. The floor shook when he dropped to one knee. He opened the box, and gemstones glimmered within, reflecting the blue Christmas tree lights. "Darling," he said, deepening his voice, "you are the love of my life. Will you do me the honor of becoming my wife?"

The unintentional rhyme reminded Caridad of the poems written for her in high school. If he'd bothered to rehearse, Harrison would have caught that. Perspiration beaded at her hairline in an itchy way, and her head buzzed. "I don't know . . . what to say."

"Say, 'I do.'" Harrison prompted her with a hollow laugh.

"It was my mother's engagement ring," Gayle murmured. "Sapphires and diamond set in white gold."

Daphne leaned in for a closer look. "Really?"

"Can I think it over?" Caridad said.

Harrison's face tightened. A purplish flush welled like a stain, spreading from his cheeks to his ears and neck. The faces that had eagerly ringed her now withdrew in puzzlement. Even Miles gave her a stunned look, and Caridad once more imagined that Cockney rasp, Moll Flanders again purring in her ear: *It lay very heavy upon my Mind too, that I had a Son, a fine lovely Boy, above five Years old, and no Provision made for it, at least that I knew of; with these Considerations, and a sad Heart, I went home that Evening, and began to cast with my self how I should live, and in what manner to bestow my self, for the residue of my Life.*

"I mean, yes, of course." Caridad extended her hand. "It would be an honor to do you the honor . . ." Here, she grew confused. "You know what I mean. I mean, yes."

Harrison grinned, his turquoise eyes full and shining. He took her hand in his and slipped on the ring. It was loose on her finger, the stones cold and sharp.

Miles glanced at her hand. "Oh," he said. "It's just a ring."

It was just a ring. When they returned home, she would hand it back. She would tell Harrison she'd felt pressured, that she'd made a mistake. But now, surrounded by his family and in the presence of her son—with Gayle and Maxine scurrying for flutes and champagne (already on ice)—she could glow as if enraptured. Harrison had given up acting, not she. Caridad could easily feign enthusiasm for his expanding bulk, his silver-tinseled hide, the knee that would creak and pop when he rose, and even those Lennie imitations that were so on-target that they must reveal some disturbing truth about the limits of his mind. She could be kind and pretend ardor for Harrison, whose large face loomed for a kiss, the quick insertion of his pointy tongue insinuating what he expected that night in bed.

For now, she would sip champagne and bear the cool weight of the jeweled band on her finger. Knowing this would be one of their last times, she would later bear the shaggy heft of his body over hers. And late at night, after Harrison was snoring beside her, Caridad would slip out of bed to take up her book and a pen. In the amber glow of the night-light, she'd flip to the last page and compose her own margin note, as if to countermand the last phrase of Daniel Defoe's novel, the final lines that read: ". . . we resolve to spend the Remainder of our Years in sincere Penitence, for the wicked Lives we have lived."

Creep, Creep

———

After she returned home one warm afternoon in June, Caridad told
Harrison about the truck driver who tried to kill her. By this time, she
was driving again, but more tensely than before, her hands slick with
perspiration as they clamped the steering wheel. She had to drive now
that they had moved to the South and Caridad traveled to temp jobs
throughout northeast Georgia. That morning, as she'd headed out to
"work the phones" for a small company in Oglethorpe County, she'd
nearly had a wreck on the two-lane highway. An oncoming pickup
crossed the center line of the two-way road, rocketing toward her.
Caridad yanked the wheel, pulling the car onto the shoulder and startling a herd of cows in a nearby field. Twangy music blared from the
truck's open windows as it whizzed past. A beer can flew out to dance
on the blacktop.

"He tried to murder me," she told Harrison after describing the
near miss.

Though it was late afternoon, Harrison remained in bed. His sky-
blue pajama top was wrinkled, the collar splotched with tea, and his
grizzled hair was oily and salted with dandruff. "No one tried to murder you," he said. "That driver doesn't know you. It wasn't personal."

"Still, he tried to kill me."

"It was completely random." Harrison massaged his temples. "It
wasn't about you."

"How is my almost being killed not about *me*?" Caridad glanced
about the master bedroom in the ranch-style house they'd bought with

her settlement money as the down payment. The room was shadowy and warm, the plum-colored curtains drawn shut. "Did you get up at all today?"

Harrison nodded. "I went for the mail, but now I feel queasy."

Months after he and Caridad had moved to Georgia with Miles so that he could pursue a doctoral degree at the University of Georgia, Harrison had been stricken with a mysterious malady that kept him in bed most days since the spring semester ended, watching television and sipping honeyed tea. Plates, a mug, several balled-up tissues, and a collection of over-the-counter medications now crowded his nightstand. A sharp eucalyptus scent issued from an open jar of salve, permeating the stuffy bedroom.

Caridad palmed his forehead. His skin felt cool, even clammy to her touch, but this was likely because she had just come in from the heat of the day. "Any test results today?"

"No."

Apart from prescribing antihistamines for hay fever, doctors at the student health center had been unable to diagnose and treat him. Harrison's parents had arranged for him to see specialists in Atlanta—a pulmonologist, an internist, even a chiropractor and a psychologist. Caridad took time off from temping to drive him to these appointments, and they'd sent Miles to stay with her mother and sisters over the summer since Harrison was not well enough to look after him while Caridad worked.

He now gathered a few envelopes from a shelf under the nightstand. "Here's the mail—mostly bills, but there's a letter from Miles."

Caridad's heart surged. She reached for the small stack, but Harrison drew it away, holding it to his chest. "You made a bad bargain, didn't you, when you married me?"

Soon after spending the holidays with Harrison's family, Caridad had been served with a court order to comply with paternity testing, an action brought by Daniel. Thinking marriage might confer the appearance of stability should Daniel sue her for custody, she'd put off breaking her engagement to Harrison. In February, at the same time the paternity test revealed unsurprising results, Harrison was accepted to graduate school in Georgia, and Caridad agreed to marry him in early spring. Before Daniel could take her to court, she'd married, changed her name, and moved with Miles and Harrison to Georgia in July, nearly a year ago. At first, they'd enjoyed the newness of the

South, the quiet college town, and the friendly inquisitiveness of their neighbors. Then they teamed up, bolstering one another against the pervasive Christianity and conservatism of the place in the way they had joined forces to evade Daniel.

But Harrison floundered in graduate school. He struggled to keep up with the reading, and his professors were unimpressed, even puzzled, by his papers. Before becoming ill, he'd earned incompletes in two of his courses, placing him on academic probation. Instead of studying in the evenings, last spring he'd begun sipping bourbon, listening to jazz on the radio, and bickering with Caridad about Miles. These days, they argued so often that they'd started seeing a marriage counselor, a middle-aged woman who'd floored them at their last session by asking, "Where do you see yourselves in ten years?" Caridad had no answer for that.

"Bad bargain? What are you talking about?" She fixed her gaze on the envelopes he held. "I don't think like that."

Harrison flashed a quick smile before handing over the mail. "By the way, darling, when you write to him, tell Miles that I'm allergic to cats."

"But you're not—"

"Please, darling," he said, "let's not bring a cat into this. Oh, and you had a call about a job. There's a message near the phone."

Caridad read Miles's letter as she made her way to the phone in the front room.

> Dear Mommy,
> I miss you. Mimi is nice. She lets me play with Smoky. Can I have a kitty when I get home? How is my tomota plant and son flowers? I am camping with Leslie and Fill in July. Mimi to. That well be fun. I really want a kitty, ok.
> Love,
> Miles

When she finished reading Miles's letter, Caridad returned the call, phoning Mrs. Peabody-Lunsford, the director of a nonprofit agency, who arranged to interview Caridad for a permanent position the next day. The agency was so new, Mrs. Peabody-Lunsford explained, that she was only now securing office space. She then issued directions to a family restaurant in Gainesville, about an hour from Athens, where she would meet with Caridad for the interview. After hanging up, Caridad set out paper and a pen on the kitchen table to answer the letter from her son.

> *Miles, my love!*
> *I miss you, too! I think of you every day and wonder how you are and what you're doing. I hope you're enjoying your visit with your abuela and tías, and Mimi, but I am counting the days until you come home. Fifty-two. When you get back, we will find a kitten for you. Your tomato plant looks great, and the sunflowers will soon be taller than you are. Harrison sends a hug. He's still not well, but he should be better soon. When he's feeling fine, I know he will write to you, too. I'm happy you wrote to me! Please share what's in the envelope with Mimi.*
> *Love forever and ever,*
> *Mommy*

She turned over her letter, drew a picture of a smiling cat on the back, and put it in a padded envelope with small boxes of raisins, colored pencils, and stickers—treats she'd been collecting to send along with her letters. Since she had writing supplies on hand, Caridad pulled out a fresh sheet of paper.

> *Dear Leslie,*
> *I hope you and Phil are well and that you are enjoying the chance to spend time with Miles this summer. Only you know how hard it is for me to be away from him, but I had to send him. I'm glad Miles will have a few weeks with you in July. He's sure looking forward to that camping trip.*
> *We still have no idea what's making Harrison ill. Honestly, I don't think Harrison was prepared for graduate school. He's enlisted me to read books for his comprehensive exam. Right now, I'm reading <u>Pamela</u> by Samuel Richardson for him. It's an epistolary novel*

about a servant girl who's trying to preserve her sense of self and dignity despite her master's advances.

My hand is cramping, and as Pamela says in the novel, "I am going on again with a long letter; for I love writing, and shall tire you." All my best to Phil, and please write!

Love,
Me

On her first day of work at the Cooperative Community Resources, Caridad slipped out of bed quietly, so as not to disturb Harrison. She showered and dressed in the front bathroom, taking care to make little noise. The last thing she wanted was Harrison flapping about like an overgrown bat in his black kimono, offering her dense buckwheat pancakes or fist-sized muffins the texture of upholstery ticking. But when she emerged from the bathroom, he was already in the kitchen, stirring a bowl of lumpy batter and humming to opera music playing on the countertop radio.

"Good morning, darling!" he said when he saw her. "I'm making oatmeal muffins for your first day of work."

"I don't have time. I have to be at work by nine-thirty, and it's after eight."

Harrison opened a cupboard and peered in. "Everyone comes in late on the first day. It's practically de rigueur," said Harrison, who, to Caridad's knowledge, had never held a full-time job in his life.

"I want to leave early," she said. "I'm not really sure *where* the office is." She flashed on her restaurant interview with Mrs. Peabody-Lunsford, a heavy woman with a black cloud of hair and a sallow face, as mealy and grumose as the mixture in Harrison's bowl. For all her volubility during the interview, Mrs. Peabody-Lunsford had been oddly evasive about the location of the new office, as well as the position being offered.

Harrison pointed the mucky spoon at Caridad. "You'll get a headache if you don't eat breakfast."

"I'll be fine." Caridad tucked a pen and writing pad into her bag.

He stared into the bowl. "Forgive me if I happen to care about you."

"I know you do." Caridad paused to issue an apologetic smile. "Well, I've got to go." She gathered her sunglasses, bag, and keys. "See you tonight." Before he could protest, Caridad dashed out the door. She glimpsed Harrison through the carport window, sadly spooning batter into the muffin tin.

Caridad drove Harrison's Mustang, hers now that his parents had bought a Lexus and given him their Lincoln. She steered the compact car, cutting through the fog-shrouded morning past the small towns— Arcade, Pendergrass, Talmo—that cropped up along the highway into Gainesville. As she drove, the mist burned away, and the landscape grew sharply green, nearly violent with color under the bright sky. Soon, the stores, restaurants, and houses thinned out, giving way to double-wides then barns, corn and cabbage fields, cattle, and even a few goat herds. Just past the Jackson County line, Caridad swerved to avoid a turkey vulture picking at a flattened squirrel near the shoulder of the highway, and she thought of Harrison.

The back of her neck tightened as if clamped. Why was he unwell? What if he had an incurable disease? What if it was fatal and these were his last months or weeks? Ashamed of entertaining and then lingering on such thoughts, Caridad regretted not being kinder to him earlier. What if instead he had a chronic ailment, a lifelong debility? She drove past a road crew, convicts in orange jumpsuits unloading rusted drums from a truck and bearing these into a nearby ravine. Sorry for these men, she imagined trudging forth, one shaky step after another, under crushing weight, and her throat clotted.

On the left, a cemetery appeared alongside the highway. Caridad gazed at a tall tombstone ornamented with gilt cherubs and nearly missed the turn that took her to the strip of office buildings in downtown Gainesville, the location of the resource agency headed by Mrs. Peabody-Lunsford. She parked behind the building that also housed law offices and a real estate agency. Finding no signs to direct her, Caridad stepped into the main entrance and was greeted by the receptionist, a young woman who was knitting something out of pink wool at her desk.

Caridad smiled at her. "I'm looking for Cooperative Community Resources."

"That's in the basement." With a knitting needle, the woman indicated the door to the stairwell. "Down in Antarctica."

"Thank you." Caridad started toward the exit.

"Hope you brought a jacket," the receptionist called after her.

As Caridad descended toward the basement, a damp chill crept up her legs, penetrating the soft fabric of her dress. By the time she reached the bottom stair, her flesh prickled with the cold. She took a deep breath, smoothed her hair, and pulled open the door to another reception area, a large space with mauve-colored walls trimmed with dark brown wainscoting. Still-life paintings of desiccated-looking fruit decorated the walls, and plastic palms stood near closed doors to inner offices. At the heart of the gray carpet, a desk was flanked by a short wall of filing cabinets. Behind the desk sat a blond wearing a sheepskin overcoat and poring over a glossy magazine. Caridad cleared her throat, and a cantaloupe-sized head capped with yellow curls popped up from behind the desk.

"Boo!" the small head cried.

"Boo," Caridad said with a smile.

"You're supposed to be scared!" The little girl wore a green hooded sweatshirt and yellow mittens. "Momma, she's not even scared."

"Hush up and stop scaring folks," said the blond woman. "I done told you about a hundred times by now."

"I don't mind," Caridad said.

"Of *course* you mind." In the fluorescent glow of the desk lamp, the receptionist's wavy hair framed her pink-cheeked face, and her violet eyes sparkled like amethysts. "Scaring folks is just rude."

Caridad ignored this. "I'm Caridad McCann."

"So you're the new one?" The receptionist's gaze measured Caridad from head to toe. "I'm Jan, and this here is Brittany."

"Nice to meet you." Caridad smiled again before glancing at her watch. "I should probably check in with Mrs. Peabody-Lunsford."

"Ha! You think I'd be reading *People* magazine? You think I'd bring my kid to work with Peabody-Lunsford here?"

"How would I know?" Caridad shrugged. "This is just my first day."

"Now, I had to bring Brittany on account of the ringworm. They won't have her over at Vacation Bible School with the ringworm. Normally, my mother watches her when there's no VBC, but Memaw's got a hair appointment until noon."

Brittany rucked up a sleeve to reveal a patch of pink blisters on her forearm.

"No one wants to see that nasty business," Jan said before turning back to Caridad. "You may as well settle in. Micah will be here around ten."

"Micah?"

"Yeah, he's the other consultant. There are three of you, but one can't start until next month. Peabody-Lunsford is in Puerto Rico for some conference, and she said for you all to read the agency information and grant stuff until she gets back."

"Is there that much material to read?"

"Nope, there's hardly nothing," Jan said, "except the grant, but no one living can make sense of that. I suggest you bring some magazines and a big old coat. It's colder than a meat locker out here, but your office is worse. That right door leads to your office. Behind me is the break room. It's slightly warmer in there. We got a fridge and a microwave."

"Got a bathroom, too," Brittany put in. "But my mama won't mop it."

"That is *not* in my job description." Jan pulled a file sleeve from the cabinet behind her desk and slammed the thick manila folder on her desktop. "Peabody-Lunsford can sure write some gobbledygook when she has a mind to."

Caridad hefted the grant. "I guess I'll go over this then."

"You can make coffee, if you want, in the break room."

"Would you like some?" Caridad asked.

"*No-o-o-o*, caffeine makes me edgy."

While coffee dripped into the carafe, releasing a burst of warmth with its rich burnt-chocolate aroma, Caridad perused the grant in the break room, which was not as chilly the office—which included three desks, a corkboard, a carton of office supplies, a filing cabinet, and a typewriter—she'd been assigned. On a legal pad she'd taken from the carton in that office, Caridad struggled to translate the vague and obscurely written grant just for her own understanding. After deciphering a few confounding passages, Caridad dropped her pen and flexed her stiff fingers. The door to the break room banged open, and Jan appeared with Brittany at her side. "Micah called," she said, a disappointed look on her face. "He's not coming in today. He's got to buy a car over in Lawrenceville. He'll be here tomorrow."

Caridad nodded.

"I'm taking Brittany home for lunch and might not come back myself. If you feel like it, you can answer the phone," she said. "If not, the machine will click on. The doors are all set to lock if you shut them all the way." Jan withdrew from the threshold, tugging Brittany by the hood of her sweatshirt.

At the mention of lunch, Caridad's stomach rumbled. She flipped through the grant to the end—one hundred fifty-three pages—and so far, she had transcribed only six of these. The small window above the sink framed two pairs of feet in high heels clip-clopping past, and a woman's laughter rang out. Someone said, "Never again!" A church bell tolled twelve times—nine o'clock in Los Angeles. Miles would be up and likely heading for his ceramics class with Mimi. Caridad slapped the file sleeve shut and shoved the grant off to the side. She flipped to a blank sheet of lined paper and picked up her pen again.

> *Dear Esperanza,*
> *I hate this, I hate this, I hate this! I don't know why*
> *I'm here or what I'm supposed to be doing, and I'm*
> *not just referring to this stupid new job. I'm thinking*
> *about my life. Why am I here when my son is over two*
> *thousand miles away? I swear there are times when I*

The phone rang in the outer office, startling Caridad. Thinking it might be Mrs. Peabody-Lunsford, she bolted for Jan's desk to snatch up the receiver. "Cooperative Community Resources," Caridad said. "How may I help you?"

"Hey, Jan, how you doing today?" It was a man's voice. He spoke with a raspy drawl, an accent different from that which Caridad had gotten used to in Georgia.

"Jan's stepped out of the office," Caridad said. "May I take a message?"

"Who am I speaking to?"

"This is Caridad McCann. I'm a community resource consultant."

"Why, I am, too. I'm Lazar, Lazar Chagall—like the painter, but trust me, no relation," he said. "I haven't started yet, but Jan needs some information for the conference we're supposed to attend next month. She faxed me the form and left a message for me to call. Do you know anything about that?"

"No, and Mrs. Peabody-Lunsford isn't here, but let me see what I can find out." Caridad rifled through the papers stacked in Jan's inbox until she found the form with his name on it. "Is it for Southeast Prevention Education Workshops?"

"That's right—SPEW." Lazar chuckled. "They ought to rethink that acronym."

Caridad picked up a pen. "I can fill in the form for you if you want."

"Okay, here goes. For occupation, put down social worker. Where it asks about education, write in MSW, and for marital status, mark single. I'm twenty-eight, so check the box for twenty-five to thirty-five."

"So am I," Caridad blurted out. "I'll be twenty-nine in a few months."

"I guess that makes you the boss of me," Lazar said. "I just turned twenty-eight." He gave her his address for the form and told her to check boxes for sessions she thought might be interesting. "It's all the same to me, and I've got to go now."

"I'll make sure Jan sees this first thing." Under Lazar's form, Caridad found one with her name on it. She would sign them up for the same sessions. No reason for her to navigate SPEW on her own.

"Say, thanks for doing this. I look forward to meeting you at the conference."

After hanging up, Caridad returned to the break room. She tore out the page on which she'd started a letter to Esperanza and ripped it in half, then into quarters, before shredding the paper into unreadable strips that she stuffed into the wastebasket. Caridad poured herself a cup of coffee and then wandered into the chilly office she would share with Lazar and Micah, remembering the typewriter she'd seen earlier.

> *Dear Mama, Felicia, and Esperanza,*
> *I hope all of you are well and enjoying your time with Miles. Thank you for getting him to write to me. You don't know how much I appreciate your having him this summer. It won't be long until Harrison recovers. Already he seems better. Just this morning, he was well enough to get out of bed to make me a hearty breakfast.*
> *Last time I called you, I mentioned that I'd found a full-time job with a nonprofit agency. Today is my first day. So far, the work is neither too hard nor too easy—it's mostly confusing, as any job is at the start. I'm sure I will soon figure out my responsibilities and find satisfaction in the work. Already it's a huge relief not to have to drive all over for temp jobs.*

I miss you all and think of you often. Please write or call me when you can. Kiss Miles for me and make sure he really is brushing his teeth and not just telling you he has. Give Mimi a hug for me and tell her I miss her like crazy.

Love,
Dah-Dah

The next day, Caridad arrived at the Gainesville office with a peanut-butter sandwich and apple tucked into her bag, along with a hooded sweatshirt. She was determined to finish decoding the grant. In doing this, she would learn her duties and begin performing these. Jan again sat at her desk and flipped through a magazine, but Brittany was nowhere in sight. Caridad asked if the little girl had recovered from ringworm. Jan shook her head. "She's with Memaw today."

Caridad pulled on her sweatshirt almost as soon as she stepped over the threshold into the office she'd been assigned, but within minutes, her fingers ached from the cold and moist chuffs of her breath became visible. She soon gathered up the grant and writing materials to move to the break room.

"Told you," Jan said when Caridad reappeared in the reception area. "That office is an icebox. Waste of energy, if you ask me."

"Can't it be fixed?"

Jan shrugged. "That's a maintenance issue."

In the break room, Caridad again set out the grant and resumed where she'd left off. She had nearly reached the tenth page when she gave up on the project. Instead, she'd attempt to read it, taking notes only when necessary.

After several minutes, the door flew open. A lanky man in his early twenties stood at the threshold, a newspaper tucked under his arm. He wore an overcoat over a light gray suit. "You're not reading that crap, are you?" He tilted his chin toward the grant. "Can you believe they gave her money for that? My lord, they should have locked her up in a remedial writing class over at the alternative school."

"Micah?" Caridad said.

"That's right, and you must be the woman whose name I will butcher if I try to say it."

"It's Caridad," she said.

With his padded coat, muffler, mittens, and hat with earflaps, he looked like an overgrown kid dressed up to go to church in a blizzard. He raised his fine eyebrows, his brown eyes shining above his long pink-tipped nose. "Carry *Dad*?"

Caridad winced. "Close enough."

"How about I call you Carrie?"

"That works," she said. "Did you buy the car? Yesterday?"

"Oh *no-o-o-o*. What a bust. I was expecting an eyeballer, but it was a total come-on."

"Eyeballer?"

"Dealer slang for a flashy thing, a sweet-looking sports car, but crazy affordable, at least according to the ad," Micah said. "Of course, once I get there, the dickhead—now I've got what you call a well-integrated personality, so I curse the same in public as in private—so the dickhead tells me it's sold, if it ever even existed outside of some hound dog's wet dream in the first place."

"Sorry about that," Caridad said.

"That's not the worst of it. Once I'm there, the dealer goes slasher on me, like I haven't been buying cars since I was eighteen, like I'm some fucking grape." Micah's eyes widened in outrage. "I didn't even want the car for me. I *have* me a damn car. I was looking at it for a guy I know who's going to pay me half what I save him off the sticker price."

"Well," Caridad began uncertainly, "maybe next time."

"To-*day*." Micah slapped the classifieds on the table alongside the grant. "I'm going to find a car for the guy to-*day*. I'm determined. Nothing's going to stop me, unless of course, you don't want me plugging a phone in here to make my calls. I'd do it in our office, but I already had pneumonia once this year."

"Go ahead. I don't mind." Caridad looked forward to having company, and another body would likely generate more warmth in the room.

"You aren't seriously reading that thing?" Micah indicated the grant. "You should bring a newspaper. I've been here a month, and one thing I learned right away is to keep occupied until Peabody-Lunsford figures out what in heck we're supposed to be doing."

"So you have no idea—"

Micah shook his head. "Not a clue. PL has only written one job description—Jan's."

"Pee-Ell?"

"Short for Peabody-Lunsford," Micah said. "There's supposedly something in the grant about us, but I've been here a month, and I haven't found it. I'm trying to get old PL to buy us a television, but until then, bring stuff to keep busy. Got any hobbies?"

Caridad nodded. She again replaced the grant in its folder and flipped to a blank page of notepaper. While Micah called dealerships in and around Atlanta, Caridad wrote letters to Miles, Mimi, Phil, and Miles again. She thought about writing another to her sisters and mother, but she had just mailed the one she'd written the day before, so instead, she started a sonnet about convicts bearing oxidized drums into a mist-shrouded ravine.

Days later, on a stormy evening in June, Caridad sat with Harrison at the kitchen table summarizing Samuel Richardson's *Pamela: Or, Virtue Rewarded* for him. Thunderclaps rocked the house and lightning illuminated the bay windows with incandescent flashes. Harrison, in his black kimono, jotted notes onto index cards, sipping wine as Caridad listed characters and outlined the novel's plot. She retold the story of the teenaged heroine resisting the advances of her new master, a man entrusted with her care after Pamela's former mistress, his mother, had died. Pamela writes about her struggles to her parents, who are unable to help her. When her master intercepts and reads her letters, he falls in love with Pamela and romances her until she agrees to marry him. Caridad thumbed through the novel, reading aloud quotes she'd marked for Harrison. Her favorite of these appeared near the ending: "I know not how it came, nor when it begun; but creep, creep it has, like a Thief upon me; and before I knew what was the Matter, it look'd like Love." Over the course of the epistolary novel, Pamela places great value on virtue and truthfulness, often signing letters to her parents, "Your honest daughter."

Harrison snorted when Caridad told him this. "Ironic!" He reached for the wine bottle to refill his glass. "She sounds like a proper temptress, a scheming little wench."

"She's only fifteen in the novel. She's an innocent—"

"You're the innocent, darling." Harrison's eyes glinted under the glow of the overhead fixture, an indulgent look softening his face. "Trust me, Pamela's working an angle from day one. He comes from money, and she wants a piece of the action. Fielding had a field day—pardon the pun—with the book when he wrote *Shamela*."

Caridad pushed back her chair and rose from the table. "If you already know what the book is about, why did you ask me to read it?"

He grasped her hand and stood. "Don't be cross. Not everyone catches the irony in it."

"But it's not an especially ironic book. That's the thing. It's about skewed power dynamics between master and servant, one a poor girl and the other a privileged man who isolates her from her family, who doesn't care that she's lonely—"

Harrison stopped her mouth with a kiss and then withdrew to say, "Oh, darling." His breath was hot and sour, and the triangle of snowy hair revealed by his loose robe smelled briny beneath the mentholated salve. "Don't you wish we were *done* with all this?"

Though certain her idea of "this" was different than his, Caridad nodded.

"Done with all the reading, the papers, the tests." Harrison closed his eyes as if envisioning such freedom. "Don't you wish we could stop worrying about the future?" he asked. "You know what? We should make a baby."

Caridad stepped back to read his expression. Was he drunk? "How does that make any kind of sense?" she asked.

"Think about it, darling. If you got pregnant, my parents would be out of their minds with joy. Their first grandchild—why, they'd set us up for life!"

"That is not one bit funny."

"I'm not joking," he said.

"Then it's a bad idea for too many reasons for me to go into right now, but the first that comes to mind is that you're not well." After a battery of tests, only the psychologist ventured a diagnosis for Harrison's condition, prescribing an antidepressant called Ludiomil to treat it.

"It's just depression. You can say it, darling. I don't mind. It's not contagious—"

"What about heredity?" Caridad said. "You told me your father has depression, and his father, too. Why would you risk passing this on to a child?"

"It probably isn't even clinical," Harrison said. "It's probably more anxiety than depression, some existential angst or ennui."

"You say you don't want to bring a cat into this, and then you suggest we have a *baby*?" Caridad gawked at him in disbelief. Harrison assumed the expression he wore when imitating Lennie from *Of Mice and Men*, adopting the slack jaw and empty eyes of an overgrown dullard, a lummox. "Maybe you shouldn't drink while you're taking those pills."

"How dare you." His face darkened. "Do you have any idea how insulting that is?" He grabbed the wine bottle and his glass before stalking off. Within seconds, the bedroom door banged shut, shaking the walls like another thunderclap.

The second week of July, attendees of SPEW gathered in the ballroom of a downtown Atlanta hotel for the plenary address that opened the conference. The presentation was given by a specialist in Native American substance-abuse prevention, an elderly white woman who wore a rawhide headband and long gray braids that rested on the beaded yoke of her buckskin regalia. The woman began by burning sage near the podium. A sweet herbal aroma wafted through the rows of folding chairs, reminding Caridad of Thanksgiving dinners at Mama's. Murmured voices blended into a low hum as more people shuffled in, claiming seats. Caridad set her handbag on the empty chair to her left, saving it for Lazar Chagall. She'd not yet met him, and she was curious, so she'd contrived to sit near him; Micah and Jan were on the right of Mrs. Peabody-Lunsford, who sat beside Caridad.

Most of the seats in the vast chandeliered room had filled by the time the braided woman finished burning sage and commenced a Native American prayer, but stragglers still trickled in. When a slender man with gingery blond hair appeared in the entryway at the front of the auditorium, Mrs. Peabody-Lunsford waved her arms overhead as if directing a plane to land. "That's Lazar Chagall," she told Caridad. "Now our team is complete."

Lazar wove his way to the seat near Caridad, nodding at Mrs. Peabody-Lunsford as he passed. The braided woman spoke in a high reedy voice, welcoming the conference attendees before launching into her speech. After a few minutes, the speaker's voice dropped until it was inaudible despite the podium's microphone. Lazar glanced at Caridad's feet and leaned to whisper in her ear. "Nice shoes."

Caridad wore black ballerina flats, the only shoes she could endure wearing all day since the accident. "Thank you," she said in a low voice.

"They look comfortable," Lazar told her.

As the speaker continued, Caridad stole a few glances at her new colleague. Lazar was only slightly taller than she, and he wore a pale blue dress shirt and an espresso brown suit with tan pinstripes. Lazar smelled minty and new. He was clean-shaven, and his fair hair was flattened with gel, his suit well pressed, and his shirt crisp, but his brown leather shoes were soft with wear and scuffed at the toes. He caught her eye and grinned. Caridad then fixed her gaze on the braided woman in front earnestly delivering a speech that no one could hear.

At her side, Lazar sniffed the air. "Turkey?"

"Sage," Caridad said in a low voice.

Lazar grinned. "Thanks."

Session after session, Caridad and Lazar, sometimes joined by Micah, sat quietly in the break-out rooms as "prevention specialists" hammered home ideas about increasing protective factors and reducing risk factors in communities and schools. Despite their various charts, handouts, and slide-show displays, they all seemed to be saying the same thing, so after the first few minutes of each presentation, Caridad would swallow back a yawn or two. Then she'd ease her notebook out of her handbag and dig out her pen.

> *Dear Felicia,*
> *Thank you for signing Miles and Mimi up for ceramics at the recreation center. Mama tells me you've paid for the three-week session and you're driving the kids to the classes yourself. Summer vacation is your time to recuperate from the school year, so I really appreciate that you're doing this.*
>
> *All is well here. My new job is interesting, and while the woman I work for is a bit peculiar, my coworkers seem fine. I'm now at a work-related conference, and I have a bit of downtime, so I thought I'd write to you. The conference is in Atlanta, and the agency is providing rooms for us in the hotel where it's being held. I'm a bit worried about leaving Harrison*

*on his own these few days, even though he is doing
better with the medication he's been prescribed . . .*

Jan returned to the office in Gainesville after she got the conference paperwork turned in and collected employment forms from Lazar. Mrs. Peabody-Lunsford also disappeared following the morning's plenary session, but she rejoined the consultants for the banquet luncheon, her black hair freshly dyed and coiffed. She sat with Caridad, Lazar, and Micah at a round table near the center of the ballroom-turned-dining-area. PL dug her spoon into a bowl of banana pudding before starting the main dish—a chicken breast with wild rice and green beans. She asked the consultants what they'd learned at the conference.

"Risk factors," Micah mumbled, his mouth full of chicken.

Caridad took her cue from him. "Protective factors."

"Prevention," Lazar said, "is the key to stronger communities and schools."

Mrs. Peabody-Lunsford dabbed her mouth, crimsoning her linen napkin with lipstick, and she smiled. "Communities *and* schools— what I want to know is who took the schools out of communities?" she said. "Still, there's much to learn here, and I hope you all are absorbing worthwhile information." A black woman wearing a lavender hat bedecked with artificial flowers, ribbons, and a twist of tulle waved the director over from across the hall. PL rose from her seat, saying, "You'll have to excuse me. The big-hat women are very powerful here."

Micah pointed to the notebook protruding from Caridad's bag. "This one's absorbing up a storm of information." He turned to Lazar. "Have you noticed her scribbling everything down in a fury?"

"A mighty notetaker," Lazar said.

A mighty letter-writer—Caridad flashed on Pamela. She smiled and sipped her iced tea.

"Are you going to eat that?" Micah indicated Caridad's pudding with his fork.

She regarded the pale gelatinous mass and shook her head. Lazar pushed his bowl toward Micah. "You can have this, too, if you want."

On the way to the next session, Lazar invited Caridad and Micah to join him for a drink in the hotel bar after the conference adjourned for the day. Caridad accepted, but Micah said he had plans to meet his fiancée that night. As the three made their way through the corridor past the many milling conference-goers, Caridad searched for a restroom. She caught sight of Mrs. Peabody-Lunsford deep in conversation with a woman donning a large scarlet hat with black feathers just outside a ladies' room. Caridad nodded at both before entering the pink tiled-room where an olive-skinned woman with graying hair was sponging the countertops. She met Caridad's gaze in the mirror and smiled as if in recognition. "Buenas tardes."

At the start of the next session, a panel presentation, Caridad whipped out her notepaper and pen.

> *Dear Mama,*
> *I miss you with all my heart . . .*

After the welcome dinner and keynote address, Caridad and Lazar marched in a great parade of conference-goers toward the lounge. They claimed a booth some distance from their noisy colleagues now thronging the long bar. Despite the crowd, a cocktail waitress soon appeared at their table. Lazar ordered a beer and Caridad asked for a glass of Chardonnay.

"Who knew," Lazar said, "that substance-abuse prevention specialists would stampede for drinks at the end of the day?"

"It makes sense," Caridad told him. "All this talk of abstinence makes a person thirsty."

Lazar smiled at her, his gray eyes wide. "Caridad," he said. "That means charity, doesn't it?"

"That's right. Do you speak Spanish?"

"I do," he said. "I worked in Santo Domingo for two years before I moved here."

"What did you do there?"

"Peace Corps," he said. "But before that, I was a dual major in college—Spanish and sociology. I've always loved languages, and Spanish is my favorite. When I found out your name, I was hoping you'd speak Spanish with me. It's been such a long time since I practiced that I worry I'll lose what I've learned."

"I bet your Spanish is better than mine. I haven't spoken it much since I was a child, but I can practice with you if you like," Caridad said. "But first, tell me about your name. I've never met anyone named Lazar before."

"It's Hebrew," he told her. "It means helped by God."

"So are you . . ."

He nodded, and the waitress reappeared to set their drinks on the table. When she retreated bearing her heavy tray of drinks to another table, Lazar said, "Micah's name is Hebrew, too, though I doubt he's Jewish. His name means one who resembles God."

"You know it wouldn't be so bad if that were true. Think of what we'd save on cars if God were like Micah."

Lazar gave her a puzzled look, and Caridad explained about their coworker's hobby. They talked about Micah and Jan and Mrs. Peabody-Lunsford for a few moments until Lazar said, "Hablame en español por favor."

Over the next hour, they spoke at first in halting and then in fluent Spanish about previous jobs, family and friends, the men and women they admired most.

"Tell me," Lazar asked Caridad in Spanish, "who is the greatest man you know?"

"Pues," said Caridad, thinking of Leslie and wondering how to put it in Spanish that the greatest man she knew—her ex-husband—was, in fact, now a woman. "Es difícil a decir."

The bar had emptied some, and the waitress returned to deposit their check on the tabletop. "Oh, it's getting late." Caridad reached for her handbag, but Lazar insisted on paying since he'd invited her for a drink.

"Ask me next time and you can pay," he said.

They left the bar and meandered toward the lobby, still speaking to one another in Spanish. Caridad appreciated that she was eye level with Lazar. Gazing up at Harrison cramped her neck.

"It's really not that late," Lazar said when they reached the elevators. "Would you like to go somewhere?"

Caridad stood with him before the elevator, the burnished metal doors projecting a quivery image of them both as if they were underwater, submerged in a silvery sea. She hadn't told him she was married, and because she disliked jewelry, Caridad rarely wore her rings. Her conscience pricked her now, and she felt wavery, lambent as her reflection. This was no lightning bolt, but it was something sparkly and thrilling. How easy it would be to step out with Lazar into the neon-lit Atlanta night. "I know not how it came, nor when it begun; but creep, creep it has like a Thief upon me . . ." Another Caridad, an earlier version, would have swept through the revolving doors with him, spinning out into the city on his arm. But this Caridad, near thirty, had a husband who was ill, a son who needed stability, and a job she intended to keep.

"Maybe a jazz club," he said, "or a show?"

"I have to call my husband," she told him, "and then I'm just going to turn in."

"Oh, okay." Lazar blinked several times and took a step back. "Yes, right—long day." He pushed the elevator button for her. "I need to get my bag. I haven't even checked in yet."

The elevator's doors parted, and Caridad stepped inside. "I'll see you tomorrow?"

"Yep." Lazar issued a quick smile and pivoted for the front desk.

The doors closed and Caridad rode up to her room on the top floor, thinking of the stationery she'd found in the writing desk—thick cream-colored pages embossed with the hotel's insignia. She pictured the faux Tiffany lamp atop this, its glow on the green blotter, a soft circle of light.

Clay and Daimon

———

It would have to be quiche. Caridad peered into the refrigerator at a dewy jug of milk, a carton of eggs, a wedge of gruyere cheese, and a cellophane bag of baby spinach leaves. She could serve the egg pie with the cantaloupe half in the fruit bin. After setting out the bowl, measuring cups, and ingredients, she flipped on the stereo. National Public Radio was broadcasting a BBC program featuring Scottish music. A lively clamor of bagpipes, fiddles, and flutes filled the kitchen, and Caridad longed to lift her knees and fling out her feet, one in front of the other, with her fingers laced behind her back, so glad was she not to have to drive to Gainesville on a Friday. Remembering that Harrison still slept, she lowered the volume, but it was too late. Footfalls pounded in the hallway, and he soon appeared at the threshold.

Harrison released a huge yawn and rubbed his eyes. "I don't see why he has to come here. Why can't you meet at Denny's?"

"Lazar's nice enough to drive out here to go to the health fair with me. The least I can do is offer him breakfast." Mrs. Peabody-Lunsford hadn't wanted her to represent the center at the Athens Health Fair, but Lazar supported the idea, offering to help Caridad set up the informational display. "Don't you want to meet him?"

He shook his head. "Look at me. I'm exhausted. I haven't been well in weeks." Though he could use a shower, Harrison appeared well fed, even rested. Caridad hoped that having a guest would prompt him to clean up a bit, the way he used to preen himself for social events. He'd had many friends before they moved to Georgia, and from ironing his shirts to patting on aftershave, he'd enjoyed getting ready for entertaining or going out with them.

"I think you'll like Lazar." Caridad measured flour into the sifter. "He's a social worker who was in the Peace Corps. He spent two years in the Dominican Republic developing a job-training program, and then he worked as a substance-abuse counselor. He's a CASA volunteer, and he teaches GED classes at the prison in—"

"Sounds like a do-gooder to me."

She shook her head. "He's not like that. He's smart and funny. Just give him a chance."

Harrison gestured at the mixing bowl. "What are you making?"

"Quiche."

"Of course, *quiche*! Do we have champagne for mimosas?"

Caridad looked up at him. "What's wrong?"

Harrison's eyes thickened. "You're going to fall in love, aren't you?" he said. "You're going to fall in love with him and leave me."

"Oh, Harrison!" She wiped her hands on the dish towel and rounded the counter to draw him into an embrace. "Why would you say such a thing?"

He clung to her, resting his chin on the top of her head. "Sometimes I get these feelings, and I don't know if it's intuition or just paranoia."

Caridad stroked his back while wondering if such worry projected *his* desire to be free of her. Remembering how he'd whistle when preparing to go out with friends prompted her to see that he had been happy before they married and moved to the South.

"Why don't you have a shower while I finish the quiche?" she said. "Lazar will be here soon, and you'll see there's nothing to worry about."

Harrison pulled a tissue from his pocket and honked into it. "I guess it might be fine to have a guest." He lumbered for the shower, and Caridad turned up the jigging music. She foresaw Harrison forging a fast friendship with Lazar, the way he had with Leslie, and in time, they would all go out to restaurants, concerts, and movies, double-dating if Lazar had a girlfriend. Maybe being with her wasn't what depressed Harrison. What if he just missed his old life, his friends? Lazar's visit would do him good, she was sure of it.

But later when he opened the door for Lazar, whose gingery hair flashed goldfish-bright in the sunlight pouring through the bay windows, Harrison seemed to deflate, recoiling from the threshold, his eyes hooded and furtive. By contrast, Lazar appeared alert and energetic, neatly dressed in blue jeans and a short-sleeved aqua-and-gray striped shirt. With a paperback tucked under his left arm, he extended his other hand to Harrison. "I'm Lazar. You must be Harrison?"

After shaking hands, Harrison mumbled something about having to leave. He sidestepped Lazar and hurried out the door. Caridad gaped after him.

"Is everything okay?" Lazar asked.

The Lincoln's engine roared in the carport, and Caridad shook her head. "I should have told you. Harrison is . . . unwell." She pushed the door shut as the car backed out of the carport and peeled, tires squealing, into the street.

"Sorry to hear that."

"He's getting better," Caridad said. "It takes time, though."

Lazar nodded. Then he handed her the book. "This is for you. It's *Justine* by Lawrence Durrell. I notice you like novels with women's names, so I thought you might enjoy this one. It's a favorite of mine."

Caridad examined the book. Its cover depicted a view from a boat: a coastal town of whitewashed edifices shimmering across an expanse of water. "What's it about?"

"It's the story of these four characters in Alexandria, Egypt. One is the narrator, who meets this woman, Justine, and she introduces him to her husband, so she's married, but they, well . . ." Lazar's face pinkened. "I won't spoil it for you. Just see what you think."

The kitchen timer buzzed, and Caridad hurried to pull out the quiche, a golden-brown pie embroidered with deep green whorls of spinach. She set it on the stove top and removed her oven mitts to prod the tawny crust. It was firm to the touch, but flaky. The lime-sprinkled cantaloupe released a sweet perfume from its bowl nearby. Even if Harrison had weirdly walked out, the breakfast she'd serve Lazar should be just right.

The Athens Health Fair—fifty or more people milling about a cluster of booths and table displays—was held at the East Athens Community Park. Once she and Lazar arrived at the park, Caridad realized that Mrs. Peabody-Lunsford had been right. There was no reason for Cooperative Community Resources to be represented here, except that Caridad hadn't wanted to drive to Gainesville and that she and

Lazar looked forward to a day of sunshine at the park. Mrs. Peabody-Lunsford had yet to compose their job descriptions, and despite her recent purchase of mobile phones for their cars, the director had grown more and more reluctant to release the consultants she'd hired from the confines of the chilly basement office.

As he propped the display board on a picnic table, Lazar speculated on Mrs. Peabody-Lunsford's reasons for this. "Maybe she's afraid we might actually accomplish something." Over the summer, Micah had been content tracking car deals for buyers willing to split what he saved them, and Caridad, who had finished two sonnets, was now composing an essay on Richardson's *Pamela*. She told herself the piece would be helpful to Harrison for his comprehensive exams, but it could also serve as a critical writing sample if she applied to the university's doctoral program. Caridad and Micah didn't much mind the long empty hours at work, but being paid to do nothing rankled Lazar.

"Peabody-Lunsford's probably worried that we'll draw attention to the fact that all she does is waste funding," he said.

"Do you really think so?" Caridad arrayed pamphlets and refrigerator magnets on the table along with a bowl of butterscotch disks to attract passersby. More likely, Mrs. Peabody-Lunsford suspected her trio of consultants would goof off if unsupervised, and she preferred to have them goof off where she could keep an eye on them. Or perhaps Micah had been right when he'd said, "She just doesn't know what the fuck to do with us." Caridad arranged ballpoint pens so these fanned out before the candy bowl. Pamphlets, magnets, and pens were all printed with the center's logo, a key inscribed with the initials CCR and its phone number, but she had no idea *why* anyone would ever call the agency.

"She takes prevention too far," Lazar said, "by preventing us from doing any kind of meaningful work."

The morning was clear and radiant, though the early warmth promised a punishing afternoon of heat and humidity. Now the air smelled of freshly mown grass, grass that still sparkled with dewdrops. A spangled knoll rose in the distance, cresting at the tree line, a cluster of pines huddled together like hooded giants. Runners jogged by on paved trails, unfazed by the fair's displays, many booths festooned with bold signs and balloons. The attendees were were mainly people from the nearby housing projects and retirees. A line formed at the blood pressure testing booth, and the candy dish Caridad had set out soon emptied. Just before noon, a gaggle of teenaged black girls emerged from the tree line and wandered to the picnic area, one of them holding a baby wearing pink barrettes in her short weave. The teenagers browsed various booths and displays before making their way to the picnic table where Caridad and Lazar stood talking.

"What do you all do here?" one asked as the others snatched up pens and magnets, leaving the pamphlets untouched.

"Well . . ." Caridad began, unsure of how to describe CCR's activities because, so far, there had been none. "It's a community resource center."

"We're *supposed* to prevent substance abuse through increasing protective factors and reducing risk factors," Lazar said.

The girl with the baby peered into the empty candy bowl. "You got any more candy?"

"No, sorry." On an impulse, Caridad tweaked the baby's bare foot, as silky and plush as a satin sachet. "How old is she?"

"Six months." She shifted the baby's weight on her hip and grinned, baring braces. "You got to bring more candy, one of those big sacks from Sam's."

Her friends laughed, and she said, "Next time, get a jumbo bag of Tootsie Rolls, a'ight?"

"Where are you all from?" Lazar asked.

One gestured in the direction of the housing projects. "Parkview," another said.

"Here." The girl with braces thrust the baby in her arms at Caridad. "You want to hold her for a little while?"

"What?" Caridad fumbled for the baby. "Oh!"

"We'll be right back," she said. Giggling, the teenagers traded looks and turned away. They hustled away from the sheltered picnic area before charging up the slope and disappearing into the tree line.

The baby in Caridad's arms watched her mother retreat with wide, unblinking eyes.

"Hope they do come back." Lazar tickled the baby under her chin, and she crinkled her nubbin of a nose, grunting with laughter.

Caridad hoped they'd take their time before returning. The warm talc-scented bundle molded as easily as Miles had into her arms. Though she loved the little boy he had become, Caridad missed his babyhood keenly and wanted to hold on to this infant as she recalled the time when her son was this small. "Wish they'd left a bottle," she said, "and some diapers."

Lazar shrugged. "They'll probably be right back."

But they didn't return, not for more than an hour. After the baby's diaper leaked on Caridad's lap, Lazar drove to the Walmart for diapers and a bottle that he filled with distilled water. After she'd changed the baby and given her the bottle, Lazar took a turn holding her while Caridad shook out her cramping arms.

He lowered himself onto the picnic bench to bounce the baby gently on his knee, and Caridad wished for a camera to take a picture of the two. Such a snapshot subverted a portrait she'd once seen in a book: the image of a tense and unsmiling black woman holding a joyous white baby. Like that daguerreotype, this composition was a study in contrasts: ginger-haired Lazar thrown into sharp relief by the dark-skinned baby in his arms, his anxious expression contrasting with the baby's calm gaze to reveal something essential yet unnamable about what was to come—a luminant glint that dissolved as swiftly as Caridad tried to grasp it. Still, she longed to capture this image before those girlish voices sounded in the distance and the teenagers appeared to reclaim her, as they would just when the baby fell asleep, taking the bottle and diapers with them before once again vanishing into the tree line.

At the end of the next week, Mrs. Peabody-Lunsford arranged to go with her consultants to a prevention workshop in Dalton, Georgia, near the Tennessee state line. She'd booked rooms for them at the hotel where the training would be held. Though no advocate of fieldwork, Mrs. Peabody-Lunsford was avid to register and accompany consultants for such trainings, joining them only for meals provided by the trainers. After the last session ended early (dinner on your own) and Mrs. Peabody-Lunsford had slipped away, Lazar invited Caridad and Micah to visit the Tennessee Aquarium in Chattanooga, just thirty miles away.

"I've never been to Tennessee," Caridad said. "I'd like to go."

"To see what? A bunch of fish?" Micah wrinkled his nose as if he could smell these from Dalton. "I'd rather hit that used-car dealership downtown while it's still open."

As Micah bounded toward the parking lot, Lazar snapped his fingers. "Oh, Caridad, before I forget—I had a call from Harrison on my car phone. Did he reach you?"

She nodded. The mobile phones Mrs. Peabody-Lunsford had purchased had numbers that were sequential, and the last digit of Lazar's was one off from Caridad's.

"Is everything okay?"

"He was just checking in," Caridad said. Harrison had suggested joining her in Dalton, but she'd discouraged this, claiming to be busy with the training. "Do I have time to change before the aquarium?"

"Sure." Lazar arranged to meet her in the lobby in ten minutes. In her room, Caridad scrubbed the makeup off her face and threw on a pair of blue jeans and a white blouse. She brushed her hair and hurried downstairs to find Lazar waiting at the front desk for directions. A group of businessmen was checking in, the clerk resolving a complication with their reservation. Caridad and Lazar talked about the training while they waited, joking about the enthusiastic facilitator, when the green blur of a bank note whooshed across the floor. Lazar snatched it up. Without missing a beat, he tucked the bill—a twenty— into his shirt pocket.

"Are you going to turn that in?" Caridad asked. "To the desk clerk, I mean?"

"Nope."

Her heart flipped.

Lazar had lifted a twenty from the floor, and Caridad bounced on the balls of her feet. Exhilaration effervesced in her, bubbling in her throat until she yearned to leap up and down. Lazar—a man who provided job training in the Dominican Republic, who was an advocate for juveniles in the justice system, and who taught basic math to convicts—had swiped twenty dollars in a hotel lobby. For all his commitment to humanitarian acts, he would take what did not belong to him. She knew this now. He'd scooped the bill up and folded it into his pocket as if it were nothing, an unthinking act of theft that was everything to her right now. *Everything!*

"What is it?" Lazar eyed her in a wary way.

Caridad shook her head. "I'll tell you later. I promise I will." Someday she'd tell him how it happened for her and that she wasn't sorry or afraid to be first. Even if it never happened for him, though she hoped it would, Caridad had at last been gobsmacked, as a BBC radio host liked to say, utterly astounded by—what was it? Could she say it? Or would it be devalued if she tried to purchase it with an inflated and overused word? She glimpsed a green corner of the bill stashed in

Lazar's pocket, and noted the date: Thursday, August 1, 1985. Caridad glanced at the wall clock behind the check-in desk. Four seventeen.

"Still want to go?"

"I do." She reached for his elbow, startling Lazar and surprising herself as she took his arm and entwined it with her own.

The next week, Caridad and Harrison had an appointment with Francine, the marriage counselor they'd been seeing. Once in the lamp-lit office with its homey living room furniture, and with Francine to bear witness, Caridad would tell Harrison she could no longer live with him because, because . . . Though determined to carry through with this, she faltered here, uncertain whether or not to mention Lazar. In fact, she was unsure about Lazar. After the aquarium, the great glass walls that seemed to submerge them in watery depths, neon-bright fish darting past, and after the drive back to Dalton, he'd stood at the threshold of her hotel room, drawing her close as if to kiss her. But then he'd pulled back. "I better not," he said. "We better not." He'd turned away to go to his own room.

After that night, Caridad made a hard choice. At work, she'd put aside her essay on *Pamela* to list pros and cons on notepaper. She'd debated herself aloud in the car while commuting to work. She'd even written a harshly worded letter to herself, to which she'd replied, writing herself again to apologize and explain. In the end, she saw that there was no way for her to continue living with Harrison. Miles would return to start school in less than two weeks; they would have to separate before then. Though she wanted to remain in the house—the down payment made from her settlement funds and monthly payments largely afforded by her salary—Caridad might have to relinquish it since she'd be the one to instigate the separation and it was closer to the university Harrison attended than to the center where she worked.

In the antechamber to Francine's office, Caridad sat reading *Justine*, her eyes tracing and retracing the same passage, a journal entry of Justine's: "'Idle,' she writes, 'to imagine falling in love as a correspondence of minds, of thoughts; it is a simultaneous firing of two spirits engaged in the autonomous act of growing up. And the sensation is of something having noiselessly exploded inside each of them . . . All this may precede the first look, kiss, or touch; precede ambition, pride or envy; precede the first declarations which mark the turning point—for from here love degenerates into habit, possession, and back to loneliness.'" She glanced up, her face warming as if Harrison, beside her, could see how these words struck her. But he pored over an issue of *Family Circle*, engrossed in an article on backyard barbecuing.

A skeletally thin man stepped out of the inner office and nodded to her on his way to the door. Moments later, Francine appeared to summon them. "Come on in," she said. "I hope you all don't mind if I eat my salad while we talk." She was a statuesque brunette who favored brocade jackets in neutral colors—mauve, taupe, puce—padded blazers that made her look upholstered, comfortable as an armchair.

"How are you two doing this week?" she asked once Caridad had settled in a wicker seat near the floor lamp and Harrison sank into the lilac-patterned couch.

"I have to say something," Caridad blurted out, her heart pummeling her throat.

Francine held her plastic fork aloft. "What is it?"

"I've had to make a hard decision." She turned to Harrison. "I've thought about this a lot, and I see now that I can't live with you anymore."

He groaned and sank his face into his hands. "I knew it. I knew this would happen."

"What's brought this on?" Francine asked.

Harrison raised his head. "Go on, tell her. You're in love with him, aren't you?"

"I'm speaking to Caridad."

"I can't stay with Harrison. I've tried—"

"That's a lie."

"Harrison, please let her speak."

Caridad dropped her gaze to her lap. The floral sundress she wore had a brownish splotch—soy sauce?—near the hemline. She licked a fingertip and daubed at the spot. "That's it. I want a separation. One of us will have to move out."

Harrison rubbed his jaw, issuing a raspy sound. "I expected this." He gazed at a framed diploma on the wall as if addressing it. "Now I have something to say, something to report, really. Francine, you'll want to write this down."

The counselor cast a regretful look at her salad. "Is it really—"

"Write. This. *Down*."

Francine pulled her writing pad near and picked up her pen.

"I witnessed my soon-to-be estranged wife, Caridad *McCann*," he said, "I witnessed this woman commit a criminal act."

Caridad perched on the rim of the wicker seat, leaning forward. Her ears throbbed, a metronomic *plumph-plumph-plumph* measuring out dull beats. What would he say? That she redeemed coupons at the supermarket past their expiration dates? That she'd accidentally brought an unreturned library book with her from California and hadn't mailed it back yet?

Harrison pointed a long finger at Caridad, as if auditioning for a role in a courtroom melodrama, and deepened his voice. "I saw her molest her eight-year-old son."

Caridad drew a sharp breath. The small room seemed to shift, the walls shuddering and the carpeted floor lurching like an abruptly halted Ferris wheel ride that left her dangling in dizzying disbelief. She shook her head to clear her ears. Surely, he hadn't said what she thought she'd heard. *Impossible!*

But Francine said, "This is a very serious accusation. Are you sure about it?"

With a sad but satisfied expression on his jut-jawed face, Harrison nodded.

"You're insane." Caridad gawked at Harrison. "You really are mentally ill."

"You may not know this," Francine told him, "but I am required by law to report this to Child Protective Services and the Georgia Bureau of Investigation."

Incredulity and outrage now collided in Caridad. Did he have any idea what he was doing? Not just to her, but to Miles? She considered what Daniel might do with such information. Caridad could lose her son!

His lips compressed in distaste, Harrison nodded again.

"So I'll need details. When and where did this happen?" Francine took up her pen again. "And why did you wait until now to bring it up?"

Caridad stared at him, as if observing a grotesque transformation, the sight of someone either losing his mind or behaving with unfathomable malevolence. "Every man is made of clay and daimon," Justine observes in Durrell's novel. In Harrison, Caridad had seen plenty of clay. Was this a glimpse of daimon, his shadow beast?

His jaw loosened, his eyes shifting back and forth in momentary confusion. "Uh, it was over a year ago, when we were living in California. I saw her touching Miles, and I told her to stop. I said I'd call the authorities and—"

"If it happened in California, then that's not a matter for the GBI," Francine told him.

"And—*wait*—it happened here, too, the touching. I saw her touch the boy." His voice broke. "It started in California, but she's done it here, too."

Caridad met Francine's eyes and shook her head again. How could anyone believe this?

"If you witnessed this and did nothing, you may be liable for neglect or charged as an accessory," Francine told him.

Harrison tilted his head back and gazed at the ceiling, his eyes tracking back and forth as if he were reading a script—the words he ought to say—written on it. "I always made her stop. I tried to protect him."

Caridad rose, clutching her book and bag. She had to get out of this room, the mad scene unfolding in it. The walls of the cozy office drew close, the flower-printed upholstery and curtains grew loud and mocking, the atmosphere charged with pressure. Caridad struggled to breathe. She needed open space, fresh air, and outdoor sounds to flush out Harrison's lies.

"Where are you going?" Francine asked her.

"I can't be here," Caridad said. "He's unwell. His mind is unbalanced, and he's being very, very . . . *hazardous*. I won't stay for this."

Francine sighed. "I'll have to make a report." She looked at Harrison. "False accusations are also punishable. If asked to testify, I will say that I don't believe you. Still, I have to report it."

"Good," Harrison said. "I want everyone to know the truth."

Caridad turned for the door, worried that he might stand to follow her, but he remained on the couch. "You can't take the car," he said. "I'll be stranded."

"That's your problem," Caridad told him, and she stepped out into the waiting area.

Harrison's voice rang out. "Did you get that? Add car theft to your report."

"Stolen cars are not my concern," Francine said, her voice weary.

Caridad drove the Mustang, Harrison's car, back to their house. She would leave it there for him, the keys on the kitchen table. Her notions about community property were sketchy, but Caridad had no doubt that he would try to have her arrested if he did not find the Mustang parked alongside the Lincoln when he returned home. She pulled out a telephone book to look up the local cab company's number. In this small college town, cabdrivers picked up two or three fares in one trip. It was likely the cab that collected her would arrive to drop Harrison at home. Still, after he climbed out, she would take the taxi to a hotel and stay there until she figured out what to do next.

Over the phone, the dispatcher told Caridad that a cab would arrive for her in about forty-five minutes. While she waited, Caridad threw clothes into an oversized trash bag and placed toiletries in her carryall. She was gathering a few books when a fist pounded on the kitchen door. Relieved that this was not Harrison, who would have let himself in with his key, she swung the door open to find Lazar standing at the threshold. Her heart squeezed, and she again felt overwhelmed by incredulity, much like the breach of reality she'd experienced when Harrison made his false accusation. "What," she said, "*why?*"

"You're here," Lazar said. "I wasn't sure, but—"

"Wait—*stop.*" Caridad raised a palm as if to halt the flow of confounding events. "Not to be rude, but why are you here?"

"Harrison called me on the mobile phone," Lazar said.

"Harrison called *you?*"

"Yeah, I was kind of surprised," Lazar said. "I was heading to my cousin's house in Oconee when I got his call. He was saying some pretty wild stuff. I thought he was drunk. I hung up and tried to reach you in your car. You didn't answer, so I thought I'd stop by to see if you're all right."

"I'm okay. I'm just waiting for a cab to take me to a hotel."

Lazar tilted his head toward the carport. "Your car's not working?"

"It's not my car anymore."

"Look, I can give you a ride."

Caridad pulled the door wide, and Lazar stepped in to help her load her belongings into the trunk of his small white car. Once they pulled onto the street, Caridad caught sight of a red-and-white checked cab approaching, the blinker signaling to turn into her driveway.

As Lazar drove them to the hotel in silence, Caridad studied the vista scrolling past: the iron works, the car dealership, the Jehovah's Witnesses Kingdom Hall, the title-pawn office, the hot-wings shack. She was snapping mental pictures, so sure was she that she would never return to the house she had paid for, except to collect the belongings she'd left behind. Hawthorne Avenue to the Atlanta Highway to Broad Street: the psychoeducational center, the Baptist church, the video rental shop, the gas station, package store, gas station. Before reaching the hotel, Lazar turned to her. "What all happened? Can you tell me?"

She shook her head.

"Say, why don't you come over to my cousin's house with me for supper?"

"I couldn't—"

"I already called her and said you might come. You'll like her and her husband. Just come on with me. It'll be good to get away from things for a while."

The thought of an empty hotel room held little appeal for Caridad, who might be tempted to call Harrison to reason with him and wind up making things worse. "You'll take me to the hotel after?"

"If you want, or you can come with me to Columbus. I've got an advocacy case out there in the morning. And it's not because you're sad or because hotels are expensive. I swear it's not. It's because I really want you to go with me."

"To *Columbus*?"

"That's right," Lazar said with a smile. "To Columbus. You don't have to decide right now."

During the drive to Oconee, Caridad again stared out the window as kudzu-covered houses, pine forests, and then fields streamed past the passenger-side window. "Bad decisions," she murmured.

"What's that?" Lazar asked.

"I have a habit," she said, "of making bad decisions."

"So what?" Lazar shrugged. "Everyone makes poor choices. The question is who's harmed by these?"

Caridad thought of Harrison, Jorge, Seth, Nash, Gray, Carl, and even Daniel. Had she harmed them, or—as the narrator considers in regard to Justine in the novel—had she pushed them to change? "But those she harmed most," Durrell wrote of Justine, "she made fruitful. She expelled people from their old selves. It was bound to hurt . . ." While Caridad doubted the men she'd left had changed much, this idea intrigued her.

In a low voice, Lazar began telling Caridad of a time when he was near the Haitian border in a jeep he'd rented for sightseeing. One of the men in the job-training program had accompanied him as a guide. Along the way, they stopped for an obstruction in the road, and bandits emerged from the jungle, bearing guns and machetes. They demanded the keys to the jeep. "I refused," Lazar said. "I didn't want to lose the rental car. I thought, what can they do to me? They were so raggedy and young, barely teenagers."

He offered them money instead. But as Lazar reached for his wallet, a blast sounded and his guide dropped beside him. The discharge, likely accidental, frightened the bandits, dispersing them into the jungle. Lazar rushed his companion to town for medical help. "Thank god the bullet grazed his scalp, and he's okay now, but he could have been blinded. He could have been killed." Lazar shook his head. "I should have given them the damn keys. You want to talk about bad decisions. There's one that haunts me to this day." He turned to Caridad. "You ever make a decision that dangerous, that harmful to another person?"

Who had her choices endangered? Miles, of course—her own son. The risk was greatest for him, but would her choices harm him? He was happy and bright, and she had woven for him a sturdy network of family and friends. Risk factors and protective factors. The jury was still out on the balance of these, and it would be for the duration of his life. When Harrison accused her of assaulting Miles, he'd prodded a tender place of conscience. Of course, she'd never molested her son. That was the cruelly vengeful product of Harrison's warped imagining. Despite this, the underlying accusation stung: Had she harmed Miles? Was she harming him still with her choices?

Lazar again lapsed into silence, and Caridad continued gazing out the window. They passed church after church. The South was lousy with churches and fast-food restaurants and dollar stores and auto-repair shops, a few of these offering "Christian discounts." Yet more churches loomed ahead and a revival tent appeared, a great white canvas shimmering in a dusky field. *Back 2 the Bible*, the banner snapping near the highway read. If Caridad were to ask the people milling toward the tent what she should do, she imagined most would urge her to return to Harrison, to make the marriage work. Good women make hard sacrifices. Caridad remembered how Esperanza had struggled in the early years of her marriage. "I have to make it work for Mimi's sake," she'd say when Felicia urged her to leave Reynaldo. What an example she was setting for her daughter, who would grow up expecting and accepting mistreatment. It was a lousy legacy to pass from mother to daughter or from mother to son.

Wasn't it better to walk away, to recognize an irredeemable situation and to leave it behind? In the novel, Justine laments that there is no choice. "You talk as if there was a choice," she tells her lover. "We are not strong or evil enough to exercise choice." Justine was wrong. There were more choices now than when Anna Karenina threw herself under a train or Madame Bovary swallowed arsenic or Edna Pontellier swam out too far to return. Caridad cast a sidelong glance at Lazar as he drove, at his well-defined profile, with the straight nose and full lips, the reddish hair that he flattened with gel. He was a slow and cautious driver. He would wait and watch and think before deciding anything.

Caridad cleared her throat. "Here's what happened."

Columbus. The swollen cloud canopy, the head-thrumming heat, the paved river walk winding along the green-gray Chattahoochee, the long-legged herons skimming over the water, the house where Carson McCullers lived, the art and history museum, the small country store and sandwich shop, the restaurant nightclub where Caridad and Lazar shared a bowl of blue she-crab soup and then blackened catfish while a drunken comic insulted diners from the stage, the immaculate hotel room where Caridad discovered the quiet thrill of whispered words, gentle touches. Again, she did not mind the imbalance of desire, knowing that she wanted him more than he wanted her.

When Caridad and Lazar returned from Columbus, he drove her back to the house she shared with Harrison to collect the belongings she'd left behind. Lazar suggested that she stay at his apartment in Atlanta. Caridad didn't want Miles to return to live with her in the home of someone he'd never met, but she might stay with Lazar until she found a place of her own. As soon as they entered the city limits, apprehension overtook her. What if Harrison barred the door and refused to admit her? What if he created a scene? What if after Francine filed her report, the police were waiting to arrest her? Lazar now steered his small white car toward the ranch-style house in Athens, *her* house, as she'd come to think of it, nosing it into the drive. The empty oil-splotched carport appeared, and within that, the front door stood open. Though it was early afternoon, the lights in every window burned bright.

He pulled into the carport and turned off the ignition. "Wait while I check things out."

But Caridad climbed out and followed him into the house. The dining table and chairs were missing from the kitchen, cupboards were open and empty, a lidless jar of mayonnaise stood amid breadcrumbs on the counter, releasing a rancid odor. Green flies buzzed about, alighting on the rim of the mayonnaise jar. Lazar and Caridad wandered through the overwarm house, one hollow room after another — nothing remained but the furniture in Miles's room and Caridad's clothing and miscellaneous belongings, which were strewn about as if in a ransacking.

"My books!" Caridad stood before empty bookshelves that gaped like mouths with all their teeth yanked. "He took my books." A feeling rose in Caridad like a bubble that she expected to pop. She waited for anger or grief, but all she experienced was that bubble expanding, the hollowness of it empty as any sorrow she had known. In the bedroom, they found a note. *Don't bother trying to find me*, it read. *I'm leaving this wretched place to spend my life with people who love me, who need and appreciate me. Find someone else to destroy. Harrison.*

"He's moved in with his parents, I bet," Caridad told Lazar. Harrison was entitled, if he was giving up his claim to the house, to take the furniture and pay to store it, even if this was done in spite. But he had no right to take her books — and not just her books, but her own words, too, written in the margins of their pages. For Caridad, who had never kept a journal, these books held the record of her thoughts and ideas.

"What will you do now?"

"I'll stay here." Caridad gazed about the empty bedroom, thinking about the furniture she'd have to buy — a bed for herself, a kitchen table and chairs, a couch, a television. She and Miles would spread a blanket on the floor for picnic-style meals. They'd sit cross-legged on the carpet in the living room and pretend they were camping indoors. "I always liked this little house." She stretched out her arms as if to embrace its empty rooms.

In thumping rain, the wiper blades sluicing water from the wind-shield, Caridad threaded a cautious route toward the airport in the Honda that Micah helped her purchase at a repo auction. This used compact was nearly as nice as the car she'd bought when she managed the Encino bookstore, the car that was totaled by Malaysian tourists years ago. Caridad parked it in the garage structure, imagining Miles's surprise at its shiny newness. Over the phone, she had told him that Harrison had moved out, that he'd no longer be living with them, and Miles had been strangely subdued by this news. "Will we *ever* see him again?" he'd asked, even though in the end, he hadn't liked Harrison much.

Caridad, hoping that they would not, said, "We *might*."

A few days ago, Caridad had run into Francine at the supermarket. After exchanging greetings, Francine placed cool fingers on Caridad's wrist. "You know, I never reported that nonsense." She had talked to Harrison for a while after Caridad left her office. When she questioned him closely, he'd become confused about the details and wound up contradicting himself. "He admitted making it up," she'd told Caridad as they waited in line to check out. Harrison had withdrawn his accusation, asking Francine not to pursue it.

Caridad wondered how Miles would adjust to Harrison's absence as she wove through the milling crowds toward baggage claim, where she'd arranged to meet him and Felicia, who'd accompanied him for the flight and a short visit. And now Caridad glimpsed Felicia's harassed-looking face among the throng emerging from the gate area. Her gaze swept down, and there he was—Miles! His handsome face bloomed with a wide grin. He dropped his aunt's hand and dashed through the crowd to throw himself into his mother's arms. Caridad crouched to catch him. "I missed you. I missed you. I missed you," he said. He buried his face in the hollow of her shoulder, his thick black hair tickling her chin. She held him close, inhaling deep and familiar draughts of his sweetly sour scent.

"Next time, Mommy," he said. "Next time, come with me, okay?"

"I will," Caridad said. "I promise."

Felicia approached, dragging a rolling bag behind her. "This airport is insanely crowded and noisy as hell." She cut her eyes to Caridad, as if to blame her for this.

"Let me get this straight," Caridad said as she reeled Felicia into an embrace. "You've just come from LAX, and you think this place is chaotic?" She winked at Miles and took her sister's bag, leading them to the carousel that would disgorge the rest of their luggage.

As Caridad steered the small car into the driveway of her house in Athens, its headlights jounced over the lawn, illuminating the overgrown grass, the ornamental pear tree, the azalea bushes, and a large rain-soaked carton that had been deposited near the front door in her absence. After they unloaded the car, Felicia helped Caridad drag the box inside. She sawed open its sealed flaps with a plastic knife. "What's with the no silverware?" Felicia asked. The box bore a sticker with Harrison's parents' return address, and it contained dozens of books — Caridad's books that he'd taken with him when he moved out. Their covers were water-soaked and warped, the pages pocked and blurry. In the margins, her pencil marks had faded and the notes she'd penned in ink had bled — most of them unreadable now.

"You've got to throw this box out or the mildew will spread." Felicia glanced about. "And what's with the no-furniture look? Don't tell me that motherfucker took everything."

From his bedroom, they heard Miles cry out, "My bed, my bed! I've missed you so much, my sweet, sweet bed!"

"Everything but Miles's stuff," Caridad said in a low voice. "At least he left that."

"So what are we supposed to sleep on?"

"I bought an air mattress."

"Great." Felicia toed the waterlogged box. "Want me to help you drag it back out?"

"No!" She pulled out books and set these on the floor, pages splayed. "If I open them up, they'll dry out. Tomorrow I'll get a fan. Help me, will you?"

Felicia grumbled, but she, too, began drawing books out of the soggy carton and opening them up so that the water would evaporate from their buckled pages.

After putting Miles to bed and settling with Felicia on the air mattress, Caridad had trouble falling asleep. They had stayed up late to help

Miles adjust to the time change, and when he'd gone to sleep, she and Felicia shared a pot of tea, sitting cross-legged on the living room carpet. Felicia told of plans for her upcoming wedding, which had been delayed by the lingering illness and death of her fiance's father, and confided in Caridad her worries about their mother and sister. Esperanza had recently been diagnosed with hypertension, and Reynaldo, after years of good behavior, had started drinking again. Esperanza, who had moved back in with Reynaldo some time ago, was ready to leave him again. "And Mama's not doing great," Felicia had said. "She's got almost no circulation in her feet and her glaucoma's so bad she's homicidal on the road, but she refuses to retire, so the neighbor dude, old Nevelson, says he'll drive her to work when school starts. And now this business with you . . ."

As expected, Felicia blasted Caridad for marrying and moving away with Harrison, for the furnitureless house, for the concern she caused, and again for the chaotic airport and its distance from Athens. "The fucking drive here from the airport was nearly as long as the flight!" she'd said. "Why do you have to live here anyway? Didn't you just move here for that asshole, so he could go to grad school? You should move back home with Miles."

"I can't," Caridad told her, thinking of Miles returning to another year at the same school, to his friends there and in the neighborhood. She also thought of Lazar, and this house, *her* house. "We live here now."

Felicia had laid into her for deserting their family, for not helping out with their mother, for being selfish and short-sighted and stupid, but now her hard words had little impact on Caridad. She'd already had a similar conversation over the telephone with Leslie, who had been kinder and more restrained, but who, in the end, had grown just as frustrated as Felicia.

"I have to do everything," Felicia said. "I have to take care of everyone."

But Caridad knew otherwise. Felicia's fiancé had long been recruited to help her out. Since he played music at night and was free in the daytime, he took Mama to medical appointments and ran errands for the household to which he did not yet belong. Unlike Caridad, Felicia had chosen once and wisely—her prettiness protected by prickliness the way cactus fruit is guarded by spiny needles. In this way, she had found a useful and devoted man and had not wasted time with any others.

Hours later, her mind a busy hive, Caridad rose from the air mattress, careful not to disturb her sleeping sister, and padded to the front room where the damp books were arrayed on the floor. She flicked on a lamp to check these for dryness. Caridad found the novel that had been given to her by Esperanza in the hospital, the used copy of *Moll Flanders*. Caridad fanned its pages before flipping to the ending, and there she made out a three-word note scribbled in the margin, an annotation to countermand the book's pious ending—the heroine's resolve to repent for wicked living. The barely legible phrase called back that night in South Carolina, the amber glow of the night-light and this nearly forgotten message penciled in as a reminder, a promise to Caridad from a former and foresighted self: *You are loved.*

Then she rearranged the books, turning pages to expose these to the air. No matter if the covers remained warped or if the pulpy mess of pages became brittle—Dreiser, Nabokov, Tolstoy, Defoe, Lawrence, Shakespeare, James, Durrell, Flaubert, Hardy, Richardson, and Chekhov—Caridad would keep these until she could, one by one, replace them. She would buy two copies of each book. They would stand on bookshelves in her office at the university where she would teach and in her home. When Miles was grown, she'd arrange them in the house she might one day share with Lazar, and in this way, she'd keep them with her always, books by all the dead men she had loved.

About the Author

Lorraine M. López is an associate professor of English and co-founder of the Latino and Latina Studies Program at Vanderbilt University. She teaches in the master of arts program at Vanderbilt and is the author of five books of fiction, including *The Gifted Gabaldón Sisters* and *Homicide Survivors Picnic and Other Stories*, a finalist for the PEN/ Faulkner Prize in Fiction in 2010.